THE MAGNA AURA GENESIS

BOOK ONE OF

THE STARGUARDS

Of Humans, Heroes, and Demigods

RAYMOND BURKE

THE STARGUARDS

Raymond Burke is a British-born author - The Starguards series being his first foray into novels. His background includes an early life in Canada and the US, employment in the British Army as an aircraft technician, an MSc degree in Archaeology from University College London, and short-article writing. He is also a member of The Mars Society. He cunningly lives without a fridge, satellite TV, iPods, and he also can't drive. He's a self-confessed 21st century caveman . . . and loves it! Through all, he has been a keen and aspiring writer. He currently lives in London.

To Peter, Georgina, and Henry.
(And in memoriam to George)
In support for the SANDS Charity

Acknowledgements

Many people have supported and inspired me over the years of writing. I would like to thank David P Perlmutter, Stephen Marriott, Guy Wainer, Jon-Jon Jones, Debdatta Dasgupta Sahay, Saiswaroopa Lyer, S. Evan Townsend, Anita Williams, Neena Katwa, Chris Bellay, Lori Buttermark, Carl Bialik, Anke Marsh, Nigel Livingstone, Gary Cobham, Dee Lobell Bratcher, and the members of the LOTNA sci-fi group for their friendship, support, advice, and readership.

Cover design by Blondie's Custom Book Covers and Jody Smyers Photography. Special thanks to KJ Waters and to Gardner Watts.

And many thanks to Narinder Singh for his formatting.

Any leftover errors are mine alone to claim.

I can spell; I just like to make words up!

FAMILY LINES

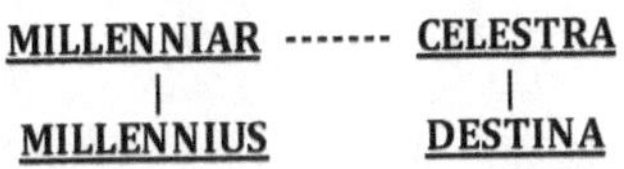

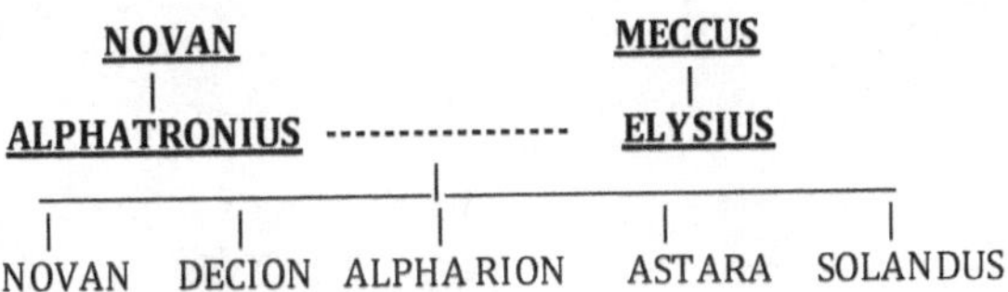

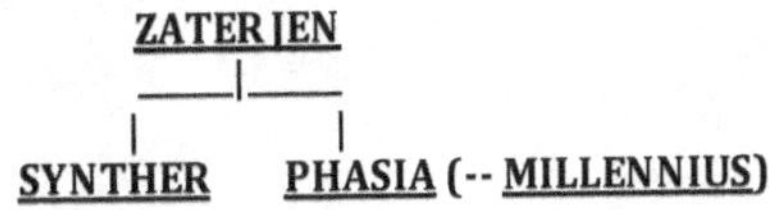

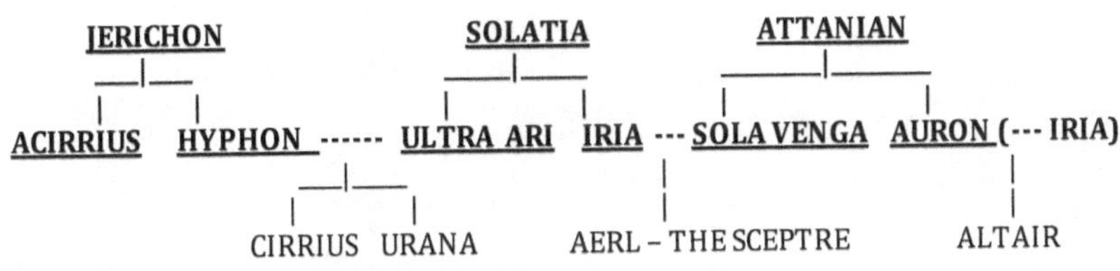

CELESTIAN KNIGHT
STARGUARD

EVIL persists.
It snakes and writhes its menacing form, eclipsing the
cosmic light of life with its shadowy wings of death.

But there is an evil which transcends all others.
An evil incarnate, slipping between the universal bonds;
a perpetual object of living darkness existing even beyond
the grasp of death, in bodies enshrouded in unholy energy.

No where, no when, is safe from them. They are the Lore. And
they are coming.

BOOK ONE

THE MAGNA AURA GENESIS
Of New Beginnings and Neverendings

Prologue: Futurepast

The Magna Aura Star System exploded, the Lore having destroyed the children of the infestations that called themselves Celestians.

But not all Lore were enraptured with their victory.

"This should not have been," the magenta one said to itself. "Time and time again, I have failed. I cannot change what has come before and what will come again—alone."

And so help had been sought.

CHAPTER ONE

The sky burned. It twisted, warped into a lurid vortex suspended like a huge, angry fist wrenching the very fabric of reality. Under the glare of the red-purple bruise puncturing the universe another battle unfurled.

"Mother, I beg of you, let me stay and fight!" Novan pleaded, arms outstretched, leaning forward and shouting to be heard above the howling hot dry wind in the intervening twenty meters between them. The dust stung his nostrils. Bitter red air swirled under the dazzling maw of the vortex hanging above the very last world, Galatia, drawing in the gleaming swordships by the dozen—their escape route.

Novan ignored the last of the armoured crew and panicked civilian refugees clutching small possessions and younglings running past him up the ramp. Dozens of other sleek cruisers dusted off in pairs to dock with the awaiting long white swordships, which majestically rose quietly upon great shafts of heavenly light toward the dark-purple cavity. But Novan's world was in front of him denying him his destiny.

"I am strong enough to stand by your side!" Unbidden tears welled up—the dust, he told himself; his balled-up fists shook in defiance, his mind's energy surged around his head like a nimbus. >*Mother!*< his psyed voice broke as he saw the look of resolve in her eyes.

She stood serenely, arms down in front of her, seemingly unaffected by the charging wind.

Somewhere in the distance, a towering silver skyhab collapsed almost in slow motion in a heap creating a billowing red and yellow dust cloud, another link to the past gone. Novan felt it symbolised his crumbling life. He turned disconsolately back to his mother.

The Goddess Elysius tilted her head, eyes glistening, admiring her son's determination—her firstborn, her beloved Novan, born of the mind like her. But he could not stay. He was not part of the prophecy.

A wisp of a woman, Elysius' glowing ethereal features belied an inner strength, and an even greater power of the mind. Her gold-tanned skin, feathery-white hair, and keen golden eyes imbued her with an exotic nature that intoxicated everyone. All that was going to end soon, but the children would be saved.

>*Novan, you must go*< she psyed to him, an urgency in her voice. >*You will lead the new Celestian civilisation. Do this for me!*< Though they were not in physical contact, Novan felt her caress his face.

Standing forlornly on the metal ramp leading to the airlock of the last cruiser, Novan knew she was right. Her psyed message was mixed with feelings and memories mere words could not convey. Novan had felt that she out of anyone would have understood his desire to stay. His father, Alphatronius, was somewhat busy keeping the vortex open and would not have countenanced such emotion and intransigence from his son, especially from Novan, who was much less his father's son in image and power than his mother's.

Another spired edifice toppled, convincing Novan even more they were representing his own personal failures.

Out of the corner of his eye, he spotted a flying figure fast approaching them. The green-clad Celestian Knight landed by his mother.

"Spheron!" Novan called out in hope, his vocal greeting whipped by the howling winds. His mentor would surely be on his side.

The dark-skinned Celestian Knight gave Elysius a supportive

squeeze of her shoulder, said a few private words, to which she nodded. Spheron advanced toward the cruiser, his great green cape flapping in the capricious winds. He was cradling an object; a book, Novan realised.

Without preamble, he said, "Your mother is correct, my young lord." Nearing him, he clasped his shoulder. "This world is no longer your fate."

Spheron, master of forcefields, was a handsome man even nearing seven hundred years old, with dark eyes and a neatly trimmed black beard and mustache wrapping his lower wrinkled face. His body was still as honed as a two-hundred-year-old's.

"Your destiny awaits on the other side of the vortex." They both stared up into the wild sky, which churned as it nonchalantly swallowed more swordships to safety.

Novan squared up to Spheron gazing past him to his mother. He would not go like this.

"I make my own fate!" he shouted, hoping he sounded threatening enough. He shifted to force his way past Spheron, but an energy trapped him in place.

Not Spheron's forcefield, Novan realised in shock, but his mother's energy enveloping him, a psychic wreath of harsh yellow light. She was shaking her head, sorrowful emotions accompanying her effort. He tried to push back, free himself, but it was no use. He grudgingly relented. Shoulders slumped and downcast he swung around to enter the cruiser, the ship's commander had been waiting in the inner airlock for almost an hour anxious to leave the dying world.

More skyhabs, spires, and a pyrathedral crashed in the distant city, dust and explosions blurring the skyline of Celestia, the capital of their world. Novan watched, detached, accepting the inevitability of The End.

"Novan."

He halted and turned at Spheron's soft voice. Spheron had his hand outstretched with the book.

"A gift," he smiled. "Read it, learn from it, and remember us, always." He embraced Novan in a parting hug.

Novan hugged him back. "Always!" he replied, feeling hot tears on his cheek.

He wiped them away. >*Goodbye, Mother*< he psyed, feeling the need to reinforce their shared connection.

>*Farewell, my son. I will always be there for you, in your mind, in your heart*< she caressed his face from afar again. >*Always, listen for me!*< she implored, smiling sadly.

It was the saddest smile Novan had ever seen and experienced. Yet it also infused him with the warmth, love, and outpouring of hope only a mother could give. It was the last thing he ever saw of his world as Novan entered the cruiser and the airlocks closed behind him.

The commander spoke quickly into his small comm unit on his forearm. The small warship immediately hovered off the ground briefly, then shot up toward its mother swordship, an elegant ten-kilometer-long shard of white light. Novan sullenly followed the commander through the endless well-lit corridors, cabins, and open spaces full of people, many of the hundreds of Celestian evacuees on board, numerous of them greeting their young lord, blessing the universe he was with them.

Novan smiled and shook hands where he could. He had to be strong for them, but inside he was rotting away with guilt. He barely noticed the rest of the journey. Up four decks he was led forward where in a large cabin aft of the bridge he joined the other Celestian Knight progeny.

The grey octagonal room was as non-ostentatious as it was

portless, with a double row of shockseats situated in a tight circle on a slightly lower circular level. It was the crash room, with emergency escape pods embedded in the walls around them. The commander strapped Novan into a seat within the inner circle, filled with the other Celestian Knight families.

By the time Novan was strapped in, they had docked with the swordship *Commandarian*.

"We will depart shortly," the commander announced. He looked at them all. "Your parents are the bravest Celestians I know. But I also know you will follow their example."

"Thank you, Commander Horp," Novan managed, his throat tight.

The commander bowed slightly, exiting the room, the door sliding shut. They were left alone as the crew busied themselves with the departure.

The other children could see the disappointment in Novan's eyes. He had failed to stay. He was one of them after all. He could see their reactions in their eyes: a glint of smug satisfaction in his brother Decion's eyes, sadness in Urana's, understanding in Aerl's. His younger twin siblings, Alpha Rion and Astara, were silent as usual sitting quietly together, while his youngest brother, Solandus, actually slept beside an oblivious Cirrius who was busily studying a crystalator's readout of the sword's telemetry. And Altair brooded opposite him, trying to ignore them all. They also did not want to leave, but they had to. The Celestian civilisation had to survive.

The last swordship to leave Galatia rocketed up gracefully to the vortex. There were minutes of serene silence. Then the ship jolted violently. Rocked left then right, Novan sat glumly, strapped into his seat. The vortex threshold bounced the swordship on a tremendous wave of energy then rolled it to one side, suddenly porpoising in the eddies of torsional currents. And then without warning, glaring lights penetrated the hull and sheared open their reality, churning them inside out, tearing at their existence. Corporeality became a memory, a painful sin punished by transit through a soul-destroying spiral. The burning sense of prevailing nothingness amid crushing omnipresence was shattering.

Novan cried out in pain, his distorted voice mingled with thousands of suffering others on the swordship. Their dying universe was extracting the last bit of energy from them, crying for its loss, birthing its former inhabitants into a new dimension; leaving the Celestian Knights to their fate.

>*Listen!*< Elysius cried out to him. >*Listen for me! Listen for my voice*< was the last thing he heard.

Novan fell unconscious.

That had been thirty years ago.

"Thank you, Spheron."

Novan, son of Alphatronius and Elysius, firstborn among the sons and daughters of the Celestian Knights, opened his eyes from his hallowed memories. He gently closed the old bound book he had been reading, rubbing his fingers over the worn leather bindings. The book, 'A History', given to him by Spheron had been his constant companion as he had traversed Alphatronius' dimensional gateway and beyond.

He read the hand-written inscription inside the front cover again, a personal message from the wizened sage, who hoped he would find solace and inspiration from his combined tales of myth and history.

"Universe preserve us!" he gave thanks to the Universe for another day in which all Celestians could dream of better days to come. "I will not forget the sacrifices you all made to save us," he promised as much to himself as to his mentor. The emotions were still raw like it was yesterday to him. It was even more so on the anniversary of The End.

Another new island settlement was being built on the crescent-shaped arc which sliced the calm blue seas. The warmth of the sun embraced Novan as his eyes caught several flocks of cackling *tarlips* swooning in the fresh salty air. From where he sat upon a high rocky escarpment it was times like these that he wished the Celestian Knights could be here to witness the rebirth of their civilisation.

There had not been any sign of surviving Celestian Knights, and Novan, still young, with centuries to look forward to, hoped one day to find out the fate of his parents and the others. But for now, he was the inspirational architect and leader of a new breed of heroes protecting the rise of the new civilisation. That the children of the Celestian Knights had been named the Starguards by the people was a testament to their heroics.

After being expelled from the vortex and rendezvousing with the fleet, they had searched for five years, before discovering a suitable star system. This had five worlds pledged to a large, luminous, yellow star. They had named it Magna Aura.

Only fifteen million of twenty-one billion Celestians had survived The End.

Most Celestians had inhabited Halcyon and Placia; the twin worlds widely circling each other like two courting Starbirds, not touching yet always near. They were nestled in between Nexa, a small rocky sphere closest to the sun, and the gas giant Magna Prime.

Celestians had never seen so much ocean before. Halcyon, was an impossibly-blue orb, an oceanic world dotted with hundreds of thousands of small island chains volcanic in origin, most islands only ten thousand square kilometers in size. Many of the hundreds of Trinari ships had been reconfigured to become the first of the majestic sky cities and a few sea-based ones, while settlements sprung up on the myriad of islands, like the one Novan had just inspected. The capital, Halcyon City, was the largest air-based structure in the system, being one of the three city-ships which had escaped. And not far away was Sky Command, the home of the Sky Warriors. Halcyon was mainly populated by Galatians and Trinari.

The small sky city of Elysian on Halcyon was Novan's home. And it was about time he returned, though he had business on Millennius City-State first.

Another bout with Altair, he sighed.

Turning his gaze up into the thick-blue plushness where the first stars had started to pin-prick their way through, Novan could just make out the glinting form of the other orbit-free City-State, Alphatron, which hung majestic-like in the skies and constituted many a Xarians' home. Novan had no doubt Decion was looking down upon him from his militaristic roost.

He found himself frowning just thinking about it. For all their hard work and fortune, Novan struggled with leadership. Or rather, others made his leadership more difficult. But it was up to him to integrate the Starguards more into society if they were going to earn the complete respect, trust, and loyalty of the Celestians and survive for long as a new civilisation.

He sighed deeply as he made ready to leave. There was still a lot of work to be done.

**

"Look, there's Novan watching over us!" gasped Classia, pointing with her chin up toward Novan's perch on the ridge. "He's a God, Deb, a true God." Her hushed voice was tinged with awe, her brown eyes wide in fascination.

"If you say so, Classie, but we'd better finish the training sessions, or old Gal Agar will find our names on report, again." *Novan and flying*, sighed Deb inwardly, *the two constant subjects in Classia's mind! And in that order!*

She nudged Classia back to reality and the two, blue-uniformed Sky Warriors began their tedious work supervising other teams of Sky Warriors in various training exercises around the building site. Lower-rank Sky-marks were helping establish several terrafarms and an aquature, the main fishery, until the protein generators were running. Luckily the long day was coming to an end.

When the sparsely spaced island-based and sky cities were first built, there had been a need to establish order and a protection force which could oversee law both in the air and on the sparse land that existed. Not that there was any rampant crime, but there were those who desired more than their fair share at the expense of others. And occasionally there were disturbances over the lack of individuals or communities not trading fairly or committing to the volunteer time-work scheme, mostly in the new settlements. And of course, there would be the pressing need for a defense contingent should an external enemy emerge.

Into this arena had stepped Cirrius, proposing the establishment of the Sky Warriors, a force of flying enforcers dedicated to his father, Hyphon the Sky Warrior and his ideals. But it would take the ambition and the ingenuity of all of the Starguards to see it come to pass, for it envisioned a force capable of natural flight, rather than depending on external mechanisms. The technology to alter themselves physically had been present for centuries, but never used, for it had not been required with the Celestian Knights around, but now things were different and extra precaution was called for.

With the assistance of the enthusiastic technophile Meccuns' genetic engineering technology, the first aeromorphically-engineered Sky Warriors had appeared, their two-toned, blue-armoured uniforms (or manoeuvre suits as they were called) fabricated from the soft-armour vortexite, a familiar sight in the skies above Halcyon. Now there were over fifty-thousand warriors of the sky, emanating from Sky Command, their vast aerial fortress.

Classia and Deb were two young Sky Leaders whose rise up through the ranks could not have been more different. Classia's Galatian parents had retained much of their noble-status after The End, based on their meritorious past rather than material wealth. They had promised that their first- and only-born would be dedicated to the service of their new world. She had undergone the rigorous and various physical and psychological tests and then the final genetic procedures. She graduated as a Sky Warrior soon after, rising up the ranks very quickly, sometimes in questionable ways. Quite haughty, living up to at least the 'superior' part of the Sky Warriors' 'air superior' creed, it was a wonder she and Deb had become best friends.

In the ensuing confusion and chaos after The End some swordships and records had been lost. Vast numbers of children became orphans. Deb had been one of them. Nothing was known about her early life, except that her name was Deneb, given to her by the orphan keepers. She had an exceptionally keen mind and soaring intelligence, along with her dark beauty and aloofness—more out of shyness than arrogance—which would later bring about resentment toward her.

All orphans had become Sky Warriors or Star Warriors, their

space-faring counterparts. Deb had shown a natural potential and with those skills and an intangible quality that set her above the rest, she had become the youngest Sky Leader, and a favourite of the Sky Commander, Gal Agar, the first Sky Warrior. It was he who had found and rescued Deb as a youngling and taken care of her in his pre-flight days, before she had been placed in the orphanment. But he had always looked out for her. The undercurrent of resentment toward her upon becoming a Sky Warrior had hardened, as her early relationship with Gal Agar had become known, as if that had conferred upon her an unfair advantage—a non-meritorious benefit. And especially when she and Classia were always leading each other into trouble, much to the chagrin of the Sky Commander, as if the life of a Sky Warrior was not adventurous enough.

"You know sometimes, Deb, I don't get you."

Deb smiled, peering over at her friend. They had been promoted the same day two years ago, not that Classia acted any more responsibly. Classia frowned from beneath her curly brown locks. Her brown eyes and pouting lips could be potent weapons, but this time there seemed to be genuine concern in them.

"What's the problem now, Class?" But she knew. Deb sighed, her eyebrows knitting together, not wanting to turn toward Classia. She let her attention wander extra-long over a distant Sky Warrior practice patrol, but Classia was still intently scrutinising her.

"I don't know, Deb. I have known you for ages and yet you're still . . . unknowable, you know? You're distant at times and I don't get it. I don't know if you mean to be like that, but it's been happening a lot recently. Is there something wrong?" Her eyes implored, as Deb's eyes searched the ground for grubmites, "Has something happened?" Classia's eyes widened in glee, "Have you and Tol Valar been . . ."

"No, we have not!" flushed Deb indignantly, yet also almost laughing at her friend. She had resisted all of his advances.

"Then what's going on? Tell me, Deb, please!" She looked so earnest this time. But just as Deb was about to tell her, Classia suddenly looked up and inhaled sharply, "Oh, look, Deb. He's going!" She pointed skyward to where Novan was a fast-receding figure in the darkening sky.

Deb slumped, not believing her friend. "You're such the universe, Classia, all cold and starry-eyed." She shook her head wearily in disbelief. Everything to Classia was superseded by Novan. "Anyway, we're just about done now. I'm heading back to Command."

Before a flustered Classia could reply, Deb launched herself into the air, flying off to visit various points on the island, advising her subordinates to wrap up for the day. Then before Classia could catch up, Deb propelled herself higher and faster executing a tight arc to spiral upward onto her back and then with an aeromorphic thrust of speed shot over the island, a classic and perfect manoeuvre, which Deb could only hope the training Sky Warriors were watching and learning from. She was so involved in her own thoughts that she had not felt Classia coast in from behind and below.

She started slightly at the sound of Classia's voice, "Sorry, Deb." Deb couldn't help but smile. She knew Classia meant it, even as Classia continued. "You know how I feel about Novan. Even the Celestian Knights married non-noble Celestians, so why can't I dream of Novan? One day he'll notice me and that will be that, we'll live happily ever after."

"Just like that?"

"Yes, just like that. I believe it, Deb. I love him."

"I don't doubt that, Class."

They slowed and stopped, hovering high over the small, smiling speck of the island. A fair breeze blew jet-black hair across Deb's eyes and she felt a chill course through her body, despite her manoeuvre suit's internal environmental protection. And Classia's concerned eyes were upon her again.

"Oh, there you go again, Deb. Something happens and you get this look in you. Really now, what is it?"

Taking a deep breath Deb shrugged, trying to tie words to her feelings, but could only manage, "I don't know, Class, I get these . . . feelings that something's wrong, really wrong, and that something terrible is going to happen." A nervous laugh escaped her as she dismissed those hazily aired thoughts with a wave of her hand. "Forget it, sounds silly I know!"

"Well . . . we all have those thoughts," Classia mused, treading warily. Then as if a new thought had struck her, her face lightened and she lifted up Deb's chin with a finger and purred seductively, "Maybe you and Tol Valar should be doing something. Could take your mind off things." Sporting a wide-mouthed grin, she sped off into the sky toward their home, looking back, taunting 'catch-me-if-you-can'.

Flustered and open-mouthed, Deb took off after her, the scene depicted by Classia embarrassingly forming in her mind. They laughed and chased their way through the darkening sky. And soon, a familiar form grew on the expansive horizon.

Deb admired the almost-translucent blue outline of Sky Command, resembling a *fragel's* tough shell, though unlike the venomous deep-sea serpent, her home was five kilometers long, three wide, encompassing twenty decks. Its pointed hemispherical outer carapaces with its distinctive saddle-shaped central bridge on top, could close upon each other in attack, the interdecks and structures collapsing within each other and the bridge receding into the skimmer bay below. Comm struts, aerials, and tertiary command habs and domes dotted the outer structures, launch and landing pads for Sky Warriors and crewed and auto-skimmers lined the upper deck with further dorsal exit points away from the four great gravity engines. Weapon ports and airlocks were dispersed around the whole fortress.

Deb tuned into her crystalator comms relaying it from her forearm unit to her ear 'conversing' with Sky Command, accepting her codes as she floated through the automated security shields. She and Classia landed on an external pad jutting out from a skimmer deck and entered the massive centre for the planet's defence via a transtube.

Once inside, Deb mentally dialled down the comms chatter, preferring the quiet walk to her quarters. She was ready for a rest after a long day. They were both exhausted and Deb was grateful for her friend's concern, but as she and Classia walked along the corridors caught up in the traffic of many returning Sky Warrior patrols, ominous thoughts began to creep through her again.

Out in the cosmos there are gaps. Some are billionths the size of atoms, while others could swallow whole worlds. Created during the exploding new-born void, where matter and energy did not quite coalesce to form ordinary matter and energy, they had developed into areas of relative nothingness. But far from being benign pools of star-lit placidity, they were raging cauldrons of whirling energy, for plugging these gaps were other universes, innocently spilling their own diverse energies into others. And after billions of years of exclusively seeping energy, something else emerged. Something screaming.

**

Two hours after leaving Halcyon, Novan coasted silently and easily through the arena that was the void. His eyes searched the cosmic horizon for a moving star that was no star, but the independent City-State of Millennius. Novan enjoyed the serenity of flying openly in space. All the Starguards possessed the indefinable energy that allowed them to live centuries or more, to fly, and to survive the open expanses of space unharmed. To them, it was just a part of life, but increasingly now, Meccun sci-techs were infringing on their territory by trying to artificially create such elements within the Magna Auran society and even asking to study members of the Starguards. This would never have happened with the Celestian Knights.

New universe, new times, was Novan's attitude, but he knew that some of the other Starguards, like Decion and Altair seemed hostile to these changes. And Cirrius seemed to outright avoid the public for just such a reason.

Maybe Solandus has done the right thing, Novan reflected, smiling at the thought of his youngest brother who had forsaken his duties. He had opted to roam the new universe in search of adventure, his parents, and his destiny, somewhere out there.

But Novan was quite different from his younger siblings, so much so that at birth, Alphatronius had been disappointed in him. While his younger siblings all possessed the black hair and dark eyes of Xarians and wore the red and black armour, Novan possessed feathery white hair and fair blue eyes enhancing his duskier complexion. His armour was chiefly white with red and black strikes and edgings. His powers, though energy-oriented like his father's, came from the mind, like his mother. And he still remembered her last words to him promising that she would return; he had only to listen for her voice calling for him to come to her. Sometimes he could hear it, but only in his dreams.

Coming out of his revelry, Novan spotted the telltale signs of the wandering gleaming City-State, just as he rounded green-hued Magna Prime. Constantly traversing the system, the city sometimes orbited one of the worlds, its unmistakable sword-like form, bristling with silver spires and transparent domes, the regal domains of its denizens. Novan had travelled to see its most eminent resident, his second-in-command, and closest friend, Aerl - The Sceptre.

Gliding through the outer-laying myriad of spires toward an entry port, Novan felt a slight tremble twist his body.

"What the. . .?" He shrugged it off, but then it returned savagely stabbing his soul. He doubled over in absolute pain, his vision blurred and a piercing scream ripped through his mind. Eyes squeezed shut in agony, his hands grabbed his head and he spun violently tumbling out of control.

He did not notice how many spires he crashed through, or how many Celestians narrowly escaped death madly rushing from the damaged spires, sending the city reeling toward the lurking planet below. He did not notice the frantic efforts to save the city or the hands, which eventually caught him, before he was lost in the deep blackness. All he knew was the scream inside his head. All he knew was in that scream, the scream Novan had waited for all his life:

His mother, the Goddess Elysius, was calling him.

The invaded gap began to rip, overflowing with resurgent constituents from an alien universe, until the cosmic effluence suddenly came to an abrupt end in a burst of spectral explosions, which for the first time ever, sealed the gap. There was no going back. The war had gone on for a very long time and they had almost lost. Almost. But now it was time to feed. And they were very hungry.

"Send Sky Leader Deneb in," Sky Commander Gal Agar ordered.

"Yes, sir," his aide, Sky-mark Aphene, responded sharp and crisp in manner as she opened the door to admit Deb, closing the door on her way out to leave the two alone.

Gal Agar had been the first Sky Warrior, genetically altered in his prime to fly and defend the skies. He was a hero to his people, the Celestians, or to the new generation who, controversially to some, preferred to call themselves Magna Aurans. An imposing figure, he was quite tall, young looking with well-weathered features, but going grey at the temples—the rewards of state he called it. Now he was entering his seventh decade and looking forward to the next half of his life, but some Celestians seemed destined to make it harder for him. Enter Sky Leader Deneb.

Before being allowed to head to her quarters, after a filling meal, Deb had received commed orders to report to the Sky Commander. Now she stepped into the familiar office of her commanding officer, noting the usual array of personal mementos, awards and other paraphernalia, like his ceremonial battle-staff, modelled on Hyphon's famous Meta-staff. Despite his rank, the office was not too airy or in fact too compact, just room enough for himself. Deb felt as if she was in a containment cell, an arm's length away from her captor.

"Take a seat please, Sky Leader." Gal Agar held out his arm indicating the chair across his desk. Gal Agar gave her his solemn stare which usually melted the wills of other Sky Leaders, but Deneb, as always, sat unperturbed and it was the Commander who let his gaze fall away first. She does that every time, he thought, suppressing a smile. Regaining his composure, he searched for the words with which to address her. Any other person and he could give them the usual speech, but with Deneb, she always required something different. She'll have my job one day, Gal Agar mused. And I wouldn't envy those under her command. That thought formed the basis of his talk.

"You know, Deneb, I've known you almost all of your life. You're one of my foremost leaders and someday, and I don't doubt it, you'll be in this seat. Even with your somewhat unfortunate record of minor insubordinations and association with the... shall we say, incorrigible Classia, your skills and intelligence should be enough to have you promoted to Deputy Sky Commander, but to take that last step, you have to start working hard now on your temperament and attention to attitude. Recently, it seems to have been getting worse, not better. I need to get inside your head. Find out what's wrong. It's beginning to affect the performance of other Sky Warriors and if it impacts on them, it concerns me. It could endanger lives and we cannot have that now." He resisted the urge to tap the desk, awaiting her reply.

Head hung in thought, Deb responded hesitantly at first, knowing she could talk to Gal Agar about anything, before finding the words. "I ... I don't know, sir. Recently, I've been having dreams, bad ones, but they feel more than just dreams. I feel like something's going to happen. I get this overwhelming sense of . . ." She shrugged, searching for a word. ". . . of doom, something beyond us all. And I'm afraid. I don't know how I know, but I do. And that's about it, sir." She sat, looking like a small child, peering out the large window at the enveloping night sky with her wide blue eyes.

"Have . . . have you ever experienced anything like this before?" Gal Agar was genuinely concerned.

"No," came a quiet voice, "Never."

"Um, well maybe we'd better get you down to the med facilities. Let them take a look at you. They might be able to help," Gal Agar said unconvinced. Then trying to reassure her, he added. "I need you. This world needs you. More than any other Sky Warrior, I feel you have the makings of a great leader. But . . . these . . . episodes are greatly undermining your chances. Go down to the medtechs and get your mind together. You'll be alright, Deb, I have every confidence in you." Gal Agar realised that his last sentence had been a thought expressed aloud. Normally, he would not have allowed himself to become so personal with anyone, but sometimes he likened Deneb to the daughter he would never have. He would never admit that to anyone, for he would never allow relationships to soil his duty. And he was not about to start now.

Deb looked at him, or straight through him, Gal Agar couldn't tell. Studying her he had always noted that her blue eyes truly matched the colour and the wildness of the sky. If anyone had been born for the skies it was her. But something was wrong. He suddenly jumped in his seat, startled. If he hadn't seen it for himself, he would not have believed it. For a second, Deb's eyes seemed to pulse a vivid blue.

And then she fainted.

CHAPTER TWO

Urana's Mountain, it was called.

The live volcano sat haunched almost six thousand meters above the surrounding plains of thick grass spread over tumulus rock. The Protectress of State had carved out her fortress from the hard yellow-brown mass herself; her base of operations and home, tapping the heat, lava, and magma chamber for energy which could be transferred to surrounding communities.

Placia had been a wild untamed rocky world wracked with torrents of volcanic magma and accompanying earthquakes, but all that ferocious physical and kinetic energy had been controlled and harnessed, powering cities around the world, without a huge techno-industrial infrastructure.

Like her younger brother, Cirrius, Urana was more at home on land rather than in space. However, while Cirrius liked his island privacy on Halcyon, the northern side of the volcano's crater held a crystalline dome. Various balconies and smaller domes dotted the sloping sides, ridges, and sheer cliffs accommodating scenic views and acting as a redoubtable defensive measure.

"I believe the chronimonum will suffice," Urana stated, tucking stray strands of long blue hair behind her ears. "Four hundred thousand techtons for my sci division and another three for the medtechs." She looked engagingly across the small low table assessing how her offer was received.

The conference room was small, but was Urana's favourite for negotiations. No windows to distract visitors and warm surrounding walls to foster engagement and comfort.

High Principal Eemom Brou inhaled deeply in thought, resting backward into the high-backed plastiform chair. Keen brown eyes met Urana's bright blue eyes as he mulled over her offer. He could surely spare the chronimonum, the Herdician Province was rich with the ore. It supplied the Trinari swordships, the Star Warrior fortress, and was traded as far as Aurana. Supply was no problem. But he wondered why Urana wanted it.

Where would she even use seven hundred thousand techtons of chronimonum? She is the Protectress of State protected by a mountain already reinforced with stellecneum! The question kept forming in his mind, but he dismissed it. Who was he to question a Starguard, let alone his world's guardian? And the daughter of the great Celestian Knights Hyphon and Ultra Ari.

Placia is blessed indeed, he thought.

Placia was slightly smaller than Halcyon, comprised of three massive landmasses encompassing several inland seas and one shallow ocean. The main occupied continent was the largest and boasted the beautiful hundred-kilometer-long Xalia Canyons, clawed out of the bedrock millennia ago, by five fast-flowing rivers which then spread through the wide plain that held the capital, Atronia. Mostly Elerae and Xarians populations had settled on the fertile plains bounded by large blue-leaved forests, while the Neb had inhabited a small southern continent to themselves.

It had surprised many that the Elerae and Xarians would choose to live together given their past histories; the Elerae having decimated the Amethystians, the one-time purple-haired inhabitants of the seventh World; and the Xarians, who were the only beings who could boast the only defeat inflicted upon the Elerae since Antiquity. But even with that violent history between them, the Elerae and Xarians had later become staunch allies.

The Xarians, besides being of a muscular ideal, were well known for their long black hair and black or dark blue eyes, a trait held by many Celestian Knights of the Alpharion clan. Some Xarian females wore ceremonial beards, known as *dreba,* while training to be warriors, while some of the older women grew real beards after attaining warriorship or to mourn certain ancestors or husbands who had died in battle. Female-bearded battle units, or the *Drebori*, were often seen in the Star Warrior ranks.

Burgeoning indigenous and imported Celestian sea life and copious amounts of small fauna and livestock, some of which became docile pets, earned Placia the distinction as the cornucopia of the system; exports its chief industry.

Urana's Mountain lay at the far end of the Xalia Canyons. She was far enough away for privacy, yet close enough to hold periodic mission briefings, though she preferred heading to Atronia if only to keep the ever-pressing Celestian folk away from her private life.

Brou had been politely summoned by Urana. And he felt he was being ambushed for the chronimonum. Even in the high-backed chair he seemed lanky within it and shifted uncomfortably, his long braided blond hair falling over his shoulders. His relative youth and openness had won him the election only two years ago and he had been thrust into the position of having to deal with weekly meetings with Urana. This had been an extra meeting with another agenda away from the rest of the council. They wouldn't have liked that. But he wouldn't have dared turn down a Starguard.

"What would you agree for compensation?" she asked, trying not to sound desperate.

Brou pretended to think about it, but the answer had always been at the ready. "My transport fleet needs servicing." He peered down at his crystalator padd, which churned out figures. "Fifteen hours per ship should suffice." He stared hard at Urana. "At the Systar docks!"

Urana hid her mild outrage. *Systar!* It was an outrageous bargain. Systar was meant for Swordships, battleships, and well, anything more than a mere trade transport, even for a High

Principal. It would take a lot of service to make up for that. But she knew the metal ore was important. She maintained a tense, but pleasant smile.

The Celestians had retained their trade and time-resource economic system. There was no shortage of resources for fifteen million people spread over four worlds and two space cities. From the raw products, whether mined or grown they could either be mass- or self-manufactured and traded. Everyone could claim their fair share. While central authorities played their administrative role, the system was run by the citizens balancing their time and resources with each other. Service, volunteering, and a meritorious character were the valued currencies. A certain amount of time and resource credits could be built up over time and by volunteering personal time with or without a trade, products and services could be paid for. This led to a less-materialist society where personal time was more valuable than amassing wealth, hence the maintenance of the meritorious system.

Urana ticked off a quick calculation in her mind. Brou's twenty ships, fifteen hours each overhaul. It could be done, but she would then have to offer the Trinari Systar eng-techs an extra service.

Teeth ground together, Urana nodded compliance to Brou, who imperceptibly breathed a sigh of relief. Just as they were about to exchange signatures on their respective padds, a side niche door slid open almost unobtrusively.

"Protectress," whispered aide Camtrin as she slipped into the room. She was quiet, slim and short, in a white and gold robe topped with a wavy bob of silvery hair framing a round face. Urana's favourite aide of the Mountain, as she called Camtrin, the discreet Trinari aide; the only one, given the history between the Elerae and Trinari. She was one of twenty-two aides in the mountain, they kept the mountain running for their Protectress, supervising the league of understaff. And they were allowed to interrupt any meeting with pertinent news.

Urana beckoned the aide over. She gave a short respectful bow to High Principal Brou and whispered in Urana's ear.

A wave of shock rolled across the Protectress' face before she controlled it. Urana tapped the comms on her forearm crystalator, listening to the communications on and off-world: Novan.

"High Principal, I am sorry, but our negotiations will have to be cut short. Please have the techtons delivered here by the end of the week. You will be compensated as per our agreement." She signed her padd. At his confused look, she added. "Please attune to Mountain comms and you will hear the news I just have. I am placing the Mountain on alert for precaution." Without waiting for Brou's response, Urana turned and marched briskly from the conference room, the doors automatically sliding up open and closing behind her, silently.

Brou's mouth opened and closed in continued confusion, his hand raised in an unasked query. As the nominal head of Placia's Planetary Council, he had expected a bit more courtesy. Camtrin waited patiently while he gathered his wits, gave her a half-embarrassed look, and collected his crystalator padd. He straightened his mauve trousers and tunic as he stood up. Composure regained, he glanced sideways at Camtrin who tilted her head in a conciliatory bow.

"This way, High Principal." Camtrin led Brou out the sliding door. Four Urana-hewn corridors away awaited the transtube chambers. Brou was surprised to see other non-staff already by the transtubes, accompanied by their respective aides.

One of the visitors recognised him before he could enter one. "High Principal, have you heard the news?" an Elerae woman asked, rushing over with concern.

Brou could only nod, automatically, his thoughts on other things.

"Such news!" said another visitor. Everyone shook their heads in sorrow.

"Were you with Urana when the news came in?" asked the first woman. A crowd was gathering around Brou now, their Magna Auran leader more accessible than their Starguard Protectress.

Brou composed himself. There were a dozen people around him. And though he felt he had been manipulated by Urana, he still had to be seen to support her. He held up his hands for quiet.

"Yes, I was with Urana when the news came in. We were in agreement on a course of action, which I cannot discuss," he smiled disarmingly as he elaborated. "But I will do everything I can to help in this crisis," he stated. *Even deliver seven hundred thousand techtons of chronimonum*, he sighed to himself.

The small group clapped in appreciation. Brou gave Camtrin a sly glance, but her face remained impassive.

A transtube arrived and the party were politely ushered into the transparent-walled carriage, by the aides. The carriage descended to a mid-mountain platform where the visitors were escorted onto the small personal flitters and flown back to their respective cities.

Camtrin sighed in relief. She loved her job, but some visitors were more troublesome, especially the political kind. She would have to inform Urana of Brou's impromptu support of her. But that could wait, she knew Urana was busy and she prayed to the Universe for Novan's recovery.

Urana rushed directly to her private quarters, located close to the heart of the mountain, via private transtube. She had many quarters around the mountain she could have utilised, most on the periphery of the mass, but now she demanded the absolute privacy in this case.

She breezed into the cool room, the natural dark yellow rock covered in places by light red wood and cut grey stone in the corners. The furniture was functional, but soft, however Urana was not here to relax. She was there to talk.

Her armour was of the same close-fitting style as the other Starguard's uniforms. Yellow sun-like rays spiked in a diagonal arc across her body painting half her armour golden and the other in white, with a narrow red sash running across the opposite way.

"Armour soft," she spoke aloud. And with a soft rush of air the armour shifted into a more causal gold one-piece outfit. She wanted to be relaxed for this meeting.

Her room's crystalator unit was located in a side alcove. A hand-sized hexagonal crystal sat within a semi-circular arrangement of six slender thirty-centimeter-high rods, fifty centimeters apart from first to last.

The crystals, which powered the crystalators came in varying sizes, shapes, and colors and powered the Celestian civilisation. So perfect and complete were the crystals in their calculating abilities and energy output upon their discovery millennia ago that many Meccun sci-techs could not decide whether the crystals were natural, engineered, or even alive. Urana was just glad her unit obeyed her instructions. There was a flashing green dot icon on the base of the control rod's pedestal. A message. Urana ignored it, knowing better than to keep the sender waiting.

"Activate," Urana commanded the unit. The crystal glowed and a virtual screen lit up between the outermost rods.

"Did you get the chronimonum?" the question immediately sparked impatiently from the screen.

Urana exhaled humourlessly as she regarded the angular handsome face on the screen.

"And hallo to you too, brother," she replied curtly to Cirrius, a bit on edge and exasperated after the day's events with Novan and Brou, respectively. "Yes, I obtained all seven hundred thousand techtons," she snapped.

"What was his price?" he asked, ignoring her gruffness.

Urana felt he already knew the answer.

"Overhauling his transports on Systar!" She shook her head, still fuming at the negotiation price. "Ridiculous, really!" She let out a loud noise of frustration.

"Of course he did," Cirrius smiled knowingly. "It was an obvious move, but it is worth it," he said, enigmatically.

Urana huffed. "Obvious, of course!" was her sarcastic reply. "What do you want them for? You have not told me!" She slapped her arms on her thighs frustrated, trying not to get up and pace in front of the screen. She liked to walk and talk, but knew her brother was a stationary and methodical thinker at best, hidden away on his island.

"Research," Cirrius answered simply. His short spiky blue hair caught the light off his screen, Urana not recognising the elaborate surroundings behind him, some sort of machinery. Cirrius, noting her curiosity, casually moved closer to the screen to block out the background. "I heard about Novan. I am sure he will be fine," he said with dry emotion. He changed the subject. "How are the cousins doing?" His smile was sympathetic, but Urana heard the mocking tone.

She also smiled to herself, knowing exactly what Cirrius meant. Aerl and Altair were cousins to herself and Cirrius, but also half-brothers and cousins to themselves. Brothers when the mood struck them, usually based upon Altair's whims, but more often than not, they were cousins. And Altair's contrary disposition was now darker than normal, seeing as Novan had just destroyed parts of his home.

Urana was rather fond of Altair. They had often played and trained together as younglings; their respective mothers remaining close as sisters. Her father, Hyphon, had encouraged an early match, but was resisted by Altair's parents. And while both Altair and Aerl were trained for command, Altair's more rebellious nature always put him in the shadow of the slightly younger, but more serious Aerl.

Urana's lips curled into a smile. "The cousins are fine, I am sure. I have not had time to comm them nor they me. You?"

Cirrius' mouth turned down in nonchalance. "I have been busy..."

"Researching," she finished.

"Researching."

"And you are not going to tell me what I have just negotiated for you?"

Cirrius shook his head. "Sister, I need to research. I have much work to accomplish." He sounded weary, but sincere.

Urana gave him a hard look. "Are you sure nothing is going on?" She tried one last time.

"Nothing!" Cirrius assured her. "Now, how soon can you have the chronimonum delivered?"

Resigned to losing this battle, Urana played out the mental calculations. "Well, once Brou gets over the shock, I can have my personal courier, Gammor, deliver in three days, maybe two at a push."

Cirrius winced, making a sound in his throat. "Three days," he grimaced, looking hurriedly at something off-screen. "It will have to do, I suppose." He returned his gaze to his sister.

"I suppose," Urana half mocked him again with a smile. "Look for Gammor in three days then." Urana regarded her brother closely, as he again monitored something else off-screen. "Are you well, brother, really?" She was not sure why she had asked, but his uncharacteristically distracted manner and actions seemed different, agitated.

Cirrius conjured another weary smile. "I am fine, sister. Just been busy licking moonbeams." He used the old-fashioned expression from Galatia, seeing as neither Halcyon nor Placia had a moon, natural ones at least.

They stared awkwardly at each other on the screen for a while neither believing his explanation.

"Fine," Urana broke the silence, hiding her frustration. Cirrius could be quite secretive at times and she never pried, much. She always felt protective of him, sheltered as he was on his island. But there was something different this time. "Let me know if anything changes."

"I will," Cirrius said cagily. "I expect the chronimonum in three days." He smiled briefly, waved his hand across a crystal, and his screen went blank. Urana was left staring as her screen shut down.

She shook her head. *What was Cirrius hiding?*

Cirrius frowned at the blank screen. He sat back in his seat steepling his hands. "Three days!" He loved his sister, but sometimes she did not grasp the importance of things, his things.

It could be the difference between life and death.

Though he was not on active everyday duty, Cirrius still wore his Supreme Commander uniform. It was a stylised Sky Warrior manoeuvre suit, light blue and dark blue in varying proportion with a black belt, an allowance of individuality accorded to Sky Leader rank and above. He was ready for battle at all times.

He exhaled heavily through his nose, more in deep thought

than anything else. He stared through the screen, his dark blue eyes visualising the mental permutations, sharpening his thoughts, recalculating schedules, rethinking strategies, manoeuvring pieces in his mind.

It was not good enough, he shook his head in frustration. Next time he would have to negotiate directly with Brou. It would risk exposing his plans, but in the end, it really was a matter of life and death.

Happy with his decision, his thoughts were cut short by a soft chiming on another crystalator array behind him. He spun in his seat, half annoyed at the disturbance, and looked at the holo-screen readout.

This is interesting! His eyebrows curved up in surprise.

"Transfer and display," he said, intrigued. A large holographic display opened in front of him; a medtech scan of a Sky Warrior. Cirrius knew this day would come. "Hmm, so Sky Leader Deneb is active." He studied the display.

Raising his hands, he reached out and touched various holographic test results and notes, slightly manipulating here, deleting there. Being the Supreme Commander of the Sky Warriors and designer of the Sky Warrior crystalator systems had its advantages. He made sure he left no trace of his presence. Satisfied, he closed the system down.

"Monitor status," he told his crystalator, which silently went to work.

First Novan, now Sky Leader Deneb. What next? a pensive Cirrus thought.

"Are you trying my patience?" The gruff voice of an irritated Decion boomed out in the cavernous training deck on Alphatron

City-State.

The second son of Alphatronius and Elysius looked more like his father every day. He was so named because his father knew he would be worth ten times more than anyone who stood before him (mostly his firstborn, Novan). His aggressive flair in command had made him Supreme Commander of the space-borne Star Warriors and an honorary commander in the Xarian warrior clan, many of whom lived on Alphatron.

And one of his many duties was the training of his younger siblings. While he had many students who came to him for training, he saw them as a chore, but he reveled in training with the twins. But the twins were having their own fun again; being individuals in his training sessions, making their own decisions.

Youth! Decion decried to himself.

The secondary dock training area was eleven levels high, thirty meters wide with various platforms, rooms, alcoves, whole and fragmented floors open to the central hollow of the dock, all ready to hone the skills of warriors. Airlocks led to external platforms for null gravity work. The decks should have been full of Star Warrior opponents, but they were either late or otherwise unavoidably summoned to other duties. Decion agreeably found himself stuck with the twins, who now it seemed had tactical ideas of their own.

"You are under my command in this scenario!" he growled down at Alpha Rion who was eight platform levels below and to the left of him and to Astara, who was crouching on the higher-most level but one, to the right.

Below, the great round dock doors were cycled closed. The air was cold and crisp, but the recyclers still wafted the mechanical scents of stowed skimmers and large support equipment around. And it was quiet. Expectantly so. The stillness demanded action.

Decion's jaw clenched as he reassessed their positions, the

unexpected absences, examining the possibilities. He smiled grimly.

Ah, now I see! They are trying to purchase wane over me! His mood turned. And he saw the twins look at each other with expectant exhilaration as they realised they had almost accomplished their goal. Decion felt a surge of pride pulse through him. He was honoured. The twins saw him as a more worthy opponent than the hundreds of live and holo Star Warrior squads he had lined up for them. And he was. Then the last piece of the puzzle fell into place. Of course, the Star Warriors were not coming. It was all part of their plans. The twins were learning.

Decion stared down at Alpha Rion. He was a cunning one, a skilled warrior, but he relied too much on his intelligence. Alpha Rion was the brains of this plan, he knew. Looking up, he knew Astara was the more able of the twins, more intuitive, instinctive, and wilder when provoked. She was more like himself.

He grinned appreciably from under his beard. "You should have kept the Star Warriors. You would have required the reinforcements," he goaded in jest. He stood imperiously on his five-meter-long platform jutting out into the central open docking area, his red and black armour, topped with his huge red helm, ringed from his wide shoulders by his bifurcated cape which swept around him. He was only missing one thing.

From within, he summoned this energy. His hand reached into the air in front of him where a small flashing portal had opened. He drew his arm back and with it his lancesword; two and a half meters of lethal black metal crowned with a fist-sized crystal resting in the vee of the pommel. Beside him lay his four-armed shield. He hoisted this up and stood ready.

The twins, like Decion and their father Alphatronius, were able to summon their weapons from a fortress hidden in another dimension. They each possessed a sword forged and handed down through each of the ancestral Alpharion clan generations, each sword as individual as the bearer.

Alpha Rion's black armour bore a torso-dominated red, broken-cross motif, which led down to a belt, adorned with the cross of Alpharion, an emblem to denote universal energy. Each hand of Alpha Rion drew an energised short meta-sword, the golden blades flaring in anticipation.

Perched above, Astara's black nexus sword was already unsheathed and held aloft. Upon her mane of long, curling black hair she wore a simple thin red crown which extended down at the sides of her head almost encircling her elfin features. A short red cape hung behind her and her short black-belted, red and black tunic covered her black armour, while long black boots ended above her knees.

Suddenly, Astara launched herself at Decion, sword first, almost taking him by surprise, just as she and Alpha Rion had practiced for weeks. Her ferocious scream, as she descended, augmented by her comms, made Decion wince. In full free-fall mode, Astara drew her arms back for maximum power. Then she wrenched her arms forward her nexus sword striking Decion's lofted four-armed shield dead centre. Decion was knocked to one knee for an instant. His shield bore the brunt of the impact, the force of the strike rebounded upon Astara who backward rolled out of the danger area, expecting Decion's next move.

Before Astara could draw back and strike again, Decion dipped his shield forward driving her back with its sharp edges. Then he abruptly brought his right arm up and around, his lancesword dropping flat-sided like a boom upon Astara's crowned head, felling her.

Astara couldn't but help cry out in pain. Followed by a curse.

Ha, Decion laughed to himself, *that will make her think twice!* He hefted the lancesword for another strike.

Trying to ignore the pain or feel for any cuts, Astara screamed; more in anger than pain, and from her prone position rolled back and out of danger rising into a crouched position. She wasn't finished yet.

Out of the corner of his eye, over the edge of the platform, Decion kept tabs on Alpha Rion below. He had not yet moved and Decion wondered what their ploy was. Astara could fight all day, but together they would be stronger.

What is their ploy? the thought dogged him.

There was a flash to the side of him as Astara charged, ran up a supporting strut, spun, and kicked Decion through the opening in his shield. Her boot caught Decion across his eye guard and he was blinded for a second, just as Astara hit the ground, pirouetted low with an outstretched right leg, and swept the legs from under Decion.

Decion went down flat on his back in a heap, shield falling from his grip, but no sooner had he hit the ground than he had kicked up followed by his torso and he was back on his feet. And almost immediately he was defending himself from Astara's Nexus sword to the head, parried; slashing down his arm, protected; jabbing, probing, swerving, Astara fighting almost on Decion's toes, too close for his lancesword to do anything, but block and parry with a virtually vertical blade and hilt, his shield still grounded on the other side of the arena.

And that's when Decion realised his back was turned to Alpha Rion, below.

Gods!

The big man turned sharply, shield-less gauntleted arm raised defiantly, lancesword pointed rearward to fend off Astara. His breath was ragged, his sweat was absorbed by his helm, but his heart was steady. So was his hand. And his little brother was not going to get the upper hand. . .

He turned and there was darkness. A weird circle of black appeared from nowhere and hurled Decion back five meters hard against the platform wall and to the metal decking. The lancesword flew out of his hand across the platform teetering on the edge.

From below, Alpha Rion stared up, a smile of astonishment on his visored face. Examining his hands, from whence the energy had come, he dissipated the portal. A little smirk on his face replaced his initial open-mouthed shock.

Astara stood frozen looking down in shock at him, motionless with caution as her instinct told her what would happen next.

Decion looked up with a grimace, tapped his helm firmly back into place, and held out his hand. The lancesword flew into it.

A rumbling grew in the room, a low roar emanating from the throat of Decion; louder as he opened his mouth, baring his teeth.

"Aaaaaargh!" the risen Decion screamed as he stormed to the edge of the platform and jumped, lancesword outstretched behind him ready for a devastating strike.

Alpha Rion stood still, transfixed in confusion and shock.

Astara shot a horrified look at her twin, willing him to do the only thing he could do. Scared to death that he would not do it! Astara jumped down.

Decion's arm brought the lancesword up and over, down upon his brother who looked up in some trepidation.

And at the last second. . .

"I yield!" Alpha Rion yelled, falling instantly to one knee, his twin gold swords extinguished to their otherworldly sheaths.

. . .just as Decion's lancesword skirted the top of his head landing in the thick metal deck beside him, point first, half a meter deep.

The reverberation sent a shiver through Alpha Rion's spine. He looked straight ahead, showing no fear; not looking Decion in the eye. Astara landed and fell in beside her twin, eyes down, her nexus sword sheathed.

"What was that?" growled Decion in as menacing a voice the twins had ever heard. He leaned on the lancesword overlooking them, flexing the decking even more.

Alpha Rion exhaled sharply. "I. . . I tried to open my sword portals to. . . be wide enough to go through it myself and exit behind you or bring you to me!" He looked up at Decion. "Obviously, it did not work. The portal repelled you."

"Repelled?" Astara scoffed, her smile evaporating quickly as Decion scowled down at her.

A face of scorn painted Decion's lower face, his lips like stone beneath his black shield of a beard. "What? You tried what?" He put a gloved hand to his beard, rubbing thoughtfully. "Why did you think you can do that?" he asked in an exasperated manner, anger slowly relenting. "It is not what the portals are designed for. They lead to our weapon sheathes in the fortress! They are not for travelling!" he roared.

"I know." The disappointment in Alpha Rion's voice could be heard. "But I wanted to see if it could be done. A surprise element in battle." He was about to say more but closed his mouth tightly.

But Decion knew what he was going to say. "You want to go to the fortress, like father."

A flicker in Alpha Rion's eyes told Decion the truth of it.

He shook his head, guffawing. "Father had the power to open dimensional portals. He could go to the fortress where our weapons are stored, at will. *We* cannot," he pointed at them. "We can draw weapons from their sheaths, but we cannot travel upon the weapon portals."

Alpha Rion shrugged. "Do you not want to see the fortress?"

Decion's shoulders slumped as much as he allowed his caped shoulders to. "I have seen it, as well you know. Father took me there when you were but week-old whelps. He used his powers from the map chamber to return!" He did not say the visit was to cheer him up after the twins had been born as he felt he had fallen down the pecking order of his parents' love.

Alpha Rion glared at him. "The only one. Not even Novan went."

Decion snorted in derision. "Novan? He is not like us. He is no warrior, has no weapon, and no place in the fortress. Why would father take him there?" His lips twisted in displeasure.

Alpha Rion bit his tongue at what was Decion's clear rhetorical question.

Decion's glare had softened, but his voice was still hard. "Training is finished for the day." With a grim smile, he extracted the lancesword effortlessly from the deck and sheathed it in a flash of portal energy. He turned and marched off, his boots striking the deck hard. The twins rose to their feet offering their brother a cursory bow. A few paces later, he stopped. Without turning he said, "You fought well today, Astara." He walked on.

Astara smiled, but then again, she always fought well. The words had been for Alpha Rion's sake.

Alpha Rion shrugged. He knew he would receive no praise today, but it did not bother him. He had his own plans. His lips curled upward slightly at the thought. Astara could see the set of his mouth. It always gave away his thoughts.

"You have already tried to enter the fortress." Astara did not have to make it a question.

Alpha Rion winked at her.

Before Decion had left the deck, there was a chime on all three of their forearm comms.

"Decion, here." He turned to the twins, a questioning tone in his posture.

"Decion, Star Commander Vander." There was a long pause on comms, the three Starguards thinking the line had been closed from the orbiting Star Warrior station of Vista Mare. Then: "There has been an incident. Novan has crashed into Millennius City-State..."

"Crashed?" Decion's retort was sceptical. "Was he attacked?" His warrior mind at work.

"We do not know. He is in their medbay, Aerl and Altair are standing by. Orders?"

Decion sighed. *So, Novan had crashed. He could take care of himself. And the brother-cousins were watching over him.* But he had to be seen to be doing something. "Raise alert status and increase patrols. I will comm Aerl for more data."

He cut the link. Turning back to the twins, he noted their genuine concern for Novan, and knew they knew he was not as concerned.

"He should have looked where he was going!" he remarked sarcastically.

He whirled toward the door, his large red cape billowing behind him. The doors to the level opened and slid closed behind him, making the dock area seem bigger.

The twins watched him go.

"Do you think we should go to Millennius?" Astara asked.

"No." Alpha Rion shook his head. "If there was a problem Aerl would let us know and if it was really bad Altair would be throwing a festival," he joked. Astara made a face at him.

"Do not even joke about that!" she chided. While she cared about their eldest brother, she, Alpha Rion, and Decion were a family within a family. "He is not as robust as us."

A knowing laugh was the reply. "Yes, he is. He's just different to us, but no less a leader," Alpha Rion said. He gave her a wry smile. "Let us clean up, renourish, then we have the tour of Systar Docks. The engineers are expecting us."

Astara groaned dramatically. The Trinari were always experimenting on new swordship designs, weapons and systems, and sought the opinions of the Starguards even though they were not engineers themselves.

"Why us? This is Cirrius's territory."

Alpha Rion gave her a look that said what she was thinking. *Because he is always on his island.*

But he said, "Probably because they want to see you," he teased.

Astara tittered. She had heard stories about the Trinari eng-techs engaging in nefarious behaviour aboard their ships with disreputable females, some known to dress up in the likeness of her or Urana. She shuddered at the thought.

Astara sucked her teeth, dismissing him with a flick of her hand. They both knew the real reason. Cirrius (and Urana) were of Elerae ancestry. And despite their respect for the Starguards, the Trinari still distrusted Elerae, due to the Amethystian genocide millennia ago. Direct relations were kept to a minimum even now. But the Trinari would deal with everyone else, even the Xarians, close allies to the Elerae.

Some of the pale, stocky, silvery-haired Trinari still retained an ancestral extra opposable thumb by their little finger. This extra dexterity had enabled them to excel in the art of spacecraft building, thereby mastering the leadership in space exploration, trading, and now crewing Swordships from the large asteroid station of Systar, orbiting Halcyon. They also allowed all others to crew their ships and access their space facilities, except the Elerae.

Astara would make sure she attended with Decion. He was enough to make any Trinari quiver in fear and thus avoid unwanted admirers annoying her.

Mind made up, she changed the subject. "So, after that spectacular failure tell me more about this portal travelling plan of yours?" she asked.

Alpha Rion looked at her cautiously. "Another time."

"No, now!" She bumped his shoulder playfully. Then she saw the guarded look he was trying to hide from her. "Universe, you've already done it haven't you?" She pulled him back by the arm to confirm her suspicions.

Alpha Rion smiled enigmatically. "We'll be late for the tour." He left the dock with a swing in his step.

"Brothers," Astara lamented, following with a head full of puzzles.

As Decion left the deck returning to his quarters, he scrutinised his and the twin's performance. He was not happy.

I concentrated too much on Astara's play; underestimated Alpha Rion. And they almost had me... almost.

But darker thoughts clouded his mind. Alpha Rion had to be dissuaded from entering the portal to the fortress. For his, and their family's own sake.

Cirrius poured over the last results from the chronimonum projections. If all went to plan, he could proceed with the engineering programmes. His crystalators had already created prototypes and his manufacturing lab under the adjacent island was just waiting to get started.

Now all I need is. . .

A loud blaring alarm from his main crystalator console froze him. He stared at it incomprehensibly. That sound was impossible. It was set to alert him in the event of. . .

"Universe! Not now!" He darted to the console, hands frantically working controls, voice commands minimal. "Confirm!" He analysed the screen, trying to collate the signals and scrolling figures. "Re-confirm. Time frame display!" His voice was raised.

He stared at the readouts. There was no question of its authenticity.

Cirrius closed his eyes, the briefest of respites in contemplation. He had much to do.

"They are coming!"

CHAPTER THREE

"So, what's wrong with him then?" snarled Altair for the umpteenth time.

While Aerl had flown out into the void and retrieved Novan after his crash, Altair had resealed and steadied the city from its drop into Magna Prime, much to the relief of the Meccuns. On returning from his task, Altair had wanted to tear apart Novan, who ever since his admittance to the medlabs hours ago, had remained unconscious. Altair had to be content with pacing up and down.

Being in close proximity to Magna Prime, the Meccuns had commed for medtech specialists, ferrying them in skimmers to Millennius City-State. Their shaved heads marked them out for their healing service, though generally most Meccuns' heads, both male and female, were adorned by long twisted locks or afros of golden, black or brown hair. Their capacity in learned-skills and advances matched the Galatians and allegedly some Meccuns possessed psychic abilities.

"You should try and probe Novan's mind for any signs of intelligence!" Altair had unsympathetically quipped, when told of Novan's condition.

Now standing in a muted blue anteroom, Sceptre tried to calm Altair down. Sometimes that was easier said than done. The Meccun medtechs had cloistered themselves in the medlabs, assessing and working on a treatment for Novan ever since, to no avail.

"They still do not know what's wrong with him," Aerl calmly stated. "The senior techs report Novan seems to have been attacked, but the city's defence forces out hunting for any intruders haven't found any signs of an attack." Aerl rubbed his face then combed his fingers through his short brown hair. "To tell you the truth, I don't think it was an attack. Something else happened to him. And if you want to help, you can by keeping calm."

"Oh, I'll show Novan calm when he wakes up. He'll be so calm when I'm finished with him, he'll never wake up again." Altair frowned, his blue eyes settling upon the double doors to the medlabs. "I'll really show him," he growled.

Aerl, the Sceptre, son of Sola Venga and Iria, and Altair, son of Auron and Iria, half-brothers and cousins, were complete opposites of each other. Aerl's calm confidence was honed into him by his father, Millennius' protégé, hence Aerl's honorary title of The Sceptre, the all-powerful weapon and symbol of Millennius, which Aerl's powers resembled.

Blond-haired Altair brooded like his father, Auron. He, like Decion, disagreed with some of Novan's policies and argued that they should be more in command. Despite Altair being almost two years older than Aerl, it was Aerl who was Novan's second-in-command.

And while most Celestians had decided upon settling on the sparkling new worlds, others wanted the freedom of space, and in time they converted ships into two vast space-faring City-States, roaming the system at will. Millennius City-State was full of magnificent spires and was home mostly to Galatians who wished a life among the stars. It was also home to and jointly commanded by Aerl and Altair.

Regarding his half-brother, Aerl sighed. He was weary of Altair's resentment toward Novan. And this latest incident did not help. Novan bore no hostility to anyone, not even toward his own arrogant brother Decion, but Altair just couldn't, or wouldn't, get along with him or anybody else. He had to go looking for a fight.

Someday, Aerl knew, someone would come along and put Altair in his place. And Aerl was afraid it would have to be him.

Inside the medlab, the medtechs tried once again to awaken Novan, this time stimulating his brain with neurowave-impulses designed to interrupt whatever was interfering with his brainwave signals, but his state remained unchanged.

Senior Medtech Ede reviewed Novan's progress with her staff. "There is no pain, no serious injuries, but his mind is systematically engaged. It is as if his mind is being held captive, his brain activity has increased remarkably. And look at his eyes," she pointed to the movement under closed eyelids. "It is as if he is receiving an incredible amount of sensory input!" She shook her head, mystified. "We just do not know enough about his psionic nature to help him. He may have to let his own mind resolve this!" She shook her head again.

The eight medtechs stood around, baffled at what could be afflicting Novan.

But Novan was dreaming.

And memories came flooding back ...

Long ago.

"We stand on a World on the threshold of total destruction ..." Millennius paused at the uncomfortable words, glowing across the crystalator screen of his padd, a reluctant admission of defeat. He adjusted the padd settings for no reason other than to procrastinate, before continuing.

"This, Galatia, was the first and foremost of all the Worlds, now we are the last remaining bastion of life in the universe. Outside our realm, enveloping death and ultimate destruction by our dark enemy, is held at bay by us, the last guardians: the Celestian Knights."

Millennius' voice tried to stay strong, but Spheron, Keeper of the Scrolls of History, heard the deep sorrow within it. He halted his rehearsal, Millennius, for all his towering leadership, had never been one for speeches and he gave Spheron a look of resignation: You can do this, Spheron.

But Spheron shook his head. It was not for him to address the Celestians.

On a kilometer-high sheer plateau over-looking the majestic and overcrowded Celestia Qor, in the Halls of Celestial Order, the young Novan sat half-slouched in a chamber seat, one of twelve ornate high-backed metal seats, circling the large U-shaped table. Millennius' raised seat stood at the head of the open end with its own raised dais. Holograms of world regions played out in the hollow of the table, Novan watching for any telltale signs of invasion. Half his mind was also engaged with listening to Millennius practice the speech he would be delivering to the world that night.

The Celestian Knights had been on varying missions around Galatia, dispersed to maintain peace, investigate enemy incursions, and show the Celestian populace a united Celestian Knight presence. Tonight, they were returning, an exciting event for Novan. And for all Celestians, a chance to hear Millennius speak to them.

But Millennius' mind seemed to be distracted by something else. Someone else.

"Has she arrived, yet?" the leader's soft voice asked.

Spheron shook his head again. Phasia was still absent. His leader's lover and blind spot. His greatest strength and liability.

Just then, the five-meter-high carved metal doors to the

Celestian Council chamber opened. Millennius' heart skipped a beat just for a second in hopes of the arrival being Phasia, but instead, a frown clouded his face as Destina came gliding in. Her long brown hair was tied up in a conical shape upon her head, wrapped in gold thread. Her green cape overlapped a silver and green loose-fitting gown. She had never been one for the tight restrictions of armour.

Millennius knew better than to mention Phasia's name now, knowing his sister's dislike for her. She was always watching, distrustfully.

"Brother," she addressed him curtly, her winsome features managing a brusque smile. "When can we expect this speech? We have to prepare and finalise the youngling's training!" she added impatiently.

Novan's ears pricked up. He knew he was included in the 'younglings' even though he was almost twenty. But he was determined to stay. He would convince them. His mother would listen to him.

Destina, Mistress of Fate, daughter of Celestra, drew close to her step-brother and kissed each cheek in a perfunctory manner. Her mother had joined with Millennius' father after both their non-Celestial Knight parents had passed. With the power of the Sight, Destina was able to see the unfolding paths of the future. She guided and advised Millennius who turned her prophesies into his commanding policy. Though she could be manipulative, her visions were true and uncompromisable, for if she were to debase her prospicience, havoc would reign.

However, even Novan knew something had happened to her powers. Even as Destina had seen the dark future forming, fate had intervened and left her blinded to the Sight. Some had said it was to ensure the prophesied fate of the Celestian Knights; others that Destina had deliberately chosen to relinquish her powers in order to not see their End. Either way, fate, it seemed, would have its way. Without a doubt, Destina was a woman all her own, her lonesome existence was all-encompassing and could drive one insane in their pursuit of her. It already had.

Millennius accepted her greeting. "The speech will be ready soon and we will have enough time for the younglings, sister," replied Millennius. "Take your seat." He held out his hand.

With a withering look, Destina glanced at the table. She stalked slowly around the heavy wood table as if looking for the optimal position, the seats not allocated to a specific Celestian Knight, a tradition so each Knight had no chance of claiming favouritism to whoever led the Celestian Knights. Destina gave Novan a courteous smile, which Novan happily returned, as she sat a few chairs from him.

Novan had heard his parents speak of Destina, how she involved herself with the intrigues of the court, scheming various fates for others whom she judged deserved her personal attention, which included almost everyone. But she had always been kind to the younglings.

Away from them, Spheron regarded his leader:

Millennius, son of Millenniar, had the magnificent bearing and stature that could have seen him live a thousand years, but that honour was lost, being the last leader of those born in the one-thousandth generation. The very light that shone out through the cosmos was at his command. He was the light, encaptured in his golden armour, and his symbol and weapon—a sceptre of light. Spheron had seen him cast his golden gaze across the lands, raise his sceptre of light and reform the land into a form that best pleased him. But as the rays of a sun blind one when glanced upon, so Millennius was blinded by his own inner pains, hidden passions, and to the flaws which lay within himself. And that is what Spheron had to mollify.

Spheron sighed, and as usual, opened the large bound book The Scrolls of History carefully emplaced on a lectern by Millennius' seat, seeking the words his leader needed. His action was an affected habit as the book could have easily been read from a padd if required. Being Millennius' First General, confidant, and interpreter of the Scrolls of History, Spheron held many secrets, many of which could destroy them all and any hope of salvation, if revealed. But Spheron, would never reveal a secret, even on threat of death; for there were some things even worse than death.

Only Millennius, Destina, and Spheron had stayed within the environs of Celestia Qor, almost thirty million inhabitants, mostly refugees trying to survive. It needed all of their attention.

Outside the chamber, fast-paced footsteps, greetings, and complaints could be heard. Novan sat up, expecting to be both warmly acknowledged by one parent and cajoled or ignored by the other.

But stepping proudly in first with a wide smile on his rough face was Hyphon the Sky Warrior, son of Jerichon. The Elerae blood within him was apparent by his flaming mane as wild and as blue as the fiery, blue-giant star that Elera sailed around. His raptorial nature and haughty loftiness was a grim reminder of his heritage, enhanced by his skysharp swooping and soaring with a grace unmatched as if he were the transformed bird itself. His strength was enhanced by the meta-staff, a gift from Millennius, capable of unleashing energies that could raze mountains or calm the seas. He was the power of the wind, his armour dark blue with red vertical stripes on his arms, torso and legs. And the only things that could capture and tame the storm that was Hyphon the Sky Warrior were his wife, Ultra Ari, and their younglings, Urana and Cirrius.

"Millennius, my Lord," he bowed graciously. "It is well met to see you again." They clasped forearms in greeting. Hyphon had just returned from patrolling Anchrus, the western continent, inspecting the shield defences across the Tannic Sea. He frowned. "It is a shame to see the Qor in such a state, but we will save as many as we can. It was a great plan you conjured, Spheron." He strode forth and also clasped the Master of Forcefield's arm.

Spheron smiled with satisfaction. "Magnanimous of you, but while I was but the architect, the engineer is behind you!" Hyphon turned knowing who he would meet.

As if on cue, the next Celestian Knight arrived ahead of a couple of others. Novan stiffened in his chair at the new arrival—his father: Alphatronius, son of Novan, warrior-sorcerer supreme. Back from reinforcing the outposts in the High Torolocos in the east, he seemed as insouciant as ever.

Alphatronius practically stalked into the chamber, his long black hair threatening to hide his face, yet never taking his eyes off Millennius, his long-term rival. Of Xarian descent, his dark features were accentuated by his heavy worn armour, coloured the red of blood and the black of death.

"Millennius," Alphatronius began, "A pleasure." He grinned, stopping short of Millennius to clasp his forearm. "I look forward to your speech as always." His words dripped sarcasm as he walked off, red cape flowing behind him. Then his eyes caught and lingered over Destina, who coyly diverted her eyes after a few seconds, leaving Alphatronius with a lecherous smile. His path took him past his son.

"Father," Novan greeted him coolly, not surprised Alphatronius barely flinched at his voice or acknowledged him with a glance. Father swept by son in silence. Novan knew Alphatronius would rather have Decion by his side, but his second-eldest and preferred son was watching over the other younglings, several chambers below them.

The warrior's powers granted him command over other dimensions and space with which he could warp around himself, expand, and create dimensional shields. It had been Alphatronius who had saved the Trinari population by surrounding their world in a shield of dimensional energies, thus allowing the inhabitants to escape to Galatia, while the creatures of darkness had become caught in a maze of energy, a feat his fellow Celestian Knights never heard the end of. He often had them spellbound with tales of other galaxies. His weapons, a myriad of swords, were sheathed in an other-dimensional fortress and commanded by thought to his hand alone.

His friction with Millennius stemmed from the fact Alphatronius was desperately in love with Destina. But she spurned his love in a toying fashion to spite him, much to the amusement of his estranged wife, Elysius. The love between him and Elysius had grown to hatred; his ego, jealousy, and cavorting combining to drive them apart. No longer a present father to his own five children, Alphatronius became mentor to Auron, whom he honed into his own image.

Dismissed by his father, Novan's spirits were raised when his mother entered the room.

Elysius, the Divine Goddess, daughter of Meccus was a treasure, a jewel of beauty. The mind was her domain, with mastery over telepathy, telekinesis, and teleportation. Elysius had long ago given up using her charms on her wayward husband, knowing too well of his indiscretions and his feelings toward Destina. Their five children were in her care and, in her eyes, better off without their father.

A wide smile rewarded Millennius, Elysius always brightening any room she graced. She kissed him on each cheek and caressed his face in friendship. She had served with Neb and Meccun priests and sci-techs across the sprawling scorched Haxhaxx deserts.

"We are with you," she said in her soft accented voice. She clasped his forearm then Spheron's. Her eyes met with Alphatronius and there was a sparse muted greeting across the table.

Novan squirmed in his chair even as his mother approached with a warm smile.

>*Never mind. This is normal*< she psyed reassuringly, standing close to him.

Novan sighed, his eyebrows raised in agreement.

While Alphatronius and Hyphon spoke in quiet tones at the far bend of the table, the estranged wife of the former was joined by the wife of Hyphon.

Ultra Ari, daughter of Solatia, was no less a Goddess herself, but whereas Elysius had the beauty and the spirit, Ultra Ari also possessed physical strength beyond all others. Her powers relied on the rays of the cosmos to radiate upon her golden mane of hair increasing her strength up to a thousand-fold, but with that power came a rage that also threatened to consume her. The beloved wife of Hyphon had rejoined them from Anchrus' neighbouring forest continent of Anturia. She and Hyphon were two of a kind, headstrong and passionate, but together managed to tame each other's primal forces enough to start a family.

She waltzed into the room, embracing Millennius with a hearty hug. She stared into his eyes. "I am ready!" she announced, just as her younger sister drew up beside her.

Iria, the Imp, was full of the energy of life. The wife of Sola Venga, Iria was blessed with the gracefulness of a starbird and could produce the most vivid spectral effects, each colour of light having a different purpose. She was the spark of life. It was said of her that during a fierce battle around Meccus, the spectrum had burst out from within her and splashed upon the unholy enemy, thereby giving each one a distinctive colour that remained ever since.

Shyer than her sister, she bowed formally to Millennius, greeting both him and Spheron. She was not as tall, nor as robustly built like Ultra Ari, but her speed was unmatched. Her only regret, she had confided once to Ultra Ari, was not marrying Sola Venga sooner and begetting him more sons. Though she had produced a son with Auron, their union had not been a joyous one. And her young, but perceptive sons fed off those misgivings.

Millennius did not have to guess what was on her mind. "I will protect your sons. I promise," he said sincerely.

This seemed to lift Iria, whose body shimmered a harmonious yellow. She patted Novan on his shoulder as she passed to join the conversation with her sister and Elysius. Her mission had ranged west across the Jenjekjo and Tannic seas surrounding Anchrus and Anturia.

Novan loved the procession of the Celestian Knights. They hardly ever entered the halls in concert as each wanted their own private entrance and an audience to speak briefly with Millennius. And none more so than the next Knight. Novan watched keenly for any signs of dissent.

Another figure in smooth blue armour marched in—Acirrius, the younger brother of Hyphon. In from the northern six-domed Opellion Qors, full of Elerae refugees, he had trained them in maintaining the forcefields over the Xaman Ice Sea.

Living under the shadow of his more famous sibling was beginning to reflect in Acirrius' manner. He tried with great care to hide that fact, but a rift had developed, which could have caused them to tear each other apart. The cause of this simmering conflict was Millennius, or rather the gift he made to Hyphon—the meta-staff. Acirrius had a great affinity with cold seas and winds able to control great masses of air, energising them to his will, whereas Hyphon used his meta-staff for that same purpose. Acirrius resented the use of the staff, which infringed upon his domain and he vowed to have it lost. Destina had foreseen that his wish would come to pass, but long after he was dead.

Even from where he sat, Novan could feel a coldness develop in the chamber. Millennius seemed to ignore it smiling cordially at Acirrius, who stared stony-faced at his leader. Well-muscled and more handsome than Hyphon, his blue hair plaited in long rows, Acirrius' sole purpose in life was to serve, so much so that he had never started a family. That had never bothered him and he had been proud that his brother had named his son, Cirrius, after him. But he would not allow anyone to distract him from his own duties.

He solemnly held Millennius' forearm and spoke quietly into Millennius' ear, "We may not see eye to eye, but I swear to you, I will do everything in my power to make sure our people survive." Without a smile he left Millennius and took a seat straight away, leaving the other Celestian Knights still standing in their private conversations. That is until the next Knight entered. And all pretense of silent conversation fell away.

If Phasia felt all eyes upon her or all thoughts directed toward her, she did not reveal it. She even ignored the cold glare of Destina. She only had eyes for Millennius. Tall, with long brown tumbling hair, green eyes, and high cheekbones, which defined her wide smile directed at Millennius, she practically danced into his arms. Millennius instantly felt the weight of the world lift off his shoulders. The daughter of the great Zater Jen and sister to Synther, she could transform herself from matter into an energy state resembling a magenta storm of energy in a woman's form, though she could not wield it as handily as her brother had.

Though Millennius could not see his own flaws and the resentment that was building toward him, notably from Destina, Alphatronius, and Acirrius—mostly because Elysius and Spheron buffered him from such annoyances—Phasia was able to smooth out his temperament, presenting him as a leader worthy of his title.

She and Millennius clasped hands and briefly joined lips, in a rare open acknowledgment of their relationship. Even the young Novan realised the significance of that. This was really the end.

And instead of joining the others around the table, Phasia took her place beside Millennius, on his right, Spheron stepping back to accommodate her.

Destina looked away disgusted, while the others tried to continue their hushed conversations.

Even Novan knew the reasons for the discreet discussions. There were rumours that Phasia's only mission to the remote southern Lostratane Mountains had been to bear Millennius' child. Her long periods incommunicado with all but Millennius and Spheron were not proof, neither was the inability to discover the child, apparently hidden for its own safety. But the suspicions still remained.

And in strode the twin sons of Attanian; youthful, brash, idealistic, but different to each other as the poles of Galatia. Both had been deployed around the Darmanon Coastal islands, southeast and southwest, ironically surrounding and overlapping Phasia's area. They had not reported being in contact with her.

The brothers could harness and wield the energies created by the universe, but not as masterfully as Millennius who had often taken the twins under his wing to hone their powers as younglings.

They were the youngest of the Celestian Knights, but made up for it with sheer courage and determination.

Auron's oft-obstinate nature coupled with a propensity for violence, the cause of the loss of his young wife, Iria and their child, Altair, to his own brother, found him more akin to Alphatronius who eventually took charge as his mentor. The twins had always been rivals and jealousies had arisen almost every time. While Auron tried to find no fault with his twin and loved him dearly, he considered Iria to be deceitful. But the apparent theft of his wife was too far for any heartfelt reconciliation.

By contrast, Sola Venga was loyal to Millennius in a way that no one else could be, though the twins both undertook training from Millennius and Alphatronius. Their shared powers were such that the raging torrent of quantum forces they controlled were unpredictable. Sola Venga always worried that his powers would overwhelm him and turn him against the others. He feared his powers. His nightmares only increased his fears as he saw himself turning into one of *Them* and destroying the others. This vision tormented him and the more he used his powers, the more he was tormented, his only source of comfort being Iria, and their son, Aerl.

Almost worshipful, Sola Venga knelt on one knee before Millennius, "I pledge I will defend Galatia to the end," he earnestly announced.

Alphatronius rolled his eyes. "Be careful what you wish for, young lord!" he laughed. There were a few quiet titters. Even Auron showed his amusement.

Sola Venga hid his emotions, but retorted. "Mock me, Alphatronius, I do not care. I will die with honour!"

Alphatronius tilted his head in appreciation. He turned his gaze to Auron in greeting who returned it with a slight bow, a small and frowned-upon discourtesy to Millennius to greet another without first paying him respect.

"You forget yourself, brother," Sola Venga whispered to him.

A brief hesitation from Auron made the watching Novan think he would not make amends, but stroking his thin-bearded chin, he faced Millennius.

"I meant no sleight, Millennius. There is no excuse." He looked down, suitably chastised, dutifully grasping Millennius' forearm.

"No offense taken," replied Millennius, accustomed to Alphatronius' ploys, pointedly looking at him. Alphatronius' sly grin remained.

Auron turned away slowly crossing over to Alphatronius and Hyphon, as Sola Venga sat by Novan. They clutched arms in greeting.

Spheron gestured and the holographic images above the table died down and the great doors closed automatically.

They had all arrived.

All but one.

Spheron inclined his head at Millennius, who motioned for everyone to sit, which they did, opponents opposite each other.

"Let the ceremony begin!" Millennius said.

Novan listened, raptly. The Recital was his favourite part of the annual Celestian Knight gathering.

The Scrolls of History were old. Long before the Decillennial War, the knowledge contained within them had been astronomical, but it had been encrypted and entrusted to the Scroll Keeper of each sequent generation of Celestian Knights, all the successive Spherons, who copied word for word the inscriptions over time.

And even though crystalators had superseded the ancient parchments, the Recitation was traditionally read from the large bound book accompanied by copious amounts of scrolls laid out in front of Spheron upon the lectern at the head of the table.

Prior to Millennius' speech to the rest of Galatia, Spheron, as all the ancestral Spherons had before him, performed the annual recital from the Scrolls of History chronicling their beginnings, an affirmation to their Great Father and Holy Mother, their Makers, and to their offspring the Storm of Stars, and the rise of the Celestian Knights.

There was a reverent hush as Spheron began with the first words that sang the Universe into being:

"Begin!"

Such a simple word, Novan thought, but it was a profound thought and concept in which to create a whole new universe and life to follow.

Novan also loved the way Spheron's voice changed to inhabit different characters and aspects of the story.

"In a blink of an eye," Spheron continued in hushed tones, "the new universe had been spoken into being by the Great Father and Holy Mother. They populated their new abode with twelve offspring: the Storm of Stars. There were six Prime Stars and six Shadow Stars, mirror-images, equal yet opposite in their argumentative and contrary natures.

"One day after an argument they gathered in the midst of the universe's hallowed swirls and boasted as to whom had achieved the most feats of power. Their tales would have gone on forever had not they decided to create lesser beings to worship them and to witness their great deeds. So from the four universal elements they created four Peoples to worship them:

First they made the People of Energy
Next they made the People of Matter
Then were made the People of Psyche
And last they made the People of Time

"The Storm of Stars were pleased with their creations, but the four Peoples did not like each other. They warred amongst themselves. They warred throughout the galaxies. They warred for a million years. The People of Energy became the most powerful and even dared to name themselves, but being so incomprehensibly evil *Their* name had been forbidden in the Scrolls of History. But it had never been forgotten. Dead to history, but alive in memory, the name had resided in the minds of those who would have dared to think it and lingered on the lips of those who would have dared to whisper it.

"*They* defeated the People of Matter, burning them from stone into metal, leaving them to drift for eternity throughout the cosmos. Next, *They* defeated the People of Psyche by spreading imaginary poison, forcing them into exile. And lastly, *They* defeated the People of Time by trapping them within crystal and casting them beyond the Realms of Futurecome. *They* were rampant and destructive, victorious, and destined to rule the universe, but their deeds did not go unnoticed. This aeons-long war, mere moments to the Storm of Stars, greatly displeased them, thus they met once again in the depths of Universe's darkest seas to discuss the development of their creations. And it was agreed to create a new People.

"And thus, from the minds of the Storm of Stars sprang champions, bred for battle, and made from the elements of the first four Peoples:

Heroes made from Matter so that they had body and strength.
Heroes made from Energy so that they had souls and emotion.

Heroes made from Psyche so that they had intelligence.
Heroes made from Time so that they knew what had come to
pass and what would come to be.

"So were the Fifths endowed, finely structured and balanced in nature to counter and defeat the People of Energy. And so had begun the Decillennial War. During that misty period of the past that was the Decillennial War, one of the Fifths came to realise that the Fifth Peoples had a greater destiny to fulfil. He was Celestius, a leader among equals, a warrior of great conviction, courage, and intelligence. Such was his character that the Fifths named themselves the Celestians. And they settled on one world they named Celestia.

"And millennia later, in the dark mythical times of the Stranger Aeons, mysterious champions arose, the progeny of the heroes and champions of the wars aeons past. With the will of the Universal Creators on their side, these champions overthrew the evil People of Energy, forever banishing them from the bounds of the universe. The Decillennial War was over.

"And yet, that defeat had unbalanced the strange symmetricism shared by the Storm of Stars and the Universe. Before they faded away, back into the universal fold from whence they had come, they infused upon the Celestian champions their legacies. But so that they would not forget themselves or aspire to universal glory, the Storm of Stars mutually agreed and saw fit that these champions would only survive for one thousand generations.

"And thus began the birth, life, and death of those who were called the Celestian knights!"

Spheron bowed his head in supplication. Each of the Celestian Knights placed a palm over their heart then raised the same hand placing their fingertips to their foreheads in sacred remembrance.

Spheron continued his recitation, the mythical past turning into recorded history.

"The first Celestian Knights: Galatian, Spheron, Statia, Ozmec, The Others, and Gen Horol were harbingers of strange and wonderful powers, mysterious, all-powerful, and worshipped throughout the universe which they safe-guarded, gifts bequeathed to successive generations. A Golden Age had followed; a time of peace lasting millennia.

"Celestia, our ancestral home world, was lost to time after the Celestians had been scattered by the Storm of Stars, diverging into differing societies. We became a peaceful union of Seven Worlds: Galatia – the world of artist-builders, Elera of the noble blue-haired warriors, Meccus the technocrats, Trinar the mighty shipbuilders and explorers, Neb the tribal priests, and Xarias with its weapon makers. The seventh world, Amethystia and her peoples, were long since destroyed.

"With their attendant colonies, Outer Worlds and territories, they had stood for countless millennia as an example of supreme excellence. And they would have existed for millennia upon millennia had not the horror from the past returned."

Spheron's voice turned harsh.

"*They*, the People of Energy, had escaped from their other-dimensional prison. Word from the Outer Worlds had told:

". . . of great creatures of black light and evil emerging from the depths of space, casting an unholy and gory glow among the stars as *They* devoured the very life from out of them . . ."

"The Outer Worlds had been slowly devoured first, as *They* had made *Their* way across the universe toward the Six Worlds, the very heart and soul of every being's life.

"*Their* evil resurgence had been swift and relentless. Whereas it had taken ten millennia to defeat them before, a mindless brood intent on survival, there was now an intangible intelligence behind *Their* actions and *They* were spanning star-years in rapid succession:

". . . skies filled with the blood of stars, suns scarred and screaming for their lives, an everlasting twilight descending bringing death . . ."

"*They* were insatiable and unstoppable. *They* had never reached the Six Worlds' frontier before, but now within a fraction of the Decillennial War's time, *They* had reached them and the final outcome was becoming inevitable. And then one by one the Worlds had fallen, leaving the survivors to flee each time, until only Galatia remained!"

Spheron's voice was husky with grief.

"Now, the universe lays dead around Galatia, burning in unnatural fires created by *Their* feeding, or dying in a cold waste; so cold that no sun's fire could ever warm it again. It pained us Celestians: those who had lived for so long, achieved, advanced and sacrificed so much only to see *Them* return to destroy it all. There was no fathomable conscience to *Them*, just an incomprehensible desire to exist to destroy.

"And throughout all of this fiery tragedy and death the Celestian Knights had battled in vain, every manoeuvre countered by *Them*, every step undermined and turned against them. They fought with fervour and righteousness, but the unnameable monstrosity continued on unabated and strengthened by Celestian Knights' failures. With Galatia the only world left, it seemed now that the greatest civilisation ever known was coming to an end.

"There had been no crisis of this like for generations, not since the Period of the Hero Siege when the Celestian Knights Priorion, Astari, Ulix, Zen Devastar, Spheron, Teo Venga, Azurzura and Thronen Kor had fought against a mysterious enemy and then just as mysteriously disappeared without a trace, a whole generation gone.

"But unknown to any of us Celestian Knights, our days in the Golden Age had come to an end on a dark day of treachery!"

Someone huffed in anger, Novan not seeing who.

Spheron proceeded unperturbed: "In all of the one thousand generations of Celestian Knights, since the end of the Decillennial War, our origins and history had been shrouded in secrecy and mysticism!" Spheron quoted from the Scrolls of History.

". . . And so it was that the Gods brought unto us the Celestian Knights, the Great Saviours," he recited.

Everyone knew that passage from the Scrolls of History. But only Spheron, the scribe and keeper, had known exact lineages. The general consensus was that the Celestian Knights were actually the descendants of the Decillennial War heroes from the Stranger Aeons.

On Spheron spoke: "But the one-thousandth generation would always be special, for as foretold by Ozmec:

"In the one-thousandth generation shall arise the most powerful generation, born and blessed with all the insight, knowledge, and power ever bestowed upon a generation. They shall be the most powerful and prolific; the most celebrated and revered. And they shall also be the last. For it is foreseen that in this same generation shall arise The Crisis of The End, a conflict beyond all others, between ultimate good and ultimate evil which shall bring about the destruction of all."

They all knew The End was near. Galatia was alone, protected by dint of the Celestian Knights having concentrated and combined their powers to create a blazing field of protective energy around Galatia, which the heartless monsters could not penetrate. This supernatural aura of protectiveness was all that kept *Them* at bay, and if it were to disintegrate as a cohesive body, then all would be lost.

Then Spheron made an admission. "We had believed we had lost one of our own heroically fighting *Them*! But that is false!"

The Celestian Knights stirred in their seats, Millennius looking hard at his exegete. A din of confusion began to rise in the chamber.

Undaunted, Spheron's voice rose above theirs. "We Celestian Knights had not foreseen one of their own turning against the others, forsaking his proud heritage..."

Phasia shot from her seat. "Spheron, speak plainly. Did not my brother die at the hands of the beasts?" She shivered in anger.

Spheron stared grimly at them all. "No!"

There was a moment of incredulous silence.

"Synther lives, Spheron?" Millennius spat through gritted teeth. His face was of dark resolve. "How? You reported he was dead!" he snarled angrily.

Spheron sighed, somewhat over-dramatically. "I thought he was dead. He could not have survived. I wanted to preserve his name, his integrity."

"No!" shouted Alphatronius, pointing at Millennius. "You wanted to protect Millennius and Synther's treacherous sister!" he accused Spheron.

Arguments broke out around the table.

"Stop!" ordered Millennius. Silence instantly followed. He shook his head in disbelief. "Then Synther is evil, Spheron. Why else would he turn against us, delving into the forbidden arts of evil and destruction... joining the enemy?"

Spheron spoke another startling confession: "But that is not why he turned against the Celestian Knights!"

More arguments threatened to erupt, but it was Phasia, not

able to abide by what she was hearing, who spoke up the loudest.

Clearly upset, she said, "I, like my brother, had been affected adversely by our father's mysterious disappearance. But while I had Millennius to console me, my brother had no one. He had been more outspoken against Millennius than even Alphatronius!" She looked darkly over to Alphatronius who didn't hold her gaze. "His inner motives and thoughts were his own. He was a law unto himself, the darkness inside us all, but, Spheron, if this was not enough to change him? Then what was?" At least a few sympathetic noises were made.

A deep breath vibrated through Spheron. "He discovered something; a simple truth. In searching for his father through the Scrolls of History, he discovered the Celestian Knights' secret, one that had affected him beyond all reason. As it has long been believed, the Celestian Knights had been sent by the Storm of Stars as saviours, our origins shrouded in mysticism. But it had been the first generations of the Celestian Knights who had expounded this myth. It had grown and become part of the legend of the Celestian Knights, but it is entirely false. And Synther, without my knowledge, deciphered an obscure inscription from the Scrolls of History, written by one of my ancestors."

Spheron glanced up from shuffling his scrolls, trepidation on his face. He was scared, Novan saw. Spheron's lips moved, but no words came out at first. Then louder, he read out:

"Know now that we Celestian Knights art no sons of Gods, but the spawn of the bane that we sought to abolish from our universe. Know now that we are kin to the Destroyers of Worlds, half-breeds to living devils, the children of death. Are They not responsible for us? Are we not responsible to Them? Are They not us? Are we not. . . Lore?"

Sharp silence spiked with incredulity descended upon the hall.

Alphatronius scoffed. "Spare us the jesting mythic testaments, Spheron..." He stopped short as he realised no one else was laughing.

Everyone turned to Millennius.

"Is this true, Spheron?" he asked his trusted friend.

With a bitter smile, Spheron nodded.

"It is part of the forbidden scrolls," Spheron confirmed with a pained voice. "Dark truths and black arts reside in these scrolls."

"What do you mean forbidden?" Hyphon exploded from his seat. "How can any knowledge be forbidden to us? How could you and your ancestors be so arrogant and so cowardly to hide such knowledge from us, for millennia!" He screamed. His wrath turned to Millennius. "How could you not know!" he jabbed his finger angrily in Millennius' direction. "This is our history! Our lives!"

Ultra Ari stroked his arm to calm him, which he unkindly shrugged off, awaiting an answer.

Spheron grimaced in an effort to explain. "The esoterics of the material demanded their removal from the public scrolls," he said. "Even I was fascinated and afraid when I first read them, but in control. I can only imagine what those words must have stirred within Synther. To be alone, different, and to discover our ancient connections to monstrous kin! What would you have done?" He let the words hang.

This time there was uproar as the Celestian Knights quarrelled amongst themselves. But Destina had kept her eyes fastened on Phasia, who now sat frozen and hadn't uttered a word since.

"And what do you think, Phasia? You and your brother's powers are closer to the... Lore," she said the forbidden name out loud before she realised, "than we are!" she added with a sneer.

The chamber went quiet. Everyone looked at Phasia.

Novan held his breath. He could barely understand what he

was hearing. How was this all possible? What was he supposed to tell the other younglings? He caught the eyes of his mother, her psi-aura, a diffuse pink colour, urging reassurance and calm across the hall.

Millennius stood up to defend Phasia, but his consort held up her hand forestalling his intervention.

"All through his life my... brother," the word reluctantly fell from her mouth, "felt apart, different, lonely. He felt that exhilaration of being pure energy, but I was still inexperienced in total transformation, still tied to the mortal world of corporeal beings. As pure energy, even I could feel the lure of immortality. But if he had fallen under their spell..." Her voice drifted off, not having to say anymore.

But more damning was another revelation from Spheron. He pulled out a tightly folded scroll from the many rolls he carried in a bundle and unwrapped it. In it was a small opaque oblong crystal.

"What trickery now, wizard?" Alphatronius contemptuously waved his hands at Spheron.

Spheron faced every Celestian Knight, his voice low and remorseful.

"This is Synther's confession!" He held it out for Millennius.

At first, the Celestian Knight leader refused to touch it, as if the contamination of Synther would tarnish him. But he knew they all had to know. He grabbed it from Spheron's outstretched hand, activated the crystal with his touch, placing it on the stone floor before him and in an instant a holographic image appeared.

Synther, son of the great Zater Jen, was a chameleon, a master of transformation, able to change his body into a fluid energy state. In this way, he had been the closest to the ancient enemy, whose energy forms were as sinuous.

Now Synther's handsome features, sporting short blond hair,

and dark eyes stared back at them. He smiled. A sad smile, indicating an acknowledgement of his actions. His quiet voice spoke:

"My fellow Celestian Knights, by now you realise I am not dead at the hands of the Lore and know what I have done! I found the forbidden scrolls. I do not apologise for my actions. They are true and noble. Though I was quite adept at deciphering the codes, the further the Scrolls of History went back, the more arcane the script became and I could not understand them. However, I sought, found, and took an ancient map from the records; an encrypted one, and that was a start.

"After a long search, I found the focal point in the region of space through which the first Celestian Knights had exiled and imprisoned the Lore outside of their dimensional plane. The breach between dimensions had been sealed by a bond of inter-dimensional energy, like a cauterized wound, strong enough to repulse the Lore's energy. But I deconstructed and opened the portal, allowing the Lore, our ancient kin, to be released.

"My first thoughts had been to unite the Celestian Knights with the Lore: a flawed ambition, I now know. The universe would have known the joys and delights of immortality, but I knew that it would not be accepted by you, especially you, Millennius. You do not have the ambition or leadership for this. So, in secret, I embarked upon my path alone to tame the savage beasts to my will.

"At once after opening the gate, thus freeing the Lore from their unjust incarceration, I, Synther, as I had been known, had died. The Lore had invaded my body, prepared to engulf me, but in that moment, the Lore, once the mightiest of the First Peoples, and I, the innocent Synther, had found ourselves fusing into something more. We were neither just Synther; nor just Lore.

"I had been chosen; chosen by the Lore to lead millions upon millions of now sentient Lore, such gifts did our fusion wrought. We absorbed all of our experiences, saw our worlds of birth, shared views of the universes. I saw them in hunger, in their drive to survive and grow. We need to survive. We need to grow. We cannot co-exist with you. Our survival demands this. We demand conquest. That is our destiny. And above all else, we demand our destiny."

And with that, Synther burst into a bright blue fiery energy being. "The Lore have returned!" the holographic image shouted. "And destiny will be ours!"

Message over, the holograph shut down.

The Starguards stared at the crystal, as if it was the embodiment of Synther, the blazing image etched into their minds.

After a thousand generations of Celestian Knights, the Great Enemy, whose name had once been a whisper on the winds of fear, became a fierce cry borne in the raging storm that would follow.

Millennius stood up and angrily crushed the crystal beneath his boot.

"Conquest! That is what Synther wants!" he snarled. "That is all!" His smile was grim, defiant. "He was bound by the laws given by the Scrolls of History, yet he still betrayed us," he lamented. With ire, he turned to his four closest fellow Knights who could have foreseen such treachery and in a fit of pique suddenly found themselves on trial.

"Spheron, Destina, Elysius, and Phasia, you are charged with the failure to detect Synther's treachery, for alone or together, you could have prevented such catastrophe!" accused Millennius. "Tell me how you could not have foreseen this?" he ordered with a demeanour which brooked no defiance. He stalked off, pacing the rear of the hall while the four worked on their defenses.

"This is crazy!" Novan overheard Sola Venga whisper to Iria.

"It is his right," rasped Alphatronius across the table.

The four accused were by themselves, preparing their statements. When the allotted time was up Millennius returned to his seat for each to address him. They each approached his seat singly.

Destina argued first; angry, forthright: "My Lord, the paths of the future are such that I can read their content, but their meaning is much more difficult. And furthermore, due to some contrivance, the paths of the future have been made unclear to me. I fear that the premonitions in the Scrolls of History were to come to pass, no matter what I saw, Sire."

Next, came Spheron; calm, logical, reasonable: "My Lord, I am the Keeper of the Scrolls of History, whose runes date to the beginnings of time. Mine is the duty to read, interpret, and scribe these runes, but at no time can I prevent others from learning the inscriptions and indeed from acting upon them. The fault lies not within the Scrolls, Sire, but within the heart of whosoever reads them."

Then came enlightened Elysius, peaceful in aura and manner: "My Lord, I am the seer into minds, but the mind of one such as Synther's was as impenetrable as the darkness that was coiled around his heart. His mind was as cold and unreachable as the creatures he now commands and I could no more read his thoughts, than he could mine, Sire."

Last was Phasia; plaintive, yet strong, determined: "My Lord, I have never been my brother's keeper and I am not now. I will not be held responsible for his actions. I have no feeling for him. I have had no contact with him. I have no brother!"

Millennius listened to all their testimonies as spoken. He stared at the stone floor, nodding to himself at each statement, deliberating on their words. After an interminably long time brooding by himself, he announced he was ready with his verdict.

Novan held his breath awaiting the verdict.

Millennius solemnly nodded to them. "Very well," he acknowledged. "After contemplation, I accept and exonerate you." This to the general relief of the Celestian Knights. But he was not finished.

"Spheron, these further words will be recorded into the Scrolls of History. Spheron readied his padd. "As leader of the Celestian Knights, I, Millennius, in my infinite wisdom, state that for his treacherous actions, Synther, shall be forever cast out of the ranks of the Celestian Knights Order and condemned; forever to be known as the Traitor Synther."

There were gasps around the chamber. Never had a Celestian Knight been cast out. But no one spoke out. No one defended the Traitor Synther. There was no coming back from this.

With those words, the Traitor Synther had been tried in absentia; there was only one punishment that awaited him, the Celestian Knights knew.

"Synther will be brought to justice. He will die for his actions!" Millennius held the gaze of every Celestian Knight. "To that end, I, Millennius, declare war against the Traitor Synther and the Lore!"

The announcement sent a chill down the spine of young Novan's back. This was the first time war had been declared by anyone since the Decillennial War and against the same foe.

The proclamation had been transmitted beyond the bounds of their unbreachable wall of energy. The Celestian Knights knew the Traitor Synther would retaliate after repudiating his offer to join him. But they had both nothing and everything to lose trapped as they were behind their forcefield. They felt like prisoners as the Lore had once been and time was running out. An eternity could have come to pass before Galatia had given in, but it was well known that this was to be the last Celestian Knight generation.

Novan, while not officially a Celestian Knight, having not been ordained into the Order or carried out a mission, was nominally in charge of liaising between the Celestian peoples and the Knights, freeing up Spheron from the role and also overseeing the other younglings, much to Decion's annoyance.

But then had appeared the most momentous occasion in the history of the Worlds.

Destina, within her private chambers, had a miraculous vision, an omen of such overwhelming vividness and eminence, that the Scrolls of History described it as:

"A visitation of significance, so unparalleled in the annals of history, its import could not be justifiably rendered by mere words."

Destina's vision had indeed been a visitation, by one of the first and most powerful Celestian Knights ever to have existed: Galatian.

Using his own and his generation's formidable powers, he had been able to project himself far into the future, through a thousand generations, to deliver salvation. Destina had been awed by his magnificent presence, but no sooner had he appeared, then he had vanished in a burst of celestial light.

Rushing into the Halls of Celestial Order and summoning the Celestian Knights, Destina had recounted Galatian's prophetic tidings:

"Behold the Voyager-Warrior come on wings of time long gone.
Our fathers are nigh, defeated not in what they have done.
When time at last shall die upon you, embrace brave blood and death.
Enter not the Gate of Spawn. Stand to, bold Knights, and hold forth The Light."

Long did the Celestian Knights ponder over these weird and twisted words, some of which were known, but others unfathomable in their sense and reason.

In a bid to decipher the words, Millennius had convened a late-night war council. Not everyone was best pleased.

"Millennius, what is the meaning of this?" Alphatronius barged his way into the chamber past Spheron and Hyphon. Even with a few meters between them, they could all smell the strong *vikinci* nectar emanating from him.

Elysius glowered at him, experience telling her that her former husband had been interrupted during one of his nocturnal dalliances. She cast a look of somewhat embarrassment toward Novan, who up until now had never seen his father inebriated.

>*Now I know, Mother*< he psyed. She closed her eyes in acceptance of the situation.

"Alphatronius, show respect to our leader," a smiling Hyphon ambled forward trying to defuse the situation. "We are all tired and battle weary, but we need to. . ."

"Silence, Hyphon!" Alphatronius whirled on him. "I am tired." He admitted, turning back to Millennius. "Tired of your leadership. You rely on whispers from Spheron, spying from your sister, and cavorting with a traitor's sister!" he spat at Phasia.

"Speak wisely," Spheron warned, "You insult us all!"

Alphatronius grinned widely. "No, not all, just him!" He pointed at Millennius, who stood impassively, with fists clenched, jaw set. "Our generation has been one debacle after another. We are trapped in a prison of our own making, letting traitors grow in our midst, and playing at puzzles from the past!" His voice rose at every accusation. "You do not deserve to lead us, Millennius, last generation or not. We need to fight, not cower behind forcefields," he raised his fists to emphasise his point. "Am I wrong?" he asked the assembled Knights.

Everyone looked at each other. Drunk or not, Alphatronius had some valid points. But was it their right to choose a new ruler? Was Alphatronius the right choice to replace him?

Alphatronius didn't wait for their answer.

"Step down, Millennius. Step down now!" he demanded, a growl in his voice. "Let someone more capable of leading take the battle to the Traitor and his Lore, instead of being self-made prisoners!" He swayed, arms on hips.

The chamber was as silent as a tomb.

Millennius stepped forward off his seat, resolute, arms by his side, eyes burning with repressed rage. Stopping inches away from Alphatronius' face, Millennius scowled at him.

"How dare you enter the Halls in your state, brandishing hate and questioning my leadership. I will not be relinquishing my leadership to anyone, least of all you!" Millennius kept his voice low to avoid embarrassing Alphatronius further, but the surrounding deafening silence served to amplify his words. "You are a disgrace to yourself and your fami. . ."

"No!" Alphatronius screamed in rage. He suddenly bared two gleaming short swords from their hidden dimensional sheaths.

In full view of the others in the Halls of Celestian Order, Alphatronius attacked Millennius.

Millennius, in turn, grasped his sceptre, his eyes also ablaze.

Novan had stood as transfixed as the others, mesmerised by the conflict in progress. They had all expected this to happen and would all now stand by and accept their fate, which lay in the outcome of this battle. It was the way of the universe.

But as the two grappled, their energies sparking and glancing off each others' weapons and armour under the barrage of the others' attacks, that is when the Great Galatian's prophesy meaning had become clear to Spheron.

In the prophecy, both had been mentioned cryptically as being instrumental in the survival of their civilisation, at least until time ended and the Gate of Spawn opened. And like lightning, that part had become clear to Spheron, too. It was all so clear. And yet he had little time. He could feel the precious moments slipping away.

Acting quickly before anyone could stop him, Spheron sealed and enveloped the Celestian Knights within individual forcefields, for Spheron was the Master of Forcefields, and such things were within his rights and realm of powers as First General.

Ignoring the protests of the others, especially a cursing Alphatronius, Spheron arranged them around himself, in order for them to hear his grand announcement and their way to victory:

"Celestian Knights, please forgive my brash and sudden manner in which I have intruded and trussed you up. But a great revelation has just now hit upon me, during this most worthy of physical debates, which to my knowledge could end our woes. Long and in vain had we pondered the words laid out before us by our great forbear, Galatian, but I have now discovered its awesome meaning."

He paused, gazing among them to see if he had caught their undivided attention. He had.

"The Traitor Synther had been right!" There were raucous shouts of denials. Spheron raised his arms to cease their worried plight. "The Storm of Stars did indeed take the spark of our progenitors, the dreaded Lore, to create us, but that is now neither here nor there, nor is this the time for discussion, for they are surely nigh and upon us, and time is running out. And you, Alphatronius . . ." he said, pointing to him, still seething in anger, "Are our only hope!"

At his confused looked, Spheron retorted, "Well, are you not the 'brave Blood and Death' of war? What have you to offer us, then? I'll tell you what: the ability to dabble with other dimensions. But have you ever tried to enter and cross those dimensions apart from the fortress?"

Alphatronius looked confused, then slowly shook his head.

"No?" Spheron confirmed. "Then I tell you, Alphatronius that you can and must. Our salvation lies within you! Let me tell you how. You all know the Story of Adantus and the Antiqchronals Quest!" Spheron referred to a mythical quest to find the First peoples. "Our children, our spawn, will lead our peoples in their wake."

A general chorus of amazement pervaded.

"But . . ." Spheron hesitated, "we are warned 'enter not the Gate of Spawn' for we are not destined to escape, I am afraid. Only the young, able, and fortunate will be able to escape, for there are not enough starcraft for all. And who will defend those misfortunate remaining at the end? We will, 'Bold Knights,' led by 'The Light,' of the universe; our own dear Lord Millennius. So, you see, my fellow

Knights, there will be no contest here today, for we will all be needed, even at The End."

A palpable, ringing silence descended within the Hall, as the truth and understanding of Spheron words sunk in, until Millennius, as resplendent as ever, had spoken for all of them:

"Then let us end this thing, forever!"

Alphatronius stared back at him and then at Spheron. "Agreed!" His voice signalled regret. But he sheathed his swords back to the fortress.

Spheron released the Starguards from their incarceration, the atmosphere still tense, but now filled with purpose. The beginning of The End was upon them.

"It is time our fellow Celestians knew what lies ahead," Millennius calmly stated, laying down his sceptre. He activated the holo-screens above the table to address the world.

At first, there had been general disbelief, outright anger, and rampant panic when Millennius had informed the populace about the Traitor Synther, the vision and the solution, but as the hard reality of the situation had taken grip, the multitudes had drawn together, united in a cause to save the cream of their once glorious civilisation. The Six Worlds would live on, but in some distant land across the cosmic barrier of dimensions.

Grudgingly working with Spheron, Alphatronius had been able to generate a large dimensional portal under the protective shielding, which Spheron shored up with his forcefields, maintained by Meccun techs and explored by Trinari probes and craft. The escape route was ready. And Celestian populations were readied for the transfer.

But disaster had struck.

Cryptic messages had been transmitted to the Hall, the Celestian Knights returning to the chambers at the urgent behest of Spheron. Taking their seats, the great holo-screens around the hall blurred, shifted and transformed into the features of a once proud Celestian Knight.

"Traitor!" accused Millennius in a great shout at first sight. "Show yourself to me, in combat, and I will end your suffering!"

Alphatronius, Hyphon, and Ultra Ari all rose from their seats ready for action.

Phasia stared in disbelief at her brother. Gone were his handsome blond features. Phasia could see no resemblance to her brother in his current form, a blue mass of energy, a caricature of a Celestian.

Synther sneered, his voice almost a hiss of energy. "Millenniussss, I am but on the other side of your great forcefield. Come, sssee me, in all my glory!"

Before he had even finished, Millennius had sprinted from the Halls, flown off the plateau and shot into the air, closely followed by the others. Novan struggled to keep up, his psi-powered flight not as strong as the energy wielders.

And what they flew toward staggered them. Not only was the dark blue spark of malice that was the Traitor Synther present through the miles of forcefields, but so was a massive force of Lore, lining the world like a stellar blanket.

The first few minutes were of silence; outright rage from the Celestian Knights, defiance from the Traitor Synther.

"Why have you returned, Traitor?" Millennius demanded.

There was a delay as the message was relayed to the Traitor Synther's comms he still wore around his forearm. His voice was as ragged as a solar flare burst:

"Join me!" his voice shattered the air. "You are trapped in your own prison. We, are free!" he indicated the millions of Lore around him. "You each have the capability to be free, like me, as the spark of the Lore runs through all of you. We were designed by the Ssstorm of Ssstars to be the sum of all the Antiqchronals, but it was the essence of the Lore which gave the Celestian Knights their powers. You know thissss!" he pointed a wavering finger of light at them.

Millennius clenched his fists, as the Goddess Elysius held back Alphatronius, and the twins Sola Venga and Auron battled against their natures with so many Lore present.

Hyphon looked at Millennius ready for any action he would take with Ultra Ari and Iria by his side. Only Phasia and Destina held back, the former out of fear of her brother, the latter out of distrust for Phasia wondering which side she would choose. Spheron braced the forcefield wary of any breaches.

"All we will speak of is your doom!" an angry Millennius retorted. "End this now! Give up!" he shouted. "Discharge the Lore and return to Galatia our prisoner. We may even forgive you in time," he lied, feeling the eyes of all the others on his back.

A noise like boiling blood issued from Synther's mouth. "No, you lie! I know you, Millennius! But one day I may forgive you," he hissed. And even from this distance, they knew he was smiling. "And I know all your secrets. Let me show you!"

While the Starguards glanced bewildered and a little nervously at each other, Synther beckoned forth a lone red Lore. He gripped the creature tightly with his hands, sculpting its energy, the Lore flickering, changing form from a Celestian-shape into a sinuous five-meter-long energy bolt.

Before they comprehended what he was doing, the Traitor Synther hurled the Lore-bolt with all his might. And to the utter shock of the Starguards, the rude charge penetrated the forcefield, sparking its jagged way toward them; toward Millennius who hovered motionless in the Lore-lightning's path.

Time slowed as each Starguard realised what had and would occur. Millennius would try to prove his power by intercepting and neutralising Synther's threat. But they each knew the Lore was also as likely to kill Millennius.

The alien projectile had astonishingly and successfully navigated the forcefield at increasing velocity, its fury rising, as the living spark expanded and reached a frenzied pitch. The Lore-bolt screamed, splitting the air as it escaped the shield, the immediate sky turning dark red, an unwavering path to Millennius awaiting. A menacing arcing mouth of red spikes reached out from the lightning-form ready to strike.

Hands charged with energy, Millennius raised his arms to counter, eyes blazing golden light. He roared in preparedness to kill or die, the lore diving to engulf him in its nebulous gaping maw.

Movement flashed from Millennius' left just as the lore lightning struck. There was a soul-churning cry, choked off suddenly as a body absorbed the entire blast, burned, crumpled, and fell from the charred-smelling skies.

"Acirrius!" Hyphon's sudden anguished shout rang out as he dived furiously to catch his brother's body, which even as it dropped disintegrated until the wind had dispersed it into nothingness.

Hyphon watched in disbelief as his hands were washed through by dust of his brother. The wind had reclaimed its champion. Hyphon stared up in torment to Millennius whose harrowed expression mirrored the rest of the Starguards.

Acirrius had knowingly thrown himself in the path of the Lore to save Millennius.

Millennius thundered, turning his violent essence toward the Traitor Synther, his whole body incandescent with rage and light. All he had to do was to convert completely and fight the treacherous coward Lore to Lore. As soon as he realised how close he was to capitulating his corporeal Celestianity, Millennius let his anger subside.

"You will not win this way, Traitor!" he sneered through gritted teeth and ragged breath. His soul burned for vengeance.

The Traitor Synther grinned, sparks flickering around his mouth, neither joyous or disappointed Millennius still lived. "Will they all sacrifice themselves for you, Millennius?" He searched out the faces of the rest of the Starguards, lingering over his sister's horrified features. He re-focused on Millennius. "I think not! Your shield energies are Lore energies. I told you we are more alike than not!" He started to back away from the forceshield. "I will return," he announced, arms outstretched. He turned to leave, but a thought seemed to fall upon him. "No matter what you do, I will know. No matter where you go, I will find you. And then I will obliterate you!" With a hissed sneer breaking the stunned silence, the Traitor Synther and the Lore disappeared into the void.

His words had chilled Millennius. *What did he mean, no matter where we go? Did he know? Did the Traitor know their plans?* Millennius' eyes were alight with energy, his grim stare threatening to bore a hole through the forcefield.

His thoughts were aired aloud by a grieving Hyphon. "He knows?" He turned to the others. "How?"

A hard shove pushed Phasia through the air. She whirled around at the culprit.

"How else?" Destina jeered at Phasia. "Like sister, like brother!" She folded her arms, case obviously closed. "She killed Acirrius!"

The words hung starkly in the air. No Starguard had ever been murdered. And no Starguard had ever murdered another. Destina's accusation was as dark a charge as could be rendered.

Still glaring through the shield, Millennius' voice was a hard strike of light: "Destina, do not make me forget you are my sister!" He aimed a glower at her. "This is all the Traitor Synther's doing! And now I do not care if he knows. Or how he knows. This is our destiny! We do this for our dear sacrificed fellow Knight, Acirrius, for our younglings' sake, and the continued existence of our civilisation. We do this right! Do you understand?" he directed at Destina.

Bravado crushed, Destina nodded in meekness. "Yes, brother."

"Does everyone understand?"

"Yes, Millennius!" had come the shouted replies.

He and Hyphon exchanged glances. "Acirrius gave his life for this. We will not forget his sacrifice," Millennius stated. "We will grieve in this world and honour him in the next.

Hyphon flew up to him. They clasped forearms. "He will be honoured," Hyphon repeated. He was the first, as the other Starguards flew to both Millennius and the Sky Warrior, clasping arms and remembering Acirrius.

Novan had joined in. He hadn't understood why Acirrius had sacrificed himself for Millennius, whom he had no great love for. But at that very thought, he realised that was the duty of a Celestian Knight. Every life was sacred. And where death threatened he would be there to defend life. It had stuck with him ever since.

Once the ceremony was over, Millennius sought out Alphatronius, "The nexus to the new universe has to be maintained for longer periods. Can you do this?"

"Yes, Millennius!" was the instant reply, positive, assured. "With Spheron's help to stabilise the vortex at such a size, it can be done." Having never generated such an immense cross-dimensional channel before, even Alphatronius had to stifle any doubts. It had to be done.

"Good," Millennius replied. "The rest of us will help with loading the swordships and protecting the forcefield perimeter."

With a last baleful look toward the forcefield, Millennius led the Starguards down to the Halls of Celestial Order. The Celestian populations would have to be told the bleak news of Acirrius and the chances of their survival. The Lore would return.

Out of the surviving two point four billion Celestians from a total of twenty-one billion Celestians before the Lore invasion, only fifteen million would be able to be evacuated. Every swordship, including three city-ships, and everything that could fly, from personal skimmers and vessels, warrior cruisers, and commercial transports, were used for passengers, food, and resource supplies. The sleek ten-kilometer swordships would go first, while the spherical personal transports would cluster together to form vast clusterships and life support vessels.

However, by creating the dimensional vortex, the Celestian Knights were destabilising the protective field around Galatia. And scores of Lore were penetrating through. They had been destroyed instantly; they had to be, because every Lore infiltrator was an eye of the Traitor Synther. He could not discover their plans or there would be no hope; he would hunt down and destroy every single living being. And they had not come so far for him to win. No matter what, the Celestian Knights had pledged, the Traitor Synther would never win.

Alphatronius, using every spark of his energy he could muster, sustained an open transdimensional portal for long periods of time, enough so that a number of scout ships could pass through untroubled. It had been tested by Meccun technology and was safe, stable, and fixed onto an area in another universe which was deemed suitable and unquestionably Lore-free. Already, the ships had been loaded and it had been hard enough for even the

Celestian Knights to let go of their children, but they would be taken care of, by trusted companions, and grow up certain in the knowledge that they were loved.

It would take three days for all of the ships to voyage through the gateway. Three days, then The End would come.

Those three days were the longest of the Celestian Knights' lives, fending off the penetrating Lore in brutal fight after brutal fight, while sending the ships through. Their future would be safe, but the Celestian Knights were coming to an end. The Lore were piercing the shield more frequently, the Celestian Knights' powers weakening from maintaining the forcefield—their prison—constantly, and they could not stop all of them. Havoc reigned.

Then the Traitor Synther had broken through.

Millennius, Spheron, Destina, Phasia, Alphatronius and Elysius had formed one defensive group, while Hyphon, Sola Venga, Auron, Iria, and Ultra Ari formed the other, protecting the remaining populace, hidden underground. However, thousands of brave souls had ventured out in determined defiance to help fight for their World.

"We *will* be the survivors!" had been their fervent cry.

Spheron's chronicle was the last thing to enter the gateway, given to Novan, as he had reluctantly boarded the last swordship, in the hopes of future generations understanding all that had come to pass, and to safeguard them in the future.

The End had come.

The dedication at the beginning of the Scrolls of History read: I am Spheron, son of Spheron and a thousand Spherons before him, Master of Forcefields, First General, Creator of the Trinar Deception, the Ring of Fire protecting Galatia, and many more feats of majesty, friend to Millennius, Chronicler, Interpreter, Exegete of the Scrolls of History. Above all—Celestian Knight. I dedicate this book to Novan, son of Alphatronius, the new lord of our progeny.

Novan would never forget the sacrifices they had all made for them to survive.

Millennius never did give the speech he rehearsed, but his last recorded words were:

"Our End has come, my Celestians; fight well and long may we live!"

In a boundless, energy-specked void, Novan floated. It was the happiest and saddest time of his life and he didn't want it to end, but he felt the rest of the data-flow coming to an end. He let his feelings flow out of him, a blue-green stream of sorrow, that was met with a rush of golden aura of sympathy and hope that no words could match in love and sincerity, and then a red aura of euphoria caught hold of him and thrust him up toward a bright light.

And then Novan awoke.

CHAPTER FOUR

Deb had regained consciousness on her way to Sky Command's medlabs, rolling off the pushed hover-cot. But despite her persistent protests that she was fine to the team of medtechs around her, Deb had still ended up being guided on foot under her own steam into the blue and white-walled med station to be tested. That's when holovids had filtered through to the med stations regarding Novan's incident.

Oh, Classia! Deb silently thought about what Classia must be going through. Her hero could be dying. Deb wanted to be there for her, as Classia had often been there for her, but the seemingly exhaustive and needless tests were still ongoing, forestalling any notion of sleep. There was no jovial banter between her and the bald-headed exacting testers as there would have been for other patients.

Deb knew they didn't like her, not since she and Classia had tormented a section of medtechs on a week-long field training course, as young Sky-marks. Not that their antics could be traced back to them, but their rebellious reputations had preceded them ever since. Added to the rumours of her blacking out running abound on Sky Command and the medtechs were keeping her at a professional distance.

What's wrong with me? thought Deb for the hundredth time. She half-hoped that they would find something wrong with her and cure it. Then she could feel normal again. Deb knew they wouldn't. She'd be like this for the rest of her life.

Feeling sorry for herself, Deb sat through the thorough probes, crystalator scans and tests; isolated, tired and alone in her thoughts for hours, until in the late hours of the day when they had decided they had finished and would await the results, during the night. Then, as an afterthought one of the medtechs, Iesse, had announced in her dead voice that Deb had a visitor.

Deb's mood picked up, knowing who had finally arrived.

A perky Classia had then glided in, ignoring the glares at her less-than-reverent entry into the hallowed medlabs. For her part, Deb was confused. Classia sported one of her classic radiant smiles that could melt moon-rings. But before she could say anything, Classia gushed:

"Did you hear? Novan's alive and well. He's on his way to Halcyon City to make some kind of important announcement. He'll be here in a couple of hours." Then she glanced around as unobtrusively as she could and said quietly, "Maybe this is what you've been somehow sensing, you know—impending doom; Novan's accident and this whole announcement thing. What do you think?"

Deb thought about it and then interrogated that place within herself where she thought this inner sense lay. A dull stabbing pain answered. "No, I don't think so, Classia. If anything, it's growing stronger. I'm sorry," Deb smiled ashamedly at her friend. *I should have lied.*

"That's okay," Classia's smiling eyes replied in kind. "You can't help it. Don't worry." She gave Deb a 'watch-this' wink. "Hey you, medtech! Yes, you, grub-face pretending not to watch us. We're going to the observation deck. Call us when you're ready." Not waiting for any response, Classia grabbed a surprised Deb's arm and practically sprinted with her out of the sterile med division. When they were safely inside an ascending transtube, they burst out laughing.

**

Altair was livid. "What do you mean he just awoke and left? I don't believe this. Who let him go?" Altair's hands glowed red with crackling energy, as his temper flared, awaiting an answer. Aerl was quite sure he wouldn't let loose his energies within the confines of the city, but just to be sure, he stood between Altair and the medtechs.

There was a clearing of a throat and Med Fortan Ede stepped forward, nervously rubbing the back of her shaved head. "Nobody let him go," she replied, indignant at Altair's accusation. "He just calmly awoke, removed our instruments and left. That's all that happened. We could not stop him."

"Pah!" fumed Altair, throwing his de-energised hands up in frustration. "Lying meds. Go away!" he shouted. Turning his back on them and their receding footfalls, Altair stared out into space as if physically searching for the errant Novan.

He and Aerl were in the main reception hall, their public forum for meetings. The circular room graced the top of a spire, which was capped with a transparent dome, to give unqualified views of surrounding space.

Earlier, he and Aerl had retired to their respective spire-top residences, where they had awaited news of Novan's recovery. But what they had since heard had amused Aerl, but outraged Altair. Novan had seemingly just awoken and left—or fled, according to Altair—for Millennius City-State, but not before announcing that he had momentous news to report upon his arrival at Halcyon City. Altair had almost raced after him, but Aerl had interceded, convincing him to wait at least until after the announcement. It could be too important. And anyway, Novan already had an hour or so head start on them, though with their greater speed they might still get to Halcyon before him. Altair had relented, but had still wanted to know who was to blame.

Now with the medtechs gone, the two were alone in the hall.

"You know, you really shouldn't treat them like that, Altair. Medtech Ede's uncle is a well-known general and their family is quite prestigious. We're not all-revered like our parents and they could cause a bit of trouble."

"And why aren't we all-revered?" Altair raised his voice. "I'll tell you why, it's because of Novan and his all-appeasing attitudes. And look at Cirrius, shut away on his own island, Solandus away universe-knows-where, and those loner twins Alpha Rion and Astara. You can't revere those not wanting to be revered," he stared accusingly at Aerl, challenging him.

"I'm not going to fight you on those words," Aerl said as calmly as he could. "But these are different times and circumstances. There's no prophecy of doom, no impending battle. We're more a part of the society than ever our parents were and Novan's trying to make us fit in. Why can't you see that and be a part of it instead of against it? If you want to be a God, then go somewhere else and do it. There's no need for them here." Silence hung between the two, Altair's heavy breathing betraying his tempestuous thoughts.

If you even try it! thought Aerl.

But all Altair said was, "One day, Aerl, you and me. It'll come down to you and me." He turned and left the room, heading for the exit port. Aerl followed discreetly and hoped that whatever it was Novan had to say, it had better be good, for all their sakes.

The clear, crisp night around Halcyon City was lit up enough to be seen from Magna City one hundred miles away, one sky city-like star to another. Everybody had by now heard about Novan's forthcoming announcement and the histographers had all spilled out of their offices to report on the event. Some waited in space, aboard their own skimmers, for the first sight of Novan approaching, occasionally showing pictures of the dazzling Halcyon City from orbit.

Millions of Celestians had personally come, hovering on their one- or two-person jet-skimmers, not able to squeeze aboard the overflowing levels of the capital's decks. And of course, millions more on Placia, the moon settlements and the City-States were also waiting. The system was buzzing with anticipation.

In the overcrowded circular upper platform of Sky Command's forward observation deck, Deb and Classia vied for viewing space among the other Sky Leaders, the Deputy Sky Leaders, the Sky-marks, and the cadets, the latter two groups confined to their prescribed and less optimal positions on the even more crowded lower platforms four decks below reached on foot at least by a wide spiral stairway, otherwise one flew between levels.

Ignoring the occasional wary glance and discreet whispers, Deb tried to concentrate on the spectacle playing out on the huge holo-screen which dominated their platform, other similar screens situated on the other levels. She felt more comfortable here, probably because she was among her fellow peers, who in other circumstances would have avoided her company. But some, like Journ and Tima had even paid courteous respect to her. And behind her, at a discreet distance, stood her admirer and the most senior Sky Leader, the respected Tol Valar. She sought his presence and found him already staring at her. His dark hair and eyes and clean-cut face standing out among the ordinary male fare. They exchanged shy smiles, disengaging before anyone made too much of it. Classia's tarnished image could handle being associated with Deb, but ambitious Tol Valar's needed to be more discerning.

But it's the thought that counts, mused Deb.

Classia had been holding her hand all this time and now Deb felt her tug hard making their way toward the steps leading down to the lower platforms.

"Deb, I want to go over to Halcyon City," she said, once they were on the descent. They had to push their way through the crowds lining the stairs. "There's nothing essential happening here and even the medtechs will be watching their screens instead of working. What's say we go over and be among the people? You know, show the Sky Warriors' colours and all that," she said honestly, trying to sound patriotic.

Deb thought about it. "If it's such a good idea, how come no one else has gone over? Even the Sky Commander's not there."

Classia feigned a frown. "Deb, you disappoint me. Since when do I think like other Celestians? I thought that's what they loved about me."

"Yeah, besides other things," Deb retorted by suggestively swaying her hips. "But you do have a valid point. Let's go!" And then just to tease Classia. "And you notice I didn't say anything about this being an opportunity to be closer to Novan."

With a straight face, Classia replied "Of course not, Little Star. I wouldn't think of it as such." But an inkling of a smile graced her face. Deb knew that they were in trouble, whenever Classia used her nickname. The last time she had coaxed Deb into a little adventure had been when they had violated a Star Warriors' ground-exercise area, disguised, comms scrambled, and constantly evading attempts at capture, while causing innocent havoc. The two had been suspected, but no evidence could be found against them. Deb remembered that that foray had been prefixed with Classia's 'Little Star' code word. Simultaneously dreading and looking forward to this adventure, Deb accepted the inevitable risks incurred when a friend of Classia.

The two turned to leave, hopefully unobserved amid the juniors, but their furtive escape was interrupted. Far across the lower platform, a wave of silence had washed over the buzzing voices and then the cadets and Sky-marks had stood and parted in unison as the Sky Commander, carrying his battle-staff and flanked by two of his five deputies, had made his way through the sea of blue-uniformed warriors. Deb watched the whole scene, inspired like all the others. If Gal Agar had been a Starguard, everybody would have been on their knees, such was the esteem felt for him. The hush preceded the Sky Commander until it had reached the limits of the upper platforms and the only sound was the footsteps of the party of three and the commentary from the viewing screens.

When they reached the rising stairways, the best vantage point over the lower platform, red-haired Deputy Sky Commander Teron turned and shouted, "Ease ranks." And immediately the warriors relaxed and awaited an address from the Commander.

Gal Agar looked approvingly over his warriors and cast his head up to where the seniors stood. His voice rang out.

"I'm not here to give a speech, but with these unusual events, I wanted to be here among you to share in this momentous event. That's if you don't mind, of course," he added, smiling charmingly. The general chorus of amusement from the floor signalled his welcome and he turned to mingle first with the nearest juniors, whose mouths immediately became tongue-tied, offering nervous smiles and eager nods.

The Sky Commander's next steps brought him close to Deb and Classia and he nodded a greeting before continuing on, while burly Teron simply frowned. But Deputy Dessa, a short, slim, unattractive brunette asked without feeling, "And how are you feeling today, Deneb?"

"Why, fine thank you, Deputy," Deb replied nonplussed.

Forcing a smile and nodding, Dessa said, "Good. Fine." She moved on, striking up yet more stilted conversions with uncomfortable junior ranks.

The trio wended their way up the spiral stairs, stopping and engaging Sky Warriors along the way.

Letting her own smile drop, Deb looked at Classia and raised a quizzical eyebrow—What was that all about?

Deputy Sky Commander Dessa (or Deputy Lesser, as the lower ranks called her) was known for her cold sternness. She was indeed the lesser of the Deputies, some feeling that she wasn't even up to the job and it was even rumoured that she and Teron had something between them, even though Teron was already married. Forcing herself to speak to Deb must have been a way of gaining some favour with the Sky Commander, but Deb let it go. It was also rumoured that Dessa would shortly be transferred to the Star Warrior Liaison Office; way out on Vista Mare and that Tol Valar would take her place as Deputy. And that it couldn't happen soon enough was on everybody's thoughts.

Taking their chances, while everyone was attentively occupied with the presence of the Sky Commander, Deb and Classia slipped through the throng of the juniors, whose male ranks dispersed this time and closed with following and longing admiring glances and wishful thoughts.

Another, whose eyes had fleetingly glimpsed their exit, was Gal Agar's and his thoughts were different: *Just stay out of trouble.*

Halcyon City was positively glowing. And crowded. Even the stage where Novan was expected to give his speech, a huge hastily emptied skimmer bay, was teeming with Celestians. But as Sky Warriors, already popular with the general populace and as two of the more glamorous members, Deb and Classia had no problems moving to more advantageous positions.

Even as Deb watched and moved through the city, she could hear excited voices, most in the common Galaxic. But Xarianese and Trinarci lingoes, loud and a touch harsh sounding to her ears, respectively, could also be discerned. She even listened as a blue-haired youngling fumbled his tongue around the rapid lilt of Eleresh. Everyone was here for this momentous occasion.

It wouldn't be long now, for a Star Warrior interplanetary observation post reporting directly to the small, moon-like orbiting headquarters on Vista Mare, had picked up the incoming near-lightspeed forms of Sceptre and Altair, followed by the slower form of Novan. And mere minutes after that report had come in, the instantly recognisable forms of Sceptre in his blue chest-plated gold armour, followed by the blue-with-gold-trim armoured Altair with his flowing blond hair, had flown into the center of the bay to rapturous applause. They were soon joined by the other dignified Starguards. Deb hadn't seen them together for as long as she could remember, and she would not soon forget this moment.

The bearded Decion stood a full head taller even with his battle helmet off as he smartly paraded on stage from the rear of the skimmer bay to join Altair and Sceptre. He was an ominous sight in his blood-red and deathly-black battle armour of the Alphatronius Clan, his long, red bifurcated cape was swept behind him. His giant lancesword, with his helmet perched on top, reached to his chin and his distinctive four-armed shield was lodged firmly on his back. He looked frightening, especially with his customary scowl.

Standing just apart from their older brother, were the warrior-twins Alpha Rion and Astara. Deb thought the two were the epitome of chiselled beauty; black cascading hair defining high cheek-boned faces with well-honed bodies, exuding confidence and nobility. They seemed distant, rarely speaking in public, but Deb wondered if their perceived introverted natures were easily pierced. They were always together—even when apart—such was the indeterminable link between them. They, like the rest of the Starguards, were single, but histographers always weaved them into romantic tales and they were adored by the younger generation. The Starguards had been criticised for not being involved in relationships. Some put this down to their superior natures and their unwillingness to associate with lesser mortals, but others commented, and Deb agreed, that with a potential half-a-millennium-long life-span they could afford to wait for what the future held for them.

Deb noticed that Alpha Rion's two golden-energy metaswords were not in evidence and guessed that they were probably tucked away in their other-worldly sheath. His sister's black nexus sword was also notably absent, though the two practically lived and breathed swords. Deb knew most of the male ranks would be more attentive to Astara's striking uniform, the subject of many a male Celestians' drinking talk. The twins were now engaged in low conversation between themselves, Astara laughing easily at something Alpha Rion said.

Just then, the savoury smell of spicy *paja* wafted through the crowd, everyone turning to find the source of the aroma. Classia's eyes widened in joy, while Deb's stomach rumbled. She hadn't eaten in ages. Presently, two vendors waded through the crowd freely handing out the small round cakes, the consumers sending discreet codes from their crystalators to token-pay or offer services in return. Spying the two Sky Warriors, one of the vendors rushed over to them and gladly offered them his wares. Classia delicately lifted a couple of the fat cakes from the out-held tray handing one to Deb. She bit into the fluffy baked treat, making a noise of satisfaction. Gratified at their contentment, the vendor bowed, smiled, and moved on, the lingering taste and smell of the *paja* lifting the atmosphere. Until there was another cheer. Urana had arrived.

Astara possessed a cold beauty, but Urana excelled in warmth. Deb watched as she animatedly talked with her cousins, Sceptre and Altair. It was not hard to be attracted to her, especially with her wild beauty and long blue hair, which won her constant adulation. Even now, her hair shimmered about her as she discussed some point hurriedly with her hands doing most of the talking.

She must be some sight in the air, Deb thought of Placia's Protectress of State, the planet's sole answer to the Sky and Star Warriors.

While Altair's powers consisted of red energy, Aerl's and Urana's were of yellow plasma energy, though her cousin's energies were more within the electromagnetic spectrum. And instead of straight beams and flashes, Urana's energy manifested itself like shards of plasma, highly dense charges of light, which among the Starguards had earned her the nickname 'Rain'. On her only visit to Placia on a training mission, while still a Sky-mark, Deb remembered witnessing Urana use her power to pulverise a small mountain for its ore resources. Deb had never seen so much power unleashed like that before, which was thousands of times more powerful than the plasma-bolt staffs Sky Warriors often carried. Deb watched Urana's conversation. She'd been described as moody, but she seemed happy enough now. And then she saw the reason why.

Entering calmly from the back of the skimmer bay from the

launch tunnel to a shower of surprised gasps and applause was the seldom-seen Cirrius. The other Starguards greeted their youngest member with friendly reserve.

His arrival had even surprised Classia, who gave a wild hoot, rising into the air, Deb having to hold her down. Being the Supreme Commander of the Sky Warriors meant Cirrius outranked Gal Agar, but he preferred and trusted the Sky Commander to run the day-to-day operations, though it was rumoured Cirrius had Sky Command's bridge duplicated on his remote island where only the Starguards and invited guests ventured.

Cirrius wore his stylised Sky Warrior manoeuvre suit, his sereneness countered Urana's animated manner, but when she gave her little brother a heartfelt embrace, his reserve cracked and he replied with an endearing smile, while she held on to his arm. Except for their matching blue hair, you wouldn't have noticed any family resemblance for Cirrius possessed his father's rough looks.

There they all were, the Starguards, together, like some exalted family. The only one missing now was Novan.

And after a few more minutes of waiting agonisingly through false alarms, the vidscreens in the bay revealed the descending form of Novan, resplendent in his white armour. A nearby skimmer preceded him, lighting the way, with onboard histographers recording the moment. It followed him all the way down, until he had touched down on the outer deck, then it had alighted elsewhere.

That left the way free for more histographers and visioners to follow him on foot through the curving corridors, transtubes, and decks, the journey remaining slow-going with all the Celestians greeting Novan, along the way. The noise was deafening both in the corridors and on the skimmer deck and Deb could see tears forming in Classia's eyes, which she unashamedly displayed. Novan seemed to have that effect on everyone, but Deb remained impassive, not because she'd suddenly realised that she hadn't slept in ages and had no energy, but because something told her tonight was going to change Celestian life forever and that she would need to save her energy.

They were still hungry. They had invaded worlds and eaten stars, but they were still hungry. Then their leader had sensed something; a reminder from the past. And it irked. Their enemy had not been destroyed. Yes, they could all sense it now: a sense of sickening hope, leaving a flickering path toward a new bastion of infestation. They would have to cleanse this universe of its unclean presence, as they had done in the last one. And then and only then would the Lore be satisfied.

Novan confidently strode into the skimmer bay to thunderous applause eclipsing the welcome of the other Starguards. He waved an arm in appreciation and the resultant jubilation of the masses exploded. The celebratory din echoed off the transparent-domed observation deck above the stage where even more Celestians viewed the scenes looking downward, joyous pandemonium circling round and about the stowed skimmers and equipment, and through the bodies of the gathered masses. The Starguards had joined in and even Altair had managed to twist his lips into a smile. Deb knew that if anyone deserved to be a Celestian Knight, it was Novan, but he himself had turned down such suggestions: 'It would be a grievous dishonour to our parents' memories and to the prophecy,' he had once said.

Standing at a podium set up for him in the center of the stage, with the Starguards and a huge vidscreen arranged behind him, he raised his hands and the raucousness died down. It was so quiet that apart from the mewling younglings, even the massive, gravity engines upholding the city could be heard. To Deb, their pulsing beat echoed the heartbeats of everyone here and the air was so still; it was as if everyone had forever held their breath together. And then, as Novan spoke, time seemed to begin again:

"Thank you all for coming. First of all, I would like to express my condolences to anyone hurt through my actions at Millennius City-State and I would like to apologise to my friends, Aerl and Altair, for my subsequent abrupt departure." He looked over at them; Aerl nodded forgiveness, while Altair offered a stiff nod. Then Novan leaned on the podium, solemnly staring at the assembly in silence. To Deb it seemed as if he didn't know what to say or how to say it. Even the Starguards looked restless among themselves. After a full minute, Novan said the words that changed Celestian lives yet again:

"My mother, the Goddess Elysius, is alive!"

The silence was stunning and deafening. Even babbling younglings seemed to sense the importance of his words and ceased their prattling. Decion and the warrior-twins, the most affected, stepped forward closer to Novan, while the others looked sufficiently stunned. With Decion just behind him for support, Novan continued:

"Yes, it is true. On my way to Millennius City-State, I received a message from her; a raw-powered telepathic message, which temporarily sent me into an unconscious state. While in that state, she sent more information, all at once and it's taken some time to unscramble, but here it is: The war went badly," he said, to general low murmurs.

"The Traitor Synther penetrated the forceshield and led his hordes down onto Galatia and into Celestia Qor, where the

Celestian Knights made their stand." Again, he looked down in sorrow and though his voice was low when he resumed, the clearness of his words resounded with thunder. "Iria was . . . was lost in the attack, Sola Venga and Auron, after slewing millions of the Lore, soon after," he said, looking sympathetically over at Sceptre and Altair, both of whom took the first-telling of the news of their parents death in public with absolute stoicism. "And Phasia disappeared, it seems to join her traitorous brother against the Celestian Knights." There were gasps of shock amid angry curses.

Again, he stopped, looking this time at Urana and Cirrius, before carrying on, "Hyphon and Ultra Ari held the Anchrusian western citadels, but disappeared." The siblings bowed their heads, Urana tightly clutching Cirrius' hand.

"There were millions upon millions of Lore. The onslaught never stopped, but my father..." Novan shook his head, as if in incomprehension, "My father, Alphatronius, and Spheron were able to convince Millennius to open another transdimensional bridge through which they could escape, trapping the Lore in the dying universe. They sought to break the prophecy!" A tinge of anger escaped him in that moment. "But something went wrong. While my mother escaped on a belatedly repaired swordship with fifty thousand Celestians, she sensed no sign of the others and does not know their fates. And she is now fighting another war.

"My mother and those Celestians are on a faraway world, surrounded by Lore who managed to cross that same bridge. And it is only through her efforts that they remain alive. They need help and as soon as I'm prepared, I am leaving Magna Aura to find them."

His last words reverberated within the gathered crowd's minds as their brains tried to digest the information. Novan made as if to back away from the podium, but the histographers, first to regain any composure, started firing questions at him:

"Where are they? Are you sure it's her? Why contact you now? Why could they not come here? Did the other Starguards know?" And they went on and on, Novan answering each one with a calm voice, while the din from the crowd began to grow louder.

Then a voice from the astounded congregation had suddenly yelled, "I'm going, too!"

Everyone suddenly went quiet, heads turning this way and that, searching for the bearer of the voice, until he, a small nondescript Galatian youth, was propped up on a couple of shoulders and he began shouting again, "I'm going, too!", which started off a cascade of "I'm going, too! I'm going, too!" The chant grew in crescendo and Deb watched in amazement as Classia joined in, fervent in voice, "I'm going, too! I'm going, too!"

The Starguards stood astonished at the sight of such emotional outpouring, the visioners panning their palm-visi-units between the superiors and the common Celestians. This was the greatest Magna Auran story since . . . well, ever, and they lapped it up, with more questions for Novan:

"What about that, Novan, are you going alone? Are the Starguards going too? Who will go? How many? How long will it take? When will you know? What if it isn't her? If it is, will you come back? Can you come back?" Novan tried to answer each question, but the background noise of chanting was too much.

"SILENCE!" roared Decion, driving his lancesword hard into the deck with a jarring effect. "My brother is talking." The silence was immediate and Decion looked pleased with himself; power and fear apparently worked anywhere for him. He nodded to Novan who answered with a wry smile.

Will wonders never cease? Novan shook his head.

Composing his thoughts, Novan eventually said, "A sizeable

force would be able to journey with me, and I will announce that at a later date, but no other Starguard will accompany us."

The clamour that ensued was mixed, cheers for the privilege of venturing into the unknown with a Starguard, but confusion over why the other Starguards would not go.

Cirrius tried to look as nonplussed as he could over at Novan, already knowing the reason why.

Novan explained: "If more Lore did escape, then they may eventually find our system. If that happens and I'm away with the Starguards and a majority of our forces, then Magna Aura wouldn't stand a chance. No, the Starguards will stay behind, commanded by my second, Aerl the Sceptre. There's already a force with my mother, but they lack the weapons and resources we now have to defeat the Lore. With our arrival, we'll be able to counter from both sides. But if we fail, Magna Aura will still be able to defend herself. Does everyone understand." Novan looked around the reasonably quiet bay. His last statement had been less a question than an order. And it was recognised as such. Even the Starguards, though looking somewhat disappointed, didn't argue, even Decion, who would have desired the command over Sceptre. The entire fate of Magna Auran civilisation could depend upon their actions and now they needed to be seen as united.

The sensational announcements were at an end.

"Thank you!" Novan graciously acknowledged everyone for their presence and for listening. He seemed destined to head for the exit, but instead leaped off the stage heading toward the crowd, who instinctively cowered before such greatness. But Novan reached out with his hand, which was instantly grasped by adoring Celestians, who before long pulled him into the gathered throng, to greet, smile and laugh with them. He was their heart.

The other Starguards slowly followed. Only Sceptre and Urana shared such wide-spread adulation and the others followed their lead, as they led them through the swelling crowds, shaking hands; listening to heartfelt condolences, anecdotes, and general chatter. While Altair was also accustomed to crowds from his duties on Millennius, it was not out of popularity but duty. Alpha Rion and Astara were mobbed by the young, admiring Halcyonites. And it seemed that only city councilors and visiting Generals from Vista Mare would talk to Decion.

Classia tugged Deb through the maze of Celestians. It seemed Classia didn't know where she was going either, but Deb had a fair idea of who they would end up by. But she'd been pleasantly surprised when they had emerged out of the crowd by Cirrius. He had been as surprised to see them as she had to see him, but he considerately allowed them to join him acting as unofficial escorts. Not a word was exchanged, but Deb could feel a tingling sensation, as if he was emanating some kind of energy. She felt charged up and looked over at Classia to see if she felt the same, but she seemed to be herself, until her eyes had widened and her lips parted in awe. Following her gaze, Deb saw that they were approaching Novan.

I should have known, thought Deb. She bit back a knowing smile.

As if reading her thoughts, Cirrius, gave Deb an enlightened look and then gazed curiously deeper into her eyes. He seemed extremely interested in her and was about to say something, when Novan appeared.

"Why, Cirrius, however did you come by such a lovely escort?" he said cajoling his fellow Starguard. And then he turned and smiled at Classia. "And you are?"

Deb thought Classia would faint, but she managed to command herself to stand straight and imperturbably say, "Sky Leader Classia, sir." And then with no hesitation, "I would like to join you in . . . on the journey, I mean," she said, her composure faltering into fluster.

"We shall see," Novan said, saving Classia from more flutter. He then turned to Deb.

She was about to introduce herself, when Cirrius announced, "This is Sky Leader Deneb, Novan."

Classia's shocked face mirrored Deb's, who managed a weak smile of greeting.

"Oh, yes," Novan said. "I have heard about you."

And he left it at that. He seemed somewhat captivated by her, shaking her hand briefly, but the eye contact between them lingered longer than Deb realised, until she felt dizzy. Novan sensed her discomfort and released his gaze. She smiled nervously again, too confused to talk. The dizziness became stronger, until a piercing ebbing pain swelled from within, shaking Deb to her soul.

And the world fell from beneath her.

The Lore attacked, undetected, sweeping through the system in a storm of energy. There were space-borne cities, moon colonies and orbiting stations, and then two blue worlds orbiting, not touching, yet always near. And they accosted the worlds, ravaging and devastating, spilling through the defences with wanton destruction, destroying the cities of the air; razing the pathetic islands and sinking the floating settlements. The sun was drained of energy; the planets eaten to the core and the infestation once called Celestians were no more. The Lore had won.

But one Lore fled the battle: This should not have been.

And so, help was sought.

**

On the holo-screens in the senior ranks' platform, all the Sky Warriors had watched as Sky Leader Deneb had collapsed at the side of their inspirations, Cirrius and Novan. Indeed, the whole system had witnessed it on their screens and nervous sideways glances were directed at the Sky Commander.

Deputy Teron fumed, muttering "stupid" and "embarrassing", under his breath, while Deputy Dessa wore a smug smile. Everybody knew that if it was up to the two of them, Deb and Classia would be severely reprimanded, if not thrown out, an unprecedented act, but all eyes turned to Gal Agar, who remained calm by comparison.

"Sky Leader Valar," he said, keeping his eyes firmly on the screen even when the said Sky Leader arrived by his side. "Take two others and after paying my respects to Supreme Commander Cirrius, take Sky Leader Deneb to the medlabs, and escort Sky Leader Classia to my office, now."

Tol Valar gave a superfluous salute, called over Journ and Tima, and the three of them headed for an airlock, taking off at speed for Halcyon City.

Gal Agar watched the screen intently. "Only the Universe can help you now, Deneb," he sighed.

Deb was in another world. Grotesque images formed before her, weird forms descended from the sky, cities plunged afire, friends annihilated, the sun grew dark and died while the seas boiled dry in the heat of war. And all through this she had watched, unable to help: This should not have been, she thought. But there was no help. No, not this time . . .

And as suddenly as that world had begun to fade, a familiar one retook its place with faces that she recognised. Classia swam into view kneeling beside her and then:

Oh, the Universe, no!

Novan and Cirrius had appeared, clouded images becoming sharp faces of deep concern. They said something, but she couldn't understand for everything heard and spoken was slightly blurred and out of sync. And then, with a great whooshing rush of air and a resounding headache, everything came back to normal. The returning noise disorientated her somewhat, but eventually, her senses came back.

"Are you okay?" asked a concerned Classia, lightly holding her shoulders, as Deb stood up shakily.

"Yes, I think so. What happened?" Her voice trembled.

Classia eyed her with some askance. "I was hoping you could tell me. Is this what's been troubling you? You could have told me!"

Deb could feel that she felt let down and could only say, "I know. I'm sorry."

Classia shook her head, a smile touching her lips and the two of them hugged, to the wild applause of the skimmer bay, who were only now hearing the passed-around word that a Sky Warrior had been overly smitten with meeting Cirrius and had fainted. The histographers had only managed to get long-range shots of the incident, but now pressed in to get the story, but were blocked by Novan and Cirrius, who calmly shepherded Classia and Deb toward an empty alcove, just as Tol Valar arrived with Journ and Tima.

Alerted to the presence of more Sky Warriors by the rowdy crowd, who it seemed didn't want to disperse, Cirrius faced the three in a slightly intimidating stance and when Tima looked behind her, the other Starguards had formed a rough semicircle around them, effectively blocking out prying histographers and intrusive spectators.

Tol Valar remained calm in such exalted company and after a curt nod of acknowledgement to the Starguards, addressed Cirrius: "Sir, I am Sky Leader Tol Valar. With compliments from the Sky Commander, I have been ordered to escort Sky Leaders Deneb and Classia back to Sky Command."

Cirrius seemed to genuinely ponder this. "That order is belayed, Sky Leader Tol Valar. My escort will remain with me, until I dismiss them, after which they will return to Sky Command with no action taken against them. Is that clear, Sky Leader!" he ordered firmly.

"Sir? Yes, sir," replied Tol Valar, snapping to attention and more than a little confused.

He looked into Deb's eyes and she could see the mixed emotions written on his face. He wanted to protect her, but was being denied by the God-like figures he had revered all his life.

Deb tried to give him a sympathetic look, but he had already been defeated and with farewell nods, he, Journ and Tima headed back past the crowds and the questioning histographers, empty-handed.

The surrounding eyes returned upon Gal Agar, as they had all watched on the screens replaying Tol Valar's brief discussion with Cirrius and then leaving Halcyon City without his mission accomplished. While he remained stoic on the outside, on the inside, he was awash with emotion. Any questions he had could wait, until he had heard what Tol Valar had to say, though he already guessed what it was. However, he was more concerned now with what Cirrius had in mind for Deb. He knew that Cirrius had kept a watchful eye on Deb, ever since her inception into the Sky Warriors. But while Gal Agar knew that there was something special about her, he suspected that Cirrius knew a lot more than he was telling. Now it was time that he found out.

Excusing himself from the gathered ranks, leaving Teron and Dessa to deal with the countless volunteers for Novan's expedition, Gal Agar briskly walked back to his office several decks up, calling in Deputy Glith, along the way. The slender pentagenerian was Gal Agar's closest aide and closest to his age. A superb listener and mentor, his cadets were most likely to be promoted to Sky leader.

"You must be desperate to call me," quipped Glith as he arrived with a smile and a voice frayed from years of bellowing orders. He casually dropped into a chair opposite his superior.

Gal Agar returned his smile. "I need to leave for a while and need a trusted hand at the helm." He sighed theatrically. "But there's only you!" The old friends laughed at the same joke they shared over the years.

"Debrief Tol Valar upon his return. Make sure he understands there is no slight on him." Gal Agar stood to leave.

"That I can do!" Glith smiled compassionately, knowing Gala Agar's task ahead. "Send my regards to his High Hallowedness," Glith saluted, as Gal Agar looked back in feigned ignorance.

Unescorted, Gal Agar vacated Sky Command through the exit port at the rear of his office.

What does the Universe owe you, Deneb? he asked himself, letting the cool night swallow him up, as he flew hard to Cirrius' island.

"It's time to leave, now," Cirrius said to them. Around him were the Starguards, Deb, and Classia. He had invited the Starguards back to his island, much to their surprise. Deb noted that Classia and Novan were having a seemingly professional discussion on aspects of flight, which Novan seemed genuinely interested in.

Maybe there's hope for them, after all, thought Deb.

But Cirrius precluded any hopes of further discussion, when he had approached them with an apologetic look on his face, "I'm sorry, Sky Leader Classia, but I no longer require your services tonight. Return to Sky Command immediately. No action will be taken against you, I assure you. And thank you for your commitment." His slight smile quickly disappeared and he quietly spoke to Novan, indicating their imminent departure, before turning brusquely, leaving a perplexed Novan to say a hurried farewell to Classia, ending in a clasp of her forearm and hand.

Classia looked ready to argue against her dismissal, but thought better of it. One didn't argue with their Supreme Commander, let alone a Starguard. So, with a furtive glance at Novan, Classia stepped aside, awaiting Deb's dismissal.

Having thought that she too would be dismissed, Deb awaited the order, but Cirrius said, "Sky Leader Deneb, your presence is still required, so if you would kindly make your way to the launch tunnel and await further orders."

Deb thought she hadn't heard right at first, but managed a snappy, "Sir".

Leaving for the launch tunnel, Deb and Classia exchanged puzzled glances. Classia then turned and followed in a somberly fashion, though Deb could tell that she was uncharacteristically angry at being humiliated like that.

After a long, gloomy walk down the darkened tunnel, they eventually came to the open sky. The wind buffeted strongly against them up here, but far below, the sea rippled under gentle breezes. They turned to face each other, Classia's curly locks whipping about her face, which was a storm in itself of thunderous emotions. Deb tried to say something, but Classia stepped off the edge of the tunnel, letting herself drop, before regaining altitude, heading back to Sky Command. She hadn't looked back, no smile of reconciliation or friendly farewell, just anger. Deb had quickly lost sight of her in the darkness.

I'll see her tomorrow, vowed Deb.

But that night would change their tomorrows forever.

CHAPTER FIVE

Standing alone at the end of the skimmer launch tunnel, Deb could hear the Starguards approaching; the lingering crowd continuing to celebrate with a raucous send-off. The tunnel illumination had been darkened for Novan's visit, signalling that it was closed down for the night, but then a radiant glow lit their way, as Aerl created a staff of solid light from his hands, his own version of Millennius' sacred sceptre. Then to rapturous applause, the Starguards with Deb in tow alighted from the launch tunnel and out across the Ocean (it had no other name being one continuous body of water occasionally interrupted by small island chains) to Cirrius' island.

Deb was still bewildered by the whole situation. *This is all some dream*, she thought, remembering how she had felt when she had collapsed, feeling as if outside her body, witnessing events beyond her control. It was like that now, flying with the Starguards, but this was acutely real. The latest dizzy spell had all started when Novan had gazed deeply into her eyes, as Cirrius had. At first, she'd been flattered for her eyes had always been admired by would-be suitors, but with those two it had been something else.

What had surprised her, however, was her own attraction to Novan. She had never felt such emotions toward him before tonight and she had the impression that Novan was attracted to her. And how had he and Cirrius known about her? Granted, he had visited her orphanment years ago, but there had been thousands of orphans there. She could only guess that Gal Agar had mentioned her to him, but why? But she had to put all that aside, for her thoughts were with Classia. How must she be feeling now? What must she be thinking?

They had been flying for some time now and Deb thought this

pace must be agonisingly slow for the likes of Sceptre, Altair, and Urana, who could fly at near lightspeed, but they showed no impatience. In fact, their emotional states had remained remarkably calm, considering they had heard the news of their parents' deaths or fates. Perhaps they had accepted the inevitable ages ago and this was just confirmation. But Deb had wondered, considering Altair's feelings toward Novan, how he felt about Novan's mother still being alive, while his wasn't. Would there be any resentment?

I suppose none of this is my business and that mine is not to reason why when concerning the Starguards, Deb concluded.

Looking around at the group, she saw resolute faces, while Altair gave her a grim smile. She smiled back in politeness looking away. Altair gave her the shivers; he was like a lair serpent, waiting until the right moment when its prey felt no danger, before striking for the kill.

As they banked left, Deb could now make out a form in the crashing waves below; a small roughly circular island with a tinier companion, just visible in the morning rays of the rising sun.

Universe! I haven't slept in ages! she realised.

The group descended now, and Deb was sure that just in front of the simple residence resting on top of a small, forested hill, someone stood waiting for them. And by the time that they had crossed the shoreline and landed on Cirrius' island, Deb could see that it was Gal Agar. She was somewhat relieved to see him; someone normal in a day that had been anything but. But, anxiously, she wondered why he was here and what he knew.

"Welcome to Aqrius, everyone," Cirrius said. Then on spotting Gal Agar, he smiled broadly, "I am glad you are here, Gal Agar. I hope that I didn't cause any inconvenience at Sky Command." He added, ushering them into his modest abode.

"No, not really," said Gal Agar, a little too stiffly. "A little bit of excitement helps now and again." He gazed at Deb more in support than anger. Deb smiled back, more relaxed.

Once inside, a modest-sized abode opened up before them. A large smooth dark-wood rectangular table with eight intricately-carved high-backed chairs of the same wood tucked beneath it resided in the middle of the lounge, which the Starguards milled around, not sure of where to sit.

Cirrius smiled at their discomfort of being in his not-so-often-visited home.

"Please, all of you, be seated. I shall return in a moment," Cirrius tried to sound pleasant. He then disappeared through a sliding door at the rear of the room. Another door to the right evidenced another part of the dwelling. Otherwise, the lounge was effectively an enclosed capsule.

Deb sensed a hint of hidden charm and wondered if tonight's events would herald Cirrius' eventual return to public life. The world could use his fascinating qualities.

While he was gone, the Starguards seemed to eye her warily, as if sizing her up: Who was she that she could share the same room as them? They sat on one side of the room in the chairs, while the two Sky Warriors sat on the other side, Decion managing to pull out a large divan from the corner to solely occupy.

It seemed that any talk amongst themselves wasn't for the ears of others, but apart from the glaring Decion and the leering Altair, the rest seemed amiable enough and idle chat began to flitter around the room, started naturally by Novan.

But now that Deb was able to relax, she found herself drawn to the room's decor. Completely contrasted to the exterior, which looked to be made from surrounding natural rock, the interior was almost antiquated, not like the standard modern abodes with their moveable plastiform interiors. A couple of standard Meccun crystalators adorned an old wooden desk near the back of the room, no doubt linked to the main crystalator on Sky Command, overlooked by a large vidscreen fitted to the wall. An over-sized rug stole the center of the floor, upon which rested all the furniture, including their table.

This hadn't been what Deb had expected. She had always imagined Cirrius in a shining residence of completely or partially recycled swordship materials and furniture as many other Celestian abodes were. And then she smelled it. The furniture was old-world, the unmistakeable deep scent of *lecker* and the carefully carved intricate designs giving away its origins. Many of Halcyon's islands retained their natural beauty so almost everything had to be manufactured. But these chairs and tables were real wood. She had ever only seen examples of such designs in the Halcyon Exposition, where other old-world artifacts were held. But then something else had caught her eyes and she had held her breath to prevent letting out a gasp, for three of the surrounding walls were lined with the grandest of paintings of the Celestian Knights.

They were the most wonderful paintings she had ever seen. Deb left her seat to view them closer. She had never seen painted art before. Everything nowadays was holographic, and she even wondered where and how anyone had procured the materials. With the archaic trappings Cirrius had immersed himself in, Deb realised that while he was the youngest Starguard, Cirrius had the oldest soul of them all. She smiled to herself at that.

All the last generation Celestian Knights were represented, except, of course, the Traitor Synther, and each was so life-like she expected any of them to actually step out from the background. She walked around the room, occasionally flicking black hair from out of her eyes, so that she could admire them properly. Then her eye caught the mark of the painter: Cirrius. He himself, had brought to life the very essence of the Celestian Saviours through the work of his gifted hands.

> "And in all the universe, there ranks not a gift
> above the one which is wrought thyself with love"

Deb remembered the quote from her days in the orphanment and could think of no truer example than this. The others had also taken a keen interest in the paintings, with Aerl and Altair in front of their mother, Iria's portrait.

As Deb stood in front of Acirrius the Sacrificed's portrait admiring his poignant eyes staring out in noble sacredness, a quiet clearing of the throat from behind startled her. Turning around, Gal Agar stood, hands clasped behind his back. He glanced at the painting and the one beside it of Elysius, which they both moved to.

"Beautiful, isn't it," Gal Agar said in a whispery voice. "They all are. Cirrius has a great talent." He spread his arm out around the room. "Cirrius built everything you see here from the habitat to the rug, furniture, and crystalators. Pity only a privileged few get to see them though." He said in that same faraway voice. He had sounded sad, and Deb had the feeling that he wanted to say something else, but didn't know how to say it. But when she had looked at his face, into his eyes they seemed to reflect the light through a moistness. She suddenly realised they were unreleased tears. They quickly disappeared in a blink, and he drew closer, holding her shoulders, gently, "You're going to be okay, Deb. No matter what anybody says, always be sure that I'll be there for you. You deserve no less."

The sincerity behind those words lifted Deb and all she could say was, "Thank you," feeling that adding 'sir' was unnecessary.

The two walked together from painting to painting, Gal Agar's presence comforting Deb and she realised that this was the first time in a long time that they'd been together outside of duty, even though she was considered to be one of his favourite Sky Warriors. Deb realised that something was different between them. Something had changed. They were both more relaxed and informal and sometimes they would talk about the paintings and other aspects of old-world art. And then Deb had found the term to explain the feeling behind Gal Agar's words, a word that hadn't been used by her before and would remain to bond them together: Father.

Once Cirrius had left the company in the lounge, he had immediately entered a short wood-lined passage leading off to other rooms, but Cirrius chose a door to what was on first inspection a storage room. Reaching out to pull on a loose wooden wall panel, a section of the false wall slid across revealing a personal transtube. Entering it, Cirrius descended rapidly for a minute, well below his island house, where his secret facility was located. He had excavated and equipped it himself and not even the other Starguards or Gal Agar knew about it. The lab was bare-walled, Cirrius liking the natural strength and colouring of the grey and black original bedrock.

In the event Sky Command was destroyed, all data could still be retrieved through his crystalators, and a chain of command could be re-established from here. But for now, from his replicated Sky Command bridge, Cirrius was concerned with other pressing matters.

"Viewers. Room one." He activated the crystalators.

Watching his gathered guests with hidden viewers, he focused in on Deb and studied her carefully, every now and again speaking commands to his crystalator, which began spewing data and projecting three-dimensional images.

The crystalators that occupied his underground refuge were more advanced than the standard issue. Their capacity was far greater than the most advanced thinking machines the Meccuns had employed back on their home world centuries ago. On Meccus, the thinking machines had been components of wires and energy currents, but there had been talk of utilising the natural amplitude present in certain types of resonating crystals with an affinity for quantum processing to create a new type of thinking machine and the crystalator had been born. The Meccuns had theorised that the crystalator processing was carried out in another dimension and they were keen to explore this possibility.

Following The End, the Meccuns had brought with them a whole harvest of these crystals, but had found similar outcroppings of crystals on Aradeal, one of the ringed gas giant Magna Prime's dozen moons. These large ovoid moons had been colonized by the Meccuns for their own purposes and because each reminded them somewhat of their dome-filled home world.

With the ability to almost infinitely decrease the size of a crystalator while maintaining computing capacity, some Meccuns had even implanted crystalators into their heads to better communicate between themselves and their external crystalators. It also enhanced their legend of being psychic. Their society on the Magna Prime moons was becoming more and more dependent on crystalators as was the rest of the system, where crystalators had been ensconced into virtually everything else from skimmers to sky cities. So, it had been to the Meccuns that Cirrius had turned to when wanting the most advanced crystalators installed on Sky Command and secretly into his own facility. But unbeknownst to them, Cirrius had also placed telepathic disrupters on both systems, so that their integrity could be secure from outside interference, especially from any Meccun 'psychic' or even a Starguard's, like Novan, intrusion.

Standing a half-meter tall, his main crystalator, consisted of a large hexagonal, prism-shaped, data-core matrix crystal which stood upright and was linked within a transparent enclosed sphere by transcendent rods networked to a horizontal periphery of a dozen processing eye-sized crystals embedded in the sphere. The central data-core crystal received and transmitted information through the transcendent rod-net work creating holographic connections and interfaces that pulsed between the crystals, like thoughts carried on the body's neurons. They were almost alive and everybody treated them as such; the Meccuns especially superstitious in this, should any of them become self-aware and vengeful if mistreated. But Cirrius treated his like a tool, albeit respectfully, for superstitions died hard, though he had declined giving his crystalator a name or personality as others had to theirs.

The final results of his analysis were revealed in holographic equations and schematics projected before him. Gal Agar had known that Deb wasn't all that she appeared to be, ever since he had brought Deb to Cirrius' attention all those years ago. Cirrius had watched over her ever since, but he had known more about her and kept it a secret, until now. As the results materialised, he still frowned on their revelations. He had discovered not only why she was so different, but also how different she was. And it was time that Deb knew the fate of civilisation depended on her.

Vacating the duplicate bridge, where all the systems shut down automatically on his absence, Cirrius ascended to his residence. On his way from the secret transtube, Cirrius detoured through the renourishment compartment, selecting a half dozen bottles of nectar, wolobean juice, and refreshments on a tray, and re-entered the lounge, excusing himself for being so long. As the others gathered around his offerings placed on the table, Cirrius prepared to enlighten them on the emergence of a new power and the reappearance of old enemies.

While Cirrius had been absent, Aerl and Altair had said their own private prayers and farewells to their mother. Now they were talking among themselves. Altair for once seemed less intense and more at peace with himself.

Maybe not knowing was tearing at him inside, thought Sceptre, but still it's no excuse for his behaviour.

Altair had been commenting on the beauty of the black-haired Sky Warrior and how beguiling her eyes were, when he had fallen silent. Aerl, sensing someone at his shoulder, turned to see Novan there.

Altair and Novan stared at each other, until Altair begrudgingly broke the deadlock, "Novan, I guess I owe you something of an apology. I had wanted to break you apart in the medlab and when you suddenly left, I was sure that you felt unrepentant for your actions and I was coming after you. But luckily for you, Aerl stopped me," he grinned bitterly. "Our mother's death wasn't too much of a shock, but it was a relief to actually know her fate. Thank you." Then he added, "This doesn't change anything between us, however, and if anything I'm watching you closer, until you leave!" With a twinge of a smile, he then walked away to the painting of his father, Auron.

Aerl had watched him go and then snuck a grin at Novan, "I think he's going to be okay. I was worried back at Millennius City for a while he was going to start vapourising medtechs, but luckily I talked some sense into him."

Novan laughed, lifting his sombre mood. "It really amazes me that you and Cirrius, two of the youngest Starguards, have such good senses about other Celestians. I could only really probably count on Urana's constancy after that, but you two, when I'm gone will have to hold everything together," Novan said.

"Do you have any idea of when you are departing or how many will accompany you?" Aerl inquired.

"Yes, I . . ." Just then, Cirrius re-entered with some food and nectar, the hungry flocking to the now-laden table. Novan continued. "Yes, I think I'll need about four or five Swordships with thirty thousand crew and support. I'll have to discuss this with Decion and Star Commander Vander for their support and to Cirrius and the Sky Commander for theirs as well," he said looking Gal Agar's way, suddenly becoming distracted.

Aerl followed Novan's gaze toward the two Sky Warriors, nibbling on something or another, still engrossed in the portraits. "You're thinking of that other Sky Leader, Classia, wasn't it? She's quite taken with you. Is she to be your first wife?" Aerl teased.

Novan tried to laugh it off and didn't answer. Aerl followed his gaze again and realised his target had been the wrong one. "Oh, I see, it's the other one; the black-haired beauty that Altair's also interested in."

Novan looked at him sharply, opened his mouth to say something, then closed it, but Aerl could see surprise and another emotion behind Novan's eyes.

Hope you're not getting too deep into something here, Novan, he thought. *Maybe you'd be better off in deep space.* But out loud he said, "Do any of them know?"

"Know what, Aerl?" responded Novan levelly.

"Oh, Universe, you are in deep," said Aerl, shaking his head. "I think I'll see how the twins are doing. I think Decion is boring them." He added *sotto voce* as he left.

Decion and the twins had also engaged in admiring the

portraits. Their mother was so beguiling, but Astara and Alpha Rion were both thinking of their father and their favourite memory of him regaling them as younglings with tales of the Knights Destina, a rival sect within the Celestian Knights Order millennia ago until they had faded from time. Decion still mentioned their battles and heretical philosophies from time to time in their training.

Deb and Gal Agar were enjoying their glasses of the dark delicious unfermented wolobean juice, the sweeter green variety, when Cirrius chimed two glasses together and everyone stopped what they were doing. Cirrius had an announcement to make.

It is time, Cirrius thought.

Everyone was now comfortable and amicable enough to hear his news. "My fellow Starguards and honoured guests, I think there are some things that you should know and we need to discuss; things that I have been aware of and have been studying and now is the time for action." There was a little stir in his audience. "Novan's news had taken me somewhat by surprise, but I had expected something like this. I believe that we will be at war again soon, which makes Novan's mission all the more imperative."

Novan seemed mystified at that remark, but remained quiet.

Cirrius then looked unexpectedly at Deb. "First, I'd like to introduce to those of you who haven't met her already, Sky Leader Deneb, one of the Sky Warriors' finest," he said, spreading a welcoming arm in her direction. "She will play a pivotal part in all our futures from now on." His smile was all but conspiratorial.

Deb looked between Gal Agar and Cirrius, confused at her inclusion. "I . . . I don't understand . . ." Her voice trailed off. She wanted to dive into the background.

Cirrius, still with his little smile, asked her, "Tell us about your dreams, Deneb?"

Deb's head tilted in incomprehension. *How did he know?* Her eyes began to sting, tears fighting to spill down her cheeks, but she held them back and looked to Gal Agar for support. He simply nodded, not too sure about what was happening himself, his eyes imploring her to tell them all. But all she wanted to do was forget about them.

Taking a breath, she said, "I sometimes see war, a war where the Lore come down and totally destroy Magna Aura. Red skies full of blood. Halcyon on fire. I see it over and over again. It's as if I'm actually there, but I can't do anything about it."

"And is that what you saw, when you blacked out in the skimmer bay last night?" Cirrius asked. Deb nodded, meekly. "What else?" probed Cirrius, urgency in his voice.

Deb's features knotted in concentration, her lips pursed together. "I don't know. I don't see any distinct faces, but there's a presence there, a presence that can only belong to the Traitor Synther." Deb wasn't sure how she was remembering all of this when her dreams had been fuzzy images. But the truth of her words seemed real to her, at least.

An air of disbelief suddenly gusted about the room and Decion laughed out loud, a rather loud, raucous, booming sound. "That cannot be," he intoned gruffly, "He must have been destroyed or he would have discovered us by now. Or else Elysius would have told Novan if he were there, would she not, brother? You're going on the word of a youngling, Cirrius?"

"I am not a youngling!" Deb fired back. "I am a Sky Leader!" She felt her face heat up.

Decion harrumphed dismissively.

But Novan agreed with Decion for once, at least on account of the Traitor Synther. "Yes, if the Traitor Synther were alive then my mother would have warned me. But she did escape before the end of the War." His thoughts were interrupted and he turned to Cirrius. "But before we go into that, I think you owe us some more explanations. I've known for some time you have been engaged in some undisclosed Sky Warrior business. Does that involve Sky Leader Deneb? I think it's time you revealed all your secrets, Supreme Commander," he finished dryly.

Cirrius sighed, half amused, half indignant for having been called out. He would have wanted to explain certain things first, to set up his finishing piece, but that was now impossible, thanks to Novan's impatience.

No problem.

Cirrius walked over to Deb, held her hand and walked with her to the rear center of the room. He looked deep into her eyes, which were valiantly holding back tumultuous emotions and then began his questions: "What's the first thing you ever remember, Deneb? Who are your parents? Why are you such a natural Sky Warrior? Why are you having such dreams? In point, Deneb, who are you?"

Every question had been delivered with a quiet voice and caring smile, but Deb had no answers for him. Her life had seemed normal enough for an orphan, until she had been plagued by blackouts and dark dreams. Deb shook her head again. She didn't have any answers, so Cirrius answered for her:

"You are a Starguard, Deneb."

The room went deathly quiet. Even Decion had been taken aback, while others stared wide-eyed. Deb stared astonished at Cirrius, then at the rest of the Starguards and Gal Agar around her. Her heart beat like thunder and she wrapped herself in her arms to keep the burgeoning muscle within herself. She looked at the floor and closed her eyes to hide her tears that were even now squeezing through her lidded barriers. She couldn't be, no, it must be wrong. And when she looked into Cirrius' face, her eyes asked the question: How?

Speaking as if they were the only two present in the room, Cirrius said, "You were born on Galatia, Deneb, just before The End, but during the voyage here your ship narrowly avoided being destroyed in a pulsar-storm. Everyone died, your mother dying in the vacuum-less bay with you in her arms; your superior nature saving you."

Cirrius shushed Deb's quiet sobs before continuing: "Once the cruiser was repressurised, a search crew boarded the crippled ship and you were the sole survivor and unaffected. The person who found you, was young Gal Agar." Deb looked at Gal Agar through teary eyes as he nodded solemnly in confirmation. Cirrius continued, "He knew then that you were special and Gal Agar was the first living person you saw, the bond between you two was forming even then. But try as he might, he couldn't keep you, for you were then placed in an orphanment. But he never forgot you and always watched over you. Then years later when he became the first Sky Warrior, he told me about you. Do you remember when I visited your orphanment all those years ago?"

Deb nodded absently, "Yes, you asked me if I wanted to be a Sky Warrior. And I said yes," she said as if in a daze.

"And then what did I do?"

"You took me someplace . . ." Deb tried to remember where, but couldn't, ". . . and I fell asleep. And when I awoke, you said that I was a Sky Warrior. And I flew about the room." She remembered that part with vivid fondness, "But—"

"But nothing was ever done to you, Deneb," finished Cirrius. "The aeromorphic process failed on you, so I had you isolated from the other Sky Warrior recruits and ran some crystalator tests. It confirmed your heritage, but your powers, apart from flight, weren't developed properly then. It's only now that your latent powers are developing."

Deb stared at nothing, reliving the life she knew, desperately trying to remember the past. She felt weak, her churning insides and erratic voice making her voice shaky, "I'd always wondered why I felt different from the other Sky Warriors. They always talked about the ways the aeromorphic procedures had changed them, how they felt, but I could never feel those changes. And now I know why." Then looking at Gal Agar, "Why didn't you tell me?" she said shaking her head.

Gal Agar stood alone confounded, stunned innocence cast across his face. "I didn't know. I just knew that you were someone special, and still are," he said with tears in his eyes. "I'm as shocked as the others, though I wish that Cirrius had told me sooner. Cirrius?" He bit back, clearly shaken, looking as if he had lost something.

"I am sorry that I didn't, universe's truth, but there is more. It was only when I was in close proximity to Deb that I could feel some energy emanating from her."

"Yes, I had felt it too," confessed Novan. "Just before she collapsed."

"Deneb," began Cirrius, "You have a power within yourself, but do not know how to use or control it, yet. These dreams that you have are not dreams, I suspect, but glimpses into the future. This attack will happen. Your powers have been trying to manifest themselves, but you've been denying them, hence your blackouts. You must be able to feel them?" She wearily nodded. "Good. Then try to use them when they come again, don't fight it. And maybe we can find out more about what will happen."

"Welcome to the family, Deneb," stepped forward a smiling Urana, with a warm hug.

Deb managed a flushed smile and a weak, "Thank you," as the others had echoed Urana's sentiments. It was almost overwhelming.

"I don't get this," interrupted Altair. "Correct me if I'm wrong, but the only other Starguard envisioned was the son or daughter of Millennius and Phasia that so far hasn't been found, right? So, if she's the long-lost daughter of Millennius and Phasia," he exclaimed with arms in the air, "Then who's this other mother who died?"

"I didn't say anything about Millennius and Phasia, Altair," Cirrius revealed. "And I have not finished, yet. If Deneb is right, and I happen to believe that she is, that the Lore are going to attack, then how did they sense us here? We've been here for thirty years and yet no sign of attack has been imminent, until Deneb here sensed it."

"Are you saying that there's some sort of reciprocal action here?" said Novan, following on from Cirrius' thoughts.

"Yes, we know that Deneb's dreams started not too long ago and now the Lore have sensed us here and I don't think that's a coincidence."

"But what's this got to do with her not being Millennius and Phasia's daughter?" asked a confused Altair.

Urana shook her head, tittering at Altair, and explained to him as if a youngling, "I think Cirrius is trying to say that if Deneb feels that the Traitor Synther is alive and leading the Lore, and that they have sensed us, then there must be some connection between her and him. Maybe something telepathic. Is that correct, Cirrius?" she stood akimbo awaiting the answer as everyone was.

"Yes, Rain, kind of . . ." he hesitated, but Decion finished for him.

"She's a Loremaiden!" Decion's hand moved so quickly that the portal flared open before anyone could stop him as the giant lancesword emerged unsheathed and wielded as if to it swing down upon her.

"Universe, no!" Deb gasped, cringing away, her world crushed forever.

Cirrius literally flew in front of Deb, as a babble of voices assailed Cirrius. "She's a Starguard, here, Decion!"

"She's the half-breed of the Traitor Synther. She should be killed as the others were." Decion protested.

"Is this true, Cirrius?" his sister asked. "You knew this and didn't say anything?"

But all Cirrius said was, "Yes, I believe Deneb is the daughter of the Traitor Synther."

Numbed to her core, not wanting to believe any of this, Deb stood in the middle of them all, shoulders slumped, the centre of unwanted attention. She wished she was back on Sky Command right now in bed dreaming this whole thing.

Novan was incredulous. "You can't be serious?" he asked. "She could be the daughter of Accirius or even Alphatronius—we all know what my father was like for Universe sake! And even then, surely the Traitor Synther would sense us, the offspring of his enemy, without it necessarily being Deneb attracting him here." There were a few noises of approval.

But Cirrius ruled that out, folding his arms. "No, you should know yourself, Novan, that that cannot be true. Spheron's Tomes you hold and always read rules that out, everyone's whereabouts were accounted for before The End, except the Traitor Synther's. We know he pierced the shield during his many attacks and disappeared frequently. He would have reverted to his Celestian form and impregnated someone, without them knowing his real identity, fathering a few younglings. Our parents hunted and killed many of the youngling loremaidens which exhibited powers early.

They could have grown up to be spies and assassins for the Traitor Synther, so we had to." He looked slightly abashed at Deb. "But who knows, there could be more Denebs, just for this purpose; so, if we escaped, he could still find us. It is Deneb's attachment to the Traitor Synther that has led him here and her dreams confirm that. I'm sorry, but it's the truth. And we have to deal with it," he said, turning to Deb. There was a slight pause for thought.

"Maybe we could just kill her," mused Decion. "It would prove these theories right or wrong—would it not?" He grinned from beneath his black beard——a sinister look. Since nobody moved or looked remotely shocked, Deb took the remark to be Decion's version of humour. But as Cirrius took a casual step toward her, Deb had the feeling that you never knew the true intentions of Decion, until it was too late. She would have to remember that.

Her head was spinning with all this life-changing news. She'd arrived tonight a humble Sky Warrior, now she was being told that she was a near-omnipotent being with the power to save worlds and the daughter of their worst enemy. At least she had stopped crying, which more befitted her new stature.

Then Altair had broken the silence. "Wait, a minute!" he said, throwing his arms up in despair. "Cirrius, you've said that Novan is to continue with his mission, knowing full well that we could be under attack. What are you doing?" he asked, pointing an accusing finger at Cirrius.

"Wherever Elysius is, she needs help. Novan must go. We have enough to defend ourselves," he replied, pointedly looking at Deneb.

"Oh, Universe, no!" exclaimed Decion. "You cannot expect her to defend us all. She doesn't even have full powers. She's a youngling!" He saw her angry expression and corrected himself, with a grin. "She's just a Sky Warrior! And besides, in her so-called future dreams, we are all destroyed!" he growled.

"That is true, but I believe that being the daughter of the Prime Lore, Deneb has the power within herself to destroy them, though she doesn't yet possess the knowledge to do so. But she will." Looking over at Novan, he said, "Novan, you have to continue your mission. It is your mother's and thousands of Celestian lives at stake. We cannot forfeit their lives, while we live in fear of attack. The sooner you go the better."

Deb felt the power wafting about Cirrius and realised that she was caught in the middle of a battle of wills. Everyone there was coming to the realisation that Cirrius hadn't stayed out of the public eye because of coyness. They all sensed the authority within him and now the would-be orchestrator of Magna Aura's future survival was flexing it.

Cirrius directed another question to Deb, "In your dreams, did you dream that you were a Starguard?"

"No," replied Deb. Never had there been that aspect to any of her dreams.

Then it seemed Cirrius had a new thought, "So now you do know, do you think the next time you dream, the outcome will be different?"

"It could be. But I don't control my dreams, they come of their own accord," she said.

"Maybe we can induce the dreams or connect her up to a crystalator to find out what happens," spoke up Urana.

"No," declined Cirrius. "It may affect Deneb or the Traitor Synther may be alerted to any changes in her."

"So, you mean to lure them here?" asked Urana, more than a little riled. "That could be potentially lethal." Her sarcasm found purchase with the others who agreed.

But Decion flexed his arms out, warming up to the idea of

fighting. "No, we can do it. We have the weapons now. The Lore are but temporalmorphic beings and we now have the weapons to fight them and more than enough willing warriors to fight them. Think of it, a united force of Star and Sky Warriors, alongside Elerae and Xarian warriors and the Starguards. Even if Novan takes an ample amount, we would still have close to a million warriors. The victory would be magnificent." His eyes gleamed at the prospect of battle and even Astara, who hadn't said a word all night, looked to her twin, who clenched his fists in anticipation of action.

Deb's memories fought to place the word temporalmorphic and remembered that it and other aspects of a Celestian's nature had been taught in the Sky Warrior's cadet training. She remembered the years-old lesson with the jaunty Sky Leader Ade.

"The Scrolls of History say that all life was created by the Storm of Stars and that they created the People of Energy, or the Lore. Our studies revealed that they were then composed of animate exotic stellar-energy, but with the merger between the Traitor Synther and his metamorphic powers, we believe that their whole nature was changed. His father, Zater Jen, had elements of chronital energy within him and could slip out of time. It was during one such temporal journey that he disappeared after the Hero Siege incident, which we'll discuss later. The Lore, existing now, are a combination of those powers and are able to travel time and as energy entities changing their shape, hence the term temporalmorphic. But although this sounds formidable, we now have the weapons to combat them. The plasma-bolt staffs and other weapons that you will be tested with, have the ability to disrupt and break apart the bonds which maintain a Lore's integrity. And the ingenious part about these weapons is that on the Lore's energy release upon destruction, the energy is captured by the staff, stored, and used again on another

Lore. Use a Lore to kill a Lore, I say. Right any questions . . .?"

Deb had liked Ade's affable ways and now he was a Deputy Sky Commander: 'Old Ade.' He always had a kind word for her. Deb's mind had drifted away from the heated discussions which had continued during her reminiscence.

". . . Forever savour that victory, Decion, but we have to think things through," replied Cirrius testily, irritated at Decion's constant battlelust. "Novan's mission has priority and you and Star Commander Vander have to sit down and decide how many warriors you can supply to Novan. Gal Agar and I will speak later. All those forces and ships will then moor off Magna Prime for training. After you leave, Millennius and Alphatron City-States will move closer to Halcyon and Placia for protection. But we have to wait until after Novan leaves to warn the system of an imminent Lore attack. We can then solidify our own forces without worrying about their fates." He paused for questions, but the looks from everyone asked the same question about him and he answered what their thoughts, not voices, had asked.

Letting out a huff of a laugh, Cirrius paused and then said, "Besides, Deneb now, and in the absence of Solandus, I was the youngest Starguard and as the youngest, I could observe things that all of you couldn't or wouldn't see on Galatia. There was so much hatred and rivalry there between what were supposed to be the all-noble Celestian Knights. You were born into that, but I vowed it wouldn't happen on our new home. But here we are and the same thing happens!" His expression was that of an earnest pleader.

"So, not wanting to become contaminated with your petty power games, I came here to my own island. I tried to ferment order through the Sky Warriors, and it works, but as to the fate of the whole system, well that was another problem. So, I set about with crystalator models and experiments, evaluating what would happen in different scenarios and right now you're hearing my scenario for a Lore invasion. And you're only hearing it now, because no one else has bothered to ask themselves what would happen or because they don't care, because they're more interested in their own personal power." His voice hadn't been raised, but the feeling of anger was quite palpable, nonetheless.

"Now, do you want to hear more on the survival of our worlds, or do you want to squabble over who rules where?" His remarks had been directed to all of them, but while Decion glared in indignation, Altair looked suitably chastised. Deb realised that some invisible barrier had been lifted from around Cirrius and now his true Starguard self had emerged. Deb couldn't tell if the others were impressed or slightly alarmed at a new emergent power. She only wondered if she could take command as forcefully. Even being a Sky Leader didn't prepare you for these kinds of decisions.

Her thoughts were broken up by Urana. "Well, looks like my little brother's grown more than others." She said, staring directly at Altair, who responded with a sneer. "Oh! Sorry cousin. Was I wrong? My mistake," she said, blowing him a kiss, which Altair ignored.

Cirrius waited patiently for their antics to finish. "Right," he continued, more calmly. "So, Novan's force is around Magna Prime and the City-States closer to us. Urana will, of course, be on Placia." He smiled briefly at his sister, who still looked pleased with herself. He turned his attention back to Deb. "Can you feel how close the Lore are now, Deneb? Do you know when they'll attack?" Deb shook her head. Cirrius continued, "That is the only problem.

Novan needs to be away, so energy isn't wasted on his departure and protection. Novan, can you depart in a week?"

Novan blew air through pursed lips. "I'll need the Swordships. There should be the reserves and out-of-rotation units docked at Systar Orbital. I'll check on their state of readiness when I depart here," Novan said.

Glancing at Decion and Gal Agar, Cirrius said. "And I'll make sure you have your forces in that time as well. Then the rest of the battle plans will be finalised. Are there any final questions?" he asked.

Still feeling out of her depth, Deb needed to know a few things. "Cirrius, you mentioned the Lore being temporalmorphic? Do you think I could be temporalmorphic? I mean I seem to remember that around the modified plasma-bolt staffs, I used to feel weak. Could that energy affect me?"

Cirrius paused to gather his words, but it was Decion who answered, "Ah, yes! I could test that theory now." He made to raise his giant lancesword, but Urana stepped in front of him in a clear stance of warning. "Look," said Decion, in his deep voice, "The crystal within my sword's pommel is energised against Lore. If Deneb is more Lore than Celestian, it would hurt her, but not kill her. Of course, it could also mean that her will to remain Celestian will negate its energies, so she won't be hurt at all. Either way, we would have more answers than before. Trust me," he said with a sly, bearded grin. Everyone looked to Deb. It was her choice.

Without hesitation, Deb stepped past Urana intent on grasping the top of the lancesword, but she froze in front of Decion, who held out the weapon tilted down toward her, which was a good half-meter taller than Deb. She stared along the black *hovric*-binding wrapped tightly around the pommel with the globular crystal entrenched in the forked top. The crystal seemed to dare her to touch it. Without realising that her hand had moved, Deb found it resting on the golden crystal.

And nothing happened. No searing pain or cry of death.

"Pah!" Altair exclaimed, both in disappointment and relief.

Deb looked at the others, who also seemed both relieved and disappointed nothing had happened. She looked at her hand, but it was unmarked. "Looks like my power's dormant, or I'm more Celestian than Lore," remarked Deb. "Satisfied, Decion?"

"My dear, Starguard Deneb, my curiosity is assuaged," he said. "For now." He bowed and gave her a kiss on the hand. Deb thought he would crush her fingers, but he was surprisingly gentle. He then turned and retired to sit in a chair, creaking under his armoured frame. He did not re-sheathe the lancesword.

Confused over a thought, Deb then turned back to Cirrius and asked, "If the Lore can time travel, how come they haven't come here by now?" The Starguards laughed as if she'd asked a relatively simple question of them.

Novan answered, "You saw the future, Deneb, so by the time your father thinks about leading the Lore here, they'll arrive in our future, but their present." Deb mulled the explanation over, nodding absently, before agreeing.

"Anything else, Deneb?" asked Cirrius.

"Yes," said Deb. "First, I don't ever want the Traitor Synther called my father again. And secondly, I like to be called Deb."

Novan laughed aloud, the other Starguards wearing broad

smiles. "Okay, Deb it is," he had said. "And I think it is time that you were introduced to your fellow Starguards properly. You already know myself and Cirrius. These two are Aerl the Sceptre and Altair," he led her to the brothers, both of whom gave her a graceful bow and kiss on the hand.

"This is Urana", Cirrius started, but Urana said, "Call me Rain, Deb." Deb had already known she was beautiful, but being this close to her was magical. Urana gave her a hug and a kiss on the cheek.

"I hope there is time for you to visit Placia. We will fly the skies together!" her warm smile invited.

Then it was on to Decion and the twins. "As you've seen, Decion may seem intolerable sometimes, but once you get to know him, you'll see he's intolerable *all* the time." Decion had tried to look injured by the remark, but the smile on his face said otherwise. He remained seated, his cape, helmet and lancesword lying beside him.

Cirrius carried on, "And these are the twins, Alpha Rion and Astara. And they're not always so quiet." Novan had finished. The two said their 'hallos'.

Astara surprised everyone with an invitation. "You are welcome to a tour of Alphatron City-State when this is all over." To which Deb nodded acceptance. She had never visited the City-States before.

Personal introductions to the Starguards over, she couldn't really think of anything to say. She felt hands on her shoulders and there behind her was Gal Agar. He was proud of her. She could tell. Deb gave him a hug. If ever she had wanted a father now, it would be Gal Agar and that's how he felt too.

Glasses of vintage nectar were passed around. First, there was a prayer for the dead and remembered. Then Deb was urged to say something by an effusive Urana.

Addressing the gathering, Deb said, "I would like to thank you all for your support and I am proud to be a Starguard. I will do everything in my power to protect our world." There was a cheer and she flushed. Then she remembered Classia. "Oh, what do I tell Classia when I see her? She's bound to suspect something," she said to Gal Agar.

"We will have to separate you two," Cirrius replied.

"Why?" Deb protested. "She is my best friend."

"The Magna Aura system means more than your friendship, Deb," Cirrius said. "Classia could inadvertently let the secret slip out. There could be other Loremaidens in league with the Lore and we need to keep your secret at all costs. Classia has to remain none the wiser!"

"She will not like this. She will probably suspect something is going on." Deb knew Classia and the fuss she could cause when she was not satisfied with something. "She will fight whatever you try to do," Deb directed at Cirrius.

But before he could answer, Novan stepped over and said, "No, she will not. As of now, she is to be transferred to my command. She'll be part of my command crew and need not know anything of what has occurred tonight."

Deb felt guilty about Classia's ignorance concerning her true nature, after all it had been Classia who had tirelessly stood by her and supported her. Now Deb felt that she had betrayed Classia, her best friend.

Novan tried to reassure her. "Deb, I will take care of Classia. Do not worry."

She smiled, putting on a brave face, but Deb knew Classia would be devastated if she found out Novan was lying to her. But what could she do?

The sun and Placia—the latter like a faraway moon—were rising together and it was time for the meeting to end. Urana said her farewells, giving Cirrius her seal of approval for his future plans. Then she flew off, heading straight toward her planet. Alpha Rion and Astara also bade farewell. They had an overdue appointment on Systar from where they would catch a skimmer to Alphatron. Decion and Novan would head for Vista Mare, the other captured asteroid circling Halcyon, and a meeting with Star Commander Vander. Decion had also promised to train Deb with a sword if she so wished. Sceptre left for an appointment on Haven City, Altair for Millennius City-State after a farewell kiss for Deb; leaving her, Cirrius, and Gal Agar alone.

"I'm sorry for the problems this has caused the both of you," Cirrius said, "But further on from that, I think we have to discuss Deb's future."

"How so?" inquired Gal Agar. Though he had always suspected another side to Cirrius, he didn't know if he trusted him now as much as he had.

"I can imagine that there will be a lot of questions on your return to Sky Command, so what I propose is to have Deb announced as my aide. That way she would have access to both of us for information without arousing any suspicions. I will not pretend not to have noticed that the two of you have become closer, that is good to see, but others would have noticed it already. But with Deb mostly in my company, she would be out of sight, out of mind so to speak. Is that reasonable?"

Gal Agar thought it over and nodded, but Deb had another thought, "Why not just tell everyone the truth; that I'm a Starguard. I'm sure they'd understand. It would explain to them all my problems recently, lessen their suspicions of me, which are bound to increase now and then I could lead a normal life, if I could call it that. But at least everything would be out in the open," she pleaded.

Cirrius considered it, saying, "After the War, Deb your powers will be known to everyone, I'm sure. We'll wait until then. Anything done now will be more of a distraction, than an asset, believe me." He nodded her into accepting.

But Deb still wished that she could run out and tell everyone what had happened to her.

Then she remembered. "Oh, Universe, the tests!" She looked between Cirrius and Gal Agar, before continuing, "The medtechs did some tests, to see what was wrong with me. The results must be through by now!" she realised.

But Cirrius didn't seem fazed. "I had already been alerted to your... incident." He raised his voice and spoke to the crystalator at the rear of the room, "Extract data, Med file, Deneb, Sky Leader." Energy crackled within the crystals and moments later it displayed the data, Deb reading it as the holographic stream materialised in the air. And there in bold letters at the end of the report were the words 'Undefined energy source.' Deb's heart leapt. "Purge extracted file and render all files on Sky Leader Deneb inaccessible, except to myself, Sky Commander Gal Agar, and the Starguards. Execute," he commanded.

More energy surged through the crystals and then it abated, only the soft hum of the crystals invading the silence of the room.

Deb thought the crystals might be singing to themselves, perfectly happy crystals. She walked around the room, again admiring the paintings, then she noticed, almost hiding in the darkness above his father's painting, what appeared to be Hyphon's metastaff, the model from which the Sky Warrior's plasma-bolt staffs derived.

"Of course, that's not the real one," said Cirrius from across the room. "But I like to keep it here to remind me. It is operational though," he stated matter-of-factly. They admired it for a while.

"I think it's time we left now," announced Gal Agar. "I'll have to also check that the medtechs didn't read the report, before we erased it. I'll see to it that everyone is informed of Deb's new position, and I will send her back over later. Thank you, Cirrius for enlightening us and bringing a little more light into our lives," Gal Agar said looking at Deb, who flashed Cirrius with a bright, blue-eyed smile.

"Farewell, Azure," Cirrius said to Deb. To the confused Sky Leader, he said, "All names have meaning, Deb. Mine means 'Lord of the High Skies', Urana's means 'Gold-sky Goddess' and if you'd been born a Starguard on Galatia, you'd have been, Azure—'Goddess of the Darkening Blue.' Fitting, don't you think?"

"I love it." Deb almost jumped with glee.

Deb, Cirrius and Gal Agar exchanged forearm clasps. Then she and Gal Agar departed to the air for Sky Command.

And some hard-earned sleep, Deb thought. But now she didn't feel tired. *Must be that Starguard blood!*

CHAPTER SIX

"So, what do you think happened?" Phorgo, leaning forward, asked in as low a voice as he could.

He and other Sky Leaders Journ, Tima, Rarla, Brace, and Kica were seated in Sky Command's main renourishment hall for morning repast before their debriefings and the rousing of their cadet charges for the day.

"I always knew Deb was Gal Agar's favourite," Kica spoke up, her red curly hair refusing to obey any semblance of order. "Bet she ends up with some special duties." She moved her tongue suggestively in her freckled cheek, drawing guffaws from everyone.

"Oh, Kica!" Brace laughed out loud, rather too loud and nervously. The others hid their amusement, knowing the large man had a big crush on Kica.

Rarla, an unlikely Elerae, rather tall and spindly with light blue hair, shook her head. "She does have a crystalator embedded up her shunter," she laughed raucously at her own joke, leaning back in her seat.

"It is a lovely one though!" Journ grinned, narrowly avoiding a not-so-friendly slap on his bald head from his partner, Tima.

Journ the Xarian, had the broody dark looks of his race, but was as extrovert as one could get. He and Tima, who was almost twice his age, had been joined the summer before. He had planned on being a career Sky Warrior, but upon meeting Tima had thoughts about settling down and living on an island.

Tima tittered at him. "You are all just jealous Deb spent time with Novan!"

Her dark skin almost marked her out as a Meccun, but they would only be half right. Her father had been Meccun, her mother

Galatian, but they had both died in The End, Tima brought up by her uncle on her mother's side. She took to the skies as a Sky Warrior to be closer to her parents. She could see them in the clouds, hear them in the winds, touch their spirits in the currents. They held her up.

She smiled at Kica, her best friend. "Besides, Classia would not like that, Novan is her territory, but. . ." she suddenly stopped as the others' stared wide-eyed behind her.

They astutely averted their gaze, Tima mentally kicking herself as she turned around seeing Classia standing five meters away with a meal tray.

"Hallo, Class, join us?" she said in her most invitingly neutral voice. She turned wide-eyed to the others with a why-did-you-not-warn-me-sooner look.

Classia's haughtiness threatened to chill them all with her frosty gaze, but with an icy smile, she sauntered over.

"Please continue," she asked of Tima, giving her a look Tima could not read. The table was quiet, trying not to set of a spark.

Brace laughed his nervous trill again. He laughed at every joke when he got nervous and some wondered again how he had been promoted as he never took anything seriously. He was not as smart or handsome or as funny as other Sky Leaders, but he was a loyal friend. He just needed to be more confident in himself.

Classia took a spare seat by Phorgo and bit into a large boiled *sago,* the spiny yellow skin sliding easily off the fruit. For some reason she looked both pleased with herself and annoyed. She sucked the pulpy fruit off the hard oval seed, licked her fingers of the lingering sweet juice, before placing the remains carefully on the plate.

The others sat, glancing in anticipation at each other for some kind of reaction.

"Any news from last night?" Tima broached the subject, her was voice tight, the others' eyes on her like a noose.

Classia finished her meal with a drink of plain water and looked into Tima's eyes, who avoided her gaze.

"I have orders," she stated cryptically. She smiled and slightly raising her voice said: "As it happens, I will be spending more time with Novan. I have been ordered to Novan's swordship!"

The moment of surprise around the table conspicuously punctuated the room, Classia realising a spontaneous lull in conversation had occurred throughout the hall.

Another table of Sky Leaders with Denzon, Terreely, and Z'Don Lar had stopped their conversation and regarded Classia from the adjoining table. Further along, Tol Valar's attention had been earned, and the ripple effect continued as Deputies Dessa and Teron's meal was interrupted by the unusual quiet.

Phorgo was the first to react, envy tingeing his voice.

"When? What orders?"

This stirred the others back to reality. Phorgo was of Galatian descent, his athletic body and handsome blond features belied a no-nonsense manner to the point that he was rather dull and uninteresting. But he was accepted into any group because of his looks, which attracted both male and female companions alike.

Classia took out a small flat crystalator from her thigh pouch and slid it to the middle of the table for anyone to pick up.

Tima was quickest to react ahead of Kica, snatching the crystal up. She was able to activate it as it was a standard issue Sky Warrior crystalator and not an encrypted personal device. She read the orders, gave a low whistle, and passed it back to Classia, via the hands and views of the others.

Journ dared bring up the *verogan* in the room.

"And Deb?" He flinched as Tima jabbed him sharply in the ribs, covering it with a pathetic cough as Classia glowered at him.

"I do not know," she said frostily. "You will have to ask her yourself. She has not commed me since last night. . ."

She looked up and behind her as she felt the presence of someone standing over her. Tol Valar's eyes flicked briefly between everyone at the table. He had strode over and now took up the crystalator and read the order, commed directly from Novan. Narrowed eyes and a slight downturn in his lips were the only indications of emotion as he flipped the crystalator back into Classia's hands. He walked off without a word.

A smile curved onto Classia's lips. "Looks like I am not the only one with territory to defend." And she, too, stood up and left, leaving behind perplexed faces and emotions.

Tima gave Journ an uncharacteristic long hug and a kiss on the cheek drawing cooing noise from the others. Brace blushed at the open affection.

"What has gotten into you these last few weeks?" Journ looked at Tima adoringly.

"Nothing, I'm just defending my territory!"

There was more laughter around the table, but it rang hollow. They knew something about their life had just changed and Classia was just the first of many.

As soon as she left the hall, Classia barely made it to an empty corridor before breaking down.

What was happening? She could not understand. It was wrenching through her mind. *Orders from nowhere? Deb with Cirrius?* She wiped the tears from her face before running into a crowd. But she could console herself with one great fact.

I will be with Novan. She smiled to herself, growing widely as she said it aloud to herself as she entered a transtube, with a light bounce, heading for the Swordship disembarkation reception centre.

"I will be with Novan!" she sang.

Cirrius watched the Placia-registered cargo ship descend with a sense of relief.

"A day early!" Cirrius rejoiced inwardly.

But what must Urana have done to expedite the delivery? He had to remember to thank her. He viewed everything from the vidscreens in his research lab.

Around thirty meters away, across a narrow channel the smaller north-side island, unnamed by Cirrius as it was just an underground extension of his research facility on Aqrius, accepted the incoming craft onto a clearing, under which lay a skimmer bay. Both his underground facilities were scan-proof and anyone approaching too close underwater would find his defenses formidable. Cirrius was deadly serious about his privacy.

The cargo ship was of Trinari design with five fifty-meter-long, twenty-meter-wide cylindrical sections connected in a tight circle by cross-struts and loaded onto an engine-bed, hauled by a command capsule, essentially a two-person tug, though the courier was alone on this particular run.

Cirrius didn't bother to attend the delivery. He didn't feel the need to see or speak to the courier, Gammor. While Urana assured him he was discreet, Cirrius knew the better part of discretion was not to be present inviting further questions or lingering visitation. From his vidscreens, the landing was perfect.

A comms link pinged his crystalator. "Delivery complete," Gammor's voice said.

"Thank you for your service," Cirrius replied curtly.

There was a momentary pause over the link, as if more was expected. Then: "Of course. A pleasure to serve." A forced injection of gratitude from the courier.

And with that, the forward tug detached from the rear cylindrical holds and engine bed, then under its own thrust began its journey back to Placia.

Cirrius chuckled to himself. Did Gammor think him a dock-tech who would meet him on the pad and converse while they unloaded the cargo. Sometimes, he agreed with Altair and Decion that the so-called younger Magna Aurans were forgetting themselves. The Starguards were still the offspring of the Celestians Knights and stood apart from ordinary Celestians. The coming war would remind them.

Cirrius programmed the crystalators to commence work. The sister island was equipped with a fully crystalator-controlled manufacturing plant beneath the surface. Even now, the landing pad was retracting into the cargo docks below where automated systems would disassemble the cylinders, remove the chronimonum, and start manufacturing what he required. And repeat, and repeat again. He reviewed the designs for the final time. The chronimonum would be more than sufficient. He was pleased with himself.

"Now to get the things made!" And hoped he was in time.

Aerl was still laughing to himself as he entered his quarters.

It had been a long morning of meetings and tours of Millennius' docking ports for swordships collecting crews, while Altair had been going over security measures with the City-State council administrators. After, they had agreed to meet to compare notes.

But then a group of five histographers had caught up to them on deck ten's eastern atrium, an arboretum dome. The Starguards found themselves surrounded.

The first histo was a blonde female, wearing a red one-piece outfit, accessorised by a traditional Trinari *tyuji*, a yellow scarf wrapped twice around her neck which crossed her torso and wrapped twice around her waist as a belt.

"Altair, how do you feel about Novan's departure?" she asked excitedly.

Altair continued walking. Aerl grinned to himself.

"He is fine. *We* are fine," Aerl answered for him, emphasising their unity.

"But, Altair. . ." continued a long-haired man, in a silver tunic and black leggons, "after Novan's collision with the city, have the two of you had a chance to talk and clear the air... well especially since he announced your parent's deaths!" He thrust his gloved right hand out, his fingers tipped with small round crystalators for sound, vision, and transmission. The others waited expectantly.

Oh, Universe! Aerl mentally chided himself for not seeing this coming.

Altair stopped walking. He was staring at the ground, his long blond hair hanging down over his eyes. His hands clenched and unclenched.

All Aerl could see in his mind was the thought of a red mist descending over Altair, a red laser mist bolting from his hands unleashed upon the histographers.

"What did you say?" Altair snapped back without looking up. His hands remained red-free, but nevertheless, Aerl could feel his half-brother's energy coiling up inside of him.

"I mean, I mean. . ." the histo had picked up on Altair's demeanour and tried to back track.

"The next person to open their mouth will be able to ask my

parents *personally* how they felt at The End!" Altair made his hands glow with red energy.

The gloved hand of the histo sparked into life and he frantically yanked it off and tossed it to the ground as the embedded crystalators blew and the glove fabric smouldered. He cursed, not sure how to respond to Altair, keeping his eyes down.

"Apologies," muttered Altair, none-too-politely. "I am still grieving." He walked off, leaving behind the stunned group.

Aerl shook his head, trying not to laugh. He knew Altair had done that on purpose and would get away with it. But he put on a serious face.

"Are you hurt . . .?" Aerl fumbled for the histo's name.

"Frojin," the histo introduced himself. "No, I am unharmed, physically, at least," he tried to smile bravely, shaking out his hand softly.

"Well, now you know how Altair feels." Aerl intimated. "He *does* feel you know." He gave the histos a steely look.

A dumbfounded silence came over the group, Frojin nodding frantically, getting the message.

"Of course, of course, we meant no offense," he smiled wanly. He motioned to the group and the histos walked off glumly, leaving a bemused Aerl to catch up to Altair.

"Well played," he grinned at his cousin, once they were alone in an adjoining corridor.

A sideways glance paired with a sneer played across Altair's lips.

"Who was playing?" he snorted and made to walk off.

"Our meeting?" Aerl reminded him.

"Later. I'm grieving," was his sardonic reply.

The residential towers of Aerl and Altair, sat atop the City-State, on opposite sides of the twenty-kilometer-wide city. They afforded wide views of space from the large encircling windows, providing privacy and secure access to the city and lower-level docking ports below via transtube and an airlock above the dwelling connected to space beyond.

Comfortable quarters awaited Aerl as he stepped out between the sliding doors of the transtube. He had opted for a conventional six-room abode with walls, flooring, and furniture that could alter upon command. For now, only his personal command centre and the recleansor were the rooms sectioned off.

Sitting relaxingly on his couch, he suddenly had thoughts of his parents. He had not for some time, not that he had forgotten them, but he had already acknowledged their deaths. Elysius' news had only confirmed his belief. But on this day, he pulled out his crystalator and keyed up the image he wanted; himself as a youngling with his mother, Iria, and father, Sola Venga. He remembered when it had been taken, on Galatia. They had flown to a mountain valley in Anturia and after taking in the sun had dined among the tall, sweet grass. Aerl smiled at the memory. Iria had laughed almost the whole day, Sola Venga regaling them with stories, funny stories of other worlds and their peoples. Even just months before The End, his parents had tried to make their young son feel safe and loved. The picture blurred as he continued to stare at his parents through tears.

"Farewell, mother, father. . ."

There was a chime from the transtube comms. Slightly annoyed at the intrusion into his thoughts, Aerl was tempted to ignore it, but the chime sounded again.

"Enter," he said resignedly, blinking dry his tears. He closed down the holographic image.

The door slid open. Altair stepped in. He was holding a transparent rectangular decanter.

At Aerl's confused look, Altair laughed.

"And what do you have there?" Aerl asked, indicating the fluted container with its dark brown contents.

A strange look came over Altair. "It is a bottle of the finest Nebian nectar, from Galatia."

Aerl whistled, impressed. Such nectar was very rare. The Neb were famous for making the strongest nectar blends, though never partook themselves. Allegedly.

"How did you acquire that?" asked a still-confused Aerl. It was not like Altair to drink nectar, preferring the grain brews. "You never mentioned it before."

As if gathering some internal strength, Altair's pursed lips parted to confess: "It is from my father." He avoided Aerl's eyes, looking at the bottle, running a finger over the star-shaped label. "He had hidden it in my belongings at The End, with a note stating to 'drink it in a time of celebration'." He peered down at Aerl.

Aerl was not sure he understood. "You have saved it all this time?"

A guilty smile creased Altair's face. "Believe me, I was going to drink this all by myself without telling you. But. . ." he paused as if about to confess something else, "But with Novan's announcement, I think now is as good a time as any to celebrate the lives of our parents... and share a drink... as brothers." He said the last part as sincerely as Aerl had ever heard him speak.

"I would like that!" he replied. He indicated the couch across from him, a low plastiform table between them. Altair placed the bottle on the table while Aerl keyed a tab on the table and two squat glasses raised from the small recessed nourishment storage unit beneath.

Altair made light work popping the cork and poured a liberal amount for each of them.

They both sipped the sweet dark liquid with a satisfying smack of the lips. Then came the bite and burn down the throat.

Aerl let out a gasping laugh.

"Universe, that is. . ." he was lost for words, gulping down air to cool his throat, ". . .is smooth!"

He and Altair shared a laugh. And another drink.

They drank in silence until half the bottle was done.

"So, what do you think about Deb?" Altair asked out of the blue.

Aerl threw his head back in amusement. "Oh, for Universe sake, Altair, not this again."

"What, what do you mean!" Altair slurred.

Aerl stared at him, surprised. Altair was inebriated. Strong nectar indeed. But it made him realise how much Altair really did miss his parents. He was Celestian after all. That thought warmed Aerl's heart. Or was that still the nectar burning?

"What about Urana?" Aerl inquired, switching subjects. "You two are close. . ."

"Rain? No, no. . . well feelings yes, but. . ." he did not finish the sentence, sighing instead. "I am not the one for her. . . too. . ." he flailed his arms around, threatening to spill nectar everywhere.

"Wild, undisciplined, opinionated?" Aerl finished, speaking of his brother.

Altair smiled congenially, allowing the tease. "Too close. She may be our cousin, but she is like a sister to us, really." He turned his head to avoid any scrutiny.

Aerl demurred, not wanting to embarrass him in their moment of amiableness. "Of course, I understand." He returned to the subject Altair had brought up. "So, Deb?"

Altair huffed through his nose. "She is attractive." His voice sounded far away as if he was out in the skies with her. "Young, but attractive. But. . ."

"But you worry if she can be trusted, being a Loremaiden." Aerl interjected.

Altair turned sharply at him, annoyance in his eyes. "You are so suspicious, Aerl!" he rebuked him. "No, I was going to say, but Novan seems to have taken a more personal interest in her."

"Ah, but he is leaving," Aerl reminded him.

Altair regarded his brother-cousin. "Are you trying to match me, brother?" he asked with little humour in his voice. "Do you think a partner by my side with younglings around my feet will tame me?" He admonished. "You are still trying to control me, run my life." He swilled his nectar as he leaned back in his chair turning away from Aerl. "Always."

There was a hard silence between them.

Aerl sighed heavily. He could not deny it. All he could say was: "You are my family."

To which Altair made a dismissive noise.

Aerl pursed his lips. "It is true. I want what is best for you, but you make it so difficult. . ." He paused. He didn't want to say the next words, but they had to be said. The words had always hung unsaid between them. "We are not our fathers!"

No sooner had he uttered those words, then Altair had whisked the bottle off the table, bounded from the chair, and half-ran, half-hovered to the transtube doors.

"Altair!" Aerl had called after him. But it was too late.

The transtube ascended to the airlock above the apartment and seconds later Altair was a red streak arcing through space toward his own quarters.

"Great!" A frustrated Aerl drained his glass. And this time he knew it was not the nectar burning him.

**

Certainty. Order. Love.

That is what Deb felt as she took to the air out in the middle of Ocean. Certainty, because she was meant to fly. She took it for granted, as much as walking, as breathing, and as much as her heart beat. It was what she was born to do. In order, she could feel her body experiencing the process of flying as never before. She had a unique place in the universe—one of deep meaning. Her destiny, her chaotic life attaining order. And she loved what she could become. She loved the sky and it loved her back. The air was where she was meant to be. It was who she was; everything was about flying. She had not realised that until now. Flying was her core, her being, and spirit. The universe had provided her with this certainty, order, and love. She was the Goddess of the Darkening Blue.

"So, let me see what I can do!"

Having finally carved out some free time away from Cirrius and Gal Agar, Deb had decided to fly out over remote Ocean and test her powers, away from Sky Command and other prying eyes. She took off in a straight vertical power-thrust upward, gauging how high and fast she could go. The nominal safe ceiling height for a Sky Warrior was eighty-thousand meters operating at peak even in the rarefied air. Her heart beat steadily though she was nervous. She had never done this before, not even in training. No Sky Warrior had to push themselves beyond that limit—they had been trained to stay below sixty-thousand meters. But now Deb knew she was no ordinary Celestian or Sky Warrior.

She hauled herself through the thinning air. Then she felt something in her body taking over, a thrust of energy, something other than the aeromorphic process other Sky Warriors had talked about, but which she had not been subjected to. There was something else inside her. She could feel the weight of the world beneath her. She looked down and could see the oceanic expanse, huge rolling waves pulled by the presences of Vista Mare and Systar, little islands dotted here and there and glinting surfaces of sky cities further to the east and of the sea-based Adantai Qor with its five distinctive silver-lobed domes in the west. She could plainly see the curvature of Halcyon.

Higher still, Deb slipped through the air, reaching what she thought was the edge of the atmosphere; close to a hundred and ten thousand meters. She was practically standing on top of the world. She could see the darkness of space. Deb could have gone on, but she did not want to be alone in that vast wildness. She wasn't that confident, yet.

She laughed to herself; great big sounds of relief and happiness rolled from her belly and throat. She felt alive. And now she knew.

"I am a Starguard," Deb told herself. "I am a Starguard," she repeated with more conviction.

She stared off into space, that foreboding cosmic fabric and tried to peer further, test herself to see if she could detect the Lore, sense their being, perceive their movement, spark some energy within herself. But there was nothing.

"Half a Starguard," Deb amended to herself. She sighed, dejected. Looking down, she decided to let herself fall back to the water below. Cutting off her internal thrust she revelled in the null-void feeling in the pit of her stomach then falling, falling, falling faster and faster; the heat around her as she reached terminal velocity not bothering her within her protective maneuver suit. She closed her eyes, feeling her weight take her down. Head first, arms outstretched, and feet together she let her crystalator guide her.

Then quite suddenly, she hit a dense wall of air which made her yelp and screech to a halt mid-air. She struggled to move, trying to barrel-roll her way out to no avail.

And there was Cirrius, hovering below her.

Bewildered, Deb righted herself.

"What do you think you are doing?" Cirrius asked, rather too harshly for Deb's liking.

Flustered, Deb floundered for words, but Cirrius was not done.

"I have had to hide and cover your flight tracks and crystalator signal from countless other prying crystalators and tracking stations. You cannot just decide to take off. You are our secret weapon! Do you understand?" he asked as if talking to a youngling.

She nodded. "I just wanted to test my powers!"

"I know how you feel. But after all this is done, you can test away. We will all help you with that. But for now--secret!" he tapped the side of his head. "Remember. Now, I believe you have duties to attend to in your new capacity!" He regarded her coolly.

And off he flew, swiftly, until he was a speck against the blue ocean, leaving a perplexed Deb to herself. She was glad Cirrius was not telepathic. He wouldn't like what she was thinking about him.

Surprise! A call. A clear clarion in the howling winds of the temporal marshes. Someone had pierced the universal folds. A piece of them, not of them, had made their presence known. A feeble soul, yet powerful, scented with the taint of. . .

The headlong Horde held fast in mid-temporal flux. They turned to their leader. Could it be? Had a daughter awoken? An emotionless euphoria swept through them, their energised cores beating faster like excited novae. If so, salvation was at hand. Their daughter would join them. She was calling them.

They shattered time once again delving through rivulets of time streams, surer of their destination, dark-heartened by thoughts of feeding, destruction, and the rebirth of the universe.

"I do not agree with you," Yons Mona stated in an even voice to his Protectress of State.

Urana sighed, Mona never agreed with her. And he was the powerful leader of Placia's planetary military council. They were at a stalemate with five votes each, Brou siding with Urana now that his fleet was being overhauled, but Mona held the deciding vote.

And my day had started so well, Urana reflected. With Novan's imminent departure, Urana had contacted Systar Docks to agree a deal for Brou's ships refurbishment. Gruff Dock-master Strortrin had at first laughably dismissed her request.

"A merchant fleet overhaul? On Systar?" he laughed over the comm screen, his whole body shaking. "Urana, you are losing your touch. Must be your Elerae nature!" he guffawed again. "There is no offer for this service."

Urana ignored his insult. "I can offer you what you desire," she replied enigmatically.

"Eh! And that would be?" A twinkle of interest creased Strortrin's worn face, silvery hair, more lined with grey, flopping over to one side.

"How about your pick of crew and swords for Novan's mission!" Urana sat back in her chair as Strortrin's eyes lit up. "Interested?" she added confidently.

Strortrin grinned widely and he combed his hair back, Urana catching a glimpse of his extra thumb.

"As I have always said, Urana, you are my favourite Elerae!" He grinned appreciably, his body wobbling in satisfaction.

High praise indeed! thought Urana.

"Deal," he agreed. "Bring the ships within the week!" He licked his lips and cut the comm line.

Grinning insanely to herself, Urana punched the air. Her euphoria was slightly tempered in that now she had to tell Novan to expect a large Trinari delegation for sword duty.

That had been then. Now hours later, she wished she was still bantering and bartering with Strortrin.

Urana gazed determinedly at Mona trying once again to convince him of her plans. She had even personally invited him to the mountain for private talks. As usual, he had arrived with a small retinue of young female aides as freshly smelling, simply but smartly garbed, and as smoothly coiffured as he was.

Urana had as usual, ignored his superfluous charms, but reluctantly accepted a kiss to her hand as was the custom. They were already at loggerheads from the beginning, but Urana had to keep trying.

"Captain Councillor, the only way to keep Placia safe is to establish and deploy the new Placia Warriors..."

Mona was already shaking his head. "No, no, no, Protectress. We will not need them. We are protected by yourself and the Neb prophesies of salvation." He spread his manicured hands and looked up at the smooth yellow rock ceiling. Then Urana spied the small discreet tattoo on his neck, recognising one of the sacred tattoos, an outstretched hand with a black star on the palm.

Universe, help us, he is a Neb convert! Urana fought to stop her eyes rolling.

Not many non-Neb converted to their strange mix of religions mostly tied to the veneration of the Holy Mother and Great Father, but those that did were certainly more spiritual than Mona.

Besides, you now had to travel half a world away to visit them, the Neb remaining as isolated and chaste as before in their stone and metal pyrathedrals, dotted along intense white-sand deserts. Diminutive, copper-skinned with green eyes and twisting bronze hair, their bodies were dotted with sacred tattoos. They were wary of outsiders and most Celestians still considered them primitive compared to the other races. But the Neb ignored the outer world, dedicated in their servitude to their religions.

However, Urana did wonder if the Neb had foreseen Deb's rise as a Starguard. Mona caught her staring.

"Yes," he confirmed Urana's suspicions, rubbing his tattoo. "I have been following the Neb for some time. They have allowed me to continue in my role as the Captain Councillor as long as I lead a more... chastened life." He looked particularly penitent, hands clasped in his lap.

An aide coughed gently behind him hiding her mouth, Mona giving her a rueful look. He swivelled back to Urana.

"Be that as it may, I fully believe in their prophesies. Our salvation is at hand. It has been seen. And it will come from the sky!" He looked up again, slicked-back blond hair shining in the lights.

The look on Urana's face must have registered a response, as Mona's eyes lit up with expectation.

"You know!" he smiled wide-eyed, his teeth glinting. "You know! You have seen it too!" He wagged a finger at her.

Urana was caught off guard. "I. . ." she groped for words, mind flying. "I have not seen anything. But," she tried to deflect attention from herself, "I would like to hear more about this prophesy. Perhaps this salvation from the sky is a weapon we could manufacture?"

Mona contemplated this. His eyes darted around on the floor as he followed his thoughts.

Urana saw her chance. "Whether it is a weapon we make or Placia Warriors or the volcanic harnesses," she mentioned an idea Cirrius had considered, using controlled cataclysmic eruptions as power sources for ground defences and shields, "It could all come from the sky!"

Mona was nodding enthusiastically. He was not a pushover swayed by emotion or even facts when they got in the way, Urana knew, but religion. . .

"I will seek counsel from the Law Gatherers," Mona referred to the Neb's higher assembly; there being no overall leader. He nodded more confidently. "Yes, I will reconsider your request, Urana."

He stood up, pleased with himself. He slapped his hands to his thighs, then held his palms out to Urana in praise.

"You are wise, Urana. Thank the Universe for that!" he vacantly smiled.

Bowing politely, followed silently by his retinue, he left the room, the sweet smell of some flowery plant lingering behind, tickling Urana's nostrils.

Urana laughed to herself as she looked up at the ceiling. "Yes, thank you Universe," she mocked his words.

She was about to leave the conference suite herself when Camtrin entered. "Protectress, you have a visitor. . ."

Urana groaned. "Oh, no, Cammie, send them away, I'm too busy!"

A look of dread flashed briefly across Camtrin's face.

"What's wrong?" Urana tried to look past Camtrin to the door. "Who is there?" Her hands glowed yellow anticipating trouble.

A massive bulky figure emerged from the doorway.

"Decion? What. . ." Urana threw her hands up in the air,

confused, damping down her energy. "Why are you here?"

Decion glared down at Camtrin who nervously looked back at Urana, who nodded her dismissal, the girl rushing out with as much decorum as she could.

"Decion, how dare you intimidate my staff!" she shouted, livid. "You can do so on your own city, but not here!" She angrily jabbed a finger at him. "What are you even doing here, unannounced?" She stood defiantly in the centre of the room.

If Decion was intimidated himself, he did not show it. Instead he withdrew his red helmet from his head and placed it on the table, his wild black hair and full beard conspiring to hide his features. He glanced cautiously around the room, Urana guessing at his reasons.

"We are alone!"

"And your Trinari girl?" he growled scornfully, glancing back at the door.

Urana stared hard at him. Everyone automatically suspected Cammie was a spy for the Trinari. And they would have been correct. They spied on everyone through their wide-spread aide and eng-tech services. They were a race of the curious, the Trinari, hence their exploratory natures even into matters of other Celestians' affairs. But Urana also knew she could use Cammie's connections with Systar and their various networks to broker deals like the chronimonum techtons Cirrius was now playing universe-knows about with, her Elerae heritage withstanding or not. Cammie was like a daughter to her and she wasn't about to let Decion smear her name.

"No one will overhear or interfere. Now what do you want?" she forced through clenched teeth.

Decion snorted dismissively at Urana's angry stance. He plumped himself down heavily on one of the armchairs. "I am here to talk," he stated. "About Deb!"

This was no ordinary visit, Urana knew, but Decion's words chilled her. She knew where this was leading. She seated herself in a chair across from him.

"Go on!"

More relaxed, Decion said, "I see Cirrius, Altair, and Novan seem to have taken an interest in Deb, for whatever their own reasons; predictable but disappointing. I see you have been spending time with her, too." His words were deliberate, questioning without an interrogative, judging. "What is your assessment of her?"

Urana stared at him. His face was a mask of inscrutableness. But she knew what his real question was.

"You mean do I trust her? That she will not turn on us when the Lore arrive?" She breathed deeply, not wanting to answer.

"Do you trust her?" Decion asked outright. His steely gaze met Urana's stony resolve.

"Of course I do," she convinced herself.

Decion smiled. "Of course." He smoothed back his hair reaching for his helmet.

Urana was not going to let him off that easily. "Why are you here, Decion? You obviously want to say something. Do not be shy!" she half teased.

The grin returned to Decion's face even to his eyes.

"I will be watching her," he said. "And if she cannot be trusted..."

"No Decion, you do not have the right!" Urana's voice was a harsh whisper.

"Yes, I do," he retorted angrily. He reached the door and turned back. "For the sake of the worlds, I will kill her myself!"

CHAPTER SEVEN

Far away, in the dead future of Magna Aura, a magenta spark of energy fled through space in a desperate search. The annihilation of the new crèche of Celestian civilisation would happen. This time. Nothing could have been done to save the Starguards from death. This time. But there were others, the sought-after legacy of the few who had escaped The End on Galatia. And it was these others who would defeat the terror of the Lore. The trail of these lost ones was faint, but detectable, another branch of Celestian Knights progeny. And the voyage stream was leading to a whirling-armed galaxy, wherein a bright, blue planet awaited.

"Universe guide you," Star Commander Nemin Vander bid Novan with a clasped arm. The gray-haired, two-hundred-seventy-year-old was still a spry barrel-chested man with bow legs. But as one of the most experienced Swordship pilots and commanders he was greatly respected, even by Decion, who delegated much of the day-to-day running of the captured fifteen-kilometer asteroid, Vista Mare, orbiting Halcyon, to the old Xarian. Though he had one, or two, foibles.

"Thank you, Star Commander," replied Novan, fearing the Star Warrior base commander would not detach himself from his arm.

Vander leaned in closer, Novan smelling the fairly reeking scent of bitter *chacan* root, which he chewed frequently; an old habit even amongst the old and bold Swordship crews. "Have I ever told you about the time I first met your mother?" The elder man's eyes sparkled.

Novan was about to say no, though he had heard the story many times.

"Nemin," Decion intervened, firmly, but with an air of practiced patience. "Another time, perhaps."

Vander looked from one brother to the other. "Of course. Of course." He smiled warmly. "When we are all reunited, I will regale you of grand old tales about your parents from before The End. All of you." He had turned to Cirrius behind him, grinning wildly.

Cirrius nodded courteously, ignoring Gal Agar's bemused expression.

"We look forward to it." Decion rescued them all from further reminiscences.

It had all been agreed. Within Vista Mare's war room; Novan, Cirrius, Decion, Vander, and Gal Agar had finalised the particulars of Novan's mission. Novan would command five Sword Warships, one-quarter of the entire Magna Auran war fleet, with a combined crew of thirty-thousand warriors and support techs, including histographers to record their experiences. Already, the orders had been sent out and all of Sky Command, Systar docks, and Vista Mare were a flurry of activity.

On Centron, Halcyon's southern-most island, the joint Sky and Star Warrior training facility was already abuzz with intense training for the cadets. With Novan's warriors on a possible one-way mission, recruitment had been increased for the Sky Warriors, while ordinary Celestians could join the Star Warriors, as no meaningful alterations to their genetic physicality were required.

Bolstered by Urana's bold deal with a favourable selection of crew manifests and Swordship development, the Trinari overseers on the twenty-five-kilometer Systar Dock installation orbiting diametrically to Vista Mare, had completed furnishing the reserve Swordships with upgraded crystalators and equipment, with Meccun assistance. The two societies had kept their monopolies over their respective trades, though a few interlopers were gradually filtering through. For now, however, the maintenance and support techs would be Trinari and Meccun. Most of the Sword crews were to be made up of Star and Sky Warriors, though units of Xarian and Elerae warriors had also been chosen, including a company of *Drebori*, and half a dozen Neb for each Sword for spiritual guidance. All six societies would be represented, so as to present a force of united peoples to Elysius' world.

Novan would command the flagship, *Sword Celectral*, while the experienced General Tecton, one of the most respected soldiers from Galatian days, was to command the second, *Sword Relentance*. General Sion, a Xarian warrior with eight sons on Vista Mare, would lead *Sword Venturon*, and General Leir Horren commanded the fourth, *Sword Confiance*. The daughter of a Xarian clan leader she was one of the fiercest combatants, whether in debate or battle. Her crew was all Trinari. Horren had tried hard to hide her disappointment about not leading real warriors into battle, especially with *Sword Venturon* and *Relentance* crews consisting of a high ratio of veteran Star Warriors. All four ships were also the largest in the fleet, each almost twelve kilometers long, after years of modifications by the Trinari; though they could never have imagined their rebirth into such a mission.

The fifth ship, though the smallest, was the most powerful ship ever built and was purposely under-crewed. *Sword Temprocity* was a weapons ship, bristling with deadly arrays from every conceivable point. Sleeker than the other Swords at only four kilometers long, *Temprocity* gave the impression of a solid shard of piercing light, stabbing through the heart of darkest space, such was its unsurpassed manoeuvrability and weaponry. It was only half-crewed, because of its complement: two thousand Xarian and Elerae warriors, with (in a rare case of unparalleled cooperation) a Trinari command crew, another part of Urana's deal. No one else was willing to serve with the fearsome warriors, especially with their erstwhile enemies in command. But two thousand warriors were deemed more than enough for *Sword Temprocity*. To make things more heated, it was under joint command by the leaders of the three factions, who so far couldn't decide on who would deliver the opening speeches for the inevitable victory feasts and tributes. It would be a hard voyage for all.

Novan's crew was mostly of Sky Warrior extract. Two days after his momentous announcement, Novan had stood before Magna Aurans again outlining the plans of his mission. He was to depart in a week's time. The crews had been selected and intense training would soon commence around Magna Prime and its moons. His own command crew consisted of his two seconds-in-command Deputy Sky Commander Drune Glith, the superb strategist, whom Gal Agar was sad to see leave, and Warrior General Veekan Vaage, one of Vander's most trusted seconds––and Novan's third was the highly-valued Sky Leader Classia. *Sword Celectral*'s lead eng-techs were the young but experienced Trinari builders Lautrin, third son of Systar's Dock-master Strortrin, and Alleguitrin. Anything that went wrong with the physical structure, they and their team could repair or manufacture, while the crystalator systems and medlabs were supervised by the Meccuns Libekka and Emkara, respectively. Two brave Neb, Fratr Nr and D'n Eld Rhir accompanied them for guidance beyond the stars. The rest of the crew were Sky Warriors.

The Swords would crew up at the central staging area on Systar, orbit around to Vista Mare for their Star Warrior contingents, then vector out to Magna Prime two days later, where all the other support forces would rendezvous before departure.

******

On board her *Sword Celectral* quarters, her new home from now on, Classia had watched as Halcyon grew ever more distant as Sword Celectral sailed through the black sea of space toward Magna Prime.

Early two mornings ago, she'd been awoken by duty Sky-marks with commed orders from Novan informing her she was to be on his command crew. Over her initial delirious shock at the order, Classia had wanted to tell Deb, but she was nowhere to be found. And that's when her mind started working overtime. Upon leaving the morning nourishment hall and her conversations with the other Sky Leaders, she had hastily packed her essentials, the excitement coursing through her like charged plasma, the imagined power boosting her confidence and dispelling her worried thoughts from the nights before. She had cried herself to sleep amid thoughts of Deb and Novan in a romantic embrace or worse.

What could they have wanted with Deb, and not me? She'd thought. *What was their interest in her?* But now, with her being on this mission, Classia was reassured that her love for Novan was not in vain.

The previous night, Classia had been furious at Deb, but on spending the night atop Sky Command in tears, had come to realise that it wasn't all Deb's fault. She had wanted to clear things up that morning with Deb, but on calling in on Deb's quarters, she'd noted that Deb wasn't there and hadn't been all night. Classia stood, puzzled, by the entrance. Surely she still couldn't . . .

Classia let her jealous thoughts fade away. There was no point in dwelling upon such things. This should be the happiest moment of her life—personally selected for a mission by Novan. She should be grateful for this chance, not preoccupied with notions of a supposed romance between her best friend and Novan. She loved both of them equally—one was a universe of constant friendship, the other one of fathomless passion. Though she and Deb had never really discussed their appearances with each other, they knew that they were two attractive Sky Warriors, but Classia didn't think Novan was too concerned about looks. He needed someone who could think like he did, to share his inner thoughts. Deb's intelligence soared off the scale at times, leaving Classia, whose own mental capacities were considered merely above normal, grasping for the simpler meaning.

That meeting between Novan and Deb had started something between them, something subtle, but nonetheless important. And it hadn't gone unnoticed by Classia, but she refused to believe that it was anything more than over-abundant politeness. Besides, Deb wouldn't do this to her. Would she? No, she wouldn't, for she knew how much she loved Novan and even if it could not be returned, surely Deb would not try to attract Novan for herself. They'd never been rivals or interested in the same male before, but, of course, Novan wasn't just anyone.

To add to all of this, was the apparent promotion of Deb to the newly created post of special adjutant to Cirrius, with duties to liaise between the Supreme Commander and the outside world. It also implied Deb's imminence as heir apparent to Gal Agar, without the need for a prior promotion to Deputy Sky Commander. The news had certainly shocked Classia, as it must have done to the other Sky Leaders and Deputies. But Classia desperately wanted to know what had happened between the Starguards and Deb on Cirrius' island. Did Novan have anything to do with this?

Classia let out a frustrated yell, throwing a cushion from her bed across her quarters, which rebounded harmlessly off the wall, much to her annoyance. She stalked around her small sparse quarters. This whole situation was irritating her and to make it worse, she was cooped up away from her family and friends, whom she had either seen or heard from in the last day or two to congratulate her. But the one Classia wanted to hear from was the most silent one of them all.

Classia had tried to contact Deb on several occasions after boarding Sword Celectral, but she'd been unavailable the past few mornings, due to duties and histographer interviews. Though Classia had no claim on Novan, she now felt close to him, but she had the distinct feeling that something was going on that had started the night of Novan's announcement and that even if it didn't involve Novan and Deb, it was being deliberately kept from her. And Classia wasn't going to stand for that. If Deb wouldn't tell her, then she would have to confront Novan.

Oh, Little Star, tell me everything's going to be alright, Classia prayed to the darkness of space.

Novan was relaxed. It had been a few frenzied days since he had announced his mission plans. Now he took a rare moment to slip away from the burdens of leadership, before returning to *Sword Celectral*. Unsurprisingly, he had found himself wending his way to Cirrius' remote island, but he sought not the presence of its owner, but the companionship of another. Novan's thoughts had been consumed with Deb. There was a connection between them, one he had never felt before, until he had met Deb for the first time. And now he couldn't get her out of his mind. He was sure that she felt the same. He hoped to find out.

Luckily, upon landing on Aqrius in a small flurry of light dust, Deb was just on her way out on another duty errand. On seeing him, she gave him a cheerful smile, all the tension having dispelled from that fateful night.

"Hallo, Novan. Cirrius isn't here, I haven't seen him for most of the day," Deb stated airily, stepping aside to allow Novan to enter the dwelling, but he stopped short in front of her.

"I'm not here to see, Cirrius," Novan replied, in what he hoped was a clear indication of his purpose.

Deb stared at him, her mouth twitching into a nervous smile. "Oh, if you want to know how I'm doing, then everything is fine. I'm getting used to my newfound heritage and my assumed position." She looked down at the ground. "I want to thank you again for all you've done. I wouldn't have had the courage to confront the truths about myself, otherwise."

She looked Novan clearly in the eyes, who was caught again by her ravishing gaze of pure-blue brilliance. There was emotion swirling within those eyes, but Novan couldn't tell what it was. He moved forward and lightly touched her shoulders. "Novan, don't... I can't. I can't." She made to leave, but Novan held her.

"What's wrong Deb? Have I done something wrong?" he asked earnestly. He let go of her, trying to read her emotions, but they seemed to be tightly wrapped up. He dared not try to read her thoughts, that would have been unconscionable to him.

"No, you haven't done anything wrong, but you are leaving, perhaps for good. And I'll be here. Universe knows when you'll be back, so it'll be better if we don't..." she couldn't finish and stepped away to look out at Ocean, with its waves crashing along the rocky shore.

Novan sighed, "Deb, I have to be honest. I haven't felt this way about anyone before. But ever since we met, I've thought about you constantly. Surely you can sense how I feel about you?" He watched the back of her for any reaction, but she said nothing. "Deb, we have centuries, perhaps a millennium to live. There must be some happiness, in that time, for us together," he reasoned.

Deb still faced away from him, her arms clasped around herself.

Her voice was quiet, just discernible above the sound of waves lapping against nearby rocks, "Nobody knows the way of the universe, Novan. But for us, I see no future." That seemed to be her final word. "Don't forget, I'm only half a Starguard, and the daughter of all that you despise."

Novan couldn't believe what he was hearing. Had his instincts been wrong about Deb? There had to be more going on he didn't know. "Deb, your heritage isn't in question. The fact you're the Celestian you are shows that. That's the person I love." There was no reaction from Deb to his forthright declaration, so Novan tried a different tact. "There isn't someone else, is there?" he asked in a vague attempt to lighten the mood.

"Yes, there is," Deb threw back instantly, her answer surprising Novan who stood agape. He hadn't realised someone else was involved, had no reason to, and curiosity urged him to discover the name of his competition.

"May I know the name of this someone?" he inquired to her back as nonchalantly as he could.

"Classia," replied Deb, with the barest hint of humour in her voice.

"Cla . . ." Novan was confused, "Classia?" *What in the universe was happening here?*

"Of course, Classia," said Deb. "She's in love with you, Novan. And she'll be with you all the way on your mission. She's really quite nice when you get to know her. Don't you find her even mildly attractive?"

"She's . . . extremely lovely, but . . ."

"Then you could learn to love her. She'd make a perfect consort," Deb stated bluntly.

"But I love you, Deb," Novan responded, feeling slightly deflated. He strode right up to her.

"Classia has always loved you and I haven't. It wouldn't be right. You could love her, for me. Do it for me," she pleaded.

"I don't understand." And then the meaning behind her words and actions became clear to him. "Oh, for all the stars, Deb, don't do this. Throwing Classia at me won't make me forget you, ever. Sacrificing your love for me just for Classia's and your friendship's sake won't help any of us. You do love me, don't you, Deb?" He felt elation returning from its eclipsed depths.

"I'm doing this for *all* our survival's sake, Novan," Deb said, her voice shaking.

"I know. And I'm doing this for my sake. If I don't make it back, I need to know." He was so close behind her that he could hear her breathing and she turned around to face him. "You do love me?" he repeated. His heart quickened, tears were running down her cheeks from those eyes of blue, half-hidden behind a curtain of black hair. He brushed it away and in that moment they stared into each other's souls. And then they kissed.

Deb felt her arms circle up and around his shoulders, while his hands caressed her face and neck, their lips mated in passion. Novan tasted the sweetness of her tears, felt the heat of her breath tickle his skin and savoured the touch of her lips, before gently meandering down her neck with kiss after kiss, eliciting a small sigh of pleasure from Deb, who tilted her head back in response, her hands relinquishing his shoulders to slide down onto his chest. His lips worked their way back up and her lips found his again in a thrall of emotion. A nearby copse of lolling *canatezeon* trees with wide blue-green leaves provided ample cover and uniform and armour soon found themselves lying on the downy undergrowth, their wearers lost in love.

The sun had wandered lazily across the sky by the time Deb and Novan had emerged embracing each other. Deb was lost in emotions she had never felt before and probably never would again; Novan, about to lose the only love he had ever found and would never have again. He unclenched Deb, looking down into her face that stared serenely up into his. This time there was love in her eyes, those everlasting pools of blueness where souls could be lost, and he wiped away an escaping tear.

"We can never be, Novan, not like this, again," Deb whispered.

Holding her face with gentle hands, Novan nodded in understanding, gave her a single kiss on the lips, before turning and departing into the air. Deb watched. Only after Novan had become a tiny figure lost among the distant clouds did she allow her tears to flow down her cheeks.

Goodbye my love.

From below in his command centre, Cirrius watched dispassionately as Novan had left. He had also watched their little frolic captured by the hidden viewers—meant for intruders—not without some interest and frowned at the vidscreen.

So, Novan and Azure are in love? he mused. Lucky, Novan was leaving, for Cirrius had plans for Azure all his own. Disregarding the screen, Cirrius tried to resume his calculations, coaxing as much material as he could from the chronimonum, but he couldn't concentrate. All he could think of was two lovers separated by their love for each other and the consequences it would have on the fate of two worlds.

Around Magna Prime, Classia was in temporary command of *Sword Celectral*, what with Novan, Glith, and Warrior General Vaage all on various off-Sword duties. She knew she probably wouldn't ever be in actual command, which suited her.

While Sky Warriors were confined to the boundary of the thin Halcyon atmosphere with little or no experience in commanding Swords, the Star Warriors were the masters of the airless sky. The bridge was their domain, under Novan's command, and she and Deputy Glith were here to command their own forces, once in the skies above the Goddess Elysius' world, wherever that was—even Novan wasn't too sure. Upon being reunited with the air, the bodies of the Sky Warriors aided by their manoeuvre suits would automatically absorb and convert air into energy for flight, but should fighting occur in the vacuum of space, then they would have to don specially-powered manoeuvre suits to compensate. That had been part of their early training and now every Sky Warrior was immersed in nauseating null-gravity training, alongside the Star Warriors, the Elerae and Xarians. If it came down to it, everybody would fight hand to whatever-the-Lore-had-for-hands to the last Celestian.

Classia sat in the command chair, a not uncomfortable curvilinear metal contraption, at the rear of the roughly triangular bridge, trying to remember every aspect of the functions and the duties of the assembled Star Warriors stood around them. Peering over to her left, she remembered that that particular crystalator controlled central mech overseeing the stellar drive, powered by an array of Qor crystals, denoting the largest of their size, while just in front of that was the weapons centre. Directly in front of her were the helm and flight-detection centres (or ship's eyes as they had been called in ancient times), which could be taken over by the crystalator in extreme situations. A pedestal with a yoke extending from its centre was to the right of Ship's eyes and could control navigation as a manual backup.

Classia had been repeatedly told by eager Star Warriors that there was nothing like manually steering a ship, especially one as agile as a Swordship, through the vagaries of the vast unknown. But Classia and the rest of the Sky Warriors disagreed. There was nothing like coursing through the naturalness of the fresh open air and being at one with the elements thrown at you. But of course, the Star Warriors disagreed and so on, leading the way to many a bold story being told as to why each force was better than the other.

All things considered though, the Star and Sky Warriors were friendly rivals and were glad for each others' company in such a historic adventure. The threat to troublemakers of being sent to *Sword Temprocity* was enough to keep that rivalry friendly.

Activity at the detection station caught her eye.

"Leader," reported a Star Warrior, "Approaching body detected—identified as…" he studied his readouts, "…Novan."

Classia's heart leapt at his name and she clearly saw the effect that Novan had on the others. A confidence swelled over them as only the honour of serving with Novan could instil.

"Thank you, Star-mark Lucun," she announced as casually as she could, hoping she had got his name right. At least their lower juniors had ranks the same as a Sky Warrior's. Classia fidgeted feeling uneasy, yet excited in the seat awaiting Novan's arrival, which seemed to be taking forever.

The next report stated that he was onboard and on his way to the bridge, so Classia pretended to be busy studying various crystalator displays, noting that *Sword Celectral* was in perfect orbit around Magna Prime with the other Swords formed up behind it and training on and around the moon Glonn was continuing. She transferred that data onto her palm-held crystalator for Novan to review and then sat back in the throne-like command chair, the only seat on the bridge. The Star Warriors believed that standing up whilst on duty implied a constant state of alert readiness and an instant aggressive stance for battle. Classia was glad to see that at least for once the Star Warrior hierarchy didn't see fit to set that example in their ships, not that the command seat was getting any more comfortable.

Just then, Novan arrived on the bridge, everyone braced up, and Classia bolted out of the chair to attention.

"Ease ranks," stated Novan. "And there will be no more of that, for my sake. Just go about your duties," he said, lazily swatting the air simultaneously, waving them back into their normal routines.

Classia noticed Novan seemed a bit distracted about something, but tried not to seem too attentive as he headed towards her. Classia welcomed him back, handing him her crystalator for him to inspect, but upon reviewing the reports his odd disinterest continued. Picking up on her scrutiny of him, Novan gave Classia a curious look of his own.

"Maintain stations; I'll be in my quarters." He then gave the bridge an approving once-over, before exiting the command centre.

Plopping back down into the chair, which seemed distinctively cold now, Classia pondered on the nature of the thoughts that could weigh on Novan's mind.

Cirrius had a visitor. He had monitored Gal Agar's steady approach and had ascended to the main dwelling to meet the Sky Commander.

After the events of the past few days, Gal Agar had felt he had just found and lost the only family he had ever had or wanted, but he was determined not to let Deb be lost from his life—*No, not now*, he thought. He'd have to have a talk with her soon, before it was too late.

Cirrius welcomed him at the door, firmly clasping his forearm in greeting. Gal Agar reciprocated with a warm smile. Gal Agar had never considered Cirrius more than a close friend. They were peers, who shared an undying belief in the order of the Sky Warriors, without which their lives would have been much different. They understood that and respected the other for what he had done to ensure that legacy of the Celestian Knights—Hyphon in particular—was never forgotten. But Gal Agar had fleeting suspicions that Cirrius harboured deeper agendas with their purposes unknown. He found he couldn't completely trust Cirrius. But he was here for other business.

"Deb's heritage is secure," he announced as they walked into the dwelling. "I had an interesting briefing from the medtechs, who claimed that their files on her had mysteriously disappeared. They had investigated crystalator functions and the medtechs involved, but nothing eye-catching turned up. They seemed satisfied for me to take the matter into my own hands, so there should be no problems from them. I happened to see Deb in flight to Halcyon City, but I didn't get the chance to tell her," said Gal Agar. "She seemed busy enough."

"Yes, though there have been a few distractions," Cirrius said, cryptically. He held out his hand offering Gal Agar a seat at the centre table, which he took, Cirrius sitting across from him.

"Oh? Nothing of concern I hope."

Cirrius noticed the worried tone. "Hmm, Gal Agar, Gal Agar, Gal Agar," he said in bored tones, slowly shaking his head. "What is it about Deb that brings to the fore emotions long buried or forgotten, hmm?" Gal Agar looked at him almost aghast. Cirrius continued, "I know how close you and Deb are and I realise that the news of her Starguard nature must have been a shock on that relationship, but really there's nothing to worry about," he said. "If she falls in love, she falls in love," he ended tantalisingly.

"With who?" asked Gal Agar, a bit too sternly. *Not you?* He thought, annoyed with Cirrius' games.

"Well, it's not me," Cirrius smiled, answering Gal Agar's thoughts, who sighed inwardly with relief. "I just happen to think that she and Novan are getting closer. Nothing too serious though," he stretched out the truth.

Gal Agar digested the news in silence: Deb and Novan. He thought that he would feel angry or envy, but he didn't. In fact, he felt relieved, comforted that even Deb would be able to experience the life he had forced away. He was proud of Deb all over again and knew this wouldn't be the last time he would feel this way about her. But looking over at Cirrius, Gal Agar discerned he had other thoughts.

"Don't get me wrong, Gal Agar, in any other time a union between the two of them would be cause for universal celebrations which would further bond all Magna Aurans, but this is the wrong time and I think they both realise that. I'm just worried about the effect these unbound emotions will have on them at crucial moments. I also happen to know Altair is interested in Deb and with his temperament and the situation between him and Novan . . ." Cirrius let the sentence hang for Gal Agar to contemplate before continuing, "We're facing a critical point in our history here and a couple of our most potent weapons have become decidedly taken with the same female. Something's going to give soon and as much as I think that Deb can take care of herself, she's still going to be caught in the middle and we can't have that. She's important to our survival," he said, staring down at nothing in particular.

"Seems to me," spoke an amused Gal Agar, "that someone else has also locked away their true feelings behind a façade of worldly concern." Cirrius tried to look offended, but in a mocking mood, Gal Agar said, "Can't fool me, Supreme Commander, I've taken that lonely path and I'm too far along to turn back now. Are you?" he teased.

"Ha! You know me better than that, Sky Commander," retorted Cirrius in a similar tone, "I won't deny I find Deb attractive. She has that effect on everyone, but this . . ." he said, standing and spinning his outstretched arms around the room, ". . . is my life." His eyes shone in passion. "No personal sacrifice is too great when in service to those who live and dream for better days to come. And until the universe takes me in her arms, I will forever stand guard till those days are realised. I owe them no less than what they deserve." He sat again.

At what future price? thought Gal Agar.

Cirrius regarded him with those gleaming eyes of his and the usual sardonic smile, which put Gal Agar ill at ease. The two of them sat facing each other in silence, two of a kind committed to the same higher purpose, but Gal Agar had again caught a shadowy glimpse into someone he didn't know. Underneath Cirrius' passion for peace and order seemed to lurk another Cirrius: one committed to the same ideals, but for different reasons. And Gal Agar was wary of that Cirrius. As if to enhance his fears, Gal Agar realised that Cirrius' apparent relaxed hands-on-hip stance was, in fact, one of extreme complacency. If he'd seen Altair in this stance, the arrogance in it would have been unmistakeable, but Cirrius hid it well, as he did most things, Gal Agar was beginning to learn.

Cirrius' smile never wavered. "I take this duty as seriously as you, Gal Agar. Things are moving fast, maybe too fast, and for the sake of our civilisation we have to monitor that."

"You seem to have everything planned to the last, don't you?" said Gal Agar, in a slightly accusing tone.

Cirrius' smile melted away, "I have had a lot of time to think things through and to remedy any problems that might arise, yes.

And sometimes I can talk things through, as I am with you now. I can always trust and rely on your judgement," he affirmed with a sincere smile.

Gal Agar was dubious he could say the same for him.

"Anyway, we'll discuss such things for later, but now," he said with a flourish, "I'd like to show you my latest device of manufacture." He voiced commands into his crystalator and an image of a small silver, multi-spiked spheroid, materialised in front of them. "It's a system-wide deployable Lore detector," stated Cirrius.

Gal Agar was suitably impressed. This was the Cirrius which inspired him, not the secretive one.

"Chronimonum has the best density, conductivity, and sensitivity properties to variances in specific multi-spectra arena. It's perfect for this kind of instrumentation allied with crystalator acuity. With enough of these spheres, the whole of the Magna Aura system could be interspersed with temporal energy detection fields that would immediately signal at any indication of temporalmorphic energy," he explained excitedly.

"Akin to the ring of protective energy around Galatia created by the Celestian Knights?" asked Gal Agar, grasping at the concept.

"Not entirely. This isn't designed to keep Lore out. No, it would give us a minimum warning time of ten seconds and a maximum warning time of thirty seconds."

Gal Agar wasn't sure he heard right and was about to ask for that time again, but Cirrius confirmed it,

"Yes, only ten to thirty seconds. The way Lore travel through time and space is complicated.

He continued, "In normal space, the Lore can travel up to lightspeed, but on hitting the detectors' energy-field, they and a secondary inner array of similar spheres will automatically emit anti-chronitons and form negation-fields around them, which might slow the Lore down, for maybe thirty seconds. If that doesn't work, then they'll be here in less than ten. On the other hand, if they are travelling through time, then they'll arrive from a dimension tangentially parallel to our own. So, the spheres also emit an extra-dimensional version of those energies, but the Lore could even by-pass them and be upon us almost without warning. Right now, I am manufacturing these spheres automatically and have contracted a few dozen Trinari and Meccun techs to disperse them after Novan's departure. The other Swords will be retrofitted with spheres to provide an extra shielding facility," Cirrius explained.

Gal Agar seemed taken aback by the scale and depth of Cirrius' plans. Cirrius seemed to sympathise with him, "I'm sorry all this information is only coming to you now, Gal Agar, but if it's any consolation, you are the first to know my plans even before the other Starguards. I will be informing them at our last gathering before Novan departs."

Gal Agar gave a nod of understanding. Some things were best kept secret. "I am honoured, Cirrius, and I understand," he said with a sombre smile. A soft chime from his crystalator alerted him and he looked at his forearm device. "It seems I must be on my way; strategy meetings with my deputies, that's if there are any more surprises you'd care to spring on me?" he half-joked.

Cirrius shook his head and with a slight smile on his face, clasped Gal Agar's arm. "I know this seems all contrived and secret, but as you know, it's better for one's enemy to see the sword within your hand, than the two hidden behind your back. We need all the advantages we can achieve against the Lore. Trust me, Gal Agar, have faith and all will be fine in the end." He gave his Sky Commander's shoulder a pat of assurance, before escorting him to the door.

Gal Agar gave his superior a courteous nod, before the door slid shut and Gal Agar found himself away from Cirrius' secrets back into the world of light and reality. Outside, he breathed the fresh air and looked up into a sky strewn with white diaphanous clouds dappling his own world of blueness, where he belonged. He thought about the war to come. Deb had seen red rain falling from blood-drenched clouds storming through the screaming skies, over lands and seas scorched into oblivion, followed by unending darkness.

Gal Agar didn't want to see that happen and if it took a whole world of Cirrius' secrets to save them, then so be it. Though at that moment, for some reason Gal Agar could not fathom, he wasn't sure of whom he was more afraid of: Cirrius or the Lore. The Lore would have all their swords inimitably displayed, but Cirrius would have more than two behind his back and each would be more lethal than the last. Just how far would Cirrius go to defend Magna Aura? *And what will happen after?* Gal Agar wondered.

While in thought, he gracefully took to the air, which welcomed back their protector with warm winds to urge him home.

They appeared without warning, diving down from out of the sun-rich afternoon: fiery demons of light, trailing thunder, drowning all in storms of chaos. The skies turned bright with fury as thousands of Lore poured in from the depths of space, lavishly extending the gift of death to all who stood before them. The upper skies were afroth and aflame in blood and fire as the Sky Warriors waged war in skies no longer fit to be called air as the Lore transformed the breathable into a suffocating mass of poisoned molecules. Bodies fell, burning along the way, rapidly descending into more fire as the seas boiled away and the land disappeared under molten waves.

A magenta star shone in the distant nether, until it was eclipsed by a menacing blaze of blue. And then he appeared, the one with eyes of fire—cold blue fire—the leader of all Lore. While Lore around him died in infernos unleashed against them by energies devised by Celestian means, his blue fiery form was inextinguishable. He hung amidst the turmoil, calm in destruction, awaiting the end of another civilisation. And then he saw her—his reason for being here—rocketing up from the churning carnage below, the billowing black smoke of falling sky-cities swirling in her wake: his daughter. She saw him, anger rising in her eyes, eyes that mirrored his.

But before she reached him, he held out two forms. They hung from his outstretched arms as if in offering, but his gravelly voice announced: "Only one, daughter, only one." Deb, regarding the term of relationship with disdain, looked at the two wretched forms recognising them to be Gal Agar and Cirrius. How had he captured them?

She approached cautiously, oblivious to the death and destruction of the world around her. She was face to face with him, his stark blue features twisting and rippling with unholy energy as his form shifted unnervingly before her eyes. They stared at each other; Deb could feel the evil emanating from him, his presence seeming to fill the entire dying sky and a gripping coldness seized her heart. Keeping a steadfast eye on him, she approached and plucked Gal Agar from his grasp. He was still alive, barely, and she held him close to her, her father in all but name.

Synther watched her, his energy-form warping into different shapes, but his blue eyes always remained fixed, watching. Watching her. And then he laughed at her, "Wrong choice, my daughter. Now everything diessss." He swooped down upon her . . .

. . . And death beckoned.

"Sky Leader? Hallo? Are you still with us?" asked Principal Larn Tula, the rotund head councilor of Halcyon City, to Deb who was seemingly lost in thought or fixated by the view offered of the skies from the conference chamber they had gathered in. Larn Tula and her four advisors looked around each other, baffled.

Then Deb had turned around, a conciliatory smile on her face.

"Apologies, Principal. I was fully aware of what you were saying, but I was caught by the wonderful view offered from here. It's not often one gets to see over the city and out to the skies this way. And I am a Sky Warrior after all," she said in a self-effacing way, gaining a few laughs among the advisors, all younger males. "But, as you were saying before, I do believe the Sky Warriors would enjoy a new liaison centre on Halcyon. So much of our time is divided between Sky Command, duties, and Centron, that it would be nice to be able to socialise with Halcyonites and other Magna Aurans. I will confer with the Sky Commander and a decision will be forthcoming. Now if you'll excuse me," she said brusquely, pretending to have just noticed the time displayed upon the wall-mounted chroner unit, "I have another pressing appointment."

"Oh. But we had planned a special tour of the city for you, Sky Leader Deneb." Larn Tula sounded crestfallen. "The younglings were especially looking forward to meeting you! They wanted to hear about your meeting with Novan and Cirrius, their heroes!"

"Deb, Principal. Call me Deb, remember?" she said wagging a jesting finger in her direction. "And I am sorry, but I really must report for this duty. It's with the Supreme Commander, you see," she lied, her stomach wrenching at the thought of letting down the younglings. But it got the desired result.

"Oh, well, yes, by all means you should report to your superior, yes. Such is the Universe!" babbled Larn Tula, bowing ingratiatingly, as if Cirrius himself could sense the action through Deb. Her advisors were more discreet, but just as amenable; all smiles. "I'll have Advisor Dham escort you to the exit, Deb," she said.

"That won't be necessary," said Deb as politely as she could. "I know the way and besides, I know you have pressing business of your own. Thank you, again." Deb took the opportunity to depart, without further delay, the door to the Advisory Chambers sliding open for her.

"Oh, well, such is the Universe," repeated Larn Tula wistfully. She sat down with her advisors. "So, to business. Advisor G'r Wel," she said grinning and rubbing her hands together in anticipation. "Tell us about your night out in Magna City!" Pulling out a bottle of nectar and glasses from her desk drawer, she carefully poured out five short quantities in each. "And how exactly did you lose your clothes this time?"

The others laughed and gathered around with clutched glasses to hear another of G'r Wel's tales of debauchery.

Outside the chamber's door, Deb sagged against the cool metal wall. During the conference, she'd somehow been able to withstand another blinding vision, oblivious to the others, and for that she'd been grateful. But she craved the solace only the soothing air could give. This time she had been able to visualise more clearly and retain significant memories acknowledging sizeable amounts of this vision. But the final instance had been less understandable. Two things had puzzled her, the first being the fateful choice demanded of her by that monstrosity history called the Traitor Synther. What had he meant by "Wrong choice?" What bearing could it have on the outcome of the battle?

Secondly, high up in the skies, just before he had appeared, Deb's attention had been detracted from the blazing lights crisscrossing the regions of space, where the mighty Swords clashed with the Lore, to a lone magenta presence. It had watched stoically as the horrific battle unfolded, with such empathy that the emotion emanating from it had reached into Deb's heart and mind with such force that she could clearly hear the words "This should not have been" over and over. Deb sensed that this entity would play an essential part in the future, but how, she knew not.

Having roamed in the general direction of the exit, recovered and unburdened by thoughts of darkness, Deb gaily alighted from the city, looped around and away from the Principal's chambers and made a sprint in the direction of Sky Command. Though Cirrius was now her immediate superior, she knew that some things would be best kept to herself. She needed time to think. For now, she would keep her visions and their revelations to herself.

Classia felt like a comedic *urake* dancer, free in motion, joining the moons, Swordships, and Millennius City-State in a stately orbital dance around Magna Prime. She was also happily inebriated, swaying about her quarters, humming tunelessly. And it was all Novan's fault.

Classia had noticed the Starguard's mood had subtly changed over the last few days and he seemed more pensive now. That day, she had plucked up the courage to ask him about Deb, but he had pre-empted her by inviting his command crew to a dinner, three days before launch. With most of the pre-mission plans accomplished, it was time for them to relax a bit. They deserved it, Novan had said. It was also the first time the ten senior staff had been on board together at once. Novan had taken time to get to know each of them in turn—Vaage, Glith and Classia, the Trinari and Meccun tech leaders—so each of them would feel comfortable with one another. The Neb had partook of the meal, but declined the after-meal drinks.

"More for us!" Vaage had hollered merrily.

Classia had enjoyed herself and found she could work with any of them. They were each fascinating characters in their own way. Unity among the seniors was important, Novan felt, and he wanted to be sure they were all of one mind for the mission. Following the after-dinner talk, when his guests were about to leave, Novan had requested that Classia remain, ostensibly for an update on a Sky Warrior personnel report she had compiled. But after the others' departures, Novan had broached the subject of Deb himself, but not as Classia had hoped.

"How is Sky Command? Have you bid farewell to your close friends, like Deb?" Classia could only shake her head 'no' to which he had looked perplexed.

Classia had considered saying something, but thought better of it. If something romantic had happened between Novan and Deb, then it seemed to be dying out. And that suited her just fine. She had exited the senior nourishment hall, leaving Novan to his own thoughts, as she returned to her quarters to contemplate the intricacies of the dance of life over another bottle of nectar.

"Yeah, all your fault," she slurred, just before crashing onto the bed, dead to the worlds. Asleep.

Alone in his quarters, Novan cheerlessly paced deliberately over to where his most valued possession lay beside his bedside, his book from Spheron. And as he began to page through its ink-scripted and painted pages, he realised that this was now his own personal journey about to begin. Out there in the vast unknown were his mother and countless others depending upon his success. He did not know exactly where they were, but his tenuous telepathic link with Elysius would guide him along the way. And he was determined he would not fail.

Soon, Mother, soon, he vowed.

The Novanian Quest—such as this voyage had been grandly dubbed by histographers and illustriously titled in the continuing Scrolls of History—day of departure had arrived.

The unrelenting tiresome work expended by the crews, techs, and myriads of supporting Magna Auran volunteers had brought the whole system together again. From Alphatron City-State, the Colcana rock and crystal miners around Aurana to the cosy homes of those on Halcyon and Placia, the system was brought to a standstill as Novan's five-Sword fleet began to move off. The last three days had been calm amid the exacting refits and crew movements with plenty of farewells, speeches announced, and hearty feasts eaten, though the *Sword Temprocity* delegation had added some not-unexpected disgrace and tense humour by ending the last feastnight brawling among themselves, filling the hall with a mess of airborne food. It had always been said that the Elerae and Xarian warriors couldn't hold their nectar and here it had been proven.

From on board their myriad of cramped bulky mining ships, the Colcana miners had watched enrapt as proud transmissions from Magna Prime had revealed the slender *Sword Celectral* gracefully sliding by the glittering Millennius City-State in a farewell salute, shortly followed by the superior *Swords*

Relentance, Confiance, Venturon and then *Temprocity*. Embarking on a stately system tour lasting a few hours, where normally the Swords could have sauntered through in a few minutes, the fleet would slowly cross the path of Aurana, the outer system world, where the rock laborers were set to parade in their small sturdy ships all lit up in their own gesture of parting salutation.

On Sky Command, Gal Agar once again stood with his warriors on the observation decks, though fewer in number than the last time he had stood here. His new First Deputy and Glith's replacement, Orman Brank, now the only senior Meccan Sky Warrior, stood on his left while the newest Deputy, Tol Valar, occupied the right side. Gal Agar could feel the combined emotions of his warriors and he was immensely proud of all of them. He'd almost wished he could have gone with Novan on the sky-mission of a lifetime, but his life's ties were rooted to Halcyon and they couldn't be cut so easily. Even with all his warriors around him, he still felt lonely without the presence of Deb, who presumably was on Cirrius' Island.

On huge vidscreens in all the homes on Halcyon and Placia— skyborne, landbased and seabound—younglings pressed against their parents, wide-eyed with excitement and wonder as they witnessed five sleek ships skate past the jewel-like City-State against the backdrop of Magna Prime in all its green glory and then into the complete blackness of space. The Swords were followed by small escort ships full of histographers. And everywhere, the fathers, mothers, sons, daughters, family, and friends wished Novan and his crews well on their journey.

Urana had remained on Placia, the Protectress of State taking part in the official farewell ceremonies with the planet's Principals and councils. The festivals would continue long into the night and around Atronia. Urana had much to cheer now that

Captain Councilor Mona had finally sided with her. The Volcano-powered shields and weapons were being manufactured and installed around the planet. And soon the official delegation would travel to the Neb heartland, on the consecrated Ve'Le'Bo Island, to pray and place tributes within the great central pyrathedral.

From Millennius City-State, Sceptre and Altair had watched from the spires as *Sword Celectral* had smoothly ghosted by in eerie silence, like some metallic spirit, closely shadowed by its mystic sisters. Sceptre said a silent prayer to the universe for their safe return, while Altair begrudgingly accorded Novan some respect with a nectar-induced libation of his own.

The brother-cousins had made somewhat of a pact of peace the previous night when all the Starguards had been gathered again on Aqrius for a short private dinner, cooked by Cirrius' own hand, with extra spicy *paja* cakes and roasted *bale*, the flightless blue-feathered birds kept wild by Cirrius on Aqrius.

Altair had noticed how much Cirrius had changed, more relaxed, though he wasn't sure if the presence of Deb had anything to do with it. If anything, Deb's presence had more of an effect on Novan—the two had hardly talked together—but Altair had noticed the surreptitious glances that passed between them. Now that Novan was leaving, Altair had made his peace with him, hopefully impressing upon Deb his own gentler side. She would need some comforting, quite naturally, and Altair knew just the person for the job. His nectared smile grew wider at the thought, as the Swords disappeared from view.

Alphatron City-State hung in the void, from where a surprisingly-contented Decion conferred upon his older brother a wish of God-expedience. They had never gotten along, but Decion acknowledged that Novan was embarking on a mission that could change Magna Auran life forever. And although he would never have admitted it to anybody, Decion missed his parents dearly, even in their cold days of disjoinment. He knew Novan felt the same, and almost miraculously and for the first time ever, the two brothers had warmly embraced each other in understanding. Once the shock had worn off the others, Decion had returned to his usual boisterous self, out-drinking them all in celebration.

Decion silently watched the Swords stream by. Once gone, the City-State's engines would be directed to change course and guided toward the inner system for safety. The twins had watched the stellar ship parade briefly, before heading away to their secondary dock training arena to resume their deadly swordplay. They had been unusually quiet since Novan's first announcement, and Decion thought this was probably their way of dealing with it. Sometimes he didn't completely get along with them either, as their official guardian and trainer, and quite frankly they often scared him. Their eerie calmness and intuitive link between them belied a frightening ferocity once provoked. And he was supposed to be the one everyone feared. And with that thought, Decion wondered with Novan gone, who would really keep everything in check?

Sword Celectral was on course, for destiny and beyond, and Novan reflected that this is how Adantus must have felt on his Antiqchronals Quest millennia ago, but he wasn't about to imitate that mission's fateful end. Novan swore that his Novanian Quest would be a successful tale of adventure for the Scrolls of History.

Around him, the bridge was silent, save for a few commands from Warrior General Vaage, who had the command chair, Novan having opted to stand. Glith, now honourably-entitled Sky General Glith, relayed Vaage's commands to helm and flight, but

Classia was not on the bridge, much to Novan's regret. His eyes kept darting to where her usual position would be at flight control, but it was inhabited by her second, Sky-mark Sujunca.

Novan had been getting used to Classia's presence and after last night at Cirrius', when he and Deb had said their final farewells, he knew that Deb had steeled herself to the fact that one or both of them might not survive what the future had in store for them. They agreed it would be best if they kept their love for each other to themselves, until a far future time when they could be reunited. Novan was heartened that Deb would wait that long, but he wondered if indeed there would be anything to wait for. In the meantime, there was always Classia, who would love Novan until the day she died.

"Tell her," Deb had urged him, "Tell Classia the truth about me!"

Novan had only nodded. "I will consider it."

But where was Classia? he asked himself.

This was no time for celebration for Classia. Earlier, her charges had urged her to lead them in voice when it was time to sing the Sky Warriors' hymn upon departure, if only to rile the Star Warriors who had no such anthemic traditions. But Classia had cried off, claiming a slight illness. She had retreated to her quarters, where she had laid down in sombre mood, sipping vintage nectar as she had done for the past few nights running, nectar which had been meant for happier times.

For the umpteenth time, she asked herself what she was doing here about to voyage forever, away from all she knew, just to follow the one she loved, but who loved another, her best friend at that. She swallowed hard, wincing at the nectar's strain on her throat. Her crystalator had then flashed, receiving an incoming recorded signal.

No rest for the lovelorn, she thought. "What is it?" she sighed still laying down. At her command, words of constructed light began to write themselves in the air accompanied by a very familiar voice. Classia sat up immediately, a slight nectar rush swirling in her head, sending vivid patterns swimming before her eyes.

"Classie,

Of anyone, there is none other that I love more than you, my universe of enduring friendship. You have been the star of constancy in my life and ever will be. But our lives are branching anew, brought on by cosmic forces within this universe we can neither change nor oppose; forces whose inexorable wake have conspired to exact a price upon our friendship, which I am not prepared to pay. Our friendship means too much to me, as tempered and as weathered as it is, and costs more than the mere triviality that is the universe.

Whenever, wherever we meet again, you will know then what I could not talk of now, but we know there is one with you who can. Go to him, Classie, tell him what I have said to you and compel him to reveal to you the way my universe has taken. He owes us both that much and the weight upon his heart will also be free. His burden is one of love, a love that has no place for the two of us, but you, Classie, have a long journey ahead and an opportunity. Show him your love, and know that mine, too, travels with you. And may all our love bring the paths of our universes to cross again. Until then and forever,

Your Little Star,

Deb"

Classia stared at the hanging words, mesmerised. She didn't know what to say, what to feel or to think, but the warmth of her tears trickling down her face said it all. As if she could embrace Deb through her words, Classia reached out, stumbling across her quarters, her hand passing through the light-projected words, distorting their form as they rippled over her skin. But she didn't care and continued to brush her fingers over the illuminated text, which seemed blurred either from her tears or from the effects of two bottles of nectar.

Oh, Little Star, everything's alright now, Classia rejoiced, her heart seeming to have just started beating again for the first time in days. Her love for Novan had always paled beside that for Deb and it had just been justified. Novan could wait, it was time to celebrate what the universe in all its complexity couldn't break— the bond of friendship. Before she left her quarters, nectar bottle in hand, Classia scribed a reply message, instructing her crystalator to send it to Sky Leader Deneb.

As she blithely strode along the ship's straight well-lit corridors and descended in transtubes towards what was euphemistically called the ship's belly, she began singing the time-honoured Celestian song of victory which had been adopted by the Sky Warriors as their own. And by the time Classia reached the crowded recreation hall, she was in full voice and unison with her fellow Sky Warriors, who on her well-received entrance raised a howling cheer.

"For Magna Aura, for Novan, for Victory!" she shouted in salute, to more rousing cheers from both Sky and Star Warriors.

The Sky Warriors chorused again, arm in arm, as Classia, in a capricious mood, hovered over them pouring nectar for each in turn, carrying out the long-held tradition of the Last Offering. After tonight, except at decreed times, no one would be allowed to drink again. And as Classia took her last-ever drink, her thoughts returned to the one left behind and she offered to her a silent pledge:

Unto tomorrow!

On Cirrius' island, staring up into the night sky, sharing twinkling stars amidst the sparkling showers of celebratory light displays, Deb's eyes searched the high horizon for the bright, greenish speck that was Magna Prime, and imagined the Swords in all their elegance as they cruised out and away. The wind cloyed around her as it grew colder by the minute, but Deb braved the chilly blasts if only to stand on the very spot she and Novan had declared their love for each other, but which she could not commit to. She loved Novan, but the time was not right, and until it was, he should love another. Deb could think of no other Celestian that she would rather have to be with him than Classia.

A plume of noisy, colourful purple and green sparks arced gracefully in the air, obscuring Deb's vision of Magna Prime, where her message to Classia had been sent. They had only known each other a scant ten years, but it had felt like a lifetime. Now she owed Classia a debt for that friendship, a debt of truth, that even if she couldn't tell Classia herself, then she hoped in time Novan would.

As Deb pondered the times ahead for them, her personal crystalator, tucked away in her manoeuvre suit's forearm, chimed softly, and after Deb initiated the device, Classia's voice resonated from the crystal:

"Forever lasts only a day when there is one such as you to return to. So look no further than the day when we shall meet again—unto tomorrow. Forever, are you my Little Star, a beacon of friendship in a void of loneliness.

So, shine, Little Star, shine in memory, shine eternal—unto tomorrow.
Classie"

Three symbols finished her signature: Sky. Heart. Love.

Deb's already strained emotions overwhelmed her. Friendship never died, it just waxed and waned in the great cycle of the universe. With a burst of pure elation, she lofted herself into the air, crying out to the whole universe:

"Unto tomorrow! Unto tomorrow!"

Tears of exhilaration poured from within, over her cheeks and lips. Hovering in the air, she felt inexplicably and completely drained of energy, but it felt good. She hadn't known it herself, but if anyone had been watching her, they'd have seen a bright blaze of azure burst from within her to light up the night sky.

A new Starguard had come of age.

Cirrius had deliberately neglected the entire sending-off festivities. Every crystalator in his main lab was operating as far over max capacity as he could push them, plotting, charting, calculating, and analysing and re-analysing every possible Lore strategy and counter Starguard offensives. The first of the deployed test chronimonum spheres had so far detected no Lore incursions, their sensor webs extending deep into space and temporal dimensions. But not a one of his scenarios returned favourable results as he sat alone, head in hands, in the underground hideaway, which was half-lit and eerily quiet.

Cirrius wouldn't let himself panic just yet, but in desperation he had his crystalators search every medtech and obscure histographic database for any other females who had or were exhibiting the same 'symptoms' as Deb. There weren't any. Deb was singular, unique. Cirrius stared bleakly at the walls. There was no point in telling anyone else the grim news. They needed a miracle.

"It's all up to you, Azure!" he whispered to his audience of humming crystalators.

Swords *Celectral, Relentance, Venturon, Confiance,* and *Temprocity* sailed on toward Aurana, the last and furthest out of the worlds, a gentle green-grey gas sphere with two unremarkable moons mined for ship-building materials and other resources. However, the other Swordfleet—*Commandarian, Vantagion, Exemplist, Ascendral, Warrious, Stardral, Despire, Palaciar, Endreadenor, Airion, Crysicity, Exire, Hyperious, Aqrius,* and *Zen Alliancer*—had formed up respectfully in opposing ranks to admit their five sister Swords between them.

General Vaage had stood to attention as Star Commander Vander and the Commander of the Magna Aura Swordfleet, General Ede of the *Commandarian,* had relayed their last farewell addresses.

"Magna Aura awaits your speedy return," Vander said.

"God-expedience to the Novanian crews!" Ede saluted, his craggy face smiling on the vidscreens of all the Swords.

"We will return in no time!" Vaage assured them, in his clipped Xarian accent.

"Time favours no one in a hurry," Novan had quipped to them all from *Celectral's* bridge, to general muted amusement. "Farewell, Magna Aura, farewell my fellow Starguards; we shall be well met again!"

His handsome face with his bridge crew gathered behind him were the last scenes from aboard the departing Swords.

Once Novan's swords had passed, the swordfleet broke formation and sped toward the inner system, each designated with a sector to patrol until the earnest work of war began.

And advancing past Aurana and the hundreds of lighted miners' ships, and with dogged histographers relaying transmissions back to the watching millions, the Novanian warriors became the first Magna Aurans to slip past the bounds of the system, to venture into new frontiers and to embark upon the journey of a lifetime.

Time also ventured forth, weaving its precious strands; a new era in the reckoning. And when those lines of time converged, it would change forever the fates of many and never be the same again.

CHAPTER EIGHT

"Clear the skies! Clear the skies! This is an emergency alert! Clear the skies!"

Warnings echoed endlessly throughout every abode, city, and skimmer on Halcyon. Citizens dropped everything, picking up younglings regardless of whose they were, and hurried into the specially shielded under-island bunkers within the land communities, while skimmers landed haphazardly almost on top of each other, their sea-going counterparts—the hydro-skimmers and mag-sailers—either docked or submerged to safety.

No sooner had the blaring warnings commenced, when familiar forms in two-tone blue swarmed through the emptied airspaces, Sky-marks, as their name implied, positioning themselves in prescribed locations, crisscrossing the entire planet in a lattice of protection. Each carried a battle-staff, the potent symbol of Hyphon the Sky Warrior, capable of ripping apart the molecular bonds which held an individual Lore together. And they were about to be used.

Battle stations on Sky Command's bridge were unbearably tense, but kept together under the authoritative control of Gal Agar as three-dimensional crystalator images of Halcyon's emplacements spun before him, every Sky Warrior, settlement, and defence grids accounted for. Extra shielding of near-indestructible stellecneum and energy-resistant alchemar metal had been bonded to all the sky cities and Sky Command, and weapons readied for war, to the detriment of the enemy.

"All systems ready, sir!" Brank announced.

Gal Agar's face was a grim mask of determination. He nodded in acknowledgement.

"Permission to engage!" requested Brank, voice steady and

clear.

Gal Agar nodded, his voice even. "Engage when ready."

In an adjacent crystalator image, three new stars had appeared, unerringly working their light-generated forms across the air toward the Halcyon light-construct. The enemy had appeared and were now entering the system to bear down upon Halcyon, but the Sky Warriors were ready.

The stars were much closer than anyone had thought. They appeared in the distant void, out-shining even Placia, casting their glow through the indelibly-blue atmosphere of her twin planet. Commanding an advance combat team, Tol Valar had no sooner seen them, when the enemy had hit the atmosphere, burning the air in their wake.

"Fire!" the countless voices of Sky Leaders commanded in unison, followed instantly by the crackling crescendos of discharging battle-staffs.

They were easy to control: just aim and shoot and the energy released automatically sought to bond with and de-cohere chroniton energy, the most dangerous Lore attribute, into nothingness. The air was crisscrossed with treacherous energy attempting to hit their targets, who so far haughtily ignored the energy directed against them.

"Can't get them, can't get them," came a panicked cry over Tol Valar's crystalator.

"Look out, Rarla, dive! Dive!" came another. And from all over, Tol Valar heard the same anxious calls, as he directed his teams to pursue and engage.

"They're too fast! Go high! High! Too late!" a Sky-mark screamed.

Until the familiar voice of Journ had come through calm and clear, "Seven Section with me; Six with Tima. Brace and Z'don take

Eight and Ten. Collapsing sector, now!"

Tol Valar could image Journ leading his section out and to the west, while the other units spread out in the remaining directions, gradually boxing the enemy in an ever-decreasing killing zone. From where he was stationed, holding a high position with his own five sections, Tol Valar could almost see the battle taking place far over the Vavashar Islands, as yellow streaks of energy raced against the unrelenting verve of the Sky Warriors. His crystalator simultaneously relayed information from the other side of the world, where Teron and Dessa tackled the enemy out by Elysian City, with a force twice the size of his.

The battle raged longer than expected until the enemy took the upper hand. "Lost them, they're gone," someone suddenly yelled. "Where'd they go?"

"Universe! Ours too," Tol Valar heard Journ say. "Anybody have them?"

Tol Valar checked his crystalator readings, but nothing appeared, except—he frantically toggled the holo-image around looking around the sky, then he saw the telltale flashes of light. They were upon Sky Command before anybody could act.

Sky Command was lost.

"We've lost, again, warriors. Sky Command is taken!" announced Gal Agar's terse voice, over the crystalators. "Exercise over. Return to stations."

Tol Valar gazed at his sections. The enemy had come straight through their position without being detected. Dejected, he led his teams back, soon joined by the rest of the forces. For the past two weeks since Novan's departure, the Sky and Star Warriors had been placed on high alert, constantly simulating a system-wide attack. Cirrius had maintained it was just precautionary, but the level of intensity stated otherwise and many suspected that something else was occurring.

The main skimmer bay under the upper deck had been transformed into an assembly deck now packed with Sky Warrior ranks and the 'enemy force' of Sceptre, Altair and Urana, holding the 'captured' Gal Agar, who had a grave look on his face.

Without preamble, Sceptre said, "You performed better this time, but after we fooled the crystalators with a subtle shift of energy to momentarily cause a time lag, you were completely lost. The Lore undoubtedly have that as a natural ability, so as much as possible try to maintain visual contact at all times, do not rely solely on the crystalators and plasma staffs; use your minds as well," he said tapping the side of his head with his forefinger. "There were only three of us, but panic was rife. Imagine thousands of them around you, behind you, who really are trying to kill you. Just stay calm, and think," he said with a tap to the head.

Sceptre turned to Gal Agar, who said a few words of encouragement himself, but Tol Valar didn't hear them, he was lost in his own thoughts. The system was on the brink of war, he could feel it, but no one was willing to divulge anything. It was one thing to train for a war declared, but another to train for a war unknown. Even the Scrolls of History extolled that, so why were they delaying? One word of acknowledgement would go far in bolstering the warriors' sense of purpose and no doubt instil some real urgency during the exercises. He almost said something out aloud, but bit his lip, hard. He'd only been just promoted and he liked it, so he wasn't about to say anything now to jeopardise that.

But he had other plans, too, for just off to one side, he could see Deb hovering in the background. *She must know something*, he thought. *Maybe it's time to re-probe the frozen landscape.*

It had been widely known Tol Valar was something of a cavorter and that one of his long-time obsessions had been Deb, but she had constantly rebuffed him, which he wasn't accustomed to. To him, she was colder than space frost, but he hoped to remedy that soon. He hadn't spoken to Deb since her promotion—in all but name—which had surprised him almost as much as Classia's inclusion into Novan's crew. Something had happened that night when Deb and Classia had met Cirrius and Novan on Halcyon City, everyone agreed on that, but the details were as sparse as an empty nectar flask. But whatever it was, it had the effect of transforming Deb and Classia from two of the more popular, though less-disciplined Sky Leaders into potential Sky Commanders overnight. Tol Valar needed to know what had happened, for his desire for Deb had never weakened and with both their promotions, he had more of a chance to pursue her at his leisure. And it could also do his career some good.

". . . And resume stations," Tol Valar heard Gal Agar order, dispersing the gathered Sky Warriors, back to their normal duties. Soon Halcyon would be back to normal again, until the next disruption and the next. Until there was war. And Tol Valar could only hope by then they were ready for the real thing.

By the time the three Starguards, Deb, and Gal Agar returned to the Sky Commander's office, Cirrius was there waiting, sitting in Gal Agar's chair, which he obligingly vacated for the Sky Commander.

"Twenty per cent better, but reaction time was inadequate, though we knew that would be the case once you produced that time-lag manoeuvre," he said to Sceptre, in his dispassionate tone, a cynical smile curling his lips.

"Don't you think it's about time we told the populace about the imminent Lore threat and Deb's part in this?" asked Urana.

"In due time, sister." This time he actually sounded bored, Urana's forehead creasing with concern. "And besides, Azure here, hasn't detected anything untoward yet, so we still have a little more time, don't we, Azure?"

Deb looked at them, a shade uncomfortable with her Starguard name being used among others, but she managed a noncommittal shrug. "They could appear before I sense them, or they could still be years away, but either way, I'm with Urana on this. The system should be warned now. Remember, it's no use trying to catch sun rays once the sun's exploded," she recited from the Book of Replenishments.

Cirrius let out an exaggerated sigh and tried to look aggrieved, and they all knew then that they'd just wasted their time, talking him into something he had decided to do anyway, but was indulging in one of his psychological sparrings.

"Okay, okay, you've convinced me. We'll have one more exercise alert in two days' time, then Aerl, if he wants, can convene a conference and announce to all that the days of war are returning, but that we also have the newest Starguard to help us!" This seemed to placate the others, and he rose from the chair, "Two days, then," he said by way of departure, exiting through the inner double-door air-lock chamber, at the office rear. The doors slid closed behind him, the outer doors opening, and he flew away, as if he had no care in the world.

"Is Cirrius all right?" Deb asked, sensing otherwise.

"You try holding all those secrets and plans to save the whole system, in your head," Altair cracked.

"Yes, just a bit of strain," Urana agreed. But she knew something was bothering him. She would have to find out later. But she returned to Deb. "Goddess of the Darkening Blue, eh?" grinned Urana, sizing her up. "It'll do, but trust my brother to come up with that one, um, 'White-star Warrior'?" she said pointedly to Altair, who visibly puffed out his chest at the sound of his name.

It made Deb smile, Altair's powers and appearance couldn't be further from that description.

Not about to be teased further, Altair, for once in a pleasant mood, excused himself and then he, too, was gone from the airlock, in a red trail of energy.

Aerl and Urana enjoyed the moment, and Gal Agar watched as Deb joined in the frivolity, as if she had known them all her life. She laughed with them, the naturalness of her movements and mood conveying an assuredness that she hadn't displayed, even with Classia.

But, almost as immediately, her mood changed and from nowhere, a cloud of darkness shadowed her features, her smile frozen in consternation, and she suddenly stared off into the distance as if listening, but not hearing properly. Her lips parted and a whisper of a word escaped: "Novan!"

Almost instantly, bursting into the office, breathless, Brank reported: "Sir, Vista Mare reports that contact with Novan's fleet has been lost. It's non-explanatory, sir, they've just disappeared," he said, waiting for further orders with rising anxiety stretched across his usually placid features.

Keying his crystalator, seamlessly attached to his visor, Sceptre contacted Star Commander Vander direct. "Star Commander, this is Sceptre. What more can you tell us?"

"There's not much, Sceptre," came Vander's concerned tones. "There was normal monitoring then the Swords just disappeared, no warning, no signs of distress. They're gone, Sceptre, I'm sorry," he sounded even more downcast.

Sceptre sighed. "I'm sure things are fine; an anomaly perhaps or unknown malfunction." He tried to sound more upbeat. "Keep trying to raise them and keep us informed if anything develops," he signed off.

"Thank you, Deputy Brank," Gal Agar said.

Calmer, Brank departed after a formal Meccun bow.

The silence heightened the unreality of the situation and Deb looked up, as if staring at the real world for the first time finding the others looking intently at her.

She shook her head. "It wasn't the Lore," she stated firmly.

"How do you know?"

Urana's question made Deb hesitate, before she said, "I felt it . . . on a more personal level."

"Oh, yes, we're sorry," responded Sceptre. "You have close friends on board *Celectral*, don't you?"

"Friends, yes," Deb blushed slightly, looking away quickly. "I do believe they are all alive," she said aloud, simultaneously praying the same to the universe.

Urana said, "I will inform Cirrius, if he does not already know. I am sure he would send a probe or discover some way to communicate with Novan."

Sceptre nodded. "Good idea, but whatever happened to them, whether good or bad, cannot affect our plans," Sceptre pondered. "I will announce to the system how deep in the gravity well we are and our chances of survival," he said. "Then we can all face it together with brave faces and fired hearts." He smiled grimly. "Besides, I don't think the system can stand seeing the Starguards all together again," he joked.

"When?" Urana asked, a little anxiously.

"We'll stick to Cirrius' timings for now. As soon as the other Starguards are notified, we'll make the announcement from here this time," Sceptre affirmed with Gal Agar. "We had better be on our way, too. I cannot leave Altair with all the security plans to work on!" He laughed and nodded in departure. Forearm clasps were exchanged before he and Urana exited through the office airlock.

Deb looked at Gal Agar. He seemed bothered by something and dark lines under his eyes had formed. "Anything wrong, sir?" she asked, genuinely concerned.

He gave her a weary smile, placing his hands upon her shoulders. "One day Deb, you and I will have to have a talk, before it's too late. These last couple of weeks have tested us all, you foremost, and for now, I just want you to know how much you mean to me," he said in a low voice.

Deb nodded, "I feel the same." And she gave him a loving hug, which he awkwardly returned, before becoming once again the Sky Commander of old.

"Now, if you'd be so kind, Sky Leader, you have duties to perform." He ordered with a twinkle in his eyes.

Deb smiled, "Yes, sir." And she was out the door, walking toward the command center. She had a long shift ahead.

Hours later, Deb had been busy familiarising herself with Sky Command bridge duty, which her new function demanded of her. The central saddle-shaped bridge stretched to two decks tall at its highest commanding surrounding views over the edge of the sky-borne structure. Deb liked the quietness of the night shift; this routine task being conducted by Tol Valar, also on assessment for his night training. But the hours had been long and the lessons extensive.

"Well, I think that's enough for tonight," Tol said, smiling affably.

"Fine," said Deb, pretending to be tired, though her system could have gone on for hours without rest.

Funny how she had never noticed that before. She smiled to

herself.

Tol Valar looked at her curiously and was about to inquire about her enigmatic smile, but Deb started to leave, intent on returning to her quarters.

"Thank you for your time, Tol," she said, walking toward the door.

He, too, quickly exited the command centre conveniently catching up to Deb outside the transtube.

"If you don't mind, Deb, I'd like to talk to you," he mentioned in an off-hand way, as they entered the transtube together.

"Oh, about?" a furrowed-brow Deb replied.

"It's private, Deb. My office isn't too far, if that's fine with you?"

Deb gave him a dubious look, but Tol Valar's face showed no sign of mischief. "Fine, your office then." She flashed a neutral smile.

Deb had still retained her quarters on deck five, but Tol Valar's office was on deck two, just under the command centre. He directed the transtube down with a press of the carriage's crystalator panel.

They walked silently through pale-blue corridors, passing other Sky Warriors on various duties. Before long they arrived at his newly refurbished office, tidy, with a large transparent screen overlooking one of the several large stubby wings of Sky Command.

Tol Valar had already heard the latest desperate news about Novan and it disturbed him. The situation was not going to plan, whatever it was. And now he finally had the opportunity to discover answers for himself. He waved her into his office, toward his desk, the door sliding shut behind them.

"What's happening, Deb?" he enquired straight away, "I heard about Novan's fleet being lost, but so far no official announcement has been made as to how or why. The rumours are also spreading amok about war!" He stepped forward, closer to Deb, hoping to provoke her into answering off guardedly.

Pursing her lips, Deb wasn't sure what to tell him, but could only say, "In a couple of days, there'll be an announcement from Sceptre regarding Magna Aura's path. So, everything will be known to you then," Deb said.

She suddenly noticed that she and Tol Valar were standing rather close, too close for her, and she moved back a couple of steps to a more appropriate distance, though his eyes still regarded her attentively. She may have been flattered in the past with his attentions, but Deb knew she still had no real feelings for Tol Valar.

"That's all I can say," she confirmed. "I'd better be going now," she made to leave, but Tol Valar stopped her, his back to the door.

"Deb . . ." he paused, gathering thoughts he'd never expressed before. "I think you know really why I want to talk to you. You've known that over the years, I've . . . admired you, maybe even loved you," he admitted coyly. "But you seemed . . . reticent to return any feeling. I thought that maybe now things had changed with our respective promotions," he emphasised, "We could get to know each other, start again as it were . . ." his voice trailed off, as he saw the answer in Deb's face: rejection.

Sensing his reading of her, Deb tried to sound apologetic, "I'm sorry, Tol. There was a time when I might have. But things have changed, more than you can know," she said, trying to leave again. But again, Tol Valar made her pause.

"There's someone else isn't there?" He sounded hurt.

Deb smiled wistfully, remembering the last time she'd been asked that question and the sequences that followed.

"Yes, there is and it's private," she replied.

"For Universe sake! Who is it?" Tol Valar's voice became more agitated, fists clenched.

"It's complicated. Now I really must go." She tried to quickly sidestep him, but Tol grabbed her arm and shoulder hard with his hands, his face barely concealing his rising temper.

"It's that old man, Gal Agar, isn't it? I should have known!" Jealousy spewed from his mouth.

"NO! Let go of me!" urged Deb, her own anger rebelling against her natural self-control.

"It is, isn't it? Or is it Cirrius? Yes, yes, it's him, isn't it, that's why you're his aide. That's why you've been promoted!" His eyes were wild as he shouted.

"That's not true!" shrieked Deb. "Now let go of me!" she spat through clenched teeth. But his grip tightened. A sharp pain shot through Deb's head and arms, clouding her vision in a cloud of blue. "Let go! Now!"

A rush of energy exploded in her mind.

Deb wasn't sure what happened next, though she had a fair idea: one moment Tol Valar had her arms gripped tighter than a *Teressian* seacoil and the next, he was across the room in a crumpled heap, the blue sparks responsible only now dissipating from her hands and before her eyes.

Tol Valar was unconscious.

Slightly flustered, not knowing what else her powers had in store for her, Deb gave Tol a few light slaps around the face, which was already showing signs of bruising. A coughing Tol slowly regained his senses, jerking sharply at the pain in his back and sides. He looked at Deb wild-eyed.

He tried to sit up, holding his right-side ribs, bruised not broken, he knew. The medtechs could sort that out in no time.

"What happened?" he finally managed to gasp after a few attempts at speaking.

"I don't know, but you were hurting me, though. I threw you," she shrugged. "My new training regime!" she smiled wanly, flexing her arms.

Tol Valar just stared silently at her, slight fear in his eyes. He let out a huff of air, resuming his prone position.

"Uh, um! Sorry, Deb," he murmured, looking quite sheepish.

"So am I," she replied with a brief sad smile, leaving his side, "But you had better see a medtech soon. And don't forget our bridge session tomorrow. I'm looking forward to it now," she said over her shoulder as she left his office.

Tol Valar lay on the ground reflecting on what could have been.

And how the universe did I end up here? he thought, looking around the room, while massaging his painful ribcage.

"Ouch!" He had just struggled to his feet when the alarms started again. "Oh, not another exercise," he groaned.

Time twisted, flowing raggedly through storms and quakes not meant to be traversed by mere mortals. But the beings swimming the Great Channel of Destiny ploughed easily through the raging temporal waves, the shores of their destination seen fleetingly through the dimensional barriers, those oscillating energy dams that kept all those solitary lakes, called universes, apart.

And then they were free of the torrents, plunging into new temporal waves that were black and dismal compared to the brightness of the timestream. But there, in the dank void were the shining beacons that some called worlds, beckoning them toward the light of the last outpost of civilisation that glowed constantly from a coast thought safe.

But now that flickering flame was to be extinguished, that beacon and all it stood for, destroyed. And in the end, the only fire still burning in the universe, the only brilliance still enduring, would be the all-consuming light of the Lore.

Deb knew before the alarms sounded. Visions had collided with pain inside her head sending her mind into a swirl. They were very close, their presence igniting every fibre of Deb's being, but she resisted their call; denied her urge to join them.

The sirens had brought her back to her senses, as she had focused on them to maintain her sanity. She sprinted to Gal Agar's office, avoiding those Sky Warriors rushing the other way to their stations. His office was already crowded with the other Deputies, all present now as Tol Valar had limped in, without time for a medtech visit, giving Deb a wary look.

Gravelly, Gal Agar looked among them and opening a planet-wide link, simply said, "This is Sky Commander Gal Agar. This is not an exercise. The Lore are attacking. Prepare for war!"

His message was automatically recorded and before it had repeated for the second time, Gal Agar was leading his warriors to the bridge, for the last time.

Bubbles. Hard bubbles floated around in the ethereal vacuum: bubbles of invisibleness rising up from the depths of the void, bubbles of death, their presence only felt at the point of destruction. The infestations had protected themselves with material devices that discharged energies lethal to them, but it would not be enough.

The signal was given and loyal legions sacrificed themselves, for their master, to clear a path to the waiting worlds. The material devices were finally destroyed and the Lore horde in their thousands poured down onto the worlds and rained death.

Thirty-one seconds Cirrius thought to himself, surprised his chronimonum anti-Lore measures had worked half that long. But now after penetrating those exotic bulwarks the next line of defence was engaged: the Swords.

"Fire!" General Ede ordered from *Sword Commandarian*, the entire fleet under his command delivering salvo after salvo against the Lore. Fifteen Swords against tens of thousands; fire spread across the heavens as Lore erupted upon death, streaks of energy blazed hot and unrelentingly, Lore and Swords alike ablaze from battle.

Nuisances. Little, shiny nuisances sped across the void spurting forth more deadly energy from their pointed, little noses. They annoyed and harassed, buzzing around like sunflies. Clever little infestations, tiny minds building tiny things, tiny things that hurt and killed, yes, clever little infestations. But these beings were also weak, they wrapped themselves in sheaves of metal for they could not stand the weather of the void, they burned at the touch of the bare sun upon their naked skin, shivered in the breeze of the particle winds, and loathed the absence of breathable air. How such a being, who could not enjoy such pleasures, could be allowed to live, was abominable. It was time to end their existence.

The nuisances scurried around, a ceaseless barrage of energy inflicting losses upon the greater beings, the master of whom led them by his own hand against the enemy.

**

Aurana had been stormed first, reduced to a mauled husk of a world by the ravenous Lore, who fed on the gaseous world's energy, the atmosphere absorbed, minerals sucked up, leaving behind a dead world, one of many for the Lore. And on they travelled.

Endreadener exploded, perishing in a burst of energy so bright that a second sun shone in the skies over Halcyon and Placia. The Swords, stretched between Magna Prime and the inner system, fought frantically. *Sword Vantagion*, crew dead, and on a rapid intercept with *Sword Palaciar*, besieged by Lore, collided with her sister Sword, the two crippled ships and Lore plunging obliviously into Magna Prime's volatile atmosphere. *Sword Hyperious* listed heavily after an attack, bravely responding to repeated attacks, until it too exploded, but was out-shone by the double explosion of *Swords Warrious* and *Stardral*.

"We're scattered, sir, scattered!" came a panicked report from one of the Swords. Then all comms cut dead becoming a despairing wail of static.

With no time for reorganisation, *Sword Commandarian* swung toward deep space dragging with them a few desperate Lore, but his ship's crystalator told General Ede that the majority were still around Magna Prime feeding upon his ships. *Swords Exemplist, Airion* and *Crysicity* disappeared from the readings; *Zen Alliancer* and *Despire* fought around the City-States; *Exire, Ascendral* and *Aqrius* were barely surviving deeper in the system.

The spires of Millennius City-State shattered. Air, Celestians—from youngling to elder—and a myriad of personnel and objects were brutally sucked into the blackness beyond, that darkness becoming light as the Lore invaded the wandering cities, hungry for food, hungry for killing, but all they found was death—their own.

Lancing energy cut through the air as Lore fought their enemies' children for the first time. Sceptre flew raggedly through the city's ruined deserted promenades, his hands charged with energy. Bright yellow streams, the power of suns, pulsed on his command destroying Lore outright as his energy countered theirs, ripping their bonds apart. He coursed angrily through sections open to space, searching for more Lore in the entire city, a blinding explosion glaring in the silence of space as *Sword Despire* lost her fight. Aghast at the loss of another Sword, Sceptre watched with furious anticipation as the Lore responsible for her loss headed toward him.

Come and get me! He goaded them.

On the opposite side of the city, Altair had his hands full.

"Haah! Come on!" Altair insisted, the Lore upon him, his surrounding energy field keeping them at bay, until in a roar of anger he unleashed a blast of red energy that obliterated everything in a ten-meter radius—both Lore and more city decks—immediately around him. Hanging in the void, he was pleased with himself, looking around at the devastation. Drifting back into the city, his eye caught movement and he looked around just in time to see *Zen Alliancer* spinning out of control. She was so graceful, pirouetting in the airless sky that it took a mesmerised Altair a moment too long to realise that he wouldn't be able to move out of the way in time.

Oh, Gods!

**

The Meccuns had provided extra stellecneum shielding for themselves, the forcefields repulsing the Lore attack. But the rampant creatures' forces were so overwhelming that the crystalators governing the shields collapsed, the sheen of protection around the Meccun moon colonies disappearing like sun-hit dew.

Magna Prime's biggest moon, Aradeal, was inundated, the crystalator's energy providing a rich source of nourishment for the Lore, which they hungrily accepted. Aradeal ceased to be a home to organic life forms, as it crumbled and broke apart. Moons Glonn and Qara were next, gobbled up as they died and split apart, joining Aradeal as a cluster of dull brown rock around its parent world.

Twelve minutes. Cirrius, still entrenched in his underground base, watched silently as his crystalator projected Lore positions. They were encircling Halcyon and Placia; Aurana was destroyed, the City-States engaged, the surviving Swords fought on, Magna Prime was lost and the circle was tightening around them, the first attacks on Placia commencing.

But what concerned Cirrus was Magna Aura. A heavy faction of the Lore had broken off and had swarmed all over the sun. Even now, disconcerting dark spots appeared and they were increasing in size. It was only a matter of time before the sun became so unstable that it would explode, whether or not the Lore were defeated in battle.

Cirrius watched briefly, then grimaced. "Death to you; death to me; death to all of us!" he recited from the Book of Rejoicements.

Leaving his replica bridge, Cirrius gave it one last loving gaze. He rose in his transtube heading up to the habitat. He faced all the

Celestian Knight paintings in a silent salute until his eyes rested on his parents. With a faint smile, he retrieved the metastaff from above his father's portrait and gently kissed it. Taking a deep breath, Cirrius streaked out into the stormy skies, generated by Magna Aura's instability. It was time to be with his warriors.

"I wish you luck, too, sister!" he entreated.

In their various skimmers, atmospheric battleships, and second-hand, jet-powered manoeuvre suits, Xarian and Elerae warriors waited alongside their Protectress of the State, Urana, for the battle that they had run from before, but which could not be avoided now. And they wouldn't have had it any other way. They were born to fight and would die the same way. Oaths to their warrior ancestors were sworn as thousands of ground-based warriors watched as the air was seared, and the Lore materialised from the upper atmosphere, savagely met by the air-bound warriors.

"Placia lives today! Placia lives tomorrow!" Urana shouted, shooting into the air. And the sky rained with plasma.

The Neb had hastily retreated deep into the dark recesses of their Grand Pyrathedral, praying for salvation and deliverance.

Sceptre strained under the burden of attack. His body ached after constant usage of his powers, the energy within him unlimited, but he had never used so much power before, even in training, and his body complained bitterly. The Lore touch didn't help either. His armour was torn, but if he had been less of a mortal, his body would have been disintegrated straight away. But even being superior, the energy of the Lore was dangerous enough and Sceptre tried to limit his exposure to them.

Half the city had disappeared, sheared spires floating around, crashing into each other and other parts of the city. Sceptre fought facing the depths of space, when a group of incandescent Lore suddenly ceased their attacks for an instant to stare—as near enough as Sceptre could tell that they had true eyes—behind him and as he turned, the wreck of a Sword came slamming through the city debris, carving a path of devastation, before careening into Sceptre and the Lore.

The stellecneum-mercron alloy Sword smashed into Sceptre, knocking him spinning out of the city. But he was able to survive the added punishment and right himself. Grabbing a jagged edge of the Sword, he tried to pull himself into the ship, but the Lore, resembling crude facsimiles of glowing Celestians, were upon him again dissolving the metal around him. Sceptre's own energy shielded him as he fired back at them.

Suddenly, red energy pierced the silent darkness and Altair, crimson blazing from his hands, emerged from the derelict Sword, teeth bared in anger. He shouted something and though Sceptre, realising his brother's comms were down, was not able to hear Altair through the void, he could definitely read his lips. The curse inspired Sceptre's efforts, dispatching the marauding Lore, until he and Altair had destroyed them all.

They stared at each other in jubilant commiseration, Altair grimacing, his armour tainted with streaks of Sword alloys from when he had burned his way into *Zen Alliancer*, just as it had crashed into him. He had ridden it all the way through the city, until it had reached the other side and Sceptre.

Sceptre clapped him on the shoulder, but there was no cheer, for their city was destroyed. Countless lives had been lost, the defence force hadn't even mobilised, but the two Starguards, tired yet upbeat, hoped the majority of their citizens had escaped to the protected city core.

But there was no time to check, for in the distance, they could see their sister-city burning away in fierce battle. Their battle here had ended, but the war went on.

Altair's manoeuvre suit had self-repaired his comms, just as Sceptre asked: "You ready, brother?"

Altair grinned, "See you on the fairer side, brother!"

They held forearms solemnly then streaked off in bursts of light in separate directions, Altair toward Alphatron, Sceptre back into the inner system.

Glorious rapture! Oh universe, give me war every day! Decion prayed.

His giant lancesword slashed through the ranks of the Lore. The swath of the lancesword gave Decion a respectful circle around him, the Lore circling him warily. He was in his element, fully armoured and weaponed-up, he was virtually invincible and he knew the Lore sensed it, so when they suddenly retreated, he was somewhat disappointed. *Damnable beasts! Cowards! Now what am I to do?* But he knew. The twins were together, somewhere, and if he knew them, they were having the time of their lives.

"*Gra'va!*" Astara whooped with joy in Xarianese.

Slash, slash, spin, slash, Astara's movements graceful and deadly, as another Lore disappeared in a flash of light. There was nothing like a hunt, and she and Alpha Rion were in the midst of their greatest foray.

They had deliberately chosen an enclosed chamber off the secondary dock from whence the Lore entered, but none escaped. It was the warrior twins' killing ground, the two working in tandem—one as bait, the other as hunter. And the Lore were falling by the hundreds. Astara's sword of pure-spun

Nexum, endowed with energies of other-dimensional origin, severed the bonds of the Lore as she evaded their deadly bursts of energy. Alpha Rion cut and thrust his way with his distinctive double-sworded blows, one gold di-energon sword twirling in one hand, the other slashing away furiously, then he would switch tactics, again and again. The Lore didn't stand a chance and soon they were all gone. The two breathed a sigh of relief and they hugged each other for victory, just as Decion burst into the chamber, killing a few straggling Lore that had pursued him.

"Oh, don't say I've missed all the fun here, too!" he said, his gruff voice sounding very, very disappointed.

Something was wrong. Cirrius could feel a sudden undercurrent of doom sweeping through his body, though he knew not why. His plans had worked far better than the crystalator models had predicted, the Lore had not reached Halcyon yet. However, he knew that a blazing inferno of a battle was taking place in the depths of space. And yet, there was something wrong, it gnawed at him, but he couldn't place it.

He had taken position with a group of Sky Warriors over southern Centron and he'd been greeted by the sound of song, resounding through the sky as every Sky Warrior aloft lifted their voice and sang the Sky Warrior hymn. Cirrius joined in, every now and again someone crying out "Sky Warriors! Air Superior! Air Superior!"

See horizons on the opening sky
See the dawn sun waking in your eyes
Air Superior, we will not falter
See horizons in the sky

To be Sky Warriors upon high
To be Sky Warriors 'til we die
For thee, forever we will fly
To be Sky Warriors 'til we die

See defenders of the darkening sky
Blue on blue triumphant colours fly
Storms will never blow in ill against us
See defenders of the sky

See Sky Warriors in the Sky Maternal
For glory, air and hard fought victory
We, the children of Lord Hyphon eternal
See Sky Warriors in the sky

To be Sky Warriors upon high
To be Sky Warriors 'til we die
For thee, forever we will fly
To be Sky Warriors 'til we die

The wave of joyous singing and chanting repeated again and again, heads raised, voices full, the last chorus bringing tears to eyes, voices becoming heavy with emotion. And then slowly the voices died down.

Cirrius looked up into the far reaches of the sky to where, piercing the blueness of Halcyon, thousands of bright lights appeared descending from the edge of darkness. The Lore were here.

Cirrius prayed for them all: "From those above, Mother Sky preserve us!"

But far from his feelings of foreboding deepening, they actually subsided and he felt strangely comforted by the appearance of the Lore, which only increased his worry. If he wasn't concerned about the Lore, then what was it?

What was it?

Something was wrong. Deb could sense it, but its precise nature eluded her, sticking at the back of her mind. Standing on the crowded Sky Command bridge now protectively recessed into the skimmer bay, orders being relayed, listening to both off- and on-world battle reports, beside Gal Agar and Deputy Dessa, Deb had resoundingly joined in singing their victory hymn.

Then Gal Agar had prayed: "For Sky, for Air, for Victory!"

The Sky Warriors were positioned throughout the skies and Cirrius had finally arrived, bolstering the confidence of the western forces led by Teron and Ade, while Tol Valar and Brank concentrated around the Magna City-Halcyon City-Sky Command axis. For a while, even with the loss of many off-world forces, the bridge crew had seemed confident, but a tense situation had developed.

"Commander, permission to join the battle," offered Deb. She was tired of bridge duty and wanted the freedom of the air; after all, she'd been born to it.

Gal Agar shook his head. "Permission denied, Sky Leader. I need your counsel here."

Dessa cocked her head. "Counsel? In what way, Sky Commander? I'm your chief advisor, am I not?" she asked, not unreasonably. The bridge went quiet in the air of settling unease, everyone holding their breath, pretending to work.

"Deputy, you're my chief advisor for battle. The Sky Leader is my advisor on the Lore, as taught to her by Cirrius," Gal Agar clarified. "Is that to your satisfaction?"

Dessa's mouth worked up and down, before she finally uttered, "Yes, sir," her displeasure at sharing the advisor's post clearly evident.

Deb was desperate to get out to the battle, but knew that her place was here, helping to coordinate the war against the Lore. Gal Agar's little lie to cover her reasons for being on the bridge only heightened her desire to be out there and also her feeling of ill-ease.

She remembered being on top of the world trying to coax her powers into fully revealing themselves, but had been unsuccessful. It was as if her powers needed a specific event to trigger them. They remained just beneath Deb's consciousness. Cirrius had warned her any powers could flare spontaneously and cause unpredictable results. He'd only hoped they would arise against the Lore, for he still firmly believed she had the power to destroy all the Lore, with no effort. But so far, Deb could only feel a tingle within herself that merely confirmed what her eyes told her.

The Lore had arrived on Halcyon.

Something was wrong. All through this war, he had had the feeling someone was watching him: one of his own. But no one would dare scrutinise the leader of the Lore. He whirled about; nothing, save the darkness of space greeted him—the glorious sight of wrecked cities, destroyed ships, barren worlds, and a dying sun, stirring his senses.

What magnificent devastation!

And now the fleshy infestations called Celestians, would die. But as his legions descended upon the two blue worlds, the feeling of watching eyes followed him.

Something was wrong. On *Commandarian* there was cause for dire concern.

"Sir! A significant amount of Lore have positioned themselves around the sun," Star-mark Oleon reported from the flight-detection station. "Readouts indicate they are draining Magna Aura of its energy. If they cause an energy imbalance," he visibly blanched, "the sun will go critical and explode!"

Bridge crew heads turned at the news, while General Ede considered his options. They were still out away from the system fighting off pockets of Lore. His was the only Sword left. However, between him and Magna Aura were thousands of Lore, but the lives of millions were at stake and he had only one choice.

"Star Leader Tann, turn this ship around. And head for the sun!"

"Yes, sir," the blonde at the manual helm replied, turning the wheel, her actions relayed through crystalators and executed. *Sword Commandarian*, still firing at the trailing Lore, swept around again on course for Magna Aura.

The whole Sword knew his order, General Ede proud of his warriors. But time was of the essence. They all knew that they were heading toward certain death, but it had to be done, if only to save precious time for others to fight or escape or even to draw more Lore away from the planets.

Smile kindly on our fates, Dear Universe, he prayed.

In the torrid air above Placia, Urana spread plasma death over the invaders. The Lore had screamed down tearing through the atmosphere. In apparent directed action they had torn straight for the forced-eruption volcanoes around the world.

They know! Urana worried about the generated shields powered by the volcanoes. But she was more than delighted the Lore were worried about the volcanic defences. It meant they were disturbed by them. And her instincts were right as a whole swathe of squawking Lore violently disintegrated in a flash as they contacted the energy shields.

Urana grinned darkly. Placia was helping to protect itself and her denizens. That furious nature could save their lives.

In that split second of thought, Urana narrowly missed being eviscerated by a dozen Lore. She hurriedly thrust her hands up in time to savagely pollute her surroundings with deadly yellow energy, dispatching the energised enemy.

Keep your head, Urana warned herself, even as another wall of Lore hared down upon her. But weapons fire from below destroyed their ranks. Huge twenty-meter ground-platform guns ringed Atriona, vast reservoirs of magma amplifying crystalator-powered batteries of chroniton energy. The guns spat shards of the vicious energy up and around Urana, who soared between the plasma rounds, the Rain within the rain. Golden rays radiated gloriously into the sky as if the sun was rising from below, shining brilliantly upward.

Urana dove and weaved between the broken strands of energy, catching out chasing Lore between the lethal beams. The skies around Atronia was a kaleidoscopic blizzard of frenzied energy, Urana finding it difficult to navigate even with her comms directing her movements. And the noise was deafening; the air popping, fizzing, and tearing. The shouts of battle or for help over comms were traumatising as brave Placians screamed, cried, and died. Then the rush of sound was sucked away and Urana realised it was she who was screaming the loudest as she lanced a Lore through its head. And then the skies were suddenly clear.

Urana twisted in the sky. The Lore *were* gone. With the geologic artillery silent, the volcanic engines were reined in and vented by the controllers operating from Urana's mountain. And with the Lore-choked atmosphere empty, the oppressive sound of nothingness pressed down on her. She almost laughed as a dozen-strong flock of white-winged, black-bodied *skops* flew by as if the war was just a minor inconvenience to them. As she followed their flight, her eyes caught the strange flickering of Magna Aura.

I hope you have a plan for that, brother! she thought.

This is it, thought Cirrius. Once again, the Lore return from dark dreams to prey upon the innocent of the universe. But this time, by the will of our forefathers, they would be defeated once and for all.

He looked around him, raised his replica of his father's metastaff and yelled, "Once for glory, once and for all! Charge!" He took off into the sky, metastaff crackling with energy.

Teron led his force upward, bellowing "To the heavens and back, almighty flight!" instilling instant confidence in his charges.

The singing had continued in defiance of the Lore attack, seeming to give the warriors an anchor in the carnage that would follow, but Cirrius blocked it out, the sound of fury the only music he was listening to. He shoved his staff straight through a Lore. It screamed, energy washing over Cirrius from an effigy of a mouth before it disintegrated, hundreds more taking its place. But Cirrius was up to the challenge.

Over the skies of Halcyon similar battles took place. Kica and Phorgo fought back-to-back, plasma staffs emitting an endless stream of energy against the Lore.

"Yeah, come on, come on!" Kica shouted.

She was scared out of her wits, sweating from the heat and light shed by the Lore bordering on unbearable levels, her manoeuvre suit's forcefield barely coping with them. Out of the corner of her eye, she could see the battles raging, many of her comrades falling from the sky and that frightened her even more.

Behind her, Phorgo shouted more profanities than she knew existed, bringing a smile to her face. But that proved fatal, her concentration lapsed and Lore swept down from above. A limb of uncertain energy sliced through her neck. Her head tumbled, still smiling as it dropped in tandem with the lifeless body, dead hands clutching the plasma staff.

Phorgo felt the heat sear his neck and looked around for his partner.

"No!" he roared. "No! No!" he continued, firing erratically, until he was engulfed by the Lore, his body burning as it fell out of the air, a defiant "No!" smoking from his open mouth.

The Lore plunged down from the heavens, met by stalwart warriors, the screams of the other-worldly striking fear into the hearts of many. The air turned dark, evil storms brewed as clouds absorbed Lore energy and thunder echoed in the distance. The wind whipped up an unsettling hot and cold mixture, often with the odious scent of charred remains. Sky Warriors lost limbs, blood raining from the skies onto others, some of whom didn't notice and fought bravely on.

Lore were corralled and unmercifully set upon, their energy forms bursting apart, the energy recollected by the plasma staffs and used again and again. One Lore exploded, but caught a warrior in its wake, the warrior's dying scream still heard even after he disintegrated.

Halcyon City's plasma guns defended the city, re-calibrated for

Lore energy, but stray and Lore-deflected strikes hit Sky Warrior and Lore alike, the action fast and furious. Lore streaked through the air, striking the city, which lurched perceptibly, flames licking the upper surface. More Lore followed, invading the sky city.

Tol Valar led his loyal Sky Warriors in after them, while Brank kept them at bay from outside. This city couldn't be allowed to fall, as had Magna City minutes ago, now a wreck sinking to the bottom of the sea.

The fierce air war raged on, with Journ and Tima leading their sections over the now vacant skies where Magna City had once hung. Half their force was gone and the battle was getting heavier. They knew what they had to do and they turned to each other for the last time. Their faces were blackened from the smoke of the burning city and fellow warriors, the air so thick with the sickening smell of burnt flesh that it was hard to breathe.

Tima held out her hand to Journ, "By strength above!" She was blinking heavily from the heavy dust in the air.

A torso fell by Journ, covering him with more blood, as he replied "Air Warrior! Sky Superior!"

And he looked up to see more torn and bloodied bodies falling toward him. Then out of the corner of his eye, something bright and massive entered the atmosphere.

The unmistakable rock-hewn form of Vista Mare rocketed down, a red-hot tail trailing behind. Towers, buildings and other structures not burned up were tumbling in chunks and broken sections off the surface of the asteroid creating smaller meteorites. Craters split apart belching forth dead bodies, exploding skimmers, wrecked equipment, and more pulverised rock. Even though it was miles away, the on-rushing wind was searing and howling. Tima and Journ watched in horror as the Star Warrior headquarters hit the ocean in an ear-splitting crash which caused underwater quakes, giant tsunamis, and huge plumes of water sizzling into the air. The sky smelled of death.

Before the super-heated cascading water splashed down, Lore ascended from the waves, leaving behind a whirlpool of a tomb for Vista Mare, the water bubbling away as it boiled. The Lore soared upward toward Journ in a solid line of fire, energy crackling around their forms, which changed from shapeless into rough caricatures of Celestians.

Journ and his sections instantly charged, plasma staffs firing away, Lore disappeared, exploding into bits of nothingness. Journ screamed; his fury fully arrayed against the Lore as he flew an intricate pattern of evasion turning, soaring, diving, firing in every direction available to him. It was getting so dark now, though it wasn't midday yet, that he shouldn't have been able to see, but the Lore were easy prey, their blinding-light forms, marking out their presence. Journ turned to see the cause of the darkness, for the clouds had not formed an impenetrable barrier. And what he saw made his heart cold. The sun had dimmed.

Dark splotches covered it and even as he witnessed that, the winds picked up and howled in unison with the Lore, as if in victory. But he wasn't about to allow that—No way was he about to

. . .

A sharp stab of pain caused Journ to look down. An arm of energy had neatly sliced through his chest from behind. He watched as if in a dream as the arm withdrew, before it ate upward toward his neck. He fell, twisting onto his back, spinning around and around, his last sight, before it went all dark, was of a bright, blue star twinkling in the distance.

What a pretty star! he thought, before death.

"Noooo!" screamed Tima, as she watched her beloved Journ crash from the sky. But she had no time to grieve. The Lore were upon her. Her last thoughts were of being reunited with Journ and telling him about his youngling she was carrying.

Brace looked around him. He was the only Sky Leader in the area. He had to rally the Warriors. He held his plasma-staff aloft.

"On me!" he commed. "On me, warriors!"

Sky-marks heard; broken sections fell into order, lines formed, and rose to the challenge. They followed.

Brace made to thrust himself through the air and take the fight to the enemy. He did not make it, riven in half by a Lore, as he turned. He had no time to scream, dying instantly.

Sky Command's crystalators registered every Sky Warrior's death, Journ's just another disappeared blue-dot statistic to them, but his fellow warriors felt it keenly. Then just as quickly, the whole of Tima's section's signals had blinked out, closely followed by Brace.

Deb looked at the floor, blinking away tears for her dying friends. She tried to feel her power, but it just wasn't coming. She needed to be out there. She yearned to be out there.

"Sir, the energy reading you were anticipating has just entered the outer atmosphere and is descending rapidly," a Sky-mark reported, just as Sky Command was rocked by another explosion.

The retort of the base's plasma weapons could be heard through the decks, their own success recorded by the crystalators erasing red dots from the screen, but not enough compared to the blues.

"Thank you, Sky-mark," Gal Agar said.

Deb could read his features and she feared for the worst. Cirrius had indicated that one Lore would have readings different to all the others and could so be easily detected. If they targeted and destroyed him, then the other Lore might lose heart and be easier to defeat. It was a dangerous strategy, but the most viable one in defeating the Lore.

As if unable to contain himself no longer, Gal Agar addressed his deputy:

"Dessa, you are in command here."

She almost stammered in resistance, but with a look of pure intimidation, Gal Agar cowed the resistant Dessa in acceptance. Gal Agar armed himself, cocking his head for Deb to follow.

The Sky Commander stepped to the nearest transtube outside the bridge and they rode up to an airlock. And with Deb by his side they flew into battle. As they hit the choking air, Gal Agar regarded the presence beside him and vowed that her father would never claim her back.

Cirrius' forces had retreated from Centron, the Lore becoming increasingly resistant. Something had strengthened them, and as Cirrius had crossed the meridian from night into day, he saw the reason why. There, materialising with another core of Lore, was their master, the Traitor Synther. He shone magnificently, apart from his followers, all the while obliterating forces in their path, and though vast amounts of plasma-staffed warriors converged on them, slaying many Lore, only the blue leader remained constant. Then Cirrius saw the distant forms of Gal Agar and Deb ascending to engage the Prime Lore.

Gal Agar valiantly rallied the forces around him, directing the attack himself. Deb had never seen him fight before, but the vigour in her commander was very evident, dispatching Lore after Lore;

his plasma-staff firing rapidly, while he swooped, twisted and turned away from danger.

So preoccupied was she by Gal Agar's skills that she didn't see the Lore behind her until it was too late. It touched her. And not even her manoeuvre suit burned. Deb and the Lore stared at each other, the moment seemingly frozen in Deb's mind. In the dimmest of notions, she felt the Lore and herself communicating; she was the one they had come for. Deb's eyes widened in surprise, her secret found out, and before she knew it, she was surrounded by others. She turned around, the Lore regarding her silently, subliminal messages encoded in energy bursts, she somehow understood, urging her to accompany them. She reluctantly followed them, not able to look back at the devastated battlefield below. After stubbornly persisting with them through a massive grey cloud, the sky turned a brilliant blue, irradiated by the presence that hovered majestically, the one history knew as the Traitor Synther; her father.

A shocked Cirrius witnessed Deb taken prisoner and urgently pursued her into the deadening sky through clouds of poisoned air and a hail of vengeful Lore. He fought them off, slashing his way through, using his powers to create a barrier of hard air around himself, to slow their assault on him, then using his staff to destroy them. It was almost pitch dark, save for the shining Lore.

Cirrius found himself surrounded and severely outnumbered.

So, it ends, he thought, readying for a fight to the death.

A piercing bolt of blinding energy destroyed the encircling Lore, as Sceptre barrelled in firing energy from both hands with wide swathes of lethal rays.

Cirrius grinned at him in gratefulness, but there was no time to dwell in reflection. He continued upward, even as Sceptre, not aware of Deb's grim predicament, reported:

"Placia's mostly under control, Swords gone, City-States salvageable. What next?" he said as Cirrius had ascended.

"The Anti-god has taken Deb!" Cirrius snarled, pointing upward.

Sceptre followed his gaze. He said nothing, but his shock and anger grew, as he trekked with Cirrius through the stormy clouds, the ravaging winds threatening to scour them. On passing through, Sceptre beheld the sight before him, the sky lit up, but further up on the edge of the atmosphere, he saw a magenta light shining away:

"Phasia?" he whispered.

But in an instant, it had disappeared.

In the distance, Cirrius saw Gal Agar approaching opposite them. Their eyes met, an instant strategy formed, Gal Agar attacking from behind, Sceptre on the flank, and Cirrius full on.

The three charged simultaneously. Deb was almost at the Traitor's hands. At full velocity, Cirrius and Sceptre fired everything they had, squarely hammering the Traitor Synther in the chest, and Gal Agar targeting the back. But with one wave of a hand, a blast of blue energy repulsed all three, sending them into free-fall.

Sceptre hazily recovered first, halting his fall, somersaulting to face the Lore again. He fired a sustained ray of energy against the leader of the Lore. That didn't seem to faze Synther. But somehow, wordlessly, instructing a group of ravenous followers to hold onto Deb, the Traitor Synther himself descended through the poisoned air into personal battle with Sceptre. Blue and yellow energies lit up the sky as energy was hurled at each other with increasing ferocity.

Imprisoned above the horrifying duel, Deb saw Cirrius and Gal

Agar trying to outflank Synther and a terrible premonition came to her. But before the two could reach the Traitor Synther, who had been toying with Sceptre, the Lore leader knocked the Starguard from the skies with a brutal punch, Sceptre disappearing into the bright burning haze below. And in one swift movement, he then suddenly reached out with his energy, catching the two new would-be attackers off-guard in blue beams of energy, pulling them toward him and certain death. Deb struggled free of the Lore and desperately dashed down toward the three.

"Father, no!" she yelled, the words sounding bitter in her mouth, but it achieved the desired effect.

The blue form turned toward her, blue eyes concentrating on her like alien blazing suns, as he clutched the Starguard and Sky Warrior. And then a crackling, hissing voice had emanated from an opening that could have been construed as a mouth.

"You know of me? You are part of me. But you are not one with me," the Traitor Synther spoke. "Join with usss," he hissed, emphasising the Lore surrounding them. "Join us and they will live," he shook his two prisoners.

"No, Deb! No! He's lying!" shouted Gal Agar, writhing in the traitor's grasp. "He'll kill us all and take your soul," he yelled through clenched teeth.

Deb knew he spoke the truth, but the fate of the system lay with her. "Let them go, leave these worlds, and I will join you," she promised, tears swelling in her eyes.

The gap on the hideous face widened into a smile. "My daughter, you will have your wisssh, but first, I must demand a sign of your . . . willingnessss," his voice fizzled, energy streaming from his mouth in laughter. "Kill thisss one." He held out Cirrius.

Deb's heart beat like never before, wanting to pound its way out of her chest and the air left her lungs as if she was breathing under water. But Deb couldn't believe her ears when Cirrius had shouted to her: "No, Deb, kill Gal Agar. It's the only way."

"Are you crazy, Cirrius?" Deb shouted.

Gal Agar tried to look across at Cirrius, but the grip on his neck increased. Deb looked from Cirrius to Gal Agar and back.

Kill Gal Agar?

"Deb, do it!" Cirrius managed to choke out. "Your powers, Deb. Emotional. . . release."

He was choked off by the grip of death, a gurgling sound ending with a quick terrible-sounding snap. The Traitor Synther released Cirrius' lifeless body, which fell tumbling through the black air.

The Traitor Synther stared at her. "Ssso, this one means something to you," he hissed, shaking Gal Agar about by his neck. "He will remain alive, as long as you do my bidding."

"No, Deb. It would be... fate worse than...coff...coff... death. D... Do... don't follow him. Do what...coff... have to do: K...K...kill me!" he yearned, tears welling up in his eyes. "Kill me!"

"I can't! I don't know how! Tell me how?" she screamed.

"Enough, daughter. Follow me, or you all die," the Traitor delivered his ultimatum.

Deb's heart threatened to out-beat its already deadly pace, her decision made quicker than its thundering rhythm. "I will do what you say, father."

It took Gal Agar and Synther a split second to realise that Deb had addressed Gal Agar. By that time, Deb had surged forward intent on killing Gal Agar with a fatal blow at that speed, but Synther was faster, his body melting into a ball of supercharged energy, engulfing Gal Agar, just as Deb reached its corona.

Deb was destroyed even before she reached the core of the being that would be the destruction of all.

As soon as the two Sky Warriors were vapourised, the

triumphant Traitor Synther sent out the final message to the rest of the Lore: "Destroy!"

Sword Commandarian was shaking itself to pieces, the intra-system engines not meant to travel at the speed at which they were now operating.

This is madness! thought General Ede.

They were almost at the outskirts of Magna Aura's flaring atmosphere where individual Lore could be seen on crystalator images. The beleaguered sun was crawling with Lore, more and more numbers pouring onto it.

Calmly, Star-mark Oleon reported, "Sir, Lore numbers increasing." Then he had looked up in complete astonishment. "Oh, Gods!"

Before General Ede could ask for clarification, Magna Aura pulsed, a giant wall of energy blowing outward. *Commandarian* disintegrated. Uncaringly, the pulse wave carried on, washing over Nexa, spreading out to the ends of the system.

On Placia, amid the volcanic cascades, Urana and her victorious warriors looked up, shielding their eyes as a giant plume of energy sliced through their world, cutting it into two, before it exploded.

Sceptre's body lay on an island, unconscious. He didn't notice as the same plume ripped apart Halcyon, the air blown away, Sky Warriors and cities alike plummeting from the sky. Spared the indignity of exploding, Halcyon was bombarded with the remains of Placia. All life extinguished, forever.

Magna Prime, already dead, save for two wrecked City-States orbiting it, was sucked of its gaseous environs. On Millennius City-

State, the survivors huddled in their shelters and were mercifully unaware when the fatal wave crashed over them.

Only on Alphatron did they see the end. Decion embraced the twins, who stood before him, as they stared out at the ever-brightening, incoming wave.

Altair's eyes itched. He hadn't wanted to lose; not this way.

"See you in the Garden of Death," he saluted the others and despite the brightness, he did not close his eyes.

The Magna Aura system died—the last inhabitants of the once great Celestian civilisation wiped out.

The Traitor Synther revelled in his greatest victory. But at what cost? He had lost a daughter. He would have valued her above all others. He wondered if other offspring of his might have survived. There had been many. But he had sensed only Deb.

Even amongst the dark rubble of the smashed worlds, his feeling that something was wrong had invaded his thoughts again. He looked around, his eyes darting heavenward piercing the void, searching for an answer. And at last, he found it. One of his 'loyal' subjects was missing. He should have known, should have realised it sooner. Treachery ran deep in his family: betrayed first by his daughter—and now by his sister.

Phasia was gone, but he could still sense her afterthought, after all she was a Lore. And all he could hear were her thoughts:

This should not have been!

The Traitor Synther stared out into the infinite void, again. There was a reckoning on the way and time would be on her side

Epilogue: Pastfuture

A sparkling globe of magenta energy plummeted through the heavens on its way toward a small blue planet, where an ordinary sun slowly rose above the mists of ancient plains.

There had been an ancient battle here once, lost in the Time of Adantus. But now a new dawn was rising over new heroes—heroes born of Celestian Knights, lost adventurers lost to history, champions of time.

They would be taught their lost heritage, guided and honed, their destiny shown to them and only then would they return to defeat the Lore.

It was only a matter of time.

INTERLUDE

Anatolia, 1201 BC

The sun slowly ate its inexorable way above the cloying mists, gradually stretching its rays over a succession of wide, grassy plains of an ancient land. As the foggy greyness burned away, long weedy grass bent in the morning breeze and the peculiar noises of myriad waking inhabitants of the land and air welcomed the day, as if a worldly veil had been lifted.

A proud stallion whinnied in the distance, its black head nudging against its reins, held by its gloved rider.

Xathanius, a noble warrior of uncertain origin, sat at the head of his band of warriors whose services he had offered to the Mycenaean King in this particular affair. His handsome weathered face and graceful bearing epitomised an eliteness rarely seen, his stature as a warrior befitting such a man who had battled hard for many and been rewarded—his leather armour was embellished with gold. And now with his hundred or so mounted men behind him and further back, with glistening swords, a thousand foot-soldiers poised on the brink of battle, he was repaying their favour. His brother Helexius, cousins Lazeron and Cal Xarien, and their great friend Halydon were lined up beside him. If only his father could have seen them. But he died years ago.

Across the wide scraggly plain, lined up rank after rank against them, were the awaiting enemy, vast in number. The stoic Xathanius estimated that they were heavily outnumbered ten to one. But he didn't care. Victory would be theirs today. The Mycenaean King's forces waited patiently ready to attack on the far side of the foreign city, whose stone-grey walls were magnificently built, massive sloping blocks protecting against all comers. Horses on both sides were restless, whinnying in anticipation. Xathanius had never observed his horse react this way before battle.

No bad omens, today! he beseeched of Zeus.

An eerie silence extended between the two armies, seeming to stretch further than the distance they had travelled to be here. Xathanius held his powerful steed back, silently soothing its jitters with calming whispers and a firm pat along its neck, his confidence slowly calming not only his horse, but his men as well. Not long now. The emerging sun had yet to reach a certain point on its unending journey, which would signal the start of their attack.

He continued watching the sun.

Any second now. Any second . . .

"Haah!" he roared, his upraised left arm chopping the air, his horse already spurred into motion, having felt the emotion of his master.

It pulled on the leather reins, bolting across the rough terrain, followed by the relentless thunder of hundreds of hooves as they beat the ground, following the order of Xathanius:

"Charge!"

They raced headlong into the on-rushing enemy, trampling grass under hoof, clumps of cold mud thrown up in the haze of the morning air. The warriors clashed with each other along a little dip in the plain, where a steady stream wended its way, the two armies mated together in a clash of masses—human, animal, and bronze metal stirred together. The clashing and clanging of metal rang throughout the land, each army beating sordid red paths toward the heart of the other. Men were trampled, caught beneath the hooves of horses, swords and spears chopped away and pierced, dropping men in agonising death. Hails of arrows killed the unwary; the unlucky wounded kicked and hacked to death as they fell. Others tried to flee the brutal nightmare of war. It was all too much for them.

Anger, greed, fear and bloodlust; Xathanius had felt such emotion before, but not like this, not all welled up into a frenzied stomach-churning knot of confusion and pain. He'd never been in a battle like this, though his father had been in worse. Blood soaked the ground, screams of terror and death seeming to match his own of rapture as he cut down another enemy warrior.

The orb of energy swung around the world, searching, before plunging into the fragile atmosphere, breaking through the wispy clouds, a sentient quality guiding it toward the right place. It spun, spiralled and crackled energy, veering down to the ground in a graceful sparkling sweep of its newly formed tail, an almost beautiful, but fearful light.

The unrelenting clamour of battle drowned out all. It filled the plains, echoing through the cowering villagers within the fortress walls, out over the surrounding hills and fertile land, toward the wine dark sea and his home islands. . .

Surely they could hear our victory in Mycenae! thought Xathanius, the murderous din thundering in his ears.

He savagely slashed and stabbed his way toward the towering walls of the city, rushing forth, spitting blood from his cut mouth, an unfortunate blow from the enemy, who had fatally paid for his transgression. In the distance, he could see the purple robe of his brother, Helexius, flying in the wind; the green of Lazeron, the red of Cal Xarien, and the black of Halydon, all four cutting triumphant paths toward the enemy's heart, the city's walls, and victory.

The magenta sphere of light rushed down in apparent glee, having found its intended targets. It spiralled down in splendid twists, meandering toward the bloody action below, increasing speed, urgent in its quest.

A glint in the corner of Xathanius' eye became reality as he spied the magenta wonder on its hades-bent declivitous path from Zeus himself.

An Omen? The Gods have come to help us? He watched in awe and bemusement, not afraid of the oncoming force.

The shiny globe beguiled him, spoke to him, as it became an awesome blot upon the sky. Every warrior had now ceased fighting. They raised their heads to the heavens bathed in a horrorful purple glare. Horses jumped, skidded, rearing up in defiance. But it was too late to escape.

Contact!

The explosion ripped the ground apart, shrouding all in darkness.

Many years before

The haze from around Xathanius cleared.

"How will we survive now, Thanni?" asked Zasandra from her rocky perch as her older brother somberly strode up beside her to give her a comforting hug.

Spheron had disappeared into the snowy distance during the night. And now he, Xathanius, in his infinite wisdom as an eighteen-year-old, announced:

"I am the leader now. We'll do what Spheron wanted us to do, so pack your things."

It wasn't much of a decision, but the answer seemed fine enough for Zasandra.

From further back in the spacious cave the rest of the youngsters stood around. Xathanius' and Zasandra's younger brother Helexius heaved a sad sigh before obeying his brother's wishes.

In their turn, his older cousins, Lazeron and Cal Xarien, their long black hair ruffled by the breeze, glared at him, before Cal, the eldest brother, turned sharply on his heels, followed as always by Lazeron. They had returned from a hunt and finished skinning the fallow deer for their journey ahead. Their bows were still slung over their shoulders, though one day they would carry the weapons bequeathed them by their mother. They wrapped those up in strong leather bindings and then distributed food sacks amongst them. Though they were older and bigger than Xathanius and prone to unjust intimidation at times, they would follow him, for now. But Xathanius wondered what would happen if they decided to really flex their powers. Things had gotten much worse since their mother had died and they were quick in exercising authority.

Zasandra seemed frail, like the native people of this world, but she had a steely determination to copy whatever Xathanius did, though she was more apt to being led by their mischievous cousins. She also had a tendency to bully Helexius who sometimes goaded her just for the attention. They missed their mother, non-Celestian though she might have been even though they had barely been old enough to remember her when their father had taken them away into the mountains all those years ago.

Halydon, though sullen, had already packed. The son of Spheron had been more fortunate than the others since Spheron had died last. Halydon's upbringing had been less affected, the young exegete becoming Xathanius' best friend just as Spheron had to Xathanius' father. On the night prior to his death, Spheron had instructed them to leave the isolation of the mountains and seek a life among the natives. He had always said that in order to learn about the world, one must live among its people. All prepared, Xathanius had led them down to civilisation.

It had been hard at first, six young adults leading a life of their own. However, soon their superior skills and knowledge as they grew older had secured them with power, wealth, and status. Without explicitly having to explain their origins to neighbours and would-be employers, they'd been regarded as journeying from places just far enough away to be plausible. Spheron had taught them everything from the sacred Scrolls of History, which somehow, even with the end of his world on Galatia, had not prevented him from parting with his most beloved memories, and spurred him to copy or recite the book to the children. At times, it had been the only thing he cared about and often he had preached endlessly to them that it held the key to their futures and that one day, their destiny would be realised.

"The Scrolls of History remembered all and foresaw all," Spheron had oft said.

He had also taught them how to use their intellect, strength, and limited powers effectively, that they could live among the people without suspicion.

That these people on a distant world existed had come as quite a shock. The End on Galatia had not been settled well. Xathanius' father had always regretted following Alphatronius' dubious claims of escape. The Scrolls of History should have been followed as written: the thousandth generation of Celestian Knights should have been the last. But they had broken that prophecy; tempted fate. And the universes would suffer as a consequence.

As the children had oft been told by their parents, Millennius, Destina and Spheron had escaped together, having lost the path set by Alphatronius and trailed by Elysius. The three had then been captured by the Lore and taken to the Helstar, the Lore's abode—a sentient star, created by the living bodies of other Lore. A daring escape and battle had ensued, but the subsequent traverse through Lore-infested portals had somehow affected them—adversely.

They had been weakened by some sickness transmitted from the Lore during their escape and battle. The three Celestian Knights had never talked about what had happened to them, only that they had wasted in the wilderness of the nether, aimlessly wandering the stars, until this tiny world had been found. Upon exploring their new world, they had discovered beings such as themselves, but much inferior. Spheron, after much contemplation, had deduced their origins: these beings were Fifth in nature, an original species, but inferior in order to Celestians.

The ancient Antiqchronals Quest of Adantus had been deemed a failure, but here was proof that Adantus had indeed found and encountered the primeval Lore in what he had called the Meriddian System and that the sole survivor Olesseus' stories had been true. The harrowed survivors of the Lore battle had then settled on the world they had called Destinia. But from the primitiveness of the current natives' societies, the Celestian descendants had either forgotten or forsaken their past heritage and interbred with this world's people. The only clues to the ancient Celestian visitation had been contained in their language, some of which the three Celestian Knights had understood anywhere they had journeyed, being derivatives of tongues from the Six Worlds.

The three had undauntedly travelled the new world for untold decades, discovering places and mysteries not yet known to the indigenous dwellers, until they had finally settled down in an area that was the nascent hub of the known world. And eventually, they formed lasting relationships with locals with whom they had children—part Celestian, part Fifth. The six children were now the first generation of a new breed.

On the children's coming of age and the emergence of their powers, the elder Celestian Knights had withdrawn them from their homes and abandoned the village along the Aegean for the solitude of the isolated mountains far to the northeast across two seas. In a painstaking decision, all human ties had been broken, and they had travelled alone; their human parents never to be seen again. It was only then in the mountains that the young children had been told of their incredible true nature and destinies. The future of this world could depend on them. And from that day, their lives had been dedicated to the ideals of the Celestian Knights.

Ten years later, their parents were gone. Millennius and Destina, as was the ancient custom, had wandered off to die and now lay eternally somewhere in those eastern mounts. Spheron had lasted a few years more, teaching and training the children as much as he could in the old ways.

His last words to them had been: "The sickness which claimed your parents has conversely made your half-human/half-Celestian selves stronger, different to all the other Celestian Knights who have ever lived. And someday, the time will come when that difference will save the universe!" His haggard face had then smiled wisely.

Two days later, the children had been left alone when Spheron had disappeared into the haze of snowy mists, forever . .

The haze from around Xathanius cleared.

He looked around him, dazed. The whole tragic battlefield had been razed, the city blazed away behind him, the walls blackened by the deadly impact of whatever had hit them. A crunching noise made him turn sharply to his left, and he saw Helexius, trudging over the charred remains of men, horses, and battle gear. Lazeron's green cape fluttered in the burning breeze as he made his way over through the rubble with Cal Xarien, followed by Halydon dusting the desiccated land off his hands. They were the only survivors. Their unique heritage had saved them. But then they realised that had been the intention all along, as they witnessed one of the most startling transformations.

From out of the blackened ground, not fifty yards away, a vaporous swirl of magenta coiled up, to be joined by another swirl from not far away, and another, until a veritable whirlwind had been created from the adjoining swirls and in a rush of energy, it had imploded in a dazzling burst, the vague outline of a woman coalescing from flames of magenta. Around her were fiery wings of radiant pink and purple, flexing for a brief moment before they melted away back into the body of the woman. Xathanius couldn't believe his eyes. His father had told him many times about this person, the one he had loved more than any other and now she was here.

This world had been graced by the presence of Phasia.

"Young Millennius, I bid thee greetings," she addressed him warmly.

He bowed slightly, indicating her perceptiveness. "I am Xathanius, son of Millennius. And it is I who is honoured to greet you, Phasia," he said as humbly as he could.

"You talk as your father would, young sire, but time is short and I need his counsel as never before." She sounded distressed to Xathanius and his awkward silence enhanced her fears. "Millennius still resides in this universe of life, does he not?" she inquired, purple flame licking about her head in consternation.

"No, Phasia," Xathanius replied. "He walked the way of death some years ago." He remembered it as if it was yesterday, but it had been twenty years ago now. "Destina and Spheron have also passed."

He looked at her carefully. She seemed in genuine need, but he didn't know if to completely trust her. The last his father had ever seen of Phasia was on her disappearance, later to appear at the side of her brother, the Traitor Synther. It had broken Millennius' heart and led to his unfortunate agreement with Alphatronius and Spheron's plans. Everything he had held as sacred, he had let go in an effort to obliterate the love he had for Phasia. Yet she still lived. Had she repented and sought Millennius' forgiveness or was this a ploy to wipe out the last of the Celestian Knights legacy?

Phasia, staring as solemnly at Xathanius as he was at her, grasped the nature of his thoughts.

"I am sorry to hear of the passing of Millennius, Destina, and Spheron. They were great heroes," she said with controlled effort, though the feeling in her voice emanated great sorrow. "I am not here to destroy, Xathanius, but to save. I did join my brother, the Traitor Synther, who used to be kin to me. I tried to save him, divert him from his monstrous course, spy on him, use him to tame the Lore for good, but it was no use! He is wild! He is evil! He must be destroyed!" she shook her head forlornly, her eyes staring off into nothingness.

The wind whipped around as if wailing in sympathy.

"So, I broke free. However, there is a problem. As you must have been told, there is another branch of the Celestian Knight progeny in the far reaches of space. They are the Starguards, the first sons and daughters of the Celestian Knights, and they had founded a new civilisation with the millions who had escaped prior to The End. They need our help, for the Lore have attacked them. It was their destruction which helped me to break free of my bonds. I had tried to alter the past, but every time I tried, I failed!"

"Naturally, for the past cannot be changed," interrupted Lazeron.

"Untrue . . ."

"Lazeron," he introduced himself, "Son of Destina."

Phasia nodded a greeting.

Phasia continued, "Doubtless, Lazeron, your mother told you of our clashes. I hope it is not the same between you and me. So, I tell you, the past can be changed. And for our sakes, it must be!"

Lazeron tilted his head in mannerly acknowledgement.

"What makes you think we can help you?" asked Xathanius.

A wide smile crossed Phasia's purple lips as if she held a secret about to be released. "As the Lore have the ability to travel time, so do you. I can sense it within you. You have either been touched by Lore nature or it seems your parents and this world have given you their strengths in all things time, but not the weakness that would turn you into Lore."

The news hit them like a sword blow.

"Really?" Cal Xarien guffawed, folding his arms, scepticism written on his smirking face.

Phasia appeared undaunted. "Yes, I can feel it. It is what drew me here from unfathomable depths of time and space. All of you concentrated here on one world. And if I can find you, so will Synther."

Xathanius deferred to Halydon, son of the sage. "Is this possible?"

Halydon, ever thoughtful like his father nodded his head and looked ashamed at what he was about to tell them. "My father knew this day would come." He sighed heavily about to release a great weight from his soul. "My father imparted to me this knowledge in the event that he could not. Long ago, with their failing crystalators, he studied the sickness that had consumed their life-force. He determined that it was a temporal virus, carried by the Lore. Synther had experimented on our parents trying to turn them into Lore. The virus was transmitted to our parents, during the pitched battle with the Lore through the portal. But those viruses became part of our half-human genetic structure. If my father was correct, then the virus has given us the ability to use our innate energy to travel time."

Xathanius stared at Halydon aghast. "Why was this not told to us before?"

His father had always told him to be wary of Spheron's words as they oft concealed the truth. And here was his son confirming that fact.

Halydon shook his head lamentably. "They were ashamed. Abjectly so. And afraid. They had broken the prophecy and this was their punishment. They did not want to taint us with their failure." He pursed his lips in regret, knowing he had lost some trust.

"Be that as it may, the rest is true," claimed Phasia, empathising with Halydon. "It is disconcerting what Synther had done, but the virus *has* enhanced your natural Celestian Knight powers and is now part of you, your siblings and the young ones—do not think that I didn't know about the others. I can feel them, too!" The five men tensed, ready to unleash their powers if Phasia uttered one word of threat against them. But she smiled. "I am not here to make threats. I am asking for your help. The Starguards and the Celestians of Magna Aura need your help. We can defeat the Lore. We can destroy Synther!"

"How?" asked Xathanius.

"I will show you. I will guide you, train you, take you on the path to destiny. But there are some things we must do first." She affirmed with a strange smile on her face. There was a hint of swift movement and before anyone could do anything, Phasia raised her arms and an enormous wave of energy spilled out of her to absorb them.

If anyone had been watching, they would have seen a blinding purple light engulf the five men and as quickly as that had happened, the six warriors had disappeared into thin air, leaving the burning city of Troy to the pages of poems and history.

Out of Time

The wonder-struck Starguards looked around at each other. One minute they had been on Halcyon going about their business, the next they had arrived here, somewhere, somehow. It was totally dark. They were encompassed by nothingness as if on the edge of eternity. They were totally alone, until they noticed the six figures who stood in even darker shadows.

"Who are you?" asked Sceptre into the gloominess, hands ready to blaze golden death.

"And where are Novan and Azure?" Cirrius inquired, quickly noticing their absence.

"We are distant kin," said a voice. "I am Lord Aeon, son of Millennius," he announced. "I come with my brother, Lord Helexius; my sister, Timechantress; Netherlord and Archron, the sons of Destina, and Spheron, son of Spheron. We have come to save you from the Lore!"

The other shadowy figures remained silent.

The Starguards, after a brief stir of bewilderment and surprise, digested the news.

"What makes you think we need your help?" Decion growled.

"And where are the other two?" insisted Cirrius, raising his voice.

"Novan has already left, as he must," Lord Aeon said. "And as for Azure, she must not be told her true nature."

"But we already have," replied a confused Sceptre.

"We will return you to a time before those actions unfold again. Everything, save disclosing Azure's true nature, will be as before," declared Lord Aeon.

"Why must she not know?" asked an exasperated Cirrius. "She is the daughter of the Traitor Synther. She can destroy him!"

"We have seen the future. The consequence of your actions will destroy Magna Aura. She must not know, until her time comes!"

"We are of equal, if not superior stature to you, *Lord* Aeon," Decion said, paying mock respect, "Who are you to dictate to us? Show yourselves!" He grabbed for his sword, only to find it missing.

"We are the Astrals," Lord Aeon declared—portentously, proudly.

And in a blink of an eye, everything vanished.

CHAPTER NINE

Magna Aura. Past time

"My mother, the Goddess Elysius, is alive," announced Novan, the following resounding silence magnifying the importance of his words.

The stunned Starguards looked at one another, each realising they had not been dreaming—the Astrals had indeed been real. And they were reliving the past.

Novan's words had come as before, the outcome of The End on Galatia, the fate of the Celestian Knights and all the commotion that followed, until Cirrius had found himself face to face with Deb and Classia.

"Why, Cirrius, however did you come by such a lovely escort?" Novan leaned enquiringly toward his fellow Starguard. "And you are?" he addressed Classia.

The brunette Sky Warrior looked faint-hearted, but managed to say, "Sky Leader Classia, sir." And then almost immediately, "I would like to join you in . . . on the journey, I mean," she said, a slight blush covering a dazzling smile.

"We shall see," Novan replied kindly and then he had turned to Deb, Cirrius resisting the urge to introduce her himself, as he had done before.

"I am Sky Leader Deneb, sir," Deb said.

Cirrius couldn't fail to notice that the two still seemed instantly captivated with each other, but before any real connection could be made, Cirrius intervened.

"Uh, Novan, we must move on," Cirrius said in exaggerated urgency. Turning to the Sky Leaders, he said, "I thank you for your service to the Sky Warriors. May your beauty instil in others the same adoration which has be-stilled my heart," he said kissing each on the hand, to their delighted and surprised glee.

The two Starguards were then lost in the multitudinous background.

"Lyrics, Cirrius?" asked a bemused Novan, once they were alone in an alcove. "That is unlike you."

"There's a time and place for everything, Novan," responded Cirrius, surprised at his own distraction technique.

"Umm, I suppose. By the way, did you feel anything unusual about Sky Leader Deneb? Isn't she one of Gal Agar's favourites?"

"She's extremely beautiful. That's all I know about her."

"You are right there, Sky Lord. Hopefully, that won't be the last I see of her."

Cirrius looked at Novan. There were some things that time couldn't change and true love was one of them.

From a place out of time, Xathanius, Lord Aeon of the Astrals avidly watched through the dimension crystal within the oracle room, as the events on Magna Aura unfolded. Beside him was Phasia, magenta flames casting eerie shadows about her face.

"Have we done enough, Phasia?" asked Lord Aeon.

He was clad in armour, inspired by his last battle at Troy. Phasia had fashioned each Astral with a similar close-fitting vortexite manoeuvre suit worn by both the Celestian Knights and the Starguards. Xathanius' basic black armour was overlaid with sim-leather and chainmail over his left torso and arm. His long brown boots were interlaced with gold inlays winding around his calves, as were his gloved forearms and wide belt. A round gold cloak clasp with an infinity symbol etched within held his original deer-hide cape trimmed with black bear fur. He had hunted the animals himself and was proud to have used all their parts for food, shelter, and for aspects of his uniform in the past. The whole ensemble was infused with his energy affording protection under temporal shields.

"We shall know, in time, young Lord," Phasia answered. She shifted views, passing her hand over the crystal, observing several key positions simultaneously.

After that fateful meeting on the battlefields around Troy, the Astrals had been born. After a quick trip to Mycenae, where all their children and Zasandra—all future Astrals—resided, Phasia had voyaged through the universe, teaching them its secrets, familiarising them with their crystalators and history, honing their powers, readying them for war. Though time travellers, it had taken ten years in realistic terms to learn everything including more futuristic battle-craft, each also gaining several degrees in engineering, chemistry, physics and other sciences and arts, travelling to uninhabited worlds to experiment with their powers. And once those feats had been accomplished they had crowned their achievements by creating a bubble dimension, undetectable by the Lore, in which to live. The fortress within was called the Chronopolis, wherein Xathanius and Phasia looked down upon Magna Aura.

With the main chambers within the Chronopolis, Phasia had helped design them, blending Grecian and Celestian aesthetics and architecture. A large dome surmounted the temple-like chamber, with tall, fluted marble pillars circling the windowless room. Crystalators provided power, computations, communications, and holo-screens, and for effect there were five fire pits among the columns for warmth providing familiarity and a humbleness of décor, which Phasia hoped would keep the nouveau-powered Astrals down to Earth.

The so-called Oracle room was off the main hall, one of many technologically-advanced equipped rooms with materials and artefacts collected from various Earth periods. In time, Spheron and Helexius, had reversed-engineered, rebuilt or enhanced the machinery to suit their needs. And so, the Astrals, once of Bronze-age Greece, were now on a technological par with the Celestians. And readily grasping such advancements was one of the many facets their new mentor admired.

The half-meter-wide, spherical dimension crystal, hovered over a simple waist-high anti-grav pedestal, which tapped into a myriad of micro-satellites the Astrals had covertly seeded around the Magna Aura system—Helexius' brainchild. In turn, smaller embedded crystals projected the holo images from the satellites through the sphere. And through some ingenious technical wizardry, Spheron could also hack into the system-wide crystalator system. Even Cirrius' clandestine labs were laid bare. But Lord Aeon was more concerned with other secrets.

Xathanius regarded Phasia closely. She was as beautiful as his father had said she was, even though she was now a Celestian/Lore hybrid—not entirely flesh; more like sentient energy. Her love for Millennius and their people had brought her back from the brink of total Loredom. But there were other things on his mind and his curiosity got the better of him.

"Phasia, my father never talked about a certain period of his life. I was, um . . . wondering if you would enlighten me."

A curious smile crossed Phasia's lips. "Oh?" she shot Xathanius a sideways glance, "And what period would that be?"

Xathanius smiled back, almost embarrassed to speak of it further.

She knew. She'd been waiting a long time for him to ask this question. But she said: "I have no real answers for you there, Xathanius."

"But the Scrolls of History . . ."

"The Scrolls of History are tainted, Xathanius," interrupted Phasia, a little too tersely, "Written by Spheron, interpreted by Spheron—history by Spheron. All of them written from their own perspective, though I don't blame them. Nothing was as it all seemed. Nothing!"

She sounded bitter, but Xathanius pushed further: "So what was written . . ."

"What was written," Phasia interrupted again, "was true. But the aftermath was again re-written, or in this case, omitted, by the skilful hand of Spheron."

"I don't understand," a completely baffled Xathanius replied.

A faint smile of melancholy touched her lips, Phasia's fiery eyes seeming to look far into the distance, or as Xathanius suspected, the past. "The answer to your inquisitiveness is yes: Millennius and I did have a child, a son called Hellennius. But after that, I cannot tell you anything else!" She closed the matter with a tone of finality.

Xathanius sighed. He'd only asked a simple question, but complications had arisen along the way and the whole answer was still yet to come. He frowned, frustrated at Phasia's evasiveness. His title of Lord Aeon had been bestowed upon him by Phasia, but Xathanius worried about the eldest son of Millennius, his nominal half-brother. Who was he? Where was he? And would he arise someday to undermine his authority?

"So, I have a brother?" he reopened the conversation at the risk of incurring Phasia wrath, and disappointment. "But I have to know, Phasia. We're the eldest sons of Millennius. Suppose someday he appears, claiming leadership. I can't have that. I won't." He grimaced at himself for sounding so childish.

"Command? Power? Is that all you are concerned about? I thought you had been taught better by Spheron," Phasia bit back with little humour. "But have no fear, Xathanius, I doubt you will ever meet my son, for he disappeared."

"Disappeared?" asked an astonished Xathanius.

"Yes!" hissed Phasia, anger tempering her words. "Disappeared!"

Though her energised state couldn't allow her to cry, Xathanius swore he saw magenta sparks flashing in her eyes like tears. Phasia calmed herself down, though she was still clearly upset, staring again into the past.

"He had been hidden away from the others after his birth in Lostratane, except for Spheron. Then one day, Hellennius had stood before Millennius and me, just stood there and announced, 'I have to go now'. He then smiled and disappeared right before our eyes. We never saw him again. Oh Gods, he was so young, still a youngling," she told the universe. "And that, Lord Aeon, is the answer you have sought. Do not ask me anything more!" She turned away, distraught, her purple fires flaring erratically.

Xathanius looked away, lost in thought. He couldn't have imagined anything like that happening, let alone to his father, the mighty leader of the Celestian Knights.

"I'm sure we'll find him someday, Phasia," he tried to comfort her.

Phasia smiled back. "Maybe."

They stared at each other, an understanding and new bond between them. They turned back together to view the unfolding scenes on Magna Aura.

"Farewell, Classia, friend forever."

"Look unto tomorrow, Deb, for that is when I will return."

The two Sky Warriors warmly embraced each other, before

Classia boarded her skimmer for *Sword Celectral*. A lot had happened to them since Novan's dramatic news. Orders had come for Classia, certifying her selection for Novan's command crew, while Deb had been unexpectedly selected by Gal Agar's recommendation to become Cirrius' aide. And with Deputy Sky Commander Glith joining Novan's crew and with Deputy Dessa's imminent transfer to Vista Mare, senior Sky Leaders Brank and Tol Valar would be promoted to take their places, respectively. Tol Valar had seldom gone a day without talking to Deb who could feel herself falling for him. But something within told her she didn't belong with him and often she would find herself gazing up into the sky and seeing the face of Novan among the clouds.

Classia's skimmer took off gently from atop a Sky Command landing platform and Deb found herself standing alone, long after the other well-wishers of departing crews had returned to their homes and duties. She hugged herself, a chill wind catching her across the face, her hair blowing into her eyes again. She was about to leave, but felt a presence behind her. She knew who it was before she even turned.

"Hallo," she said, shyly, a different kind of sensation prickling her skin.

"Sky Leader," Novan said formally. They stood silently watching each other, the wind whistling about them. "A fair breeze for farewells is it not?" he offered.

Deb nodded. "I love the open air. I feel that I was born to it sometimes."

Novan smiled, looking away and out, over the edge of Sky Command and the endless ocean below.

Still spying the distance, he said: "This may sound sudden, but I've always believed in the power of one's own feelings, especially love." He smiled, a bit embarrassed. "Maybe it's my psi-self speaking, but my feelings since I met you are telling me that I'm in love; that I'm in love with you," he said looking straight at Deb.

Deb's lips parted in surprise. In her dreams, which seemed so real, she'd wanted to hear those words from Novan. However, she could never remember answering him, as if she was not meant to and their love was not meant to be. Now, here she had the chance.

"I don't know what to say." She really didn't. "But I know I have also thought about you constantly since we first met."

Novan strode across to her. "I wish you could voyage with me, but in the time I have left here, I wanted to tell you that when I return, I want us to be together," he said.

Deb nodded, tears tingeing her blue eyes. Novan cupped her face and gently brushed her hair away from her eyes. And then they kissed. It was the most intoxicating sensation Deb had ever felt, like a raging lightning storm inhabiting her body, his lips like burning embers threatening to ignite her soul, their fire of love lasting forever. But just before that spark erupted, the kiss ended, Novan peering into her eyes as before. Her eyes were like everlasting pools of blueness, such that he could lose himself in them forever if he looked too deeply.

"There is something about you Deneb, something that cannot be seen as you stand before me. I feel that we belong together. We shall be together!" Novan avowed. He studied her eyes again, but something was troubling Deb. "What is it? Have I done something wrong?"

"No, no. I just sometimes. . . I have these bad dreams . . . and well, if you can't make it back, don't let our love stand in the way of future happiness. There are some onboard *Celectral*, I'm sure, whom you could love," Deb said, feeling a little guilty, not forgetting about Classia's love for Novan.

"Nothing in the universe could assuage my love for you, Deneb.

We will be together again. I swear it!"

A tear escaped from her eye, Novan wiping it away. Holding her face with gentle hands, Novan nodded in understanding and gave her a single kiss on the lips, before turning and departing into the air.

Deb watched. Only after Novan had become a tiny figure lost among the distant clouds did she allow her tears to flow down her cheeks.

Goodbye, my love.

Alone in the oracle room, Xathanius pondered the future. The Astrals were now, as far as he knew, the most powerful beings alive. The ability to travel time had granted them dominion over time as well as space and the temptation to imagine themselves as Gods was all too real.

Cal Xarien and Lazeron had taken to their titles of Archron and Netherlord, respectively. Xathanius could sense their eagerness to unleash their powers upon the universe and already Lazeron's daughter, whose powers of manipulating dimensional portals were extraordinary, was following in her father's and uncle's worrying mode.

It didn't help that his own sister, Zasandra the Timechantress, had chosen sides to be with them, as Netherlord's wife. Her natural blue hair had returned after having to crudely dye it while on Earth and she took to wearing blue and purple armour with a purple cape stylised to include a pair of blue wings, as if competing against Phasia.

Phasia had also warned Xathanius about the possibilities of old hostilities and grudges passed down from their parents flaring up, his cousins leading the way. He knew Archron had some plan in mind and the opportunity to implement it may come at his expense. Leading warriors against humans was one thing, but up against their own kind was another. As children, they had promised their parents they would never war with each other as previous Celestian Knights had, and Xathanius could only hope that Archron and Netherlord would honour that oath.

At least I can count on Helexius and Spheron, Xathanius thought. His brother and best friend were his constant companions. The three of them had children around the same ages and they got along perfectly. Xathanius' son, Aristedes, exhibited powers reminiscent of Alphatronius' powers, albeit on a temporal plane, while his daughter Zane's powers seemed to be somewhat late in developing. Both the daughters of Helexius and Spheron were strong-willed and independent. Their confidence in their powers sprung from having fathers who taught them well, while allowing them to experience the freedoms in several future Earth periods they would never have been able to participate in while living in ancient Greece.

And in the back of Xathanius' mind, he had to wonder if any kin had been left behind. Well before Troy, he and the others had helped wage war across the ancient world. They had also encountered their first loves, only to leave them behind for the next campaign. If offspring existed, then these lost Astrals were being denied their birthright by dint of not having been with them at the time of Phasia's arrival.

One day, Xathanius thought, *I will search them out and complete the Astral family.*

He waved his hand over the giant, spherical crystal, shifting the floating holographic controls to survey Magna Aura.

It would not be long now.

Sword Celectral, followed by her sisters, sailed past the boundaries of the Magna Aura system to chart courses unknown on a mission to save their beleaguered Celestian kin. Novan stood on the bridge, eyes staring through the black haze pictured on the screen.

However long, whatever it takes, I will be with you again, he vowed, not only to his mother, Elysius, but also to the one he loved waiting for him back on Halcyon.

"So, what do we do?" asked an exasperated Cirrius of the other Starguards.

They had all gathered again at his island home the night before to see Novan off, but not one of them had said anything to him about the existence of the Astrals: 'It was not in his interest to know' the Astrals had insisted, but Cirrius was suspicious of them, especially with his own plans for Halcyon nearing fruition.

He again sat at the head of the table, Sceptre opposite, the twins and Urana on either side, with Decion in what now seemed to be his favourite corner chair behind Sceptre; and Altair, as always, pacing the room. Novan had left early to oversee the final preparations.

"Well, I'm not going to sit idly by while they have all the fun fighting the Lore!" sneered Decion, who seemed to be shining his helm with the end of his cape. "That's if they intend on fighting them and they're not Old-World Lore sympathisers planning their own attack."

"Decion's right," agreed Altair, stopping to randomly rock a free chair back and forth. "We have no reason to trust them, kin or not. And who made them lords over us? We were first! We were!" he thumped his chest with his fist.

Cirrius exhaled wearily, finding Altair's actions irritating. Altair, noticing Cirrius' annoyance left the chair alone, backing off to lean unobtrusively against the wall.

Stoked up into a rare state of agitation, Alpha Rion spoke up, "I agree with Decion and Altair; to a degree. I think the Astrals have an agenda of their own. But there is no denying the power they possess. They can do things with time that the Lore cannot and if they wanted to, they could have destroyed us long ago or changed our paths without us knowing. But they came to warn us, albeit in their own unorthodox method and in the end, that could save us all."

Astara smiled in agreement. She was with him on this. Alpha Rion looked at every one of them, seeing if his point had been made. They all looked unconvinced, such thoughts having already crossed their minds.

"Well, I don't like it," snarled Urana, standing and angrily pacing the room between Altair and Sceptre. "They're using us. Who's to say it won't happen again and how are we to stop them? I'm not happy about this. Not happy at all."

"Maybe we should try and talk with them." The room went quiet as the Starguards looked at Sceptre, who shrugged at his own suggestion. "What else is there to do? And they might even answer some of our questions."

Altair laughed. "There are times when I call you brother, though very rarely, and times when I call you cousin. And this is one of those times, cousin!" he said in mordant tones. "You think they would condescend to appear before us at our request? Pah! That's a cousin of an idea if I ever heard one." He finally sat in a chair, defiant, arms and legs crossed.

Urana's facial expression wasn't as contemptuous as Decion's or the twins', while Cirrius' dubious expression wasn't exactly helpful, all politely hidden upon down-turned face. But Sceptre knew their thoughts.

"If you don't try, you'll never know," he said, serious. Then looking up at the ceiling, for what reason he didn't know, he said: "Well, if you can hear us, we'd like to talk."

There was utter silence.

A minute or two passed by with idle fidgeting beginning.

Suddenly Altair stood bolt upright from his chair, the others bracing up in their seats, even Decion in the corner stared in glowering fashion behind him. Sceptre slowly craned his head and looked behind himself.

There was a young girl standing there, calmly, unafraid, with a slight smile on her face.

"I am Lightstream, daughter of Helexius, brother to Lord Aeon. I am the messenger between you and the Astrals. While my powers allow me to remain undetected by the Lore, more so than the others, my time is limited. What is it you wish?"

Sceptre regarded the young girl, and she was young, not more than sixteen even by Celestian standards, but her precociousness marked her out as other and more than Celestian: she'd grown up on distant soils. Her long blonde hair, flowing down onto a short red cape, enhanced startling grey eyes, her appearance completed with a short-skirted red armour, adorned with gold-leaf. She was a warrior.

What more could one expect from the granddaughter of Millennius, thought Sceptre.

"You Astrals have the advantage over us, but there doesn't seem to be much trust between us. We're all the children of Celestian Knights, yet you seem to presume yourself greater in nature. Are you?" Sceptre challenged her.

Lightstream smiled again, rather too much like Urana's sneer for his liking. "We do not presume anything. We just are. While you can live in the open universe, we are confined to shadows even darker than the Lore's, lest they detect our presence, to all our detriments. We watch and we act..."

"For what?" interrupted Altair.

"For events such as this. The Celestian Knights betrayed the words of the Scrolls of History and defied the prophecy by escaping, thereby allowing the Lore to escape as well. This universe throughout time and space is now endangered and we must be on constant vigilance. You are known to the Lore, but they do not know or sense us Astrals, yet, and that will be to our advantage when they arrive here. We fight the war secretly: Is it not better for all that the Lore fight what they know not?" she asked.

"Only if we're not next," said Urana, still upset.

"Oh, I don't know, Rain, I'm beginning to like their tactics," Decion grinned, warming to the idea of fighting against the unknown.

"So, after the war, what's next for us then?" asked Sceptre.

Lightstream smiled again, quite disarmingly this time, "You'll know in time," she said even as she faded away, the air faintly rippling without light, as if she hadn't stood there at all.

Altair cursed. *So much for trust!*

Lightstream appeared from her ripple-portal in the columned main hall of the Chronopolis.

"Well done, Lexa," offered Phasia, giving her a hug, "Your first mission completed," she told the beaming girl.

Xathanius, also congratulated her, while they observed the Starguards through the Oracle crystal. Xathanius had much respect for Sceptre, now leader of the Starguards in Novan's absence. He comported himself with dignity and intelligence, which had compelled him to send Lightstream to comfort him somewhat. Xathanius had watched Sceptre throughout, remembering the first time he had seen him, dead, upon land destroyed by the Lore.

To show the young Astrals what they were up against, Phasia had taken them to the destroyed past-future of Magna Aura. There they had found the frozen Decion, Altair, Alpha Rion and Astara floating in space after the sun's explosion had destroyed Alphatron City-State, leaving only their bodies amid minute debris. They had never found all of Urana's body, just parts of her uniform submerged in the charred volcanic landscape, mega eruptions having ripped apart the continents.

Then they had descended through the dead air of Halcyon, the Lore not interested in flesh, having left the dead strewn as they were. Cirrius was presumed lost forever under the ocean. And then they had come across Aerl - the Sceptre, bloodied and broken upon an island shore, the bracken waters washing over him.

Xathanius had felt the most compassion for Aerl, for it had been his father, Sola Venga, who had sacrificed his life so that Millennius, Destina and Spheron could escape through the gateway. Xathanius had wanted to tell him how heroic his father had been.

I owe your father my life. Next time, I'll tell you, he had vowed.

Then Phasia had told them about the hidden Starguard: Azure; how she had the power to destroy the Lore, but for now could not be allowed to possess that information. They had asked why and Phasia had told them; Xathanius' heart tore at the unknowing sacrifices Azure would have to endure to save the world. But the Starguards would not be finished yet, there was a lot more in store for them from the Astrals.

"And what happens after the war?" Spheron had asked.

"When we win. . ." Xathanius began.

"If we win," Lazeron interjected. He always felt the need to needle at inopportune moments.

Cal Xarien clapped him on the shoulder. "Have faith, brother, Xathanius knows what he is doing. Phasia told him!" He and Lazeron laughed with Zasandra stifling a grin. Helexius clenched his fists ready to stride forward to defend his brother, but Spheron held him back.

"Easy, Helexius!" he cautioned quietly.

Lord Aeon took no notice. He knew what they thought of him and he didn't care. Phasia had got them here and she would save their kin.

"Think what you will, Lazeron, Cal, but we have to win. We cannot afford to lose or we forsake everything our parents sacrificed for us." He looked them straight in the eye.

The sons of Destina were not ones to forsake their mother's oaths she had sworn or the weapons she had bequeathed to them.

Casting a serious glance around the hall, Xathanius carried on. "Are we clear on the next part of the plan?"

"You mean Phasia's plan to use the Starguards as canaries?" Zasandra smirked.

Xathanius stiffened, pursing his lips. He hated that term, but that, in essence, is what they were planning.

"After the war, we will be known. The Lore, Synther, will know us if we fail. They will search for us, for Earth, so it will need protecting. You know we cannot do so or the Lore will detect our temporal presences, so it has to be the Starguards!" he tried to convince himself.

"It still does not make sense!" Lazeron argued. "If we defeat the Lore then they won't know either way!" he laughed.

"But there are still other Lore out there, attacking Elysius and

Zeus knows where else!" countered Helexius.

Lazeron grimaced in reply, taking the point.

"I still don't like that we cannot tell the Starguards about it; They might cooperate willingly," Sola said.

"Perhaps," Xathanius replied to Spheron's daughter, the first-ever female of the Spheron lineage, "But not all of them. No, we will need to move quickly after the war. Remember," he reminded them, "keep the Starguards separate and isolate the Lore to the sun and to Halcyon. Then Azure will do the rest!"

"Are you sure?" Lazeron spoke, scepticism still in his voice. "We are entrusting the whole of our survival to a Loremaiden!" His long purple-bladed nethersword chipped at the ground.

"Phasia. . ."

"Yes, yes, Phasia sees all!" Lazeron mocked Xathanius. "Fine, the Loremaiden saves Magna Aura somehow and then we deal with the Starguards.

Lexa sighed, exasperated. "They will detest us even more." She stood, arms folded, by her father.

"That is why you will be paving the way. The Exmoors will need to be prepared," Helexius told his daughter.

"Can we still trust them?" Spheron asked. "We have not contacted them for centuries, relative to their time period."

"They are warriors," Cal Xarien said. "When I first discovered them, I knew we could trust them. "They will follow our wishes." He nodded at his brother who grinned knowingly back.

Xathanius watched them. Clad in their respective grandiose armour they would make great bookends for Decion.

Zeus knows what the three of them would get up to together, he mentally laughed to himself for still thinking of Zeus as a real god.

Xathanius looked for and embraced his children. "Aristedes, Zane, look after each other while I'm gone." They looked at him glumly. "Yes?" he asked for their confirmation knowing they wanted to join him.

Only Celestra, daughter of Lazeron and Zasandra would be in the battle, as the oldest of the Astral children. Her ability to alter spatial dimensions would come in handy to disorder the Lore.

Aristedes sighed. "Yes, father."

Xathanius could see his Earthly wife's qualities and features in his son's diligent mind and brown eyes while the young teenager Zane held back her tears.

"Yes, father," she also replied, her black hair partially hiding her face. Aeon knew how they felt, but they were too young for battle.

"Perhaps when I return we could settle here," he soothed them. Turning to the other gathered Astrals he said. "Maybe we can all settle here in the Magna Aura. We may call ourselves Astrals, but we are all Starguards and we are here to save our kin!"

"Hear, hear," Spheron commented, hugging his daughter. "Do not worry, Xathanius, Sola will also watch over yours, as will Lexa," he winked at Helexius' daughter. "The children will be fine." He grasped his leader's arm in a promise.

Xathanius realised they weren't alone and looked behind him to see Phasia. She threw fiendish shadows across the hall from her fiery magenta Loreself.

"It is time," she said. "I sense the Lore horde's presence." She sighed in sympathy. "I wish I could be with you, but I would be giving your presence away and crossing my own timeline. Protect the rest of the system, leave the Traitor Synther to Azure, and most of all do not interfere with my past self or I won't be here when you get back. Remember what Spheron's father and I have taught you." She sounded like their mother, to Xathanius. "And don't worry, we will be here when you return," she indicated the four youngsters.

Xathanius strode over to the others, a confident smile on his face. "Then let's go."

And the Astrals were in the war.

CHAPTER TEN

A great hush fell over the Sky Warriors as thousands of Lore shrieked their way through the Halcyon skies, great trails of fiery energy burning in their wake.

Ahead of the Sky Warrior forces, Cirrius charged perilously upward threading a tortuous path through the ranks of venomous Lore, combating each one he met with unforgiving punishment. Plunging his metastaff into the heart of the enemy, teeth clenched in anger, mind and body fuelled with fire to match the potency of the Lore, Cirrius fought with singular determination, wild with rage. This was his world and the Lore would take it over his dead body.

Well, not this time! he thought with grim humour.

He sliced through another Lore, its energy form disintegrating, but replaced by ten more Lore.

Bring them all on! raged Cirrius.

The Sky Commander had kept his jewel Sky Leader by his side and now with Deputy Dessa, they watched the progress of the war on the vidscreens around operation control.

Deb desperately wanted to join the war, but to no avail. She wasn't to know Gal Agar was under strict orders from Cirrius to keep her by his side until he himself entered the war.

Even Gal Agar itched for combat, but he understood Cirrius strategy, if not entirely his reasons. When the Traitor Synther arrived, fresh warriors and resources would be required. And Gal Agar would lead that vital charge. He would engage the Prime Lore long enough for the Starguards to arrive. Gal Agar was honoured by the duty accorded to him and knew he would likely give his life for that cause. But he was ready. He glanced at Deb beside him, eagerness for action straining her very being, and recognised the most important reason he would fight for Magna Aura.

Conflicting feelings surged and ebbed within Deb as she observed the battle slowly being won. Cirrius' strategy seemed to have worked and he himself was holding the far side of Halcyon almost single-handed, while Tol Valar's forces were ably defending further west over the Sea-City States.

And though Halcyon was engulfed by Lore, their presence was almost negligible outside of Halcyon, except for the sun. The Swords were being swamped by Lore, barbarous wave after wave of cruel Lore descending upon the graceful ships, but something strange was happening.

Sky Command's crystalators revealed it themselves: unseen forces were repelling the Lore.

Sword Commandarian was shaking itself to pieces, the intra-system engines not meant to travel at the speed with which they were now operating. They had almost lost shields; the Lore draining power from them. They were almost at Magna Aura's flaring atmosphere where individual Lore could be seen on crystalator images. The under-siege sun was crawling with Lore, more and more numbers pouring onto it.

"Madness!" cursed General Ede under his breath.

Amid the chaos, Oleon, the calm Ops Star-mark reported, "Sir, Lore numbers increasing." Then he had looked up in complete astonishment. "Oh Gods!"

Before General Ede could request a more concise report, a giant wall of energy blew toward them; a bulwark of Lore crashing through space like an undulating out-of-control wave.

"Universe!" someone screamed.

Just as Ede was about to order full reverse, a blinding flash burst onto the bridge. A man appeared out of the light, crouched low, one knee upon the deck, palms flat upon it before him. A glow surrounded him and his eyes were closed as if he was concentrating and had not even noticed where he was or the crew.

A black cape covered his green and black armour with a thick red emblem covering his torso like a geometric lightning bolt. Ede did not recognise this Celestian, but he looked of Meccun descent. He was not a Starguard.

Bridge sentries, side-arms unholstered, rushed to assault the intruder and protect the General, who was already half out of his chair. Startled bridge crew looked from the stranger to General Ede. But it was Star-mark Tann, still attentive of the controls and approaching Lore, who spoke.

"Sir, the Lore are being destroyed. Our shields are back up to full strength and disintegrating them!" He glared at the intruder. "I do not know how that is possible!"

Everyone looked at the unknown warrior.

Still in the kneeling position, eyes closed, Spheron said, "You are safe, commander. Continue firing. You are under my protection!" He had not moved, opened his eyes or given any other explanation.

The bridge was silent, save for frantic comms chatter demanding explanations on sudden power grid increases and elated commentary on the unexpected Lore deaths.

General Ede looked down upon the trespasser-warrior in front of his seat. He had to trust this person was here to help them. Questions could come later.

"Whomever you are, thank you. We owe you our lives!" He stared around the bridge, standing down the sentries with a cautious nod, bringing general calm to the chaos.

Ede eased back restfully into the command chair, keyed his comms, and opened a channel to the rest of the ship. "Crew, we are continuing to orbit the sun to destroy the Lore. Stay alert and hit every single one of those evil profanities of life we can!" he ordered. "Then we are going home!"

Tann smiled. She saw the same smile reflected in the faces of the bridge crew. The glowing man on the bridge was still motionless, but they had to trust him.

Onward thrust the *Commandarian*, stealing into the flaring arms of their mother sun.

Tachscreen, polarity-vert, sub-darken, transcendent slip, glance, glance, slingshot, glance, hold!

Archron softly uttered the commands to himself, hands manipulating timefields in sync. He found himself standing mere meters, relatively, above the stellar tumult of Magna Aura, the giant yellow orb seething under the hissing blanket of Lore. He was invisible to the Lore, hiding in phase space, the time between time; behind space.

Cal Xarien had a love for the Roman Empire, wishing he could have lingered in that period for more training, combat, and living the life of an Imperial warrior. Hence Archron's penchant for his stylised Roman armour, which he wore complete with a preference for a blood-red chain-mail tunic ending in the pleat-like *pteruges*, partially overlayed with a gold-trimmed leather breastplate girdled by a gold belt. The long leather-like boots matched the red-topped gauntlets. However, upon his head was an oddly-stylised, Corinthian-style, blood-red spiked helmet which paradoxically kept his eyes and nose hidden in darkness despite that part of the helmet being open. A black cape swirled around him. He likened himself to the first space Roman.

His temporal shielding further protected him in phase space hidden from the Lore. His voidspear, a gift from his mother, Destina, radiated in his hands. The long steel grey-purple staff had runes carved into it—ancient spells, his mother had told him and his brother to ward off the Lore—surmounted by a crystal orb which in turn was encased in a thin lattice with two sharp pointed blades jutting out at the centre on either side, the longer forward-facing pointing downwards, the rear blade hooked upwards. It was a chaos energy entrapment weapon, an entropy vane. And Archron was about to work some magic.

Aloft, the voidspear crackled and a gargantuan flare from the sun washed over him and charged the spear, drinking the discharge into the orb. It channelled the energy, shaking the arm of the Astral as it drew in more and more energy.

Detecting a noticeable depreciating change in their surroundings, the thousands of Lore in the area stopped feeding. They cast about trying to discover the source of the disturbance.

Archron grinned to himself. The orb was using the chaotic transformative energies of the sun to charge up and produce an anti-chroniton wave. The Lore would not know what hit them.

Before the voidspear could fly from his hands in an uncontrollable spiral, Archron released the energy.

"*Nike!*" he gleefully shouted, invoking the Greek Goddess of victory.

The shooting black particles could hardly be distinguished from the background of space, but the Lore could unquestionably see them like densely-lit bolts of dead time or chaos flak.

Thousands of Lore dissolved into nothingness. There was no time for them to escape to, to exist. Time was rendered asunder as Archron let the anti-chrontions flow around the sun. Even Magna

Aura baulked at the notion as it shuddered with core-felt star quakes under the rough sea of forbidden energy it should not have been able to exist within.

Still, the Lore came. Archron knew the voidspear would not be enough. But that had been the plan. He and Spheron were drawing the Lore away from Halcyon.

And on cue, he could detect the displacement ripples of a Swordship approaching.

"Fire!" General Ede ordered.

Energy-cannon fire lanced from all ports of the *Commandarian*.

Spheron's fingers dug into the deck plating as his forcefield enhanced the ship, offering more power to shielding and weapons. As if responding to his touch, the ship lurched forward blazing away as it rounded the sun like a bullet from infinity. Magna Aura was encased within a Lore mantle who in a frenzy desperately tried to pierce the Swordship's shields.

The more Commandarian fired, the more Lore flocked to them.

From his screens, Ede could see that the Lore were concentrated on two main areas; his ship and an area around the the sun. He did not know how much longer they could hold out. They did not seem to be winning, but they were not losing either. Without the stranger they would have been destroyed many times over.

"Now what?" he asked aloud at the crouching intruder.

A slight smile tugged his lips. "We hold, General. We hold for the light!"

Everyone's eyes turned to Ede. The General felt he should say something snappy. He shrugged, hands outstretched.

"You heard our saviour. We hold! Keep firing!"

I hope you know what you are doing, he silently beseeched the stranger. *I hope I know what I am doing*!

Even the City-States, despite the Starguard presence, were besieged by Lore, only for them to be destroyed by unseen hands. Around Alphatron City-state, Helexius was a blur of energy. The muscular, long blond-haired warrior was garbed in dark purple, gold-embroidered armour diagonally crossed at the waist by a double gold belt, cape flying behind him. Using his temporal powers, Helexius could twist time, moving himself in the blink of an eye.

Lore were torn apart in unforeseen temporal storms, other Lore were disposed of in time loops eroding Lore energy away into other dimensions, while more unfortunate Lore were doomed to essentially die of old age, time ravaging their energy into nothingness. Heat and light into dust and ashes, semi-consciousness washed away into oblivion. Helexius rampaged across space, racing unfettered across the smooth surface of *Sword Despire* reversing its terminal damage around its rear-based engine core before it could explode catastrophically in the environs of Alphatron. The wrecked, but serviceable Sword turned and limped toward the heart of the battle continuing its fight for Magna Aura's continued survival.

Helexius raced on.

From the vidscreens on Sky Command, Deb could see that the Lore at the sun were being greeted with an insurmountable resistance. She wondered what miracle Cirrius had conjured to save them all. The Lore were forming a ring around Magna Aura trying to penetrate an invisible barrier. But for some reason, Halcyon wasn't accorded the same protection and the Lore were sweeping in, down from the now-blackening skies.

The Lore were scorching the very life from the skies. Sky Warriors, even with their activated personal force-shields had choked from the poisoned air, dropping from the dead skies. The battle turned, the fire of the Lore killing the air, and the Sky Warriors found themselves turning back in retreat.

Descending from the void, the blue presence that was the Prime Lore assessed the fields of battle. There was something wrong. There was another force at work—alike, yet different; felt, but unseen; all powerful and in opposition: Anti-Lore.

Timelines had been crossed, he sensed.

But they would still fail, he snarled. This was but a battle, the true war had barely begun, a war of eternity.

The Traitor Synther dove into the once-was atmosphere of Halcyon, the blackening air churning in his wake. There was still the matter of the Starguards, especially the one born of him that he could feel within the planet's care.

The main ops crystalator heralded the approach of a Lore different to the others: the Traitor Synther. He burned fire that fanned out like wings of blue flame, vapourising anything in its path.

Deb watched as Gal Agar clenched his fists at the sight of the Traitor Synther. They flexed and tensed as if he could grip the Lore around his neck and choke the very life-fire from out of him. His eyes were all but afire at the sight of him. Not able to contain himself any longer, Gal Agar paced over to his command dais and armed for battle, snatching up his metastaff and heaving on a heavier torso-armour pack.

"Dessa, you are in command."

Before awaiting an answer, Sky Commander Gal Agar indicated for Deb to follow him, and she in turn gestured to his personal guard to fall in behind her. They entered a transtube to the upper deck, rising into the airwreck of Halcyon, and into battle.

Magna Aura was awash with Lore, raging in waves like malignant flares and fractured lightning. They were under assault from three shadows that fought from the darkened recesses of time, flicking in and out of temporal pockets only on the point of inflicting death upon the Lore.

Netherlord, a figure in silver and green medieval-type armour hovered in the cosmic firmament, green cape billowed around him. The rune-etched nethersword in both hands delivered blow after blow of sacred de-salvation, striking fear into the hearts of beings that had no hearts with which to fear. The nethersword pulsed runic-energy again, glowing before discharging the pent-up energy into the despicable Lore, Netherlord feeling the energy coursing through him—it was almost intoxicating. Mad with delight, he swung and slashed his way through the legions of Lore around him.

Archron burst through the bodies of Lore, his voidspear obliterating the forces of evil before him. The blade-encrusted globe atop his staff charged again and temporal energy flowed from within, tapped from the entropic fluxes around him. The darkness of space around him lit up and he became like a sun, eclipsing even the merged power of the Lore, who burned away in the wash of energy created. Archron, finished, coasted over the pole of the sun, to see his brother, Netherlord, polishing off the last of his Lore. He patted his brother on the shoulder, the younger grinning back at him; a strange glint in his eyes. Their mother's weapons had exceeded their expectations. They would serve their cause in the years to come. But on looking out into the void, their euphoria seemed to be short-lived, with thousands more Lore encroaching once again.

Ravenous Lore scoured the sun's environs, converging upon the two brothers, who raised their weapons for another battle for survival. But just before the Lore entered the full glare of the sun, a horrific wave of brutal entropic energy poured around the brothers' temporal shield to engulf the unwitting enemy, casting their atoms into non-existence, a familiar figure in purple and blue winged armour swooping in to greet the two.

Timechantress yelled in triumph, her Spell of Entropy working first time. She stopped short of her husband and cousin, her blue hair still seeming to flutter even without the aid of any wind.

The three regarded each other, their jobs were done, but the war continued. It was time to indulge themselves and have a little fun, before the next battle.

Sceptre started on his way to Halcyon, he and Altair having defended their City-State, even with Helexius, whose powers of light exceeded his own.

These Astrals were truly powerful, he thought. *But where was Lord Aeon?*

"Umph!" Sceptre hit a solid barrier in space. His astonishment passed quickly as he realised he was encased in some form of energy sphere, his visor crystalator confirming detection of a force-net around him.

"You cannot enter Halcyon, Sceptre."

He spun at the sound of the female voice behind him to find the Astral, Lightstream.

"Watch," she said and he twisted again within the sphere to see Halcyon pulse once, a vivid blue. He had wanted to ask what had happened, but she had smiled her little girl smile and said "It is over. Here at least. But we have other things planned for you," she smiled again.

Before Sceptre could do anything, he disappeared.

On Millennius City-State, orbiting Magna Prime, Altair welded extra decking to holes all over the city with his energy, pleased the majestic spires would rise once again. He turned to look out at the majestic sight of Magna Prime rising, but he never saw it, disappearing in a blink of light.

It was gone! Astara fell to the ground distraught, trying to heave herself back to her feet. Her link with Alpha Rion had just been cut off. She'd only just left her brothers in the main observation chamber. She raced back, sword in hand, ready to avenge her brothers' deaths at the claws of the Lore. But upon entering the chamber, it was completely empty, with no sign of a battle or her brothers. She sunk to her knees, the realisation of what had happened dawning on her. She cast her head upward toward the universe, just on the other side of the city's metal skin.

"I'll kill you all," she swore, "If my brother dies for your cause, I'll kill every single one of you. Do you hear me?" Her breath was ragged. The impudence of these upstarts was staggering. "Do you hear me, foul Astrals? I will kill you all!"

Alone, really alone, for the first time in her life, Astara broke down and cried.

Urana soared heavenward. Her body ached, her soul ached, even her hair ached. The Lore had fixated on destroying her, always seemingly starting with her blue locks. The Protectress of State surveyed Placia from above, her warriors having begun the hard tasks of restoring order below, leaving her free to thank the universe personally for this second chance—if what the Astrals had said was true. She combed her fingers through her hair, clumps of blue pulling away to her disgust.

A bright, pulse of blue in space caught her eye.

That could only have been Halcyon, she thought, quickly determining the flash's trajectory. Despite her fatigue, she set off to investigate, but never made it another metre, before vanishing into nothingness.

Gal Agar rallied the warriors as they crushed their way through the Lore, who seemed to withdraw ever higher into the black skies, where the ashes of fallen warriors swirled in the deathly breeze.

Deb had never seen Gal Agar fight this way. He breathlessly led the way, screaming thunder and dread, unleashing the emotions of countless years spent as the stoic Sky Commander. She herself had fended off countless Lore, but she hadn't felt tired. Now she had noticed that the Lore had seemed hesitant to engage her, which had aided greatly in her efforts.

Maybe they're afraid of me, Deb mused.

Thick musty air surrounded them, the light of the Lore making for eerie shadows against the black clouds. But one chiefly light stood markedly out from the meager ordinariness of the Lore and the sight of it paralysed Deb as she stared at the spectacle that was the Traitor Synther.

With a wild yell, Gal Agar charged the leader of the Lore, followed by his personal guard, but Deb was rooted to the spot.

Her head spun, eyes clouded over, the breath stuck in her throat. Tormented memories, sundered dreams, and fractured nightmares flooded her mind. Images, dark and distant, past and future, far and near assaulted her conflicting senses. She held her head, the searing pain swelling up, waiting to burst out. The world smelled dead, like burning blood.

Deb opened her eyes for a split second and the world turned dark with horror as she saw the charred body of Gal Agar crumple and fall from the sky at the smouldering hands of the Traitor Synther.

She could have saved him, the only father she had known, if only she had been able to move. But she couldn't. And she still couldn't move, even when she found the Traitor Synther hurtling at speed toward her. The moment had been lived before, Deb could feel it, but didn't know how or why.

"Come to me my daughter," the blue presence commanded, an outstretched hand beckoning her forth.

Deb recoiled from the monster before her. She knew his words to be true just as a fleeting wisp of memory or a dream or neither, flooded her mind. And there was something else. She hadn't felt it at first, but the burning sensation within her had become a fire of erupting rage, an emotional fire sweeping through her. Deb trembled with the power within her, the leader of the Lore still approaching, until she could hold it no longer.

Deb screamed.

Cirrius streaked across the skies, having vanquished the last of the Lore over Vavashar. He had arrived in time to witness Gal Agar's forces engage the Prime Lore himself. Cirrius expected the rest of the Starguards and Astrals to arrive imminently. The Traitor Synther would then die. Cirrius could sense victory at hand.

But then an unexpected horror had unfolded before him as he had watched dumbstruck and with a heart of searing coldness as Gal Agar had been struck down

And Deb was next.

"Nooo!" cried Cirrius, storming toward Deb.

Where were the Starguards? Where were the Astrals?

Even as he neared Deb, he found himself hopelessly surrounded by Lore. But what he saw next would be scorched into his mind for the rest of his life.

A spark of blue energy broke the bonds of Deb's mind, becoming a flame so fierce that it suffused Deb and pushed outward enveloping all the Lore in a blue conflagration. Raw psychic chroniton energy, like for like in Lore nature, burst forth like fingers of lighting and cleansed the realm of the Lore, ripping them apart with their own energy. They dissolved under the onslaught of the vivid blue pulse that washed the planet and beyond in the span of a thought.

Cirrius' vision cleared. Manically, he scanned the clearing skies with his eyes and crystalators. Of Deb there was no sign. The Traitor Synther and his Lore were gone. They'd been defeated. Deb had saved the world. Cirrius hung in the air alone.

"You will never be forgotten, Azure," promised Cirrius.

He flew disconsolately back to Sky Command from where he would spread the news of the Starguards' victory and their sacrifices. Magna Aura would rebuild.

Azure had burned blue destruction.

The power within Deb became a living force, slaved to her will, fervid in its desire to do her bidding. Azure held the power until she could no longer contain the fire, her soul. She let go, the multi-forked torrent of energy manifesting around her and for a brief second, she was a Lore, majestic blue wings combing the air, her transformed head and body aflame in Lore fire.

Azure screamed in pain, in anger, in the sheer joyous freedom of being a Lore. She didn't want this feeling to end, ever. The coursing energy within her felt like oblivion neverending, a darkness lifting her toward the light, that same light of infinite exaltation plunging her back into black eternity. What seemed like gazing through millennia to Azure were mere seconds to mortals. And what she savagely embraced shattered and decohered the Lore into the universal grave like primordial failed mini-universes winking out of existence, like imploded sunlit shadows, until they were no more.

Betrayed! The thoughts of the Traitor Synther echoed from the edge of the void of extinction, feeling the wrath and power of his daughter's reach beyond her grasp and years.

All Lore in the Magna Aura system were destroyed in a conflagration of what amounted to anti-Lore fire.

Then all was quiet again.

Spent, even as the dark blue flames subsided within her, Deb fell through the sky, half dead. But she was caught in the gentle temporal field. She half-opened her eyes, the shimmering form of Lightstream cradling her in the air.

"What happened?" a groggy Deb asked the Astral.

"You just saved your worlds," Lightstream said simply, by way of congratulations as she gazed down upon her. "Now it is time to save another!"

"No!" Deb tried to struggle her way free.

She had to find Gal Agar. But it was too late.

The cosmos split asunder and the two disappeared into the rippling portal.

There had been much celebrating throughout the Magna Auran system to their epic victory over the Lore, until it had been found out that not all the Starguards had survived the battle.

Their bodies had never been found, though the only two survivors, Cirrius and Astara secretly suspected they were still alive, somewhere, somewhen.

But the mystery of their disappearance would go unanswered for a long time.

The light of a portal flashed within his underground lab.

Cirrius smiled. He had been expecting this visit since the others had disappeared.

Behind him, as he calibrated a new crystalator module, Zasandra sauntered around the lab, lightly touching various instruments and furniture. It had been a few weeks since the end of the war. And while rebuilding had been taking place and order restored, the system was still mourning for the loss of the Starguards. Now Cirrius, taking time away from his duty as the Supreme Sky Commander, hoped he would get answers. But he was mistaken.

"Hallo, Timechantress." He greeted her without turning. "Come to tell me where the others are now that Synther is dead?"

The slightest of hesitation in her movements, made Cirrius frown deeply.

"Synther is dead, is he not?" This time he did turn to search Timechantress' face.

"Of course he is," Zasandra assured him with a straight smile, staring him unflinchingly in the eyes, which made Cirrius even more suspicious. "I would not be here if he was not!" she calmly said without falter.

Cirrius studied her closely. She was not without charm, but her technique had much to be desired.

Zasandra walked up to him. A subtle seductiveness in her movements enhanced by her winged cape sweeping gracefully between the work stations.

"I have a proposition for you, Cirrius!" she stated, enigmatically.

"Oh, and here I thought you were now going to tell me what happened to the other Starguards," he reiterated sarcastically, cleaning the crystal before setting it back in its round housing.

That should counter their surveillance of me, Cirrius consoled himself as the new crystalator hummed into life.

"That and more!" she replied.

And she told him.

Cirrius stood stunned. She had technique after all. He put down his tools and stared at Zasandra. Then he laughed. Long and hard.

Once she knew she was not being insulted, Zasandra joined in.

They clasped arms in agreement. Things were changing in the Magna Aura system.

EPILOGUE

Deb woke up. Or at least she thought she had. One minute her world had transformed into a blue cosmos within her and the next she was. . .

"Where am I?" she croaked, sitting up, blue sparks still subsiding from her sight. The room was dark and bare, surrounded on all sides by a meter-wide strip of reflective glass along the centre of the walls. And she was not alone.

Three forms moved toward her. She held up her hands to defend herself.

"It's only us, Deb," she heard Urana's voice, soothing.

Presently, her vision cleared and she, Sceptre, and Altair were before her. Altair was scowling.

"It's those Astrals," he growled, lighting up his hands, the room glowing red. "They took us!"

"We don't know. . ." Urana began.

"Yes, we do!" Altair cut her off. "We have been captured by them! Look at this prison. Pah! Where are you?" he shouted out loud.

Sceptre spoke to Urana. "Altair's right. It was Lightstream. She was the one who took me!"

"And me!" Deb was able to speak better. "Something about. . . saving another world." She remembered.

Just then, a scrabbling noise was heard on the wall ahead of them, like a locking mechanism being released.

"Remain calm," Sceptre whispered to Altair, who glared at him with a cousin-look.

But while he kept his hands lit, he took a breath and stepped back.

"I will talk," Sceptre added.

The door opened and a man walked in. He was no Astral. And certainly not a Celestian.

He was tall, bearded, with short black hair. His clothing was unfamiliar to the Starguards. Rich dark cloth material with thin white stripes on his long-sleeved, buttoned-up and collared garment were coordinated with matching legwear, ending in hard shining black footwear. A thin strip of red material hung smartly around his neck over a white lighter-material vesture, beneath the over-garment. He entered slowly, smiling confidently, hands up in a non-threatening position in front of him.

"Who are you? Where are we? And how did we get here?" Sceptre demanded authoritatively.

The man in the suit continued smiling and replied. "You already know how you got here. As for me, I am Bastian Exmoor. And welcome to Earth!"

APPENDIX A

IN THE BEGINNING
A STORM OF STARS SHALL GATHER

Begin!

Energy filled the void, elementary forces coalesced and collapsed, vibrant particles formed and collided in universe-spanning filaments of quivering strings until they were torn apart by the expanding cosmos.

In a blink of an eye the new universe had been spoken into being by the Great Father and Holy Mother.

They populated their new abode with twelve offspring: the Storm of Stars. There were six Prime Stars and six Shadow Stars, mirror-images, equal yet opposite in their argumentative and contrary natures. One day they gathered in the midst of the universe's hallowed swirls and boasted as to whom had achieved the most feats of power. Their tales would have gone on forever had not one of them said:

> We need other beings; lesser beings; weaker beings;
> beings to worship us, fear us and to see our great
> deeds. Then would we all be great in their eyes.

The others agreed and so from the four universal elements they created four Peoples to worship them:

> First they made the People of Energy
> Next they made the People of Matter
> Then were made the People of Psyche
> And last they made the People of Time

The Storm of Stars were pleased with their creations, but the four Peoples did not like each other. They warred amongst themselves. They warred throughout the galaxies. They warred for a million years. The People of Energy became the most powerful and even dared to name themselves. They called themselves the Lore.

They defeated the People of Matter, burning them from stone into metal, leaving them to drift for eternity throughout the cosmos.

Next, they defeated the People of Psyche by spreading imaginary poison, forcing them into exile.

And lastly, they defeated the People of Time by trapping them within crystal and casting them beyond the Realms of Futurecome.

The Lore were rampant and destructive, victorious, and destined to rule the universe, but their deeds did not go unnoticed. This aeons-long war, mere moments to the Storm of Stars, greatly displeased them, thus they met once again in the depths of Universe's darkest seas to discuss the development of their creations:

> *How shall we stop this bitter war that has raged for this short time?*
>
> *We dare not interfere or we shall ruin the course of destiny.*
>
> *Thus, we shall create a new People, one created from each of the other Peoples, one that shall decide the outcome of this war.*

And thus, from the minds of the Storm of Stars sprang champions, bred for battle, and made from the elements of the first four Peoples:

Heroes made from Matter so that they had body and strength.
Heroes made from Energy so that they had souls and emotion.
Heroes made from Psyche so that they had intelligence.
Heroes made from Time so that they knew what had come to pass and what would come to be.

So were the Fifths endowed, finely structured and balanced in nature to counter and defeat the Lore. But fearing that the Fifths People would become too powerful and even turn against them, the Storm of Stars took action:

The Shadow Stars decreed:

> *If these beings were to flourish and become too powerful they may take themselves to be beings such as ourselves. That must not be so. We shall therefore cast these Fifths far across the universe into an abyss so they could never return.*

But the Prime Stars disagreed having compassion for their new creations:

> *No, let these Fifths contend for themselves in war. If they be vanquished, then we have nothing to fear. Be they victorious, then we shall teach them, lest they forget themselves.*

In the end, it was decided that the Fifths' fate would be decided upon by the outcome of the war. And so had begun the Decillennial War between the Fifths and the Lore.

The Fifth Peoples had been a space-faring warrior race long before finding the path to peaceful civilisation. The Storm of Stars had made them solely for their pleasure and for the purpose of war, giving them great ships of power that harnessed the stars and weapons of potent destruction, but no guidance as to the nature of their being, nothing but the knowledge of war. But sometime during that misty period of the past that was the Decillennial War, one of the Fifths came to realise that the Fifth Peoples had a greater destiny to fulfill.

He was Celestius, a warrior of great conviction, courage and intelligence. Even in a universe where every Fifth was created equal by the Storm of Stars, Celestius stood out among them. Such was his character the Fifths named themselves the Celestians. And they settled on one world they named Celestia.

But the Storm of Stars had not been pleased and as was their way, contrived to cause misery for the Celestians. They split the People. The Decillennial War had covered every corner of the Universe and the Storm of Stars used this to scatter the warriors, so that they could not find their way home. These people had then settled on different worlds in distant parts of the universe, creating seven separate races of Celestians with differing cultures, languages, and beliefs.

They were the Galatians, the Elerae, the Amethystians, the Xarians, the Meccuns, the Trinari, and the Neb.

The Galatians, bless their glory, were the perfect specimens of physique and beauty. Their combined wealth was beyond calculation, which was evident in their dress, art, and culture. Their cities, from the tallest spire to the deepest walks, were designed by artists and built to perfection by architects whose blueprints looked like sheets of divine music, the finished product a shining chorus in an orchestra of stars. Truly were they works of marvel and wonder. Galatia, the only world in its star system, was also the seat of the ruling government, a fair and just society—the Guiding Light of the Six Worlds. Many a Celestian Knight claimed heritage from Galatia, the golden jewel in all civilisation.

The Elerae were no less noble, but were highly feared and fiercely loyal to one another. Their uniqueness was shared in an extraordinary trait in that to the last one, they all possessed long, flowing blue hair. Their world was one of arduous cold domains from towering mountains down to the deepest of the magenta seas, which had given birth to the Elerae warrior states. And all beneath the glare of a fierce, blue star, which Elera shared with three gaseous spheres. Now, the reason why the Elerae were so feared and mistrusted stemmed from their treatment of the Amethystians, the one-time inhabitants of the seventh World. Long ago, so it was written, an Elerae had been unjustly killed on Amethystia. The killer was never found or given up. The grievously loyal Elerae had found fault with this, and as one, had travelled the vast scape of space to Amethystia and annihilated the whole world in revenge. Total decimation. Amethystia still hangs around its sun, but as a disjointed ring of loose rubble and dust.

The Elerae had never been forgiven, nor had they ever apologised, and nor had they been punished; the other Worlds fearing the consequences of another war. But from then on the Elerae had always been treated with caution. And the Elerae would be judged. The universe was the Great Judge of all things and the day would come when Elera would be judged. It was the way of the universe.

The Xarians, another warrior-class society, were the beings who could boast the only defeat inflicted upon the Elerae since Antiquity. An industrious and once peaceful people, the Xarians were the most superb weapon forgers, making weapons for others, their skills unsurpassed, but they began to feel that their skills were going unappreciated and so started making weapons for themselves. There had been an uproar from the other worlds as their supply of weapons had been cut off and the Xarians had armed themselves. The Elerae had then taken it upon themselves to restore order, but had been humiliated in battle and repelled by the upstart warriors. Fearing further battles, the remaining worlds had negotiated a settlement between Elera and Xarias, restoring calm. Even with that violent history between them, the Elerae and Xarians later became two of the closest allies among the Worlds.

The Trinari excelled in the art of spacecraft building, thereby being the leaders in the explorations to and of the Outer Worlds. They also controlled the space trade, allowing all others to crew their ships and to access their space facilities, except the Elerae. Out of all the worlds, the Trinari had more reason to hate the Elerae, for the Trinari had been close kin to the Amethystians, the two worlds being close to each others' star system. No direct relations existed between Trinar and Elera.

Meccus, the smallest world, was a world of intellectual wonder. Their capacity in learned-skills and advances matched the Galatians and allegedly some Meccuns possessed psychic abilities. Meccus, like Galatia, had been named after a hero from antiquity and was also a single-world system. Meccus was also the most inhospitable of the worlds and was adorned with thousands of vast inhabited domes and underground cities, linked by thinking machines and crystal tunnels, which the Meccuns were deeply proud of. It was a triumph of what could be accomplished by mind and science. But underneath all this visage of wonderment lurked a tangible air of sadness, for the universe held secrets that even they could not fathom.

Neb was a world of boundless nature with endless forests and rivers, a world alive with the vibrancy of life. The few large, inland seas and mountains that existed were sites of majestic monuments and pyrathedrals, for the Neb were a very ritualistic and religious race. They were wary of outsiders, and hardly a one of them had ever left their world, though they had the technology and capability to do so. Their Book of the Ages had prophesied total destruction if they were ever to leave their world. It was their most sacred law.

One thing that had remained a link between these different peoples had been the stories and legends of their past heroes. Only fragments of the Decillennial War chronicles survived and they were passed down through the ages in the Scrolls of History during the Stranger Aeons, that dark time which preceded the Golden Age.

It was a time when great heroes arose to teach, to battle the dreaded enemy whose name was never uttered, to explore, and to search for the other three Antiqchronals races, as the First Peoples were now called. The Celestians had almost been destroyed by the People of Energy and had vowed never to rebuild again until their enemy had been completely destroyed or ultimately purged from the light of the Universe.

This period had brought forth great questions about the nature of war as epitomised in the *Tomes of War*, philosophical preachings and practices revered by a sect called the Knights Destina. These elders and warriors upheld the Storm of Stars as their Gods, revering them above the Great Father and Holy Mother, a heretical tradition. The Knights Destina awaited the Storm of Stars to embrace them in godliness, once the war was finished. But as the War wore on, the Knights Destina's power diminished and they gradually disappeared, becoming the Forgotten Ones. For all Celestians, belief in the Universal Father and Mother was paramount, and they prayed and waited through the darkness for salvation to appear.

And in the dark times of the Stranger Aeons, mysterious champions arose despite the interventions of the Storm of Stars. With the will of the Universal Creators on their side, these champions overthrew the evil People of Energy, forever banishing them from the bounds of the universe. The Decillennial War was over.

And yet, that defeat had unbalanced the strange symmetricism shared by the Storm of Stars and the Universe, for shortly after, the Storm of Stars faded away, back into the universal fold from whence they had come. But the Storm of Stars had not left their existences without infusing upon the Celestian champions their legacies.

The Prime Stars granted:

Champions; Fifth in nature, but superior in being.
They will flourish, be powerful, and victorious.
They will protect our creations and their destiny.

But the Shadow Stars declared:

But these champions will forget themselves in our absence.
They will seek to vanquish us and shoulder the universal glory.
Hence they will only survive for one thousand generations.

This was mutually agreed upon. And thus began the birth, life, and death of those whom were called the Celestian knights.

APPENDIX B

THE DECILLENNIAL WAR CHRONICLES

Celestius at the Gates of the Universe

During the ten thousand years of war there arose a champion from the ranks of the Fifths. His name was Celestius the Wanderer—the light and the sword—who slew creature after creature, those evil beings of fire-energy, till they hid in the shadows, afraid of this mighty warrior. His fame was known throughout the Universe. He was superior and evil feared him.

Celestius had learned much in his wanderings and had grown strong with many followers. Though he loved his people they were not his to lead. He told them this, but they did not heed him. They were the domain of the Gods, fit only for war and death. He told them this, but they did not believe him. "Lead us, Celestius," they cried. "Lead us!"

But Celestius was still not convinced. He alone had amassed great knowledge and ability. He alone now stood above the other Fifths who clamoured for his leadership. But his was the voice that should command them when a higher voice of authority existed? And so Celestius had built a boat to sail the heavens until he had come to the place that were the Gates of the Universe, home of the Gods.

At once, in the presence of the Place of the Gods, Celestius was assailed by the Storm of Stars, those of enchanted birth, who demanded of him the reason for daring to present himself before the Great King and Holy Queen. "Were you not created by us?" They thundered, "How come you to us, to our very steps and demand an audience with those beyond your imagining?"

Unafraid, Celestius answered in earnest: "I come to seek the wisdom of the all-knowing, all-seeing Great Father and Holy Mother, those who hear the voices of all with compassion and justness. Are we not more than vassals of war? Do we not possess a destiny befitting a People who in total are greater than the sum of their parts? Give us the means to survive beyond the war."

The Storm of Stars swirled around Celestius in anger: "How dare you demand this of us, we who gave you being. Be gone from here lest we destroy your bones." But still undaunted, Celestius answered with passion: "No, I seek the guidance of the King of All and the mercy of the Queen of Life that I may lead my People to their destiny, surely foreseen by the Great Makers."

The Storm of Stars fell silent, flashing in deafening silence. They argued amongst themselves, as was their nature to, then their voices thundered again and their tone was ominous: "Give you more and you shall wont, whet your tastes and you shall hunger, let you see and you shall go blind. All these things we hold from you to protect you. What you seek is not real."

The Storm of Stars sparkled in unwavering brilliance, conspiring, mesmerising, warning—Be gone or be destroyed. But Celestius was undeterred: "If it is my fate to be destroyed for my People, then so be it. I will not journey back through the void to my People who await their destiny. I plead for the judgement of the Immortal Lord and the Timeless Majestrix."

Thrice, the Storm of Stars flared amongst themselves then the voices thundered: "Your life is not price enough for what you would demand for your People. Your being is not worthy enough to be allowed to stand before us as an equal. Your kind is not esteemed by us, those who were made to pique our interest, and now we are piqued—our interest gone. Prepare to be destroyed."

But the Great Father—King of All—and the Holy Mother—Queen of Life—had compassion and mercy for Celestius and intervened: "HOLD," they boomed in twin voice greater than that of the Storm of Stars, their offspring, "There will be no destruction. You out-step your warrant we fear. Be gone now, our children, and we shall tend to the needs of this noble being you have created."

Celestius felt their invisible eyes turn to him. "Have no fear mortal. We have heard your plea. Our fear is not for your protection, but for the protection of ourselves: It is foreseen that you shall grow; grow into beings such as us. And we fear that from beings made for war. Yet, we have seen the love and nobility that your kind can show, so we shall grant you what you have so dearly sought."

And all at once, Celestius was struck in the mind with the seed of knowledge: of writing, of reading, and of the secret of numbers, of science, of the art of reasoning and understanding, of culture and industry, and all things necessary to grow off the land, and to build great cities that would be the culmination of all the knowledge in the universe interwoven into the fabric of reality.

And the seed of Celestius' knowledge flourished to encompass the spirit world and the known in the corporeal world, so that they knew the call of the Starbird; the path of the Moonwolf; the way of the Skyserpent; the sign of the Rockmage and the magic four elements—Matter, Energy, Psyche and Time—that which they were made from and which were transmutable.

Celestius had brought forth the knowledge thereby giving the Fifth Peoples a destiny beyond the war. But it had come at a price. For his courage, Celestius had been taken by the Great Father and Holy Mother so that through his sacrifice, the Fifths would never forget them and their humility before them. And so that the Fifths would forever honour Celestius the Destiny Bringer, they had named themselves the Celestians.

Taken from the Celestius Chronicles

Adantus and the Antiqchronals Quest

In the year 8,002 of the Decillennial War, Adantus gathered us together and told us that he was going to seek out the Antiqchronals—those who came before us—to reunite all the peoples in peace. But not everyone wanted to undertake this hazardous and seemingly impossible task and after a vote, only five thousand of us volunteered to accompany the illustrious Adantus and his companion, Xal. We would be venturing into realms never before seen, and though it could be a lifetime before we returned, the all-glorious journey to find our forebearers was too great a temptation for many. Adantus was granted leave by the High Generals of Celestia and after a mighty feast and tribute, we bade farewell to our homes and set sail into the stars.

We forged ahead and decided to search the Stars of Blood, in the area called The Father's Hands, a far-off place of foreboding doom, where stars disappeared and reappeared as if the Great Father himself was raking his huge hands through the stars, hiding their light behind his long fingers. Great nebulous rifts streaked through this place and filled us with fear, but our sturdy ship of stars kept us afloat in the eternal darkness. We travelled for endless days, rocked to and fro by the stellar waves from this chaotic region that was tearing itself apart. Xal, the blue-haired second of Adantus, had the strength of the legendary People of Matter and kept us together with his tales of heroism and magic. But even that didn't save us from what happened next.

We were swallowed—engulfed by a hole the size of a star that appeared from nowhere, like a ravenous maw. There was no escape. But dauntless Adantus steered us straight down its black heart. We were torn apart, stretched to infinity, compressed into nothingness. We were everywhere and nowhere; screams shattering the aeon-long moments of madness, until suddenly we were on the other side of the monster. And we were somewhere else. Somewhere faraway. In that moment we truly comprehended our predicament and gloriously praised the Great Father and Holy Mother as we rejoiced and wept. Ever since our creation we had sought a purpose beyond the War—our destiny. And here beyond everything ever known to us, we had surely found ours.

Before us lay a vast expanse of deep black fields, littered with brilliant points of light that did not embrace us in death upon our arrival as our enemies, the People of Energy, would have done. These lights were not alive. We were alone. In our wanderings of this new place, we came upon many spectacular sights, but crossed no others, no one else to share our stories, glories, and adventures with. Despite the abundance of stars, worlds, and lifeless dust, we found nothing save emptiness and desolation; a magnificent universe devoid of life. Adantus led us to the zenith. He ordered us to the depths, to the furthest points athwart of us and then to the furthest reaches beyond and back. And in all these places we saw no sign of the Antiqchronals.

We saw galaxies eating galaxies; pulses of light shining so far away, yet so tantalizingly close that we despaired in ever reaching them. Adantus led us through countless starscapes of pure-spun golden light; through seas of magenta stellar storms; past holes of black darkness; around swirling gaseous pools of red-hot ember. Yet there were no Antiqchronals. Around and around the hub of galaxies our ship of stars sailed, great shards of broken worlds streaking by with their menacing tails of fire flickering. Some roamed alone, other in scores or hundreds. We left them to their fates and resumed our course, Adantus charting our way. But still our beloved forebearers were not to be found, until . . .

It had beckoned us. A white swirling arm of a distant galaxy had seized our attention. It was not a worthy space, yet it had called to us, our senses overwhelmed by a burning desire to seek out this unassuming clump of whelpling stars. We surged across the boundaries of the galaxy, Adantus sparing no thought besides the pursuit of this venture. We slept for neither day nor night until we had reached the place that had so beseechingly called to us: a small system lying on the milky outskirts. A small yellow sun held sway over ten magical worlds and as we sailed into the system, five thousand minds contemplated the meaning of our existence as we prepared to encounter our destiny.

Of the small worlds in the system we called Meriddian, only the third was inhabitable and we named it Destinia, after Celestius' mother. Divided into groups, Adantus explored the world, while Xal and the other leaders Orizel, Herm, and, Azirius explored the outer worlds. We should have known then that we sailed among evil and that death stalked us.

But it was too late. We should have known. From the beginning, all life, whether Celestian or Antiqchronal, had been inextricably bound together. We had all been cast from the four universal elements which represented the four fundamental aspects of the universe, yet were immutably one. We were as much a part of them as they were of us and, of course, we could sense each other, that is what had drawn us here so strongly, but we had expected to find the exiled Antiqchronals. But they had never been here, only evil had. They had acted like a beacon, luring us here, and now they were flooding the system.

Azirius saw them first. They rose from a giant clouded world in a swarm that caused a giant red scar to boil and swirl like a storm upon its surface. The Fire was upon us. Divided as we were, we fell like skystones. Azirius, Herm, and their forces were swept away in a wake of obliteration. Our ships were attacked; air was ripped asunder so fast that others were sucked into the blackness. The enemy next swooped down upon my domain like raining stars, drowning all in seas of unbridled fire. Some of us escaped, only to see distant battles raging. Then a bright light erupted upon one of the worlds where we knew Adantus' ship to lay. Adantus was dead. I knew not Xal's fate. We were lost.

What was left of us awaited for the Fire of Hel to attack from the deceptive calm that now prevailed, but they did not come. Our ship's eyes told us no People of Energy survived. We then journeyed to Destinia to find Orizel, the sword second only to Xal, and his one thousand warriors. Orizel related to us how Adantus had used his inner energy, the primordial elements that we all were, to lure the Lore to him on his ship where he had destroyed them all. But what would we do now with Adantus and Xal with his five sons gone? Destiny was sweet in invention, but cruel in fate.

But Orizel had decided. The war still raged, but in a different place. Evil still reigned even here in the furthest of horizons. A constant and fervent vigil would be needed to detect and defeat the People of Energy. And here, on Destinia, he would continue Adantus' dreams of searching for the Antiqchronals while starting a new

Celestian civilisation in the distant reaches of space. Anyone whose destiny belonged here was welcomed to stay and those who did not would journey back to the home worlds and tell them of their heroic deeds and sacrifices. I, for one wanted to remain, but the voyage back would be crucial, and if Destinia was to thrive for future Celestians to return here someday, then I would command the voyage back.

I and two hundred departed in a ship rebuilt from the wreckage found after the battle. But the omens were not in our favour and the journey back was not a joyous one, fraught with danger and catastrophe. We'd been ravaged by starstorms, battered by starfalls, stuck in whirling maelstroms, left drifting on desolate worlds having to repair our wounded ship, become lost in a maze of galaxies so compact and strung together that beginning, end and middle had no meaning, and fought creatures and forces beyond our comprehension. I lost Celestians in every single encounter and after twenty-five years found myself alone in the void. I despaired, wandering aimlessly around the universe, lost. I was far from home, far from my companions, and I would die a death alone, by far.

I awoke from a sleep that I did not know I had fallen into. A voice had called to me, but search as I might I could not find the source. It was everywhere and nowhere, a reverberating buzz that chorused into a thousand or more voices, voices that I recognised as those of my companions, all of them. The ship's eyes and functions were long dead, but I suddenly knew where I was. I was at the bridge, the edge of reality that had swallowed us all over a lifetime ago and the voices I heard were the echoes of our first passage through. They had brought me home. I sailed through the

Sea of Voices, down through the turbulent black maw and after emerging from the outer realms, steered homeward, with sadness and joy in my heart—destiny's door waiting.

Olesseus

+

But history was not kind to Olesseus. The portal to his so-called Sea of Voices, the mysterious gateway to another universe, was never rediscovered. Adantus' quest for the Antiqchronals had been deemed to have ended in failure and Olesseus, a disillusioned wanderer, had returned with stories to glorify what had actually been a disastrous journey. The Antiqchronal Quest quickly turned to myth. Its inclusion in the Scrolls of History added just for the rich tapestry of Celestian life.

The Knights Destina Tomes of War

The Tomes of War were the great Articles of Faith for the Knights Destina, a secret order within the Celestian Knights. They were destroyed once the Decillennial War was over and the Storm of Stars cult died out. However, particular war poems and philosophies still existed after becoming part of Celestian folk tales. If any parts of the Tomes of War did survive, they were in the hearts and minds of lingering adherents.

O, the war, like constant twilight falling
O, the war, eternal darkness rising
O, the war, shadow of the Cosmos dreaming
O, the war, the war, the war, the war

O, the war, more than death; life's length and breadth
O, the war, of blood and doom and fatal thunder
O, the war, echo of the Cosmos screaming
O, the war, the war, the war, the war

O, the war, immortal fire, forever fire, the final fire
O, the war, the dawn, the coming, the future, the end
O, the war, memory of the Cosmos dying
O, the war, the war, the war, the war

The first War Poem is interpreted as the Prophecy of the Return of the Lore. It was written by an anonymous Knight Destina who allegedly had the power of sight, strong among many members of the clan. Their goal was to produce at least one such member per generation who could foretell the calamities ahead and watch for the signs leading to the return of the Storm of Stars.

RAYMOND BURKE

The Four Stages of War:
Purpose: to drive us
Death: to hold us
Victory: to remind us
Life: to let us go

What is War?
If not a way to fight for what one knows not
then what is war's worth in the cosmic scale of things?

What is Evil?
If not a way to seed menace and to proliferate chaos unseen
then tis to openly flaunt as enemy to none when thou art to
all?

What is Secret?
If not the elusive answer behind the Universal Truth
then what is the question inherent in the Cosmic Lie?

War is secret. Evil is secret.
Yet they yield and perish in the wake of the all-enduring
Secret. In the eternal struggle, only the Secret survives,
outlasting the cycle of War and Evil, which cannot exist
without the Secret; forever sought by constant vigilance
forever opposed to War and Evil. But the Secret wears on.
It is the Way of the Universe.

The Knights Destina were obsessed with the belief that
something else was happening beyond the war: The Secret. They
believed that this secret was the reason for Evil's existence, for Evil
had always tread the unknown, and nothing else could generate

such ceaseless capacity for war, unless something, somewhere, somewhen was at stake—a Secret existing within the all-powerful Cosmic Machine that Evil sought at all cost. It was seen as the Universe's Great Leveller; its way of keeping everything in balance in a universe where everything was in chaos. The Knights Destina believed that long after the war had ended, the Secret would still be there. Central to their philosophy were the two Principles of the Cosmic Lie and the Universal Truth.

The Cosmic Lie was the Knights Destina heretical line of reasoning stating that the Celestian's divine creation was true and that the veneration of an organic universe was a Cosmic Lie to deny their true heritage. The People of Energy were real, but they had been mythologised by ancient peoples to explain their existence. Although no one—outside of ancient texts— had actually seen the Great Father and Holy Mother or the Storm of Stars they had been portrayed as real entities throughout history. But the Knights Destina awaited the return of the Storm of Stars at the end of time. The whole war was a lie to cover up the non-divinity of the Celestians. So, a perpetual balance of war was kept to preserve the Cosmic Lie—a sin of the past.

The Universal Truth was the unknown factor, for it existed beyond the known future. The Truth would be revealed when the War had been won, but Evil and the Cosmic Lie prevented such an outcome. For now, war existed to protect the Secret, whatever it was. So, it was thus reasoned that if the Celestians were fighting to preserve a known lie then the Knights Destina might as well fight to preserve an unknown truth. The Universal Truth was the hope of the future.

War existed to protect the Secret and destroy Evil; Evil existed to prolong the War and unravel the Secret. Both were the spawn of the Secret; one could not exist without the other two. But it was the Cosmic Lie and Universal Truth, the past and the future that held the key to the Secret. Reveal the truth of the Cosmic Lie and unveil the Universal Truth then the Secret would be discovered. And in that time beyond past and future would War, Evil, and the Secret be bound together in the ultimate fate of the universe.

Whether the Secret existed or not the Knights Destina firmly believed it. But their days were numbered as the Decillennial War ended. However, the Knights Destina spirit secretly lived on and they waited for the time they could rise and claim the Universe for themselves. It was destined.

O, the war, like flame of blood descending
O, the war, from tide of poison vengeance
O, the war, future of the Cosmos changing
O, the war, the war, the war, the war

O, the war, order of the heartless stone
O, the war, where ether drowns the newborn souls
O, the war, chaos of the Cosmos veering
O, the war, the war, the war, the war.

O, the war, destined fearless suns and sons of suns and sons
O, the war, lost in memory of forgotten remembrance, no more
O, the war, crescendo of the Cosmos 'wakening
O, the war, the war, the war, the war.

The last war poem is interpreted as the Prophecy of the Return of the Storm of Stars and the Antiqchronals, whereupon they would rebirth the universe with its chosen Peoples, the Knights Destina. Only time would tell if the Knights Destina were right.

APPENDIX C

PROPHESIES OF THE END OF TIME

I can see things. I can see more, a power to see things not visible in this world that ever since I was born and thereafter, I have seen things that no one else can ever see. I thought that I had seen everything, but then one night, I saw ever so much more, more than I ever wanted to see. And it scared me.

And so I had called the others: Galatian, Spheron, Statia, and The Others, even Gen Horol deigned to appear. And I told them what I saw:

"I saw four shadows, four distant darkened forms, reflections in black, but I saw their eyes, only their eyes, eyes that were windows into their souls.

"The First One, his eyes were blue. Ice blue. Ice cold. Worlds froze under his gaze. His eyes were like summer in winter, ice like fire. Scorching, burning, cold blue fire. Undeniable. Inextinguishable. His eyes burned. And all afire and unholy, he looked at me and I burned and burned and burned in his icy flare.

"The Second One, his eyes were black. And a voice said unto me: 'Look into my eyes.' I did. And I was lost, for they were deep. I saw a galaxy in each eye, one spiral arm in one corner, the far side in the other, the pupil a glowing core. He blinked and the galaxy exploded. And began again. He blinked and the galaxy exploded. And began again. Over and over and over again. They laughed at me, those black eyes.

"The Third One, his eyes were gold. Devastating. Fascinating. Lightning-bringing. Crackling starbursts. Fierce and noble. Flaring points of omnipotence. Conflict raged within those eyes. Light hailed. Darkness assailed. Then pain rained down, chaos screamed, and the gold bled, dead. In a rage of light he turned to me. He had terrible eyes. And I was afraid of him.

"The Last One, I knew his eyes. I had seen them before. My father's eyes. His eyes were death. There were tears in his eyes. Tears of death. He cried death, one drop after another, dealing death. Death to all, until no one was left. And it was then that I knew I had seen the end of the universe. I had seen the end of future's end."

And so I had called the others: Galatian, Spheron, Statia and The Others, even Gen Horol deigned to appear and I told them what I saw. And they believed me, even inscrutable Gen Horol. And they prepared, and hoped we were in time.

Ozmec

APPENDIX D

FAMILY LINES

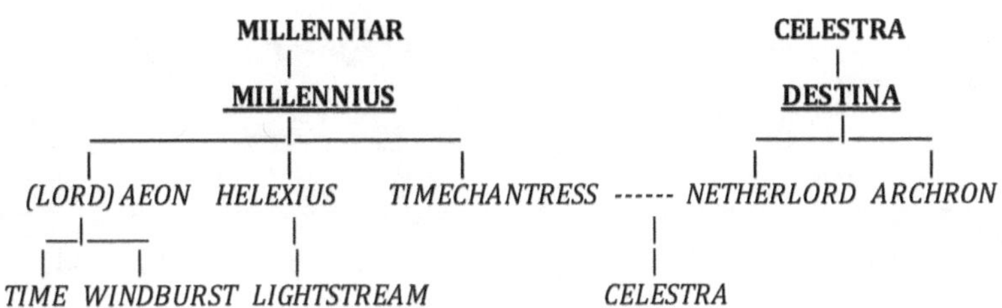

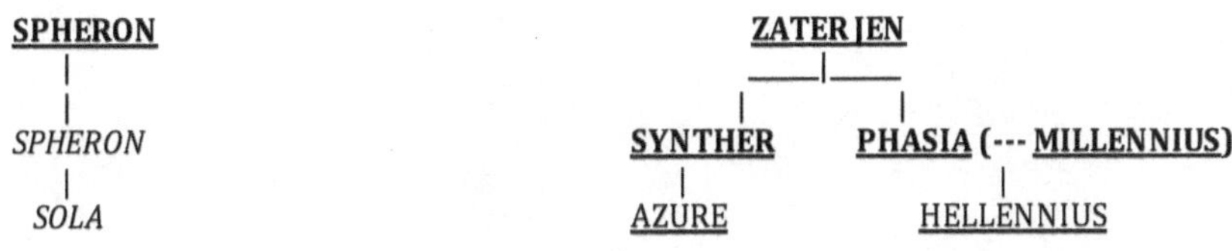

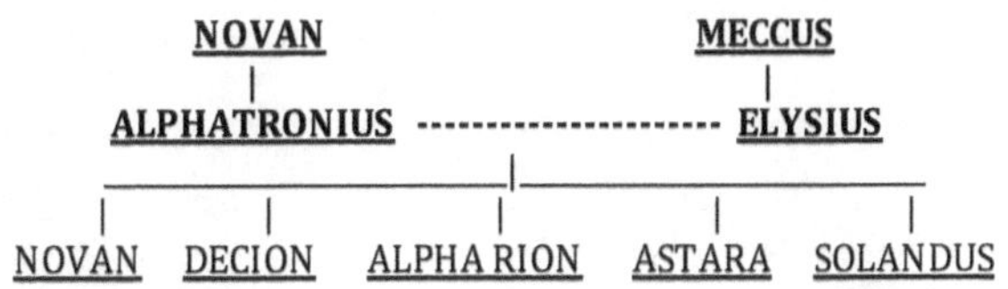

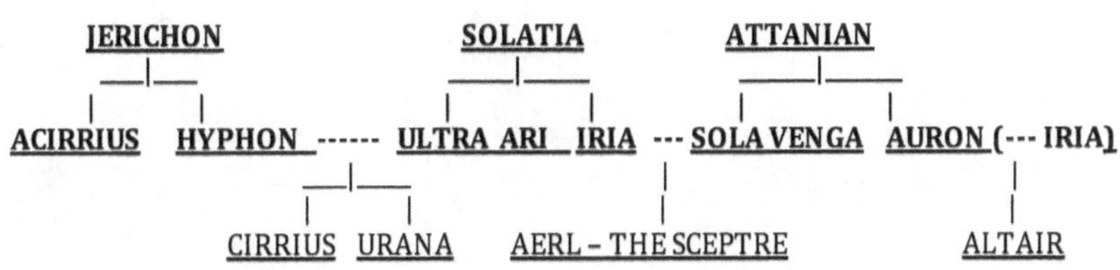

CELESTIAN KNIGHT
STARGUARD
ASTRAL

Have you enjoyed this book?
If so, why not write a review on your favourite website?

THE STARGUARDS
OF HUMANS, HEROES, AND DEMIGODS

continues in

BOOK 2 – THE AXALAN REVELATION

The Planet Chryria, the Fourth Cycle after the Expulsion

>*Escape! Escape! Escape!<* The word flitted around the disembodied consciences of the thousands of survivors.

They babbled and squabbled, scurrying about the last of the Great Psionic Temples that had not yet been destroyed by the invaders. There was no one left to fight for them, too few of themselves to restore order, and they had no allies, having subjugated everyone into slavery. It was over. Their Second Great Age had now ended and escape was their only option. They agreed to fling themselves upon the mercy of the universe and seek forgiveness. After advancing through their galaxy conquering and enslaving with their formidable psi powers, establishing an order that had lasted millions of years, they had finally come to their own end.

Their most feared weapons had been their slaves, the Surge. These space-borne, nomadic creatures could survive in the cruel vacuum of the void, their metallic bodies absorbing all forms of energy for sustenance, allowing for various energy discharges, or to change shape at their extremities, especially in flight. They were sentient, telepathic, and they travelled in hordes of up to five thousand, there being in excess of one million such hordes. To the Chryrians' regret, they had been deceptively-looking gentle creatures, but their ingrained sense of justice and order would be turned against the psi-beings, the Chryrians having taken advantage of their telepathic nature and enslaved them, ruthlessly using them to wage war.

The end of the Chryrians had come to an end by way of invasion and rebellion. A virulent race of energy beings had emerged from the depths of eternity—the Lore. But the Chryrians had had the perfect counter-weapon in the form of the Surge who could absorb and repel the Lore's energy. After an eternity, the Lore weakened, as did the Chryrians. And that's when the Surge had revolted; a three-way battle ensuing, which destroyed the Chryrian's world. Homeless and defenceless, their great civilisation in ruins, the remaining Chryrians had taken to the cosmic unknown, floating on the universal currents.

The journey had been very long, many dying along the way, many lost or left behind in the dark sea of stars or on other worlds. But others had persevered, surviving the perils of space for aeons, until they had detected the faint presence of life on a small, blue world, still in its primacy.

They had arrived in clusters, in a wide arc across three great landmasses, and in time they had encountered some of the indigenous life forms, isolated tribes who had worshipped them as Gods. The Chryrians, now benign and repentant for their previous imperious actions had befriended the inhabitants, but the exhaustive journey had robbed them of some of their lifespirit and they were dying. Their hope of being remembered in this universe and their renewed commitment to preserving life was now in jeopardy.

But a grand solution had been hit upon. Their worshippers had minds like their own, though on an order much more primitive. If agreed upon, a merger of minds could be formed, the hosts also bestowed with the memories of the Chryrians and their incredible psi-powers. The Chryrians wished to share their wondrous powers in an effort to help these primitives understand their world and ensure a secure future, without making the mistakes that they had. These powers would also enable the hosts to live for millennia.

But the Chryrians had also left their new flesh-bodied hosts with powerful enemies—the Lore and the Surge—who they knew would come searching for them. The future of this world and the Chryrian-minded beings would now be fraught with unimaginable danger.

However, not all of the empowered corporeal-beings could cope with their powers and madness ensued, causing the near annihilation of some tribes, the survivors scattering themselves around the world. But on the plains of a hot, dusty continent, one dying member of a tribe held on tenuously to life.

CHAPTER ONE

The Sahara, 2403 BC

Aranu of the D'anaa people lay among the desert rocks for days, his life slowly ebbing away in the unrelenting heat of the day and the deadening cold of the night. Only those few days ago, he and his older brother had clashed over the leadership of the tribe, Aranu wanting to live by the peaceful ways taught by the repentant Chryrians. The aliens wanted this world to benefit from their mistakes and sacrifice. But his brother had resisted, wanting to conquer their rival tribes and then beyond. Their young sister, who could have ended such quarrels, had embarked on another of her explorations that she revelled in so, and had not been there to pacify either of them.

A tremendous psychic battle had ensued between the brothers and their allies; psychic bolts hurled, among the wooden clubs and clattering sticks, and stone weapons, as fighting raged in the physical and psychic worlds, combatants on both sides killed, until only the brothers alone fought for their lives. And then Aranu had been felled by a vicious assault, which left him more dead than alive. His treacherous brother had disappeared, leaving him for carrion.

His lips were dry, his blistered tongue unable to move, the pain in his body hampering his already laboured breathing, his psionic energy draining away so much so that he couldn't heal himself. There was not much time left. In a last effort, he gathered together all his remaining energy and hurled out a desperate psychic scream for help. The light was fading fast, or were his eyes closing for the last time? Aranu did not know. But just as his eyes were closing in a final sleep, he hallucinated: the air beside him sparkled and shimmered and then split open. Then a young, pale boy

333

emerged from the ripped sky. He looked down and smiled at Aranu, who tried to smile back at his vision, but passed out instead.

Consention Military Base, Earth Frontier, AD 2216

Aristedes stared down at the young African. If he had been any later, he might have died, but then again, being an Astral he could have gone back earlier. He ran through the gun-metal grey corridors with the medics as they rushed the half-dead casualty to the medical bays, where among the late-shift medical staff, Commander Lynn Kellis awaited him for a report.

"What're the stats on him, Aristedes?" she asked, her British accent cutting through the surrounding medical techno-babble. She had just rushed in herself, sweeping her brown hair back into a ponytail. "I don't see any markings on him. Hell, he hardly has any clothes on!" She said, staring at the mystery man.

To Aristedes, Kellis was an enigma herself. At a young age, well thirty-five-ish, she was the overall commander of the research departments on all Earth bases, but kept her own life as secret as her work and experiments in her own secret facility at Zero Star, where she was something of an expert on aliens and extrasensory powers. Though how she came to be so, Aristedes did not know.

Kellis, Aristedes and his sister Zane, her two aides, had been visiting the twenty-two forward deep-space bases all the way from Bleakstar Base, Starfalls Command Base to Fort Barnard, and toward the January Satellites in such a way as to firmly make Consention Base the last stop before heading back to Zero Star. On the previous bases, Kellis' team had been officially collecting data for Earth Command, but unofficially they had been conducting an unauthorised mission for another group. Their actions were under need-to-know orders, and the commanders of these bases did not need to know. On Consention, however, they were also visiting the base's commander, Commander Xaul Relentus, who knew something of her covert enterprises. Kellis and Relentus were not only old friends, but also members of a secret elite group that even the Earth Council knew nothing of. How these two knew each other and how they were involved in the other secret group, Aristedes also didn't know. But he wanted to find out.

Kellis waited for Aristedes' answer. The rescued man was placed in an isolated medbay as the doctor arrived. She knew Aristedes secretly had a crush on her and found it difficult to fully express himself when alone with her. It must have been especially difficult now, having thrown everything into disarray by bringing onboard a severely injured stranger, Kellis certain to have to invent a cover story for her aide's discovery. Aristedes and Zane had been with her for a couple of years now and would probably stay for at least the duration of the war, but then he and Zane did have their own personal mission to accomplish. At twenty-one, his mature bearing belied his age, people mistaking his attitude for haughtiness, but Kellis knew better, Aristedes had been bred for leadership. And he was still learning.

For Aristedes, this was another of those awkward moments. His whole life so far was one chaotic moment after another, even for a time traveller. The aftermath of the Magna Aura battle had been as mysterious as The End on Galatia, for Lord Aeon, the Astral leader, Aristedes and Zane's father, had disappeared during the battle though he had not been directly involved. Blame had fallen on Netherlord, Archron and even his sister, Timechantress, but they had pleaded innocence. It seemed that some other dark powers lurked in the void.

The war-weary and wary Astrals had then been dispatched by Phasia to find Lord Aeon, but the brothers Archron and Netherlord had rebelled; Celestra, the latter's daughter, and Timechantress following. The Astrals were split. Helexius had taken over, and with too few to search, efforts to find Lord Aeon had been hit hard. Aristedes and Zane had then left the Chronopolis to mount their own search, declaring that they would never return until their father had been found. The two had been strangely attracted back to their home world of Earth, in the future, only to find it at war with the Axalan Empire. They had elected to stay, whilst searching for a possible time-displacement theory to their father's whereabouts, all the while trying not to influence the outcome of the war. But now Aristedes had rescued this refugee from time, whose mental scream he had somehow heard in the temporal void. And he had to explain this to Commander Kellis.

"Er, Commander, I think we should talk in private," Aristedes said sotto voce.

Kellis rolled her eyes and indicating an empty examination room, shoved him in. Normally, in delicate situations like this, Kellis would have activated a sensor inhibitor, scrambling any listening devices that may have been concealed. One could not be too careful, nowadays. But Aristedes and Zane emanated a natural force which functioned the same way.

"Speak!" Kellis barked.

With no sign of his usual nervousness when around Kellis, Aristedes said, "That man has no uniform markings on him, because ... he isn't in the military. And ... umm ... he isn't from .. . this time." He winced, waiting for her reaction, which he knew would not be slow in coming or nice to watch.

There was a momentary shocked silence, then "Go on ..." she said, folding her arms, surprising Aristedes with her calm response. Aristedes told her about hearing the mental plea and saving a man from over four thousand years ago. Kellis smiled, ever fascinated by Aristedes' tales of time travel, talking as if he had just walked across a room and picked the man up.

That's what was so charming and innocent about him and his sister, she thought, though she had a soft spot for Zane for other reasons. Out loud she said, "So, the upshot of the story is that this man is strongly, hell, extremely telepathic, eh?"

She rubbed her chin in thought, Aristedes watching her thought processes, her dark brown eyes seeming to follow the visuals of her mind. She was so different from the women of ancient Greece, yet with her beauty and grace, she would have fit into the old-world society perfectly. He would have to take her there, someday, after the war.

A smile, as always, ended her brainwave. "It's a bit late, but we'd better go see the main man." They exited the room. Kellis, knowing Doctor Brosus would be busy with the patient, asked a nearby nurse about the casualty's prospects, which seemed to be fifty-fifty at the moment. "Thanks, Rannie, we'll be 'at top'. Call us if we're needed." They then proceeded into a lift, "Command Deck." Kellis ordered it and they rose swiftly.

This could work, Kellis told herself. If this person survived, was as powerful as she thought he was, and could also be trusted with her other assets at Zero Star, they could go on the offensive, but it would take a lot of selling to the Earth Council. If all else failed, she could play her trump card.

They owe me. Those bastards on Earth owe me, big time! And she would not let them forget that.